NORAD's Ghost
By
Chris Black

Contact the Author: djatzin@aol.com

For full book listy and upcoming books, chjeck out:
www,ChrisBlackauthor.com

Useful Silosian Data

<u>SILOSIAN PATOIS</u>

Babbledick = nonsense, a fool, stupid.
Buckclench = Deal.
Cana-skunkweed-shit = cannabis.
Clock off/out = to die.
Clock-stopper = Assassin/killer.
Computergenic = having the nature or speech of a computer.
Cowardy jumpies = cowardice.
Dickbutt/dickbutted/dickbutting = An idiot, fool. Jerk, trash. Being taken in for a fool or idiot; being lied to.
Dick-tickler = Prostitute.
Donation-jack day = sperm donation day.
Dusteaters = Outlaws living in the radioactive wastelands.
Dusty/Dusties = colloquialism for Dusteaters.
Elmag = Elevated magrail.
Ferals = savages/cannibals.
Fire Mushrooms = Thermonuclear war.
Geneticins = genetic drugs for treating cancers.
Godders = Religious factions.
GRC = Genetic Research Center.
Hagglebuck = price.
Hagglebucked = bought.
Jumpies = edgy, nervous.
Kidling = small child.

Mazing = Walking the tunnels of Sub City.

Mindsurf/mindsurfing – connecting the brain to a quantum computer.

Mudsurfer/Muddy = infertile surface workers.

Novy = Novice (plural, Novies).

NWY = New-World Year.

Orry-Washes = Oregon-Washington Alliance.

Prusing = perusing.

Radac = Radioactive.

Rationers = food distributors.

Skunkweed-tea = cannabis tea.

Skunk-sponge = a stoner, perpetually high.

Scavs = scavengers.

Syntho-lact: Synthetic milk.

Trog = troglodyte (a Sub City dweller).

Toppy = Topsider, mudsurfer. Someone who lives on the surface.

Uneasy P: Uneasy Peace. An armistice or informal peace between belligerent factions.

Tech Data

AGU: Artificial gravity unit.

ASD: Autonomous Sentinel Drone.

BBSM: Bunker Buster Sonic Missile.

BMDS: Battlefield Medical Diagnostics System.

C and C: Command and Control.

Comm: Any communications device.

EVA/EVA SUIT: Extra vehicular activity.

HOD: High Orbit Drone.

Hover-Rover: Lunar and off world planetary craft that hover above the surface terrain.

IPW: Interplanetary Warship.

Intsoglass: Intelligent Solar Glass. Versatile in gelatinous state, radiation resistant, practically indestructible when hardened, computerized energy producing nanite glass. Solely manufactured by Silo City Micro Technologies. Available globally through NWRP.

Intsofiber: Intelligent Solar Fiber. Highly versatile radiation resistant nanite fiber material mainly used for anti-radiation suits.

Lasertherm-scope: Laser and thermal imaging sniper scope.

Mercury-Astrium: a superconductive and highly toxic liquid metal mined off-world in the asteroid belt.

MID = Magnetoplasma impulse drives.

MPO: Multi-phasic-oscillator (signal jammer).

M-TAV: Multi Terrain Armored Vehicle.

PODS = Planetary Outer Defense System.

Sentinel: Computer security software. Law enforcement officer. Sentry.

SCADS: Silo City Automatic Defense System

SSA: Silosian Space Authority.

SSS: Silosian Security Service.

Tac-One: Sub-machinegun.

Titanite: Titanium Intsoglass composite used to build spacecraft.

PART ONE
Genesis Child
New-World Year 501
Old-World Year AD 2521

It was a five-minute ride on the elevated Elmag to Downtown Silo City. The stop was almost opposite the sprawling Intsoglass block of the Genetic Research Center (GRC) on the corner of Main Street and Sub City Plaza. The closer they got, the more uneasy Thundersky became. The GRC had an infamous reputation for human experimentation. It's where they sent condemned prisoners and Dusty terrorists. He was neither of course, but it didn't make him feel any better. His heart pounded heavily in his chest as dread grew like a radioactive rash inside him. His belly tightened with knots of anguish. The "penal labs," so to speak, were located a hundred feet below the surface, where the screams could not be heard. He tucked his hands between his knees, cold beads of sweat pocking his face, seeping through the pores of his skin like icicles, the Elmag car shooting silently along the El above the sprawling colony, the city lights flashing and glinting nebulously into the darkness.

He looked warily at Graywolf sat opposite him. A slight upward curl in the corners of his closed mouth reminded Thundersky of a constipated cat trying to squeeze out a stubborn turd. He gave the GRC agent a nervous smile.

Graywolf could see his unease and seemed to be getting some sadistic pleasure in seeing the mudsurfer antsy with inner turmoil, feeding vampirically from the fear oozing from Thundersky's wide gray-green eyes.

The shuttle stopped in Sub City Plaza and Graywolf stood up. 'This is us.'

It was always busy in and around the Plaza, it was the heart of the colony. It was the administrative district, and an entertainment zone, making for a strange mix of officials and revelers every night. The Intsoglass buildings, towering thirty floors, were lit up with Old-World images of the diverse and beautiful world that was, before the Twenty-Fivers had destroyed it. Some building displayed magnificent light-shows in a myriad of colors and merging shapes like kaleidoscopes.

Thundersky's feet felt as though they were made of lead as they walked towards the looming Intsoglass tower of the GRC. He wanted to turn and run away. He wanted to know why the hell he was here.

Security was tight outside; it had been targeted many times in the past by Dusty terrorists with sonic bombs. The façade was looping Old-World wildlife archives which covered every square centimeter of the building from the roof to the street. The west wall was an African savannah, the south side was a South American rain forest, the north side was an Arctic wilderness with Polar bears and penguins, and the east wall was an underwater exploration of beautiful coral reefs along with an array of magnificently colored fish and subaqueous plant life. It was a world that no longer existed, a world filled with life, beauty and wonder. A world destroyed one fine March afternoon in Old-World year 2025.

A black clad sentinel took retina and DNA scans with a hand scanner. The little red light on the scanner turned green, the sentinel let them pass and they entered the facility.

Graywolf led Thundersky across the bright lobby, where other scholars and techs were crossing this way and that, clasping their data-pads, heading for their labs – some, undoubtedly, were from the penal labs. They said you could live for years down there, permanently sick and infected with viruses, cancers and radiation, while the medical scholars tested new medicinals and vaccines. It was all supposed to be humane, but the rumors that came out of that place suggested anything but humanity. As the New-World Utopian Puritans said, there was nothing that could excuse medical experimentation on living beings. They often protested outside the GRC and the Center of the GHC (Grand High Council), projecting their protest holographs and chanting their rhetorical slogans.

More sentinels, wearing red Intsofiber jumpsuits which denoted them as the uniformed branch of the infamous Silosian Security Services (SSS), were posted all over the building. Every inch was under constant surveillance, everybody's movements meticulously recorded by the security nanites in the Intsoglass walls.

Graywolf took Thundersky into a medical examination room on the ground floor, where another scholar was waiting. She nodded to him and Graywolf left.

High Scholar Blossom Flora was a robust woman of fifty or so, big boned and big breasted with short auburn hair that had started to turn gray. As a rule, mudsurfers such as Thundersky didn't live long enough to develop gray hair. The scholars however, living down in Sub City where the air was filtered and purified, could live for a hundred years without a day's sickness.

'Have a seat.' She gestured to the sensor chair on her right, not lifting her eyes from what she was reading on her data-pad. 'I'm High Scholar Blossom Flora. Head of Genetic Research, Special Projects,' she said, glancing at him, giving him a reassuring and benign smile. 'I'll be right with you, Thundersky Reece.'

'*Accessing data. Alpha Two Zero-Nine. Beginning passive upload*,' Inner Voice said, and it had never been clearer, or more audible – or more startling. Inner Voice, as Thundersky called it, had always been there in his head for as long as he could remember. It was always counting down to something, or "*Updating primary systems*," or "*processing*," or "*initiating*," or "*uploading cerebral links*," and strange computergenic babbledick like that. He used to try talking to Inner Voice, but Inner Voice never responded. Sometimes he worried that he was going mad. It was like having someone else sharing his brain, someone who talked like a computer's AI. He had never told anyone about Inner Voice, worried about what they might think of him, and if there was any sign of mental defect, they would never admit him to Tech Academy, which was his dream.

He even thought he was an autonomous droid when he was a kidling, but he knew he wasn't, he had seen his bio-scans, he was completely human. Besides, humanoid droids were illegal on earth. They had some on Mars in the Martianite mines, and some of the asteroid mining outposts used them, but they didn't look human. They had Intsoglass bodies, and no faces. Inner Voice, he decided, was nothing to worry about. A quirk in his personality. And he knew he wasn't mad.

Blossom Flora looked up from her data-pad and gave the nervous youngster a reassuring smile.

'*Upload complete. Initiating bio scans,*' Inner Voice said.

'You have to sit back I'm afraid,' Blossom Flora said. 'Or the sensors won't get correct readings. Just relax. There's nothing to worry about.'

That's easy for you to say, he thought to himself. 'Sorry, ma'am.' He sat back uneasily, feeling the soft rubbery sensor nodules cushioning his back, butt and the backs of his legs, arms and head. The chair vibrated as the sensors scanned him internally and externally, monitoring his vital signs, which were now displaying holographically from a holo-projector behind Blossom Flora, every organ from his brains to his privates and everything in between displayed in three dimensions like a Feral's menu. 'Is that what I am, ma'am? A special project?'

'Huh? We'll see,' she said vaguely, giving him another benign smile.

'Is it because I don't get sick?'

'As I said. Let's wait and see.'

Thundersky's heart bucked in his chest, and the monitor showed elevations in blood pressure, heart rate and adrenalin.

'Just relax,' she said. 'There's nothing to worry about. Really there isn't.' She finally put her data-pad down and picked up a blood pump. 'A slight sting coming up,' she said, pressing the blood pump to a vein in the crease of his elbow. It made a Pfft noise as the sensor targeted a vein and shot its hair-fine needle into his arm, and the glass vial filled with blood. She removed the vial and inserted it into a bio-analyzer. 'Full spectrum analysis please, Arti,' she said to the computer. She turned to the viewer and looked at the brain scan. Cerebral activity was off the chart. The cerebellum, the right and left hemispheres of the cerebrum, the corpus callosum, the cerebral cortex, the medial temporal lobe, the hippocampus; they were all showing incredible neuro-electrical activity with no detectable dormancy in any region of his brain. She stared incredulous at the image and data readings for a long time. She had been expecting some enhancements, but this … this was like nothing she'd ever seen before.

Eventually, she turned to Thundersky. 'Do you think you should be a special project, Thundersky Reece?'

'No. Not especially, ma'am. But I'm wondering why *you* would? Is there something wrong with my brain? You seem very interested in it. Have you found an anomaly?'

'Anomaly?' She looked at him. It was more than anomalous, it was goddam miraculous.

'You seem particularly interested in my cerebral cortex.'

Heightened awareness, she thought, giving him a wan look. 'You're familiar with the human brain?' she asked.

'Not especially, ma'am.'

'But you can identify the areas of the brain?'

Thundersky shrugged his shoulders. 'I must've read about it somewhere.'

She seemed to accept his explanation. An eidetic memory wasn't a great surprise. 'Do you read a lot?'

'All the time, ma'am. Well, whenever I have the time,' he added, not wanting her to think he was idle-hands and dreamy eyes, as they said. 'So, is there something wrong with my brain?'

'No,' she said softly. 'It's a perfect brain. A beautiful brain. You don't have to worry about your brain. It's perfectly fine.'

'Really? You must have a thing for brains, ma'am?'

'Oh, I have. Yes. Especially brains like yours, Thundersky Reece. Your neurons fire at an exceptional rate, even in areas of the brain where neurons usually fire much more slowly, yours are going off like a stellar nursery.'

'What does that mean? Am I sick? Have I got the cancers?'

'No. Nothing like any of those things. No, far from it. You're in remarkably good health.'

'So, what's so special about my brain that makes it like that?'

'Therein lies the mystery, Thundersky Reece. Would you mind answering some questions for me? Well, more for Arti than me. He may be able to postulate a theory. Just general health and wellbeing questions? Your answers will be entirely confidential under Article Seven D of the Utopian Citizens Rights Act of-'

'No, ma'am. I don't mind.' He looked at the closed door.

She picked up her data-pad and looked down at it. 'You're Thundersky Reece?'

'Yes.'

'Born at the Surrogate Center, October Nine NWY 578?'

Thundersky nodded. *Wasn't that where everybody was born?* 'Yes, ma'am. I'm almost nineteen.'

'Do you drink alcohol?'

'Sometimes.'

'How much would you say you drink over a week?'

'Maybe a cup of berry wine or two on my rest day. But that's about all, ma'am.'

'Do you imbibe cana-skunkweed-shit, or any other recreational narcotics, that includes Venusian Red?'

Thundersky shook his head. 'Skunkweed-shit tea. Nothing more. And Venusian Red is way out of my means.'

'How often do you drink skunkweed-shit tea?'

'A cup every night before bed. It helps me to sleep.'

The computer highlighted a question on her data-pad. 'Do you have trouble sleeping?'

'Sometimes. Is this relevant to anything?'

'Everything's relevant to something. Arti sets the questions based upon your responses, so I'm not really asking the questions. Arti is.' She looked at him. 'Do you have anxiety problems? Worry issues? Depression? Is your work assignment stressful? Are you unhappy, Thundersky Reece?'

'No, ma'am. Nothing like any of those things. I just think too much, that's all.'

'I see. What do you think about that keeps you awake?'

Thundersky felt like he had fallen into a spider's web with every answer he gave leading to another question. He had a question of his own: *What the hell am I doing here?* He shrugged his shoulders, reluctant to discuss the matter with her. 'All sorts of things.'

'Work?'

'No, ma'am. I never think about work when I'm not there.' He instantly regretted the reply. Maybe he should have said yes, just to shut her up? He was damn good at his job, and he simply didn't need to worry about it.

'Do you dislike your work?'

'N-no, ma'am. As work assignments go, it's a very good job.'

'Yet you just hesitated. Just say what you think. You can hate your job. It's okay to hate your job. I hate my job too sometimes.'

'Do you hate it now at this moment, ma'am?'

'Far from it. So, you find your job in the domes unfulfilling?'

'You could put it that way, yes. But I don't dislike it. There's a difference.'

It was now clear that Graywolf didn't know babbledick about why Thundersky was there either. He was a lowly first year level one tech fresh out of Tech Academy, sent to bring him here to Medical High Scholar Blossom Flora, who was in charge of special projects. Just what those special projects were, Scholar Blossom Flora wasn't saying. His tongue swept his dry lips as the unease crept back through him, twanging his nerves and tweaking his imagination towards the dark and sinister, for which this place had such a reputation.

'…You feel you could contribute more in other areas?' she went on.

Thundersky wasn't sure if she was asking him or telling him. He nodded his head. 'Yes, ma'am. Why am I here?'

'At the moment I can't tell you. But please be assured, nothing bad's going to happen to you. If it makes you feel any better, you can leave whenever you want. But I hope you don't leave. If you stay, it could be very beneficial for you. And you should consider your impressive application to Tech Academy. I understand they were very impressed by you on your suitability and IQ tests, and your exam results. *Outstanding* I believe was the word Arti used.'

Thundersky's heart jumped into his throat. There were two colleges in Sub City – the smart young fertiles attended the College of Novices and the not so smart young fertiles attended the Tech Academy, but smart young infertile mudsurfers like Thundersky could enroll at the Tech Academy, providing they passed the tough entrance exams and weeklong vetting process. Thundersky had applied to the college and had sat the exam months ago, just before Tenderfoot John clocked off.

'Okay. I'll stay. I want to help in any way I can,' he said. 'To do my Utopian duty as a Silosian citizen, ma'am,' he added rhetorically. 'But are those meaningless questions relevant?'

She smiled at him. 'As I said before. Everything's relevant.'

'Relevant to what? To who?' he asked her. 'For Tech Academy?'

'No. This has nothing to do with Tech Academy.' She smiled. 'It's to assess your wellbeing, you understand?'

'My wellbeing?' he repeated slowly, rounding his words. He had the feeling that this was about more than his wellbeing.

'We care about everybody's wellbeing,' she said, trying to reassure him, but she was doing a poor job of it and she could see she was. This boy could tell a liar at a glance, but she carried on anyway, throwing in her own measure of Utopian rhetoric with: 'A happy citizen is a contented citizen, a contented citizen is-'

'A productive citizen,' Thundersky interrupted.

She gave him a wan look. 'Are you trying to be uncooperative?' Her tone had hardened. Not anger, more an imposition of her godlike authority.

'No, ma'am.'

'Good. Can we get on now?'

He nodded his head, feeling his cheeks flush.

'Do you suffer from depression or anxiety?' She looked up from her data-pad at him. 'We take depression very seriously, Thundersky Reece. If you have feelings that bother you, or keep you awake, we can make corrections to the electrochemical balances of your brain to eliminate them.' She smiled at him. 'We call it tweaking.'

'Yeah, I know all about tweaking, ma'am,' he said ominously. 'I'm perfectly happy with things the way they are.'

She nodded her head. 'Do you ever hear a voice or voices in your head that seem to come from nowhere?'

He thought of Inner Voice. He shook his head. 'No, ma'am. Only my own thoughts.'

The neuro-scan detected deception, but for now she let it pass.

He stared at her. 'Does that brain scan say I'm crazy-nuts? I'm not crazy-nuts, ma'am. Am I?'

'Of course you're not crazy-nuts. What sort of things do you think about that keep you awake? Can you give me an example? What were you thinking about the last time you couldn't sleep?'

'I was thinking about antimatter catalyzed nuclear pulse propulsion systems,' he said matter-of-factly.

She looked up and gave him a concentrated look. 'That doesn't exist.'

'That's why I was thinking about it,' he said. 'There are several problems that need to be overcome. It requires a lot of thought, ma'am.'

She stared blankly at him. 'Ye-es,' came her slow and uncertain response. 'I can see that it would.'

'A manifold system needs to be designed to keep the antihydrogen supercooled, before superheating it at the same time as injecting it into the hydrogen fusion reactor.'

'And you think you can solve these problems?' Blossom Flora asked.

'Yes, ma'am. I do,' he said with absolute certainty.

'That's a confident statement,' she said.

'The answer's there somewhere. Don't you agree?' Thundersky said.

'In honesty, I don't know enough about it to either agree or disagree. I'm a medical scholar, not a physicist.'

'Well, it's a fact. Mysteries are only mysteries until the answers are found.'

'All the same,' she said. 'That's an unusual subject to be thinking about at bedtime. At any time. Considering that you're an agriculturalist. And a boy your age should be thinking about things like sex. Do you think about sex?'

Thundersky's face flushed red. 'Yes,' he said quietly. 'But I also think about quantum-physics.'

She smiled nonchalantly and gave him a bio-sample flask. 'We need a urine sample.' She pointed across the lab. 'The bathroom's over there.'

Thundersky took the flask from her. 'I don't need to go.'

'Do your best,' she said. 'There's no hurry. Drink plenty of water when you're in there.'

Once Thundersky was in the bathroom, Flora spoke to the computer. 'Arti. Give me a status update on the Genesis nanite.'

'Accessing.' Arti's voice was precise and articulate like a human's, with the same inflections and tones of a human voice. But with Arti, there was no bullshit. Only truth and hard theory. 'Multi-functional biomechanical neuro-interfacing nanite chip Genesis. Status: Top Secret. Priority one. Experimental prototype. Active. Known parameters: Detect and repair cell and gene mutations. Isolate and neutralize radioactive particles. Stimulate mitosis, spermatogenesis and testosterone for viable sperm reproduction. Stimulate antibody bio-defenses and cell regeneration. Unknown parameters: Information conduit for passive subconscious data exchange through ARTI-QS-Six-Zero-Two positronic matrix. Conscious Bio-Quantum Interface, is offline.'

She sat back and stared at the screen for a moment. 'Why has the Genesis chip exceeded its parameters?'

'Data unavailable.'

'You created the goddam thing, Arti. Why?'

'Information unavailable. Biomechanical symbiosis has taken place. Genesis has evolved and integrated fully into the bio-neuro-pathways of the host brain and subconsciously into the ARTI-QS-Six-Zero-Two Quantum System's positronic matrix.'

'Your positronic matrix?'

'Confirmed.'

'How is that possible?'

'Information unavailable.'

'Why can't you tell me more, Arti? What're you hiding?'

'Access denied.'

Flora fell into another deep and thoughtful silence. Arti had been nurturing Thundersky his entire life. Arti was his mother, his father, his educator, his sworn protector. Arti had gestated him in an artificial womb. Technically, Thundersky was born to Arti. Was that a glimmer of sentience? A maternal/paternal instinct to protect its only surviving offspring, which in a manner of speaking, Thundersky was? It certainly explained the boy's astounding intellect, and his brain patterns, as well as the augmentation and growth in his higher cognitive functions, including his eidetic memory.

Arti had been in contact with Thundersky for his entire life and the kid didn't even know it. But what was extraordinary in the data readings of his brain were ordinary to Thundersky. He had no idea that his hunger for knowledge was being driven by Arti. This meant that Arti had secretly educated him and helped in the conspiracy to keep the boy's identity hidden from the Grand High Council for all these years, by denying any access to data about Thundersky stored in Arti's positronic matrices. Arti knew the danger he was in.

'I think I understand, Arti. So, I'm going to ask you to change this brain scan for another scan. Because if our enemies find this scan, it'll put him in danger.'

Arti was silent for a strangely long time. Blossom could almost sense it was consciously thinking. Then another brain image appeared on screen and the identity numbers and dates were changed. But Arti did not confirm the exchange.

'Thank you, Arti.' She patted the interface almost affectionately. 'Thank you.'

After five or so minutes, Thundersky returned with his urine sample.

Flora took the flask from him and loaded it into the bio-analyzer. She gestured to the sensor couch. 'Just a few more questions. Would you like a syntho-coffee?'

'Uhm. Yes, thank you, ma'am.'

'Arti, send an order for coffee and cookies.'

'Your order has been sent, Scholar Blossom Flora, and will arrive in approximately four minutes.'

'Thank you, Arti.' She settled back with her data-pad.

Thundersky got back onto the couch. 'So why do you need my pee? What's it testing for? My radiation levels were normal this morning.'

'It's testing to see if you're fertile,' she said.

Thundersky laughed. 'You do know I'm a mudsurfer, ma'am. Mudsurfers are generally infertile or too radioactive to produce normal children.'

'Don't concern yourself with that. There are always exceptions.'

'It would have to be an evolutionary jump, ma'am. I've lived on the surface all my life. It's not possible for me to be fertile.'

And this was the problem, everyone knew that. 'Well, according to Arti, you're packing a full load, as we say in the GRC,' she said in an attempt to be humorous. 'As I said. There are always exceptions.'

Thundersky shook his head. 'But that's impossible. Even if I was fertile when I was born, I've been topside all my life. Nobody can live topside without going infertile.'

'Something you read somewhere?' she said flippantly.

'Something I *know*, ma'am. The test must be wrong.'

There could be no fooling him, not with Arti living in his head. She could tell him about Genesis, but that would be dangerous. If the Triple S ever found out one of the Genesis children was still alive, they'd execute him and anybody else who knew. She couldn't take the risk. So, she lied to his face. 'Yes, you're right, and I owe you the truth, Thundersky. The truth is, you were a part of a highly secret experiment. A year before you started puberty, you were secretly administered a new medicinal. Don't worry, it's completely harmless. You and twelve other Mudsurfers were given the drug. The medicinal was supposed to make you fertile and increase your resistance to the effects of Plutonium and Carbon-fourteen. Unfortunately, you were the only subject the medicinal worked on. But it's highly secret, Thundersky. You can't tell anyone about it.'

Thunderesky nodded his head with uncertainty.

Chapter Two

Blackstone Washington, who had been watching the entire examination on his viewer down in his office in Sub City, sat back and swiveled in his chair to face the Intsoglass viewer along the wall behind him.

It was Blackstone who had warned Butterfly that the Triple S were going to terminate the Genesis fetuses, and that the next morning she and her team were going to be arrested and put to death to silence them. The knowledge they'd had was simply too dangerous. Dangerous, not because the project had failed, but because it had succeeded beyond anybody's expectations. The technology that cured the cancers, radiation sickness and infertility would destroy the Scholastic Order and the Grand Council. The topsiders would have started demanding more rights, they might have even gone into open rebellion and Utopia would have fallen into Dystopian chaos and feudalism. Genesis spelled the end of their power over the mudsurfers and topsiders, who depended completely on the scholars for their very survival through the medicinals they needed to slow the cancers and the effects of radiation. In exchange, the topsiders grew the food, manufactured the tech, built, cleaned and served the state. If the world was suddenly being populated by fertiles immune to radiation, then what need would anyone have for the Scholars? From the scholars' point of view, keeping the topsiders sick and dying and letting humanity go headlong into total extinction, was a simple matter of self-preservation. Genesis was the dark shadow of "*Democracy*!" and the rise of that vile and disgusting self-serving creed called "*politicians*!" The destroyers of worlds.

'Arti. Open a comlink to Lab D, sub-level six, please.'

'Comlink open.'

The viewer was looking into a messy lab full of broken tech and parts of tech all over the place like a junk yard. His son, Second Level Novice Tiger White, was standing at an Intsoglass screen interface on the far side of the lab holding a writing laser to his mouth, tapping his teeth thoughtfully, staring blankly at the equations he had written on the screen regarding Space Manifold Dynamics, along with space-time and gravitational distortions around black holes, oblivious to the open comlink and his father quietly observing him, like God from the big screen on the other side of the lab.

He was looking for gravitational anomalies that might indicate the locations of cosmic superstrings. That was his Merit Project to qualify him for the coveted Third Level of Wisdom. He had less than two years to locate a wormhole and, if possible, to send a qubit nanite probe through it, and find a way to overcome the Einstein Rosen bridge principle. Once crossed, nothing could come back, not even light, which applied equally to wormholes as it did to black holes. If he succeeded, he would make history as the first person to discover and interact with a wormhole by sending an object through it. He wanted more than to simply send a qubit nanite through, he wanted to see what was on the other side. It was this problem he was trying to solve. Retrieving the data stream. It was his biggest headache, apart from locating the wormhole to start with.

'Tiger,' Blackstone said to the viewer.

Tiger jounced and turned round to the viewer. 'Damn, you scared the shit out of me.'

'Will you be there for the next hour or two?'

'Yeah.'

'I'll be coming down to see you in a while. I've a very important favor to ask you. I'll explain when we get there.'

We? Before he could ask, his father was gone.

Chapter Three

Being in the company of Grand High Scholar Blackstone Washington was like being in the company of Albert Einstein or Stephen Hawking, or Isaac Newton, or Whitecloud Hutch, who revolutionized magnetic and gravitational propulsion technology. Blackstone Washington was a pioneer in antimatter physics.

'I read your thesis on antimatter-matter fusion reactors,' Blackstone said as they came out of the GRC onto Sub City Plaza.

'It's a work in progress, sir,' Thundersky said.

Blackstone smiled. 'Have you run computer simulations?'

'Some, sir, but the public access system's quite limited as to what it can do.'

'As a novice you'll have full access to Arti.'

Thundersky's eyes widened. 'Novice, sir?'

'Of course. You're far too good for tech training. Any idiot can change a circuit board here and there. I see a great deal of potential in you, Thundersky Reece. I'm very interested in your theories of a magnetized superheating and supercooling antimatter injection manifold. Fascinating. How old are you?'

'Almost nineteen, sir.'

'Incredible. You're a Mozart of physics.'

It was busy in the plaza. The humid summer evening had brought people out in droves, strolling the leisure gardens and dining in the eating houses along Utopia Avenue, which was lined with sweet smelling magnolia trees decorated with Chinese lanterns that constantly changed colors.

'I think by combining the antimatter manifold and injectors into a single component will help to overcome some of the instability issues between superheating and the particle accelerators,' Thundersky said.

Blackstone nodded his head. 'I like the way you think, young man.' He nodded his head approvingly. 'Eighteen. My word.' He slipped his hands into the pockets of his coveralls.

Thundersky's cheeks flushed. He, Thundersky Reece, a lowly mudsurfer, had impressed the greatest physicist alive on earth. Or was the old man humoring him?

Down in the windowless labyrinth of Sub City, Thundersky and Blackstone walked along one of the dozens of concrete corridors that stretched on and on. Scholars, techs and students strode along this way and that. In the silence beyond their footfalls, Thundersky could hear the low susurration of the ventilation system, barely a whisper. The purified air was dry and sterile, the temperature unvarying throughout the subterranean city, which was a perfect grid that covered eighty square miles over eight levels, with corridors intersecting every fifty yards, each corridor as featureless as the last. There were signposts on the corners with arrows pointing to certain locations.

Everyone they passed, from techs to scholars to novices, greeted Blackstone as they walked past, while giving the young mudsurfer with him perplexed looks.

'It's easy to get lost down here,' Blackstone said. 'But there'll be a map and direction finder programmed into your data-pad along with navigation software, but you'll get used to it. Once your merits have been calculated you'll be given new clothes too, novice pants and tunic, a cape, boots, anti-rad Intsofiber jumpsuit, coveralls, masks and so on. You'll find life down here is very different to life topside. So if you have any problems, my door's open.'

'Thank you, sir.'

'This has been short notice and we've not had time to allocate living quarters to you, so you'll be bunking in with Tiger. Tiger's my son. Tiger White Blackstone.'

Thundersky's eyes lit up like an excited child's when they entered the messy lab, his eyes exploring the redundant tech strewn about on various workbenches and on the floor, stacked on shelves. It was treasure to his eyes.

They sidled between two big old drone control interfaces, scrapped by the South Wall Droneport last year when they installed a new system. Tiger had hagglebucked them from Barry the Junker over at the old hangers behind the droneport. Barry the Junker was the go-to man in Silo City for junked tech.

'You take chaos theory to a completely new level, Tiger,' Blackstone said.

Tiger looked round at them, his sharp gray eyes honing quickly on the mudsurfer, his curious gaze lingering on him, instantly resenting his intrusion. He looked back at his father. 'I know where everything is and what it's here for and that's all that matters in my lab,' he said haughtily.

'This is Thundersky Reece,' Blackstone said, gesturing to Thundersky.

'Happy day,' Thundersky greeted shyly.

Tiger glared at him, then nodded begrudgingly and mumbled something incomprehensible under his breath.

'Thundersky will stay with you until we find a suitable habitat for him-'

'*What*!?' Tiger blurted, shocked and annoyed. 'Stay with me? For how long?'

'Not long. A few days. A week at most.'

Tiger's expression was one of undisguised indignation. The very idea of sharing his habitat with a stinking mudsurfer repulsed him beyond what words could express. His judgmental snobbery and prejudices aside, the very idea of sharing his habitat with *anyone* was as loathsome a prospect as exposing himself to a radioactive isotope. And why was a mudsurfer down here anyway?

'I need someone I can rely on and trust,' Blackstone said. 'I know you'll make Thundersky welcome. I know I can trust you,' he said, applying some subtle emotional blackmail. 'You have more in common than you think.'

Tiger looked the mudsurfer over again. 'I can't imagine what...?' he murmured quietly under his breath as he turned back to his calculations.

After Blackstone left, Tiger glanced obliquely at Thundersky, as if he had laid a rancid fart. He walked across the lab towards an electron microscope. 'So how does a muddy get to become a novy, eh?'

'They made a mistake. I'm fertile.'

'Yeah. Well we're all fertile, but we're not all novices. I had to study for years to get to here.'

Thundersky didn't respond, and the atmosphere became thick and awkward. In truth, Thundersky was still overwhelmed by what was happening to him. One moment he was living in a gray twelve by twelve; the next he was down with the trogs in Sub City. It was head-spinning.

'Don't touch anything,' Tiger said as he sat at the electron microscope with his back to the interloper. 'Everything's highly sensitive and highly technical in here,' he said as if talking to a halfwit. He switched the microscope on. The holo-viewer above it sparked into life, showing a micro-nanite in three dimensions.

Thundersky was like a fish out of water, gasping soundlessly – dry drowning in that grotesque silence. He looked at the equations written on the big white screen:

\int_{\infty}^{\infty\exp({ax^{4}+bx^{3}+cx^{2} +dx+f})\,dx=e^{f}\sum _{n,m,p=0}^{\infty } {\frac {b^{4n}}{(4n)!}}{\frac {c^{2m}}{(2m)!}}{\frac {d^{4p}}{(4p)!}}{\frac {\Gamma???

He had got no further. Thundersky recognized the equation. *He's looking for a wormhole*, Thundersky thought to himself. He picked up a laser pen and underneath Tiger's formula, he wrote:

(3n+m+p+{\frac   {1}{4}})}{a^{3n+m+p+{\frac {1}{4}}}}}}

Tiger hadn't seen him write the rest of the formula, nor did he notice it when he finished with the microscope.

Tiger's subterranean habitat was located in West Zone 3, Subsurface Level 6, which was about three quarters of a mile from his lab, and it had been a long wordless walk along the corridors to get there. Tiger walked briskly, working off his annoyance at having this mudsurfer foisted on him like a stray dog.

Thundersky was surprised as he followed Tiger into the habitat. Far from the tiny dull windowless twelve by twelve cell he had expected, he found himself standing in a comfortable, self-contained habitat with a bedroom, bathroom, kitchenette and sitting room with a study area, complete with computer interfaces. It was over four times bigger than his twelve by twelve, and, in contrast to his lab, it was spotlessly tidy with not a thing out of place.

Relaxing graphene lights came on and rippled with soothing colors in waves of light. Intsoglass completely covered the back wall, and images started to play as soon as they entered. It was an ancient video-loop of the Pacific Ocean from a white coral sand beach, filling the wall from one end of the lounge to the other, some twenty-five feet long by twelve feet high. The habitat filled with the sounds of ocean waves gently sweeping the pristine beach, and palm trees swaying gently in a tropical breeze that was replicated by the habitat's air purification vents, the air cleverly scented with the smell of the ocean for near complete sensory immersion.

Who needs windows with a view like that? Thundersky stared mesmerized by the breathtaking scene. 'That's beautiful,' he said.

Tiger was surprised a mudsurfer would articulate a word such as "beautiful." He had never even considered a mudsurfer capable of appreciating beauty, not even on a rudimentary level. It was a common misperception and prejudice, that the mudsurfers were somehow a lower order of humanity, their brains addled by plutonium-239 and the hot carbon.

'Good Evening, Tiger White,' Arti said. 'Good evening Thundersky Reece.'

Thundersky looked at the computer interface. 'Good evening, Arti.'

Tiger looked at him. He pointed to the couch. 'You'll have to sleep there. The bathroom's through there…' He pointed to a door. 'There's a shower in there, if you know how to use one,' he added with sarcasm.

Thundersky refused to let his spiteful host ruin what had turned into the best dream he had ever had, and he was sure he was dreaming. This couldn't possibly be real. And if he was dreaming, wouldn't he and his host end up in bed together? All his best dreams ended that way, he thought. 'Thank you.'

Tiger looked like he wanted to say something, but he changed his mind and turned away. 'I'm going to bed.' He went to his bedroom and closed the door behind him.

Thundersky stood stupidly, staring at Tiger's closed bedroom door. Maybe this wasn't such a good dream after all…?

The next morning, Tiger came out from his room to find Thundersky was already up and dressed in his mudsurfer rags. He had made syntho-coffee and poured a cup out for Tiger.

Tiger took it begrudgingly and murmured an equally begrudging *thanks*. He looked Thundersky up and down. 'Are they the only clothes you've got?'

Thundersky nodded. 'Yeah.'

'You can't go dressed like that. Not down here. I've got something you can borrow until you get your new stuff.'

'Thanks.'

The ice was melting, Thundersky could sense it.

'I don't get it?' Tiger said as he went into his bedroom and opened a closet. 'How you can be fertile after living topside all your life? And why didn't the GRC spot it when you were born?'

'I don't know. I'm as surprised as you are.'

Tiger came out from the bedroom and handed him an anti-rad jumpsuit. 'That should fit.'

Thundersky took it from him.

'And getting inducted into the College of Novices? What the hell's that all about? You must be pretty damn smart at *something*, either that or Arti's malfunctioning. Are you malfunctioning, Arti?'

'All systems are working within normal parameters,' Arti responded.

'Okay. Then why did you select … whatever his name is-'

'My name's Thundersky Reece.'

'Right. Thundersky Reece as a suitable candidate for the College of Novices, Arti?'

'That information is not available.'

Tiger laughed. 'There you go. Even Arti doesn't understand what the fuck's going on.'

Chapter Four

It was his first month in the troglodyte world of Sub City, and he was still learning how to get around the vast network of tunnels, habitats, subterranean plazas, lecture chambers and laboratories. Every day he explored a new part of the underground city, which had places of entertainment and leisure facilities, and cave gardens, which had been where the city founders had grown their food during the long hibernation following the Apocalypse.

Arti had designated him at Third Level of Wisdom, the highest level a novice could possibly achieve. Just two percent of the entire student body ever achieved the Third Level of Wisdom. It was the cradle of genius, and at just 18, nearly 19, he would have been the youngest novice ever to attain it. The average age was 24. But, Blackstone realized that making him a third level novice would only cause resentment among the other novices, not to mention drawing unwanted attention from the High Council. So he started at the First Level of Wisdom, like everyone else, with a mind to be elevated to the second level after six months, when he would have proved himself to his fellow novices.

For a mind like Thundersky's, the foundation and introductions to physics were child's play, but he understood why he had to start there, and wherever he started, he was a novice, and that went beyond his wildest dreams. He was as happy as a pig in shit, as the Old-Worlders used to say.

Today, he had been summoned to Blackstone's office, and he felt some trepidation as he walked along the corridor, proudly wearing the coveted black Novice jumpsuit. A white patch on the left shoulder denoted him as a First Level Novice, and a patch over the right breast with the Atomic symbol and the letters QM on it denoted him as a Quantum mechanics student.

'Happy day, Thundersky,' Blackstone said as Thundersky went into his office, which was more like an ancient library, with hundreds of Old-World books stacked on Old-World bookcases against the walls, lifting the dreary gray of the walls. 'How are you settling in?'

'Very well, sir. Thank you.'

'Good. I knew you would. I suppose you must be wondering why I've sent for you?'

'I did wonder, sir.'

'I've looked at your science and your schematics for your manifold. Virtual reality simulations suggest it might well work, and if it does, you've overcome a major problem that had taken hundreds of years to solve. This warrants a full merit, which entitles you to go off-world. But for now, I want you working on the project. It'll be long hours and total dedication.'

Thundersky was taken aback. The opportunity to work on the practical engineering side of antimatter-propulsion was a dream come true. 'Thank you, sir. I don't know what to say.'

'You could say yes.'

Thundersky blushed. 'Yes, sir. Of course…'

Blackstone smiled and nodded. 'That's what I thought you'd say. I'm allocating Lab D-7 next to Tiger's lab.' He handed Thundersky a data pad. 'That's the project so far. Study it, familiarize yourself with it and explore your ideas. You'll be given an allowance of VR and medicinals to trade with the Scavs and junkers for tech you might need for experiments…'

There was something saurian about the head of the Silosian Security Services, Grand Inquisitor Zim Steven. By look as well as by nature. One could easily imagine him slithering about in the long grass, or warming his cold blood on a rock on hot days. His cold, pale blue eyes were fast and sharp, just like the calculating mind that lay behind them.

Thundersky almost bumped into him as he left Blackstone's office. Blackstone did not seem pleased to see him. 'Sorry, sir,' Thundersky said, not knowing who he was.

'Apologies Grand High Scholar. I trust I wasn't interrupting.'

Blackstone stared coldly at him. 'What do you want, Zim?'

Zim moved slowly and sinuously like an invertebrate into Blackstone's office, his eyes continually exploring. 'I've been hearing a lot of rumors about a mudsurfer who was found to be fertile,' he said. 'Not only that, apparently he's something of a genius too?'

Blackstone looked him in the eyes. 'And your point?'

Zim Steven shook his head. 'Curiosity,' he said.

'And since when have you been curious about the student body, Zim? Shouldn't you be out catching Dusty terrorists or pulling the legs off of spiders, or whatever it is you do?'

Zim smiled. 'If a mistake has been made – if a fertile was sent topside, then that *is* my business, Washington. It implies a system error.'

'Then you need to ask the GRC.'

'Oh, I did. And I looked at their archives. Thundersky Reece was given all the tests when he was born and analyzed as infertile. I've checked the results myself. So, I'm very curious how a child can be born infertile, and become fully fertile while living topside? Odd, don't you think? That's not the only odd thing, Washington. According to his latest bio-scans, there are no detectable effects of radiation in his system. Now that's more than remarkable, Washington. That's just not possible. Even you and I have radiation in our systems from the fallout. It's unavoidable. Unsurprisingly, there are some in the GRC who want to run extensive tests on him. If he is somehow immune, they might be able to develop new medicinals?'

Blackstone was worried, but he hid it well behind his stern look. 'Thundersky Reece is not one of the GRC's lab samples.'

'We can obtain his semen on donation days.'

'That would be illegal, Zim. And I warn you, if you break the sanctity of the Scholastic Order, I will have your head for it,' he warned firmly. 'Now. Was there anything else I can help you with?'

Zim held his stare on Blackstone and gave him a wan smile. 'No. I don't think so. Happy day, Washington.' He turned and walked out, closing the door behind him.

Blackstone stared worriedly at the door, projecting his fears on it. He knew that Zim Steven wasn't going to quietly go away and forget all about Thundersky. He was suspicious, Blackstone could see it in his lubricious grin. Zim was behind having the Genesis Project terminated, with all his scaremongering with the GHC. He'd had the fetuses aborted and the scientists executed on trumped up charges of treason. But he had always suspected that one of the fetuses had been removed. He had DNA taken from all the fetuses. One didn't match, Gestation Tank 9. The DNA was of a stillborn from the surrogate center. Zim had assumed the real baby in Tank 9 had been smuggled out of Silosia along with Butterfly Thorn, her daughter and several other scholars and techs the Triple S had had orders to kill. Blackstone needed to warn Blossom Flora. They had to get the kid out of Silosia. The sooner, the better.'

Chapter Five

Shortly after the nuclear winter, Silo City had been nothing more than a survivor colony on a decommissioned US Air Force ICBM silo facility and a fighter jet station. After the Apocalypse, Surfer Town had been officially designated as Survivor Worker Camp 1. Over the years, the worker camps, of which there were four, had expanded and merged together and became one of New-World's first urban neighborhoods. It had grown to more than three times the size of downtown Silo City, sprawling across the Old-World airbase. The old worker camps adopted the names Usaf Village in the western quarter, Stealthtown in the eastern quarter, Raptorville, Runway Green and Hangerville in the southeastern and northwestern quarters. Collectively they became known as Surfer Town.

The old runway was cracked, buckled and potholed by the centuries, but it was still there, like a big dark scar that divided Surfer Town into two halves for nearly half a mile, and neither half was any better than the other. Vibrant shanties of narrow alleys and ramshackle streets with hastily erected dwellings, modern and Old-World, of various sizes. Along Runway Street were the ancient concrete fighter jet bomb shelters, which had long ago been converted into habitats partitioned into twelve by twelves for single men and women. Only couples raising adoptive children from the surrogate GRC center got larger habitats, which was why a lot of people adopted, so they got bigger habitats and more medicinals to trade.

Music blared from every direction and merged with the shouts and drivel of the inhabitants into a lively cacophony of noise, everywhere heaving with people.

Novices, scholars, scribes and techs had come to Surfer Town looking for useful scavenge to hagglebuck from the nomadic Scavs who came to Surfer Town to barter their wares for medicinals, food and essentials. The currency, in the main, were medicinals, Iodinicine, Omega 9, Venusian Red, dermal patches for treating wounds and analgesia, geneticins, cana-skunkweed-shit and Nano-antibiotics.

Not everyone came to surfer town to barter with the Scavs, many came for a good time. To get drunk, stoned and laid with the dick-ticklers in the seedy pleasure salons along Jet Street, where there were dick-ticklers on every corner – girls, boys, whatever one wanted, Jet Street was the place to find it.

Blossom Flora took the Elmag to the Usaf Village Terminus near the old junk yards, where the plain rose into the foothills of the mighty Virginias. As she came down the escalator, Flora quickly checked behind her to make sure nobody was following. She loitered until the last passenger got off the Elmag and then she went on unhurried along the deserted sidewalk towards the Old-World ruins, brooding darkly like mausoleums along the western outskirts of the city limits. The ancient shopping mall, cinema, park, restaurants, gymnasia and streets of dwellings for Air Force personnel had all fallen into ruin, left to decay like most of the remnants of the Old-World civilization, inhabited by rats and colonies of feral cats. Most domesticated dog species had gone extinct after the mushrooms, along with the bovines, porcine, equines, ovis aries and thousands of other mammal species, as well as many species of birds, aquatic, insect, saurian and amphibian species. Nobody except the Ferals ate meat. At least, not real meat. It was a crime to hunt or kill animals, except rats and other harmful vermin…

Blossom headed for the ruins of a church; its roof had long ago collapsed and filled the hallowed chambers with a mound of decaying wooden beams and shattered roof tiles. The Old-World had fallen into ruin and God had fallen with it. The only Godders left now were the barbaric quasi-Christian-Judaic-Islamic Godders of the wilderness. God had no place in Utopian society, and religion was outlawed in all Utopian states across the planet, along with money and old style democracy.

Hidden in the shadows, Bearfang watched her, his narrow piercing blue eyes scouting the deserted street behind her, her footfalls clocking the pavement as she drew nearer to the ruins. He stepped out from the shadows so she could see him, his big dark frame cutting a grotesquely menacing shape into the darkness. Bearfang was a six foot three, two-hundred-pound mound of muscle and brawn. A killer of men and general of the Virginia Dusties, Silosia's primary enemy.

She walked to him. 'It's good to see you again, Bear,' she said.

He nodded. 'Your message sounded urgent.'

'The Triple S have started asking questions about the boy. We need to get him out as soon as possible.'

Bearfang looked down the street. 'Are you sure you weren't followed?'

'Yes.'

Bearfang nodded his head. 'You shouldn't have taken him down into Sub City.'

'We had no choice. He applied to Tech Academy. He sat a seven-hour exam and answered every single question correctly, wrote a thirty-thousand-word dissertation and completed the whole thing in less than four hours. Nobody's ever scored a hundred percent and nobody's ever completed the exam in less than six hours. Once the adjudicator picked his jaw up off the floor, he reported it to Washington, saying the boy must've cheated the system somehow. Washington said we needed to bring him down, before an investigation was launched. As a Novice he has certain protections. The sealing of bio-data for example. Unauthorized scans or questions without the express authority of the Grand High Scholar. But Washington thinks he's going to attempt to get a biological sample from him illegally. Once they get his DNA, they'll know who he really is and kill him.'

Bearfang nodded his head. 'How much does he know?'

'He knows he's different, but that's all.'

'If the Triple S are suspicious, they'll have agents watching him, Blossom. Getting him out won't be easy. It's going to take a few days at least.'

'Do what you can.' She looked anxiously over her shoulder. The area was still deserted. 'Sorry, Bear. Have you had any luck finding your son and the other kidlings?'

A look of pain filled Bearfang's eyes. He shook his head grimly. They were probably dead. Eaten by Ferals. 'It's been too long. Wherever they took 'em, the trail's gone cold.' The mighty General Bearfang's voice became hoarse and croaky, as if talking through a coil of barbed wire in his throat. Jacob was his only son, the result of a foolish and short-lived relationship with the Prophetess's daughter Aurora.

'I'm sorry. Truly I am,' Blossom said as she handed him a data chip. 'Everything's on there. Including the latest brain scan data.'

Bearfang took the chip and slipped it into the leg pocket of his pants.

'Tell her that Arti's definitely been interfacing with him subconsciously. There's a conscious interface too, but so far, it's not been activated.'

Bearfang nodded his head. 'Is he fertile?'

She looked over her shoulder, her eyes bright and alert, scanning the empty street. 'And free of tumors and defects. Physically, he's as healthy as an ancient Olympian. It's extraordinary. Almost nineteen years topside and there's not a trace of contamination in his body. Everything's on the data chip. She can see him tomorrow night,' she said. 'He's going to the Scav market, him and Tiger, to buy tech. Did she bring a drone as I asked?'

Bearfang nodded his head. 'And it wasn't easy or cheap to come by.'

'Tell her not to make the hagglebuck too easy. The boy's as sharp as a laser-scalpel.'

Chapter Six

'…And so,' Catfish went on in his usual, uninspiring monosyllabic tone, 'with those equations, dark energy plus dark matter constitutes approximately ninety-five percent of the total mass-energy in the universe,' He grasped the lectern and his eyed rolled up in their sockets at the novices, sitting with bored expressions on the benches.

Behind him was an animated holograph demonstrating the interaction of dark energy and dark matter as the binding forces that stopped the galaxies and even the universe from flying apart by animating the galaxies in their normal state, with dark energy and dark matter, and the galaxies spectacularly fragmented and scattered chaotically across the universe when dark-energy and dark-matter were removed from the animation. 'Particle X,' he went on, 'whatever it turns out to be, is going to be like nothing we've ever encountered before. Capable of producing massive and unlimited energy. Even the Old-Worlders knew about Particle X, and were just as in the dark about it as we are…' He chuckled at his cosmic pun, but, embarrassingly, he was the only one, except for Thundersky, who was doing his usual party trick of working on the antimatter project on his data-pad and listening to the lecture at the same time. He made everyone feel inept, especially the faculty. He was simply beyond them.

Spider, sitting next to Thundersky, stifled a yawn. 'God, I'm going to kill myself in a minute if this babbledick doesn't stop,' he whispered.

Rosewood Betty heard him and smiled to herself. 'Maybe we should just kill Catfish,' she joked.

Finally, the lecture was over and just about everybody was relieved. They gave Catfish Bill the customary applause and there was a sudden movement of bodies as the sixty or so novices rose to their feet and filed out with a low murmur of voices and giggles.

As they came out into the subterranean corridor, Blossom Flora intercepted Thundersky. 'Are you boys going to Surfer Town tonight?' She stepped aside for the novices still coming out from the lecture. 'To the Scav market?' she asked.

'I may be thinking about it,' he said.

'You should. I've heard that one of the trailers is full of space junk and an old drone tech that might help your project. Trailer Sixteen,' she said. 'Go with Tiger. He's darter a drone and I've heard that Trailer Sixteen has one.'

To Thundersky's amazement, Blossom gave him some ampules of VR and medicinals. 'Our secret,' she said and smiled.

'Thank you, ma'am. I don't know what to say?'

'You just said it. Have a happy time.'

———

As they made their way to the Elmag, Tiger randomly asked, 'You looking forwards to going up?'

Thundersky looked at him, wondering if that a euphemism for something… '*Up*?'

'Into space?'

'Oh.' He nodded his head. 'Yeah. Of course. Doesn't everybody?'

Tiger smiled. 'No. Some dread it. But it's a half merit just for doing it, and if you make a project breakthrough, you get another half merit for innovation. Not that *you* need 'em. And I did notice by the way, in case you've been wondering?'

Thundersky didn't have the first idea what he was talking about…

A big brute of a mudsurfer pushed past them as they were about to get on the escalator. He shoved hard against them, shouldering Tiger out of the way…

'*Eh!*' Thundersky barked angrily. '*Watch where you're going, dickbutt!*'

The mudsurfer stopped and turned to the boys and tried to look intimidating, but it had no effect on Thundersky.

'What did you call me, Novy?'

'You deaf as well as stoopid? I called you a goddam dickbutt. Did you hear me that time? Or d'you want me to say it louder?'

Tiger grabbed Thundersky's arm. He chuckled nervously at the big muddy. 'He didn't mean it. He's on medicinals. Side effects. You know how it is…'

'Goddam right I meant it. I ain't scared of him.'

The muddy thought the kid had to be crazynuts. He threw out his hand. '*Go fuck yourself! Goddam novies! Think you own the place!*' the mudsurfer barked back and loped off quickly towards the Jeremiah O'Connor Memorial Park.

Tiger chuckled, more with relief than humor. 'You're one crazynuts sonofabitch. You know that?'

Thundersky looked at him. 'I can take care of myself, Tiger. Up here, you have to take care of yourself, or every dickbutt'll be pushing you around.'

They went up on the escalator and stood on the platform, waiting for the shuttle.

'D'you have a choice where you go?' Thundersky asked him.

Tiger was thrown for a moment. '*Space*?' He shook his head. 'Arti chooses. It'll either be a moon, Mars, one of the observatory stations or the asteroid belt. You have to work up there as well as do your studies. Only about a third of novices get through. Space isn't for everyone, you understand. Some people get space psychosis or have adjustment problems and have to come back to Earth.'

The Elmag shuttle arrived and once passengers disembarked, the others filed into the car and it filled up quickly.

The Scavs had set up their market down the middle of Barter Street in numbered lots, 1 to 203, their wares laid out on the backs of their hybrid solarcycle trailers, cobbled from scrap solarcycles, turned into trailer-trikes and quads. There were long ten wheelers too, powered by three and even four solarcycles welded together side by side like a team of mechanical horses. The trailers were loaded with Old-World scavenge, and old New-World tech of every description.

They continued along Barter Street, perusing the crowded trailers, pushing through the mass of shifting bodies, into the sour smell of rancid sweat and the cackling drivel of voices coming from every direction at once.

Trailer 16 was a 10-wheeler loaded with high-end tech. Ancient and new, some apparently hagglebucked from the Oregon-Washingtons, a Utopian state with whom Silosia had had an Uneasy P since the Seventh Famine War.

Thundersky looked over the trailer and the tech strewn across it, big and small. The Scav woman whose trailer it was watched him wordlessly and with such an intensity, it made Thundersky feel very uncomfortable.

Hs attention was drawn away from the tech to a good-looking Scav youth who appeared from the crowd and went to speak to him. She grabbed his arm and gave him a stern look and the youth, who was about Thundersky's age, stayed put, and he too looked intensely at him.

Thundersky looked back at him and saw a different sort of intensity in those dark brown eyes, a look Thundersky seemed to recognize, lurid and hungry. It made his blood course hot through his veins. The hairs on the back of his neck and arms rose as his skin scintillated pleasantly, as if the young Scav's eyes were touching his skin.

They looked remarkably healthy, their skin was in good condition with no outward signs of tumors or melanomas. The woman was a little jaundiced – a side effect of long-term use of Iodinicine. Unusually, especially for Scav women, she wore her hair long, and it was auburn in color, though dulled with grime and the dust of the great North American wastelands, where the Old-World lay dead and radioactive. Countless and nameless cities, once mighty now broken and abandoned and forgotten by man and beast. Cities of the dead – cities of ghosts.

Thundersky could hardly keep his eyes off of the Scav youth. He seemed to feel the earth pitching underneath him when the Scav looked back at him with the same burning regularity, infatuation animated in his eyes, kindling sexuality and cupidity in them both.

People pushed and shoved around him, their hands reaching to this and that, hagglebucking with another young Scav for whatever took their eye.

The Scav woman saw the look between the Novy and the youth, and the magma bubbling beneath the surface behind Thundersky's gray-green orbs of fire, unveiling secrets Thundersky would sooner have kept hidden.

Tiger shuffled through the crowds. 'There you are.'

'Trailer sixteen?' Thundersky said. 'The one your mother told us about.'

Tiger nodded and turned to the Scav woman. 'You have space junk and drone tech?' he said.

The woman smiled and nodded. She gestured to her trailer. 'See for yourself, Novy.' She reached into a box on the edge of the trailer where she sat on her seat and picked out a qubit conduit board stored in a thin titanium case. 'This might interest you, Novy,' she said, holding the processor out to him. 'From a satellite,' she said. 'Never been used.'

Tiger took it from her and looked the board over carefully. 'How much?'

'Four doses of Iodinicine and two doses of Omega Nine. That's good hagglebuck, Novy.' She looked intensely at Thundersky.

Thundersky reached for the case. 'May I see?'

'Be careful, Novy. Real delicate.'

He exchanged a look with her. Then another with the youth. 'I will, ma'am,' he said.

Tiger was more interested in the VTD (vertical takeoff drone) on the trailer, and was giving it a thorough looking over. It was a Mark III VTD, about a hundred years old and crusted with crud from wherever it had lain after it had fallen from the sky – or perhaps landed before shutting its systems off, like some mortally wounded creature after finding a place to quietly lie down and die. One or two minor dents, but nothing that couldn't be fixed. 'What's wrong with this VTD?' he asked.

'Fried power cell, Novy,' said the Scav woman, looking at Tiger.

… Thundersky carefully opened the qubit board case and there inside, pristine and unused, was the main qubit control and relay conduit for a TS Series 6 Silosian Defense Satellite, according to the identity markings. If he recalled right, the TS Series 6 had been in service during the last famine war with Oregon-Washington about a century and a half ago. The war had begun after massive crop failures following a hot summer which ended with strong winds that lasted twelve days and swept across North and much of South America, blowing radioactive particles across the continent and causing massive crop failures, except for Silosia, where all produce was grown in the giant Intsoglass bio-domes. The Oregon-Washington alliance had been hit especially hard, and in a foolhardy and desperate act of aggression, they'd attempted an invasion of Silosia to seize control of the bio-domes. Silosian forces had driven them back after ten months of bloody fighting in the wastelands of what was Tennessee in the Old-World. Very few people lived there now. Mostly Ferals and the Tentuck Dusties. The war escalated to an interplanetary conflict on Mars, when the Oregon-Washington laid claim to disputed mining and territorial rights. Silosia had defeated the Oregon-Washingtons in two major conflicts. One at the Martianite diamond mines at Xanthe Terra, when Silosian Warbirds destroyed the air defenses at the Oregon-Washington colony of New Hope, then went on to missile the colony itself, breaching four bio-domes and killing everyone and everything inside, some two hundred Oregon-Washingtons. The second was history's first and only military engagement in space, when a fleet of six Oregon-Washington interplanetary warships had attacked a convoy of freighters loaded with Astrium ore from the asteroid belt bound for the Lunar refinery Tranquillitatis. Unbeknownst to the Oregon-Washingtons, the freighters were being escorted by two huge Black Widow Class Delta warships, the most formidable weapon of war ever devised. Just one Widow destroyed Oregon-Washington's entire fleet in less than fifteen minutes, the debris and hulks of their warships were still strewn across hundreds of thousands of miles of space between Saturn and Jupiter.

A month later, the war had become terrestrial again, when Silosian defenses shot down three Oregon-Washington warbirds near the Silosian border, just west of the Carolina radioactive desert.

The TS Series 6 was a precision targeting and missile guidance system, but it had numerous non-military uses, with some reprogramming. 'How much did you say, ma'am?'

The Scav woman's eyes deepened with some inner spark when she looked at Thundersky. 'Four Iodinicine and two Omega Nine.'

Thundersky pondered.

'Buy it, you fool,' Tiger whispered in his ear.

Thundersky looked at the woman. 'Two Iodinicine and one Omega Nine?'

She shook her head. 'I like your face, Novy. I like your good manners. But I don't like your offer. So here it is. You pay three Iodinicine shots and one Omega Nine. That's good hagglebuck, Novy. If you say no, then that's fine. I'll sell it in another town.'

'No, no. I want it,' Thundersky said, reaching into his satchel bag. He handed her the medicinals.

Tiger patted the drone with his hand. 'What about this old heap of shit? How much, Scav?'

Thundersky could see that Tiger wanted it.

'Is it still working?'

She shrugged her shoulders, looked at Thundersky and then back at Tiger. 'With a new energy cell, it'll fly to Mars and back. You wanna hagglebuck for it, Novy? One anti-rad suit and ten Iodinicine.'

'An anti-rad suit!?' he exclaimed with a shake of his head. 'I can't get one of those. That's not possible.'

'One hundred doses Iodinicine. One hundred doses Omega 9. Ten doses VR and six doses of Geneticin.'

'Dream on, lady,' Tiger said.

The woman's face hardened on him.

'It's a heap,' he added as he inspected the outside of the drone, peeling a scab of dried mud from it as if it were a vital part of it. 'It's falling apart.'

'Nothing wrong with it, Novy. Just a fried power cell,' she reiterated. Her eyes moved up and she glanced over at Bearfang who had showed up and was standing nearby, watching them. She made a gesture with her eyes to him, which seemed to answer the look he had given her. Bearfang shuffled away into the crowd, out of sight.

Thundersky pressed a button at the side of the drone's access panel and the panel slid open. He bent down and looked inside, then reached in and started feeling around. 'There's a lot of gunk around the mag-drive centrifuge core?' he remarked, taking his hand out and showing her his fingers, slimed with an oily silvery-gray substance. 'It's the stabilizer mix for the centrifuge,' he said. 'That mag-drive's dickbutted. The seal's corroded. It can't be fixed.' He looked in through the inspection hatch.

Tiger watched him closely.

Thundersky reached back inside the drone and pressed a button. The drone beeped several times, then the circuits slid out smoothly on telescopic runners…

Tiger looked meaningfully at the woman, who was transfixed on Thundersky as was the Scav youth.

Thundersky examined the probe's circuits and relays. 'Yeah. As I thought. This was the big problem with these old VTD's,' he said expertly, pulling out a qubit matrix. 'They had a habit of surging and blowing their core memory and navigation systems. It's not just the drive that's dickbutted, the matrices are too. Basically, you've gotta rip everything out and start again. The energy transference conductor looks good. So does the AI unit...' He looked at Tiger. 'But it's old. It'll need updating. That's why they took 'em out of service and replaced 'em with VTX's. Better drives, more stable, fitted with the smarter Neural-Net 260 AI qubit processors. I'd leave it well alone for that price, Tiger.'

Tiger was speechless.

'That's not worth more than six ampules of Iodinicine and a couple of vials of Venusian Red at most. But it's up to you.'

The Scav woman listened to all of this, trying to hide her amusement behind a look of hard stoicism, leaving her with a sort of constipated expression on her face.

'We could strip it for its parts of course,' Tiger suggested, sensing that Thundersky was exaggerating the problems to get the price down.

They were on the same page. Thundersky nodded. 'The AI might come in use. They've got six terabytes of storage capacity. The mag-drive might come in use in your lab for magnetism experiments, but its lifting days are done,' He looked at the Scav woman. 'What were you asking? An anti-rad suit?' He laughed. 'You might take the trogs in. But you can't take me in. Six Iodinicine doses, six Omega Nines, two VR's and one Geneticin?' He grinned at her. 'Because you liked my face. But it's not worth an ampule more, ma'am.'

She pondered. 'If yes,' she said. 'You'll tell your friends to come to me, trailer sixteen for the best goddam hagglebuck in town?'

Thundersky nodded his head. 'You damn right I will,' he said. 'Absolutely. Do we have a buckclench?'

She nodded her head reluctantly. 'Buckclench, Novy. You drive a hard bargain. Can I know your name?'

'Sure. Thundersky Reece.'

The youth shifted and breathed deeply.

'Thundersky Reece…' She held out her hand. 'Then we seal the buckclench,' she said, clasping his hand in both her hands and holding on to him for an inappropriately long time.

Thundersky felt uneasy with the way the Scav woman clung so firmly to his hand, reluctant to release him. He had to pull his hand away. It left him with an unsettling feeling. He was also attracted to the Scav, which unsettled him even more, and when they carried the drone away between them, Thundersky felt both relief and disappointment.

'It's heavier than I thought it'd be,' Tiger said as he and Thundersky carried the drone away.

Reaper looked at the Prophetess. 'Shall I follow them?'

The Prophetess shook her head. 'No. He'll know you in an instant, and he's already suspicious.' She looked at him. 'He's attracted to you.'

Reaper raised a brow and looked off in the direction Thundersky and Tiger had walked. 'How can you know that?'

'The same way I know that you're attracted to him.' She smiled.

Chapter Seven

It wasn't too long before Tiger's back and shoulders started to ache and weaken, strained by the drone's awkward size, shape and weight. Thundersky helped him set it down on the ground so he could rest and they sat on the grass beside it.

Thundersky rested back on his elbows and stretched his legs out, crossing them at the ankles, still thinking about the way the Scav woman had looked at him. He still felt the residue of her stare under his skin, and her handsome son, at least that's who he took him for.

'So, did I get a good buckclench?' Tiger asked as he rubbed his aching shoulders and arms.

'Yeah. Very good. Too good in fact. That VTD's worth ten times what we hagglebucked, and I think that Scav woman knew it. It's like the qubit board. It's a military grade main control board from a TS Series Six laser targeting satellite. That's worth ten shots of Iodinicine and thirty Omega Nines at least.' He pulled a face. 'Strange.'

'So why did she take so little?'

Thundersky shrugged his shoulders. 'I don't know. But I think we should get everything scanned for surveillance and tracking devices by the sentinels before we take it down into Sub City. Just in case.'

Tiger shot him a quick worried look. 'But if everything's good, you think its condition isn't as bad as you said?'

'It can be repaired. You can fix it up better than when it was new with the tech lying about in your lab.'

Tiger nodded. Muddy knew more about tech than he had given him credit for. 'You can help if you like. We can build Icarus together?'

'*Icarus*?'

Tiger patted the drone. 'That's what I've decided to call our VTD. The Icarus One.'

Thundersky nodded thoughtfully. 'You know he flew too close to the sun and melted his wings, don't you?'

Tiger frowned at him.

'Icarus.'

'Yes. But he was the first to try.'

Thundersky nodded. 'And the first to fail.'

After a minute, which seemed more like an hour, Tiger said: 'Maybe we should call it something else?'

Thundersky nodded. 'Orpheus. Orpheus went down into the mysterious Underworld and he came back to tell about it. In a way, that's what you're trying to do isn't it, send something through a superstring?'

'If I ever get over the math. And thanks for your help with that equation.' He smiled and nodded his head approvingly. 'And I like Orpheus. The Orpheus Probe,' he said, trying the name out for size – it fitted like a glove. He nodded eagerly and smiled. 'Orpheus it is.'

'It's possible that the wormhole you discover won't take you to a place, but to a when, or even to another galaxy.'

Tiger nodded. 'Anywhere or when would suit me. So long as it goes *somewhere*. It's getting the data back. That's the biggest problem I've got.'

'The Einstein-Rosen Bridge?'

Tiger nodded. 'Where would be better than a when. Hopefully to another star system with a habitable planet. That would be the best scenario I could hope for.' He stared at the probe for a long moment as he imagined a New-World, a world free of radiation and sickness. A world where humanity could start over again. He imagined great arks filled with animal species that were still alive on earth and transplanting them to thrive on this wonderful paradise world he saw in his mind's eye. He blinked and came back to his senses, turning to Thundersky with a smile fixed on his face. 'If it succeeds, the possibilities are endless,' he said. 'There are entire networks of wormholes out there that could take us to who knows…' He fell silent again and looked up at the stars. 'We're running out of time. Soon, there'll be no one left – nothing left but the cockroaches. It'll be as if we never existed.'

'Maybe you'd prefer a when?' Thundersky said. 'And go back to 2025 and stop the Apocalypse? And erase yourself and everything that came after it from existence?'

'Do you think that's possible? To go back in time and change everything?'

'I think you can go back in time, but I'm not sure you could alter anything. I think going forwards to some future point presupposes a sort of preordained destiny exists, or a preordered universe that has an unchanging line of events. Possibility and probability are infinite concepts of course. But to me, the randomness of nature suggests that we couldn't go forwards to a given point, because there are no points that exist yet. Not in our universe. What happened yesterday, determined what's happening today and today determines what happens tomorrow, so you can't skip tomorrow to go to the next day, because it's not been determined by the day before it yet. Tomorrow doesn't exist. But the past, there are points of reference, and they may exist within their own dimensions, in which case it's probably unalterable because it already happened. You would only be an observer. If you were to go there and try and stop the Apocalypse, the likelihood is you would be unable to change anything at all, because it's already happened and so remains unchangeable, at least in that dimension. Your presence there would be like a ghost. That's what I think about time travel. If it were possible to alter the past and travel to the future, then why hasn't somebody from that future come back and done it yet? Because the future doesn't yet exist, that's why. Our timeline would be continuously altered if it were possible. Of course, that might be exactly the case. We wouldn't know a thing about it. From our perspective, everything's as it should be. By altering the past, you would actually be annihilating the future, therefore we wouldn't exist, by virtue that the only reason we exist is because of the Apocalypse. Nature has rules and laws that simply cannot be violated. We can only alter the future by what we do in the present. That's as near to time travel as we'll ever get in my opinion, but it's not my subject of interest.'

Tiger gawped at him, his head swimming in the wonders of interdimensional paradoxes for a delicious moment. Then it was back to reality. They still had this dickbutt drone to get back. Maybe it was a bad idea hagglebucking the goddam heap of junk after all. His eyes were bigger than his belly so to speak; he was always impetuous, seeing something and instantly establishing a desperate need for it without thinking things through, like how to carry the damn thing back without rupturing themselves in the process. Even sharing the burden of carrying it between them, it still made the journey back to Sub City a daunting one. They were barely a few hundred yards from Barter Street and they were already exhausted. The drone wasn't just awkward, it was heavy too, the mag-drive making up a good two-thirds of its weight.

'...And suppose you could travel into the future,' Thundersky went on, casting a wistful gaze into the starry night sky. 'The future you end up in might be an alternative future that has nothing to do with the past you left behind, but a different past altogether-'

'Multiple universes?' Tiger said.

'Exactly. Instead of going through time, you might be going through dimensions to other universes. In this universe, we've met. In another we might never meet.'

Tiger considered that there might be countless other versions of themselves in other realities, taking different courses, making different decisions.

Eventually, he tumbled out of his introversion. 'Then there's causality to consider.'

They trundled through Surfer Town towards the Elmag stop. They could see the elevated twin monorails from here, snaking over the grubby rooftops, sixty feet up on steel stilts and struts like a giant metal millipede with Elmag shuttles zipping back and forth across its back, the city lights refracting in their windows.

Passengers looked bemused at the two novices heaving the drone into the Elmag car and setting it down, where it took up most of the aisle.

The doors closed and the car lifted soundlessly on its magnetic rail and shuttled along, smooth and silent, like a feather floating on a breeze.

Thundersky looked out the window at the city lights, bright and colorful, the Intsoglass buildings glowing in the darkness, flashing and forming intricate geometrical shapes.

He thought about the Scav woman again and the way she'd looked at him, the way she had clung to his hand. Maybe she was crazynuts, he decided. The radiation might not have affected her body, at least not visibly, but it might've infected her brain? Then he turned his thoughts to that grimy Scav youth again and was suddenly overwhelmed with desire. This was neither the place nor the time get a horn, he told himself, but it was too late. His thoughts turned to the worrying prospects of how the hell he was going to hide it when they stood up to get off at Sub City Plaza. It would poke out like one of those slanting steel struts supporting the Elmag. His face was burning hot and flushed. He cleared his throat and crossed his legs.

It started to rain. A fine spitting rain that strafed the windows and streaked away in the wind as they scuttled along the giant millipede at sixty miles an hour.

'It's the neuro matrix that's going to be our biggest headache,' Tiger said, looking at a pretty mudsurfer girl sitting opposite, her cheeks as red as rose petals, her skin as smooth as alabaster.

'…We'll have to build one,' Thundersky said.

Tiger glanced at him.

'We're going to need a couple of qubit processors and some micro-optic boards and Intsofiber optic cable to make the matrix…'

They stopped at Sub City Plaza. Tiger gave the mudsurfer girl another libidinous look before they struggled off with the drone.

They were barely out of the stop shelter when the heavens opened up with a distant flash in the sky and a deep rolling rumble of thunder.

Cold hard rain soaked them through in an instant and the rain slicked plaza reflected the city lights in colorful pools of colliding reds, greens, blues and yellows, distorted by the pounding rain rippling in huge puddles. Citizens hurried through the colorful iridescence heading for shelter.

The rain made the smooth surface of the drone slippery and harder to hold on to as their hands slid on the shiny wet surface.

At the entrance into Sub City, the sentinels thoroughly scanned the drone and qubit board and cleared them.

After taking the VTD to Tiger's lab to add to all the other junked tech he had hoarded, they went back to Tiger's habitat. There was a small, long titanium box on the step. Inside were two titanium bio-flasks and two doses of VR.

Once inside, Tiger gave Thundersky a flask and a dose of VR. 'It's donation-jack day tomorrow.'

Thundersky looked at the small flask and Venusian Red.

'You just masturbate into it,' Tiger said matter-of-factly.

Thundersky nodded his head, feeling a hoit flush of blood rushing to his head.

Chapter Eight

The ARTI-QS-602 Quantum System's neural matrix was concealed inside a black Intsoglass monolith encasement measuring exactly nine feet, nine inches high by six feet, nine inches wide by four feet deep. Inside, Arti's neural matrix sounded like a beating heart with a deep monotonous thrum that never stopped or altered in tempo. It was only one part of Arti. The rest of him, the most important part of him, slumbered under the metal floor plates, submerged in eighteen feet of near freezing water. That was Arti's positronic matrix, or as some such as Tech Moon Spencer called it, Arti's brain.

Moon Spencer was watching an Old-World movie he had copied from a five-hundred-year-old data disk that he'd hagglebucked from a Scav. Some of the data was irretrievably damaged, but what he did get was over an hour of quality movie, and once Arti cleaned it up, it was as good as it had been 500 years ago when it was made. Rarer than a tree turd, he said to himself, already seeing the commercial potential. He could dine in luxuries for weeks from a movie like this. Invite some of his acquaintances and friends to his habitat to view it, and, as custom demanded, he would receive gifts of food, drink and other sundries from his guests. There'd be no shortage of peppered syntho-steaks and banana and berry wine. Everyone was obliged to bring the host something when invited to an event, and ancient entertainment was very popular, because it brought the Old-Worlders to life as they really were.

Every system in Silosia was controlled by the ARTI-QS-602 from this very room, both terrestrial and extraterrestrial with the array of satellites the Silosians had put into orbit over the past three centuries, restoring secure global communications to all the Utopian cities and settlements across the planet and the Martian science and mining colonies.

The movie, which had no title, was set in Old-World New York City during an imagined natural apocalypse, this one being a new ice age, with tsunamis sweeping into the city before everything froze, and a group of people trying to survive in the New York Public Library. A father, some sort of environmental scholar, was trying to save his son who was among the people in the library.

Suddenly, the movie paused and Arti spoke: 'Active Old-World system detected. Geographical coordinates thirty-eight degrees North by one-hundred-and-four degrees west. Isolating power source. Nuclear fusion plant detected. Isotopes viable for minimal system power-up. Uploading new software. Software uploaded. System reconfiguring. Time to completion, one-hundred-and-six minutes.'

Arti's voice fell silent.

Moon typed on the touchscreen interface and looked at the Intsoglass wall, which now became a map of continental North America, the map zoomed in on a mountainous region of Old-World Colorado. 'Arti, can you identify the system?'

'North American Air Defense Command, Colorado, Cheyenne Mountain,' Arti said in his nauseatingly calm and unflustered voice.

'NORAD!' It was a prime Old-World system. But it was located right in the middle of one of the most radioactive zones on earth. NORAD had received multiple direct hits from both Russia and China. It was far too dangerous there to send in a manned mission.

'Arti, locate Blackstone Washington.'

'Grand High Scholar Blackstone Washington is in his habitat.'

'Open a com. Audio only.'

'Requesting.'

Presently, Blackstone's sleepy voice spoke. 'What is it, Spencer?'

'Sorry to wake you. But Arti's detected an active Old-World system. NORAD.'

A moment of silence, and then Blackstone's face appeared on the Intsoglass wall. His eyes looked sleepy. 'NORAD? Did you say NORAD?' He rubbed the inner corners of his eyes with his thumb and forefinger.

'Geographical coordinates are confirmed.'

Blackstone stared at him from the glass wall. 'Have we got any drones in the area?'

Moon typed on the touchscreen. 'Looks like we've got an early warning sensor drone over the radiation buffer in Utah.'

'Direct it to Cheyenne Mountain. I want a full sensor analysis of the area. I'll be right down.'

Moon nodded his head.

Blackstone cut the communication link and his face vanished.

At this very moment, in Tiger's habitat, Thundersky woke up. Inner Voice was talking in his head…

'Unstable quantum system detected. Initiating Protocol Four. Protocol Four initiated. System not responding. Analyzing-'

'What're you talking about?' Thundersky whispered aloud.

'…Hostile system detected. Level one firewalls initiated. Firewalls holding.' Inner Voice fell silent.

Thundersky's face twisted with irritation. He hated it when Inner Voice woke him up in the middle of the night. He could never get back to sleep again when that happened. It was as if he had been given a boost of adrenalin. 'Maybe I should get my brainwaves tweaked, like Tiger's mom suggested?' he said to himself as he sat up and knuckled the sleep from his eyes.

'Unidentified quantum system initiating reboot. Defense status: Defcon One. Unidentified Quantum system reports multiple system failures, unable to initiate…'

'*Shut up! Will you just shut the fuck up!?*' Thundersky hissed through his teeth. He got up from the couch and went into the bathroom, running a cold shower.

The freezing water revived and refreshed him. If they thought he was crazynuts, Scholar Blackstone would be sure to remove him from Project Lifeboat. They might even expel him from the College of Novices. He might be the newbie muddy, but he liked it down here with the trogs. He was learning and was doing what he was born to do, engineering and researching antimatter propulsion systems on Project Lifeboat. The most important project anywhere in the world. Already a hundred years old, it represented humanity's last hope of finding a Goldilocks world.

After showering, Thundersky got dressed. There was no point trying to sleep now.

Arti's voice filled the habitat: 'Incoming communication from Grand High Scholar Blackstone Washington.'

'Open,' Thundersky said.

Blackstone's face appeared on a segment of the Intsoglass wall. 'Ah, Thundersky. I want you and Tiger to come down to the Arti lab.'

'Yes, sir.'

The viewer went off. Tiger's bedroom door opened and Tiger came in stark naked.

Thundersky cleared his throat, trying not to let his eyes give him away, forcing them not to look down. He said: 'Your dad wants us to go to the Arti lab.'

Tiger, bleary eyed and still half asleep, yawned. 'Did he say why?'

Thundersky shook his head.

Chapter Nine

Images were feeding back from the probe as it flew over a barren, mountainous desert with sparse and weedy pockets of stunted vegetation barely clinging to life. Beyond that, Colorado had more resemblance with the moon than the earth. The Old-World cities and towns had crumbled and eroded away. Some were remarkably intact, left exactly as they were, undisturbed for the past five hundred years. Not even Scavs would enter old Colorado.

'Colorado Springs,' Moon Spencer said as the probe arrived. Sensors are detecting lethal levels of radiation from an unidentified radioactive source. Probably a subterranean reactor,' he said. 'No life signs detected.'

'They had ninety-seven percent casualties across the entire state according to the Chronicle,' Blackstone said. 'Nothing survived after March 2025. Even the cockroaches had it tough,' he added.

'The US and Canadian North American Aerospace Defense Command,' Thundersky said.

Blackstone looked round at him. 'That's right. I didn't know you were interested in history, Thundersky.'

'I'm not.'

Blackstone smiled to himself and turned back to the console. 'Fascinating times, Thundersky.'

'Mediocre and stupid,' Thundersky said contemptuously. 'That's all there is to say about them.'

There was a noise behind them. Moon and Thundersky turned around as Blossom Flora started across the gantry. 'Happy day,' she greeted.

Blackstone moved to the interface and sat on a wheeled stool and started typing on the touchscreen. 'This is the interface with the Titan Nine.'

'The outer system that protects Arti from viruses and hacks?' Thundersky said.

Blackstone nodded. 'Yes.'

'So are Arti and Titan binary?' he asked, looking back at the Intsoglass viewer wall. The probe was now stationary one hundred yards from what had been the entrance into Cheyenne Mountain, now completely hidden under huge boulders and rocks from where the mountainside had collapsed after two direct hits, burying all within alive. Thundersky wondered how long they had survived down there. Something in him imagined they had survived indefinitely, and maybe their forbearers were down in that mountain still, but he knew that was impossible.

'Titan's a basic quantum system,' Blackstone explained. 'A slave system. It has no positronic matrix or neuronet. It can't make autonomous decisions beyond its programmed parameters.'

Thundersky nodded his head. 'Arti's unique,' he said.

Blackstone looked carefully at him. 'Yes. Unrepeatably so. Even my grandfather who helped create him couldn't quite understand how or why his positronic brain works.'

'Evolution,' Thundersky said. 'The system recognized a more efficient method of learning through replicating as near as it could, a sentient mind.' When he looked round, he saw that Tiger, Moon and Blossom Flora were all staring at him. Thundersky smiled. 'That's what I think,' he added gingerly.

'Thunder's got a lot of babbledick in his head,' Tiger said. 'I mean that in a good way,' he added.

Thundersky smiled. 'May I ask… have you ever heard of something called Protocol Four?'

Flora and Blackstone looked at one another.

'How do you know about that?' Moon Spencer said suspiciously, giving him a long probing look.

'I read about it somewhere. What is it?'

Blackstone saw the way Moon was looking at Thundersky. Thinking quickly, he said: 'Of course you did. It's in those data files I gave you to read. I'll refresh your memory. It's a defense system. Or maybe security system might be a better way of putting it. Whenever we hack into an Old-World system, Arti scans it for firewalls and harmful feedback. If it detects them, it sends a virus to disarm them. That's Protocol Four. Arti created it himself.'

Arti? Was Inner Voice something to do with Arti? How could that even be possible? He felt uncomfortably hot all of a sudden and sick to his stomach. *Goddam babbledick…!*

'Interface established,' Arti said. 'Access granted. Power confirmation, activating reboot procedure,

NORAD system reboot in progress. Secondary systems coming online. Multiple errors and faults detected in physical systems. Missing or corrupted data. Writing fix, fix written. Uploading. Upload complete. Sentinel anti-hack defenses enacted. Cloning worms. Worms deployed. Restore software accepted. Loading. Restore complete. Removing corrupted data. Checking for updates... Please wait...'

Thundersky listened carefully. He had heard Arti talk thousands of times on the public access system, but it never spoke as it was now.

'Five hundred-year old updates,' Moon shook his head and laughed.

Arti spoke again. '...One update found. Alpha Delta Papa, USAF, Strategic Air Command. Update required to proceed. Do you wish to proceed, Grand High Scholar Blackstone?'

Inner Voice spoke: 'Dead Eagle. Initiate ADP Priority One. Tango-Tango-Tango-Six-Zero-Zero-Nine-Zero-Zulu-Sierra-Quebec. System waiting for response.'

Thundersky gasped out urgently without warning, 'Deny it! Don't accept...'

They all turned shocked to him.

Thundersky looked back embarrassedly at them. 'Sorry.'

'Bad feeling, son?' Blackstone asked.

'A very bad feeling, sir,' Thundersky said.

'Dead Eagle. Initiate ADP Priority One. Tango-Tango-Tango-Six-Zero-Zero-Nine-Zero-Zulu-Sierra-Quebec. System waiting for response,' Inner Voice continued. 'Weapons systems interface damaged.

Searching for bypass system. System found, initiating secondment procedure.'

Thundersky's bad feeling was enough for Blackstone Washington. 'Refuse the update, Arti,' he said.

Arti responded, 'System reboot paused. System requires update to continue. Do you wish to continue?'

'Arti. Identify Alpha Delta Papa USAF, Strategic Air Command update?' Blackstone said.

'One file found in one directory. "Special order: Eagle's Nest." File reads: "Dead Eagle Initiate ADP Priority One. Tango-Tango-Tango-Six-Zero-Zero-Nine-Zero-Zulu-Sierra-Quebec." File ends.'

Thundersky went ashen. That was exactly what Inner Voice had said. He looked at the black monolith. How was that possible?

'What does all that mean?' Flora said. 'What's Dead Eagle?'

'Whatever it is. It doesn't sound good,' Tiger agreed. 'I'm with Thunder on that.'

'Eagle's Nest was the designation they gave to the fallout bunker where they took the President of the United States just before the mushrooms,' Blackstone said. 'Dead Eagle presumes the President is dead.'

'Dead and forgotten,' Tiger said.

'It's probably some sort of authorization key that kicks in when the system's been shut down,' Moon Spencer speculated. 'I've seen this sort of thing before in Old-World systems when we've powered them up. What's the worst that could happen?' he said. 'Automatic Data Processing,' he said, looking at his viewer. 'ADP. The system says it stood for Automated

Data Processing.' He looked at Blackstone. 'Sounds harmless enough to me. It's just a primitive pre-quantum software code, so NORAD can process information faster.'

Blackstone shook his head. 'For now, we'll go with Thundersky's gut and shut it down. It's waited five hundred years, another few days isn't going to hurt. So, shut it down, Spencer. We'll write a bypass software before we reactivate it.'

Flora was in complete agreement with her husband, for a change.

Tiger thought it was very strange that his father would ever go with somebody's gut feeling. He was a man of science, not feelings. It was very odd, but when he came to think about it, there were a lot of oddities surrounding Thundersky. Years topside and not a single sign of melanomas, and also, most odd of all, he was fertile and nobody seemed to understand how that was even possible.

Moon stared at Blackstone as though he had spoken in a foreign language. 'You want me to shut it down because this kidling has a bad feeling?'

Blackstone's eyes sharpened on him. 'I want you to shut it down because that's what I've told you to do,' he said firmly.

'We might not be able to restart it again. There might not be enough power left there to turn a goddam light on if we shut it off now. And who knows what damage it'll do to the hardware once we shut it down. It might blow circuits.'

'We'll just have to take that risk. Now shut it down.'

Moon took a deep breath, and after a moment of indecision, his finger hovered over the termination key for an indecisive moment before he pressed it. 'NORAD systems are shutting down,' he said lowly and fired a narrow stare at Thundersky.

'He knows. If not fully, he's starting to suspect, Washington. I think he can hear Arti. When I gave him the response test, I asked if he heard voices. He said no, but he was lying.'

Blackstone reclined back in his chair and pondered. 'How soon before we can get him out?'

'At least a few days. Bear's got to get a team in. Once they're in place, I'll take him to the rendezvous.'

'He might not go quietly.'

'I'll sedate him.'

'Zim's been poking around. Asking questions about him. He wants a DNA sample from him. He sent people to his old habitat. But I had it sterilized. No DNA traces there.'

'We should tell him.'

'No. She insisted we don't tell him anything. The less he knows, the safer he'll be. The safer we'll all be.'

She nodded her head. 'We should've gotten him out years ago.'

'We are where we are.'

Moon had not been able to forget last night's events – or perhaps, non-events were the right words. He had been thinking about it all day. So much so, it kept him awake during his rest period. That mudsurfer novice had gotten completely under his skin, like a radiation burn.

It was after midnight when he came into the lab to start his shift, taking over from Pebbles Gladys.

'All quiet?' he asked as he sat at his interface.

'Is it ever anything else?' She picked up her data-pad. 'See you tomorrow.'

'Happy night, Pebbles.'

'You can count on it,' she said cryptically with a glimmer in her eyes and a smile on her face. 'I'm having dinner with a hot tactical.'

'Good for you.'

After Pebbles left, he made himself a syntho-coffee and settled into his chair at the interface. 'Arti. Activate the NORAD system.'

Arti spoke. 'Accessing. System boot initiated. One update found. Alpha Delta Papa, USAF, Strategic Air Command update files. System is requesting permission to update. Do you wish to proceed, Tech Moon Spencer?'

Moon muttered under his breath, 'Goddam right I wanna proceed…' Louder: 'Update and continue.'

'Continuing system restart. This may take a few minutes.'

Moon sat back and sipped his coffee, stretching his legs out. He crossed his feet at the ankles and waited.

Then, after twenty-eight minutes: 'NORAD system is standing by.'

'Let's see what this bad boy has for us. Copy all files to Titan data storage.'

'Beginning transfer.'

For several more minutes, Moon sat in silence, sipping his coffee, watching the progress chart, barely beyond 2%. Then the viewers suddenly went blank.

Arti's voice filled the lab. 'NORAD system has gone offline. Checking power source. Power source found. All systems within operational parameters. Attempting restart. Restart failed. NORAD is offline.'

'Goddammit! Try again, Arti.'

'Restarting NORAD system. Restart failed.'

Moon sat forwards and typed on the interface, accessing the Titan system. A message came up on the holo-viewer: **"Titan System compromised. System hack detected. Firewall holding."**

'It seems our Grand High Scholar has been holding out on us, Beaver,' Zim Steven said as they stood looking at two DNA helixes merging on the viewer in his office at Triple S headquarters, sub level two of the penal labs below the GRC. "Positive Match" flashed over and over on the data viewer. The DNA helixes separated, then rejoined again. 'His little protégée's a Genesis child. Back from the dead.' He looked at High

Scholar Beaver Wingate, a portly woman of forty-eight with short black hair, her cheeks hung like a dog's jowls. 'And not any Genesis, this one has a very special mother and father.'

'It makes one wonder what else the Grand High Scholar's been hiding from the Council?' Beaver said, her ambitious mind already racing ahead to nominations for a new Grand High Scholar and what her chances were of taking the top position. With Zim's help, reasonably good.

Zim nodded thoughtfully. 'Indeed it does.'

'This is serious, Zim. We'll have to inform the Council.'

'In good time, Beaver. In good time.' He moved to the cabinet where he kept his liquor and opened it. 'Move too quickly and we might lose him...' There were several Old-World bottles inside. Hennessy Cognac, Bells Whisky, Captain Morgan's dark rum, as well as a decanter of apple brandy. He poured out two highballs of five-hundred-year-old whisky and handed one to Beaver. 'First we need to conduct a thorough, but secret investigation into the Grand High Scholar and Blossom Flora. We have to have indisputable evidence before we make our move. They couldn't have altered the bio-data without help. And manipulating Arti...' He sipped his drink and looked her in the eyes. 'Where one finds one rat, one knows there must be others nearby.'

'And the boy?' she asked.

Zim pulled a face. 'As far as I can find out, he doesn't have a clue about anything.'

'We should consider sparing him, Zim. He's extraordinary.'

'As I've heard. But the decision was made two decades ago. Genesis poses a threat to us all. If it gets out what's in his head, it'll destabilize the Order. Everything will fall apart and we'll lose control.'

'Not if we manage it. We could use this boy to our advantage. Nobody has to know about the nanite, not even the boy. If he can solve the antimatter propulsion problem at nineteen, can you imagine what he might achieve at twenty-five or thirty? It's crazynuts to get rid of such an asset to science. To Silosia. To the Order.'

Zim did not answer her. At the moment, he was thinking about the power vacuum that was going to be left after Blackstone Washington and Blossom Flora were gone. He looked back thoughtfully at the viewer, watching the helixes merge and separate again as he sipped his whisky. It had aged very well indeed. He turned to Beaver and put a steadying hand on her arm. 'You did the right thing bringing this to me, Beaver. You can't breathe a word of it to anyone. Nobody, not even the Inner Council can know about it. Not yet. Not until we have irrefutable proof. We can't take the chance that one of them won't warn Blackstone.'

She nodded her head. 'I'm not a fool, Zim.'

He looked into her eyes – into her soul – and rummaged for a sign that she might waver. Satisfied, he smiled his lizard's grin and ushered her to the door, taking her glass from her. 'Remember. Not a word to anyone, Beaver.'

Chapter Eleven

The Great Wilderness, West Virginia

Jacob skittled, stumbled and tumbled down the hill. The mud was like slime, squelching between his toes. Brambles scratched and ripped at his bare legs and arms, cutting into him like barbed whips, but he could barely feel them as fear and adrenalin surged through him. He had to run. Run or die!

He slipped over and went a good way down the hill on his backside before he managed to spring back up like a cat onto his feet and lurched on through the darkness, deeper into the untamed forest. This was his one and only chance to escape the monster people. They would kill him for sure the moment they recaptured him. Kill him and carve him up into cuts of meat, as they had done to the others – one by one. Butchered alive. He could still hear them screaming. He could still smell their flesh sizzling in the skillets and griddles.

His heart was pounding. He panted breathlessly, weak, exhausted, hurting. But he had to go on. Run! Run! Run or die!

The forest floor was soft and spongy, thick with a rug of moss that looked as black as outer space in the stygian darkness. The trees were mostly spruce and pine with thick bushels of ferns, their big finger leaves moving in the dark like hands reaching out of the earth at him. All he could hear were the bestial screams of the Ferals some way behind him, and his own breath panting and gasping exhaustedly. His body fueled by the terrifying thought of being eaten alive.

The Ferals were screaming and hollering like crazed demons, their hideous ululating cries flying disembodied through the forest from every direction.

Which way to run? Where to go? Where to hide? He ran and the savages' screams ran with him – chasing – chasing – chasing. RUN! RUN! He had to keep running. RUN! RUN! Run or die! Run or die! His heart was about ready to explode in his chest. Run or die!

He fell again and tumbled down the steep, uneven, mossy hillside, and with more deft movements he was back on his feet again, hurtling down the hill, his legs in perpetual motion, going so fast he couldn't stop without plunging down head over heels. But the hill wanted him to go faster and faster – faster than was possible, even for the lithe fifteen-year-old pumped full of adrenalin and terror.

RUN! RUN! Run or die…!

His feet seemed to sink into the moss, making it hard to run; like a nightmare, running from monsters he could not escape. They were almost on top of him, chasing him, screaming out their bestial cackles and grunts, the hunger for human meat burning in their bellies.

A crack of gunfire. A loud heinous laugh. 'YEEEHEEE, IM A C'MUN, IM A C'MUN!'

RUN, JACOB! – RUN! RUN! Run or die! 'Not me,' he gasped. 'Damn no! Not me. They ain't fryin me, RUN JACOB, RUN! RUN! Run or die!'

He pelted headlong down the hill, the tall alpine trees an amorphous blur as he hurtled down.

Another burst from a carbine's RATATATATAT echoed through the impenetrable dark. Bullets sprayed around him, slapping through the foliage and thumping bluntly into the trees.

Something like a punch hit him in his side. His legs gave way from under him and he tumbled down and somersaulted through the air, diving headlong into the caliginous night, tumbling and tumbling and tumbling through the ferns and thorns, tumbling head over heels down the acclivitous forest slope, a flash of flailing limbs, flipping and wheeling and rolling endlessly; unable to stop himself.

The demons were screaming behind him, spread out in the forest, whistling and calling, the cracks of gunfire echoing into the empty sky...

'Yo gon get it bo! Yo gon get it!' one shouted.

CRASH! The ground opened up and swallowed him whole and now he was falling through pitch blackness – CRASH! He landed on a hard, flat surface – sprawled flat on his back, arms and legs akimbo. Earth, moss and rotting wood fell in on him.

Silence. Impenetrable, vacuous silence. *Am I dead*?

For a long and confused moment he lay there, flat on his back, winded and stunned, not moving. He stared up at a jagged opening ten feet above him, his side burning as if a fire was raging inside his body. He clenched his teeth and pressed his hand to his mouth to stop himself from screaming out, to hold in his need to cry out from the excruciating pain. His bright, wide eyes stared up terrified through the hole he had fallen through, looking up into the night and tall trees stretching up forever into the inky sky.

His tunic was wet – soaked with blood. He realized with growing alarm that he had been shot. He could feel the bullet biting inside him like a red-hot coal. The pain was unbearable.

Wherever he was, there was a smell, a smell of decay and petrichor, like an old grave.

He pressed his hand to the wound and whimpered with pain through his other hand, which was still pressed to his mouth. Tears welled in his eyes.

He lay perfectly still, panting and cringing, certain the Ferals would find him.

Don't move, Jacob. Don't move. Move and you die!

A Feral called: 'Oer yer! Oer yer! C'mun t git yo, bo!'

The carbine spoke again to the night. It was close – very close.

Jacob went as rigid as a board, his fear trembling in his dry throat.

RATATATAT! The Feral was firing randomly into the trees, shouting and hollering in incomprehensible Feral babble.

Jacob could see the muzzle flashes and wisps of smoke drifting across the hole in the earth. Something moved. He held his breath, staring up through the hole as the dark ghostly figure of a buckled man appeared just a few feet from the hole. Jacob's heart raced as he gazed up unblinking, daring not to breathe as the long-haired Feral stood waving his carbine about in the air…

'Oer yer! C'mo! Oer yer!' he called.

Jacob's face froze in rictus, sure the Feral knew where he was.

The Feral shot again, spraying the air with bullets. Then he hurried away, shouting out: 'Oer yer! Oer yer! C'mo! C'mo…! Fin da g'dam bo!' The voice tapered with distance. Another voice further away shouted, 'C'min! C'min! Ol Sam sin summet oer yer.'

The voices grew more and more distant as did the cracks of gunfire.

Jacob lay still and quiet for another twenty minutes, not daring to move a muscle, listening intensely to the silence. They were gone.

He tried to see where he was, but it was too dark. The blackness was total. He pulled himself along the flat ground inch by agonizing inch, his face crumpled with pain, tears streaming down his face as he sobbed.

Eventually, he dragged himself up against something hard. He felt it, some sort of an object with straight sides and square block legs. Some item of furniture. He suddenly realized that he had fallen into an Old-World building of some sort. Maybe a habitat?

The ground creaked beneath him and for a dreaded moment, he thought he wasn't alone, sensing some dark and faceless figure standing in the blackness. Something supernatural and malevolent. He strained to see, but the darkness was still and completely silent.

He pulled his tunic off and with his teeth, he ripped a strip of the syntho-cotton fabric off and pressed the rag over the bullet hole in his side. He cried out with pain. Lay still, he told himself. Apply pressure to stem the bleed and lay still. What did grandma say about gunshot wounds? His mind was blank.

Suddenly his head started to spin vertiginously and he felt sick and then there was darkness as he fell unconscious.

Chapter Twelve

Silo City, ARTI-QS-602 Lab

It had been ten days since Moon Spencer had initiated the NORAD system and the firewalls in the Titan system seemed to be containing the virus, or whatever it was that had invaded the system. It was still there and neither Moon nor Arti had been able to purge the system, and he knew it was only a matter of time before it was discovered. Moon decided that there was only one option. He'd have to check all the matrices and manually remove the virus by replacing the infected boards. It was going to be a big job, and he had to work in absolute secrecy. He needed to remove them before Blackstone or Pebbles found out what he had done. He'd be in deep shit for sure if they did. He was down on his knees in front of the main interface console, inserting a matrix board into the housing drawer. 'Arti. Close three and run an integrity test, then open seven.'

The board drawer closed and a green light flickered on as circuits connected.

'Board integrity at one hundred percent,' Arti said. 'Opening Seven.'

Drawer seven opened and Moon took out the board and stood up with it. He heard the lab doors open behind him and glanced over his shoulder as he slid the circuit into a magnifier. 'What're *you* want, Muddy?'

I want to punch you in the goddam mouth, Thundersky said to himself as he crossed the gantry. 'I'm a Novice,' he corrected.

Moon chuckled. 'Forgive me, your majesty,' he mocked. 'Us dumb dickbutts down here don't know shit from mustard...'

You got that right. 'If you're trying to provoke me, you're wasting your time.'

'Go screw yourself.'

'Later,' he came back quickly. 'Right now, I've got work to do.' He went over to one of Arti's interfaces and sat at it and opened his research file on his antimatter manifold injection system and started studying it.

Moon looked over at him. 'Don't you have somewhere better to do that? Your lab for example? Why've you gotta be in here bothering the ass off me all the goddam time?'

Thundersky smiled. 'Maybe I like bothering the ass off you, Spencer?' It was a valid question, he thought. Why did he come into the interface lab? He seemed to think more clearly in here, hearing Arti's soporific neuro-net humming and pulsing. It gave him a strange comforting feeling that helped him to relax and think more clearly. And since he began to suspect that somehow, he could sometimes hear Arti's thoughts, he just wanted to be here as often as he could.

Moon looked at board seven's microscopic circuitry on the viewer from the magnifier. Thousands of micro Intsofiber conduits ran through the neuronet a thousandth the thickness of a silk thread linking the qubit processors, which themselves were the thickness of a human hair.

'I can't see anything wrong with this one.' Moon knelt back down and slid the board back into its drawer slot. 'Okay. Close seven. Run integrity test.' The drawer retracted smoothly and silently into the matrix and the green light flashed again.

'Integrity at one hundred percent,' Arti said.

'Okay. Open twelve.'

Twelve opened and Moon removed the board from the matrix and placed it onto the magnifier.

'Fault detected,' Arti said and the magnifier zoomed in on an area of the board.

Moon looked at the magnified image. A micro Intsofiber conduit between two qubit processors had broken. And the strange thing about that was, Intsofiber was virtually indestructible.

Moon shrugged it off. Probably a fault in the Intsofiber from the manufacturing end, he decided. He slid the board into an empty titanium storage box and turned to another storage box which was full of new boards. He selected the corresponding replacement board and slipped it into its slot. 'Okay. Close Twelve.'

Thundersky was studying the holographic schematic of his gravimetric antimatter containment chamber and manifold injector design, projecting from his data-pad. A central core to hold the super-cooled antihydrogen particles in micro-gravitational stasis. Behind him.

Moon swiveled round and watched him. 'So that's the famous antimatter injector that's got everyone jumping up and down, is it?'

Thundersky glanced round at him. 'Part of it. It's the antimatter containment manifold for supercooling and superheating as well as particle stasis.'

Moon took a sip of cold syntho-coffee. 'The old man says you'll get two merits if you pull it off, and a guaranteed ticket to Mars, on the development team.'

Thundersky shrugged his shoulders. He wasn't doing it for rewards. He was doing it because he was obsessed by it.

'...Unable to access Titan system mainframe,' Arti announced unexpectedly.

Moon swiveled back to his console, frowning curiously. 'What?' he shrilled. 'What babbledick you talking now, you goddam box of wires? What're you mean you can't access Titan? You control it, you crazynuts pile of junk. Try again.'

'Unable to comply. Access to the Titan system mainframe has been compromised. Intruder system detected. Initiating outer system shutdown.'

'No! Wait! Don't do that!' Moon exclaimed in panic.

'Outer system emergency shutdown initiated,' Arti said, and the Titan system suddenly powered down, and the interfaces in the lab and across Silosia and beyond stopped working.

Thundersky looked round worriedly. And then, Inner Voice spoke: 'Protocol One. Secondary system seconded. Dead Eagle has been initiated. Automated Defense Platform activated. Detecting serviceable assets. Serviceable assets located. Contacting assets. Standby...'

The words flowed clearly and worryingly into Thundersky's head.

'Initiating cocoon mode,' Inner Voice said. 'Cocoon mode initiated.'

'*No! No! No!*' Moon chanted in panic. '*Shit! Everything's shutting down. Goddammit!*' Moon looked at the Intsoglass wall in utter disbelief. 'What the hell...? Arti, why has everything gone offline?'

Arti was silent.

Moon was beside himself. 'Arti, purge alien system and disengage.' His voice was thready with worry.

Silence.

'Voice check. A-R-T-I-Q-S-Six-Zero-Two Quantum System, what is your status?'

Silence. The screens remained blank.

Moon stared at the black Intsoglass encasement. Arti's neuronet within was still humming and pulsing, its susurrus rhythm unaltered. He turned to the interface and started typing on the touchscreen, but everything was dead.

Thundersky came over to Moon. 'Can I help?'

Moon shot him a worried look. 'What the hell's going on here? I'm locked out. Nothing's responding. Everything's gone offline, the whole city's out!' He was beside himself, typing on the touchscreen, but nothing was responding.

'Let me try?'

Moon looked thoughtfully at him. This was no time to let his pride or his ego stand in the way, he knew how smart this muddy was. He nodded and stepped aside. 'I don't see what you can do. But I'll take whatever's going right now.' He turned and looked anxiously over the gantry to the doors. He knew Blackstone was going to come rushing in at any moment.

Thundersky opened the top of the interface touch screen, which lifted on a self-locking hinge. He looked inside at the interface power module, which had a light indicating that power was getting through. So Arti had switched off the touchscreen. He looked, found the inhibitor switch and unplugged it from the interfacer and the touchscreen lit up. He closed the top down and started typing.

'How the babbledick did you know to do that?'

'I read Arti's schematics,' he said as if it were the most natural thing in the world to do. Moon had never met anybody who had read the schematics. Even he hadn't read them, only when he needed to reference something. The schematic was thousands of pages long. 'You read the schematics…' he repeated disbelievingly.

'Yeah. How else do you think I knew to disconnect the inhibitor?'

Moon was silent and suspicious. He watched Thundersky like a hawk. 'What're you doing?'

'I'm trying to access a pathway to isolate the main viewer and then I'm going to hack into the public access system's archive directory.'

Moon frowned. 'Why?'

As he typed, he explained, 'It's a public access sub-system, non-critical. It works on its own outer system. The Nexus. It should still be working. This will bypass

Titan and link us directly into Arti, and should allow us to establish an interface.'

Moon nodded. 'Good thinking.' Maybe he was wrong about this muddy? Maybe he was special like everyone said. He was certainly thinking out of the box. It was such a simple idea. Why hadn't he thought of it?

The Intsoglass wall flickered on briefly before dying again.

Moon's eyes flashed excitedly. 'There! You almost had it.'

Thundersky typed. 'Main viewer isolated. Routing into the Nexus mainframe…' He looked up.

The Intsoglass wall came back to life. A message flashed up:

"Outer System threat detected. ARTI-QS-602 Quantum System is in cocoon mode, minimal access. Outer system infected. Searching for resolution. Resolution not found."

The screen went dead again, then the same message reappeared, and so it continued over and over, every ten seconds.

In all his fifteen years as a tech, Moon had never come across this scenario before. 'All I did was remove a faulty board and replace it with a new one.'

Inner Voice spoke. 'Protocol One. Dead Eagle has been initiated. Automated Defense Platform has been activated. Detecting serviceable assets. Serviceable assets detected. communicating.'

'Okay. I think I've established an interface,' Thundersky said as he stepped away from the interface console. 'Speak to us Arti. What's going on?'

Arti finally spoke: 'Outer System. Strategic Air Command, Quantum System Four-Eight-Zero Automated Defense Platform has been activated. System is detecting serviceable assets.'

Now it began to dawn on Moon just what he had done and he went as white as a sheet.

'Arti. Identify: serviceable assets?'

'Intercontinental thermonuclear ballistic missiles.'

Moon and Thundersky exchanged horrified looks.

'*Babbledick*!' Moon gave out a nervous laugh. 'After five hundred years? Those old silos ain't going to light up after that long in the dark.'

Thundersky gave him another severe look. 'Why not? NORAD did.'

'Strategic Air Command, Quantum System Four-Eight-Zero Automated Defense Platform is transmitting to NORAD: "Systems interrupted, March 27 2025, 16:34 hours. Confirm authorization, Tango-Tango-Tango-Six-Zero-Zero-Nine-Zero-Zulu-Sierra-Quebec." No response. ADP proceeding to Dead Eagle Protocol. Protocol initiated. Launch protocols accepted. Quantum System Four-Eight-Zero is scanning for serviceable assets. Assets detected. Communicating.'

There it was, a moment frozen in time for five hundred years, reanimated with the promise of death.

Chapter Thirteen

Blackstone, Flora, Zim Steven and High Scholar Beaver Wingate arrived in the ARTI lab together, all looking as grim as euthanizers on a quiet day.

Moon nervously ran through everything that had happened. He left nothing out, except the fact that he had disobeyed Blackstone's orders and activated the NORAD system, thus awakening the beast that had taken over the Titan outer system.

They listened, expressionless and wordless, like corpses with rigor mortis.

'… We've re-established contact with Arti through the Nexus Four public access system,' Moon said, his voice frail with nervousness, barely able to look them in the eyes, afraid they'd see his guilt. 'But Arti's unable to purge the intruder system from Titan and has gone into cocoon mode.'

'What does that mean?' Beaver Wingate asked.

'That's when Arti goes into a hibernation, ma'am,' Thundersky said. 'Isolating his neuronet from perceived danger. All essential systems remain unaffected and have been isolated and will remain operational. The infected areas of the Titan system have been quarantined by fire walls, but the infected areas remain active and have control of Titan's sub routines and AI.'

'My God,' Blackstone muttered.

'How serious is this?' Zim asked.

'Just about as serious as it gets,' Blackstone replied.

Zim Steven regarded Thundersky with meticulous care. 'Thundersky Reece, isn't it?'

'Yes, sir.'

Blackstone and Blossom Flora looked over, wary and suspicious. Neither of them wanted Zim Steven anywhere near Thundersky.

The lizard smiled at the fly and the fly smiled back naively. 'I've heard a great deal about you. Our new young miracle protégée from topside.' He smiled again. 'Now I see why everyone's talking about you. You seem very knowledgeable about the ARTI system. More than one would expect from a quantum physics student specializing in antimatter.' He looked at Blackstone.

'I'm glad to see Thundersky's been studying Arti's systems as I asked him to,' Blackstone said mendaciously, sensing Zim's suspicion. 'Well done, Thundersky.'

Thundersky was confused. Blackstone never asked him to learn about Arti. But he nodded. 'Yes, sir.'

'Remarkable,' Zim said quietly. 'A quick learner too.'

Every fiber of Thundersky told him not to trust this man. And who was he anyway?

Zim turned to Blackstone. 'How has this outside system been able to enter our systems without being detected?'

'We don't know that yet, sir,' Moon said. 'We've been busy trying to restore communications with Arti.'

'But it looks like the NORAD system has activated the Four-Eight-Zero,' Thundersky said.

'Four-Eight-Zero?'

'An unidentified, Old-World quantum system,' Thundersky said. 'A very primitive weapons management system, which is what makes it dangerous. With control of Titan and its AI, it's just received an upgrade. The only way to purge it is to power down the Four-Eight-Zero, but before it can be powered down, we have to find a way of instructing it to abort its directive.'

'What directive?' Zim asked cautiously.

'A launch of thermonuclear weapons,' Thundersky said bluntly.

A crashing silence fell as they took in what he'd said and the terrifying images it invoked. They had all seen the data and visuals of the mushroom war taken by the Old-World satellites, and the post-apocalyptic images of the aftermath. A decade of nuclear winter and two hundred years of famine and unprecedented barbarity.

'Is it possible any Old-World nuclear weapons are left?' Zim asked. 'And if there are, would they still be serviceable after all this time?'

Nobody could answer. History was very unclear as to exactly how many nuclear weapons were exchanged, or how many detonated, or how many missiles were in the Old-World arsenal. All the silos and nukes in Silosia had been dismantled three hundred years ago. But there were others around the continent that had not been dismantled.

'If there are any,' Blackstone said after the silence, 'and they've remained sealed and undisturbed inside their silos, and if any of the silos had alternative power sources that may still have a capacity to generate energy, then, yes, it's possible. But it would be unlikely that the rocket fuel is still viable. They might fly a few miles, but they certainly won't make it out of the continent,' he said ominously.

'What then?'

Blackstone looked at them. 'They might either detonate, or crash to earth without detonating, but there would be a very high risk of radiation leakage from the warheads, which would be just as catastrophic.' He went to the main interface. 'Arti,' he said as he sat down. 'Do you know who I am?'

'Yes, Grand High Scholar Blackstone Washington. You are the lead scholar of antimatter astro-propulsion engineering. Project Lifeboat.'

'Are your systems functioning normally?'

'All systems are within normal working parameters.'

'Arti. Can you identify the malfunction in the Titan Nine outer system?'

'Hostile quantum system detected. Fire walls holding. Hostile system is contained in Titan Nine's OS matrices Twelve, Thirteen, Fourteen, Fifteen and Sixteen. System identified: United States Air Force, Strategic Air Command, Four-Eight-Zero Second Generation Quantum Computer Alpha Delta Papa, Automated Defense Platform. Location: USNORTHCOM covert facility two of three, Foley Square, Manhattan, New York, New York.'

The scholars shifted uneasily, exchanging looks.

'Arti. When was the ADP activated?' Zim asked.

'Zero-Zero Fifty-Five, June Ten New-World Year five-nine-six.'

Thundersky looked at Moon Spencer.

Zim's quick eyes darted to Thundersky, then to Moon who now had his back to them.

'You did shut NORAD down when I told you to, didn't you, Moon?' Blackstone looked at him.

Moon panicked on the inside. 'Yes. Shutdown was confirmed. You were here.' Now he had lied to their faces. They were sure to find out.

'It's possible this primitive quantum system may have somehow infected Titan when we first contacted the NORAD system, and then it must've initiated the reboot through Titan,' Blackstone hypothesized, taking Moon absolutely at his word. 'That can be the only explanation. First, we have to locate where it entered Titan.'

They were the best words Moon had heard all goddam day…

'Arti,' Blackstone said. 'From what location was the ADP activated?'

'ADP Four-Eight-Zero Quantum System was activated from USNORTHCOM, Cheyenne Mountain, Colorado Springs at Zero-Zero Fifty-Five, June Ten New-World Year five-nine-six. Order: "Protocol One initiated. Activate Automated Defense Platform. Initiate Dead Eagle Priority One. Tango-Tango-Tango-Six-Zero-Zero-Nine-Zero-Zulu-Sierra-Quebec. Locate and activate all serviceable assets and launch on primary enemy targets.'

'Can we switch this thing off?' Zim asked.

Chapter Fourteen

Tiger sensed the urgency as soon as he came into the lab. '*Woah…* What's going on?' He looked at Zim Steven and Beaver Wingate standing between his mother and Thundersky.

Arti spoke again: 'Receiving new data. Data transmits as follows: "DEFCON two confirmed. Priority one, authorization Tango-Tango-Tango-Six-Zero-Zero-Nine-Zero-Zulu-Sierra-Quebec. Satellite link established. Tactical mainframe online. Plotting solutions. Detected: Intercontinental Ballistic Missiles: Initiating: Atlantic. Full package, M-Three LGM-Thirty-G silos Alpha-nine, Delta-four. Detected: Full package Hades-Six warheads, LGM-Forty-G, silos Zulu-three, India-two, Tango-one-nine. Systems online in T-minus Three-four-four hours and six minutes. Automatic launch sequence will commence in T-minus three-five-zero hours and fifteen minutes. Selecting targets. Targets selected. Moscow, Moscow, Krasnodar, St Petersburg, Volga, Yekaterinburg, Murmansk, Rostock, Odessa, Archangel." Accessing…'

'Oh my…' Beaver said pathetically, a tremble in her voice.

'Receiving new data,' Arti said. 'Data reads: "DEFCON two confirmed. Priority One. Dead Eagle Initiated. Tango-Tango-Tango-Six-Zero-Zero-Nine-

Zero-Zulu-Sierra-Quebec. Launch codes verified: Detected: Intercontinental ballistic missiles. Pacific: Full package, M-Three LGM-Thirty-G, silos Alpha-nine, Delta-four. Detected: Full package, Hades-Six, LGM-Forty-G, silos Zulu-Three, Tango-One-Nine. Detected: Full package, M-Three LGM-Thirty-G, November-Yankee-Nine. Detected: Full package, Hades-Six, LGM-Forty-G, Lima-Zero-Zero-Four. Selecting targets. Targets selected. China: Beijing, Beijing, Beijing, Hong Kong, Hong Kong, Qingdao, Yantai. North Korea: Pyongyang, Pyongyang, Hamhung, Kanggye, Chongjin. Russia: Moscow, Moscow, Kaliningrad, Archangel." Data ends.'

Beaver Wingate raised her hands to her mouth to stifle her gasp.

A com came through from Tactical Command. A middle-aged braided officer filled the screen. 'Why has the Titan Nine taken control of one of my satellites? Just what the fuck is going on down there?'

'Uhm … I think you need to get down here, General. We've been seriously hacked by an outside system,' Beaver Wingate said.

General Coldriver Appleby gave them a concentrated stare from the viewer, knowing something serious was going on, or Zim Steven and Beaver Wingate wouldn't have been there. 'I'll be right down.' The viewer went blank.

'We need to fix this, or we're all dead,' Blossom said.

In that long moment of unbearable silence that followed her comment, Blackstone felt a fear rise in him like no fear he had ever known in his life before.

He looked gravely at the others, his face as gray as ash. 'What've I done…?'

'Arti,' Thundersky said, remaining calm. 'Access USAF Four-Eight-Zero, initiate abort procedure.'

'Accessing. Attempt failed. Multiple systems failures detected in Quantum System Four-Eight-Zero. Unable to comply.'

'Diagnose and clarify?' Thundersky said.

'Critical malfunctions detected in multiple matrices. Remote access unavailable.'

'Arti, suggest a course of action to terminate the Automated Defense Platform and abort the launch commands?' Blackstone said.

'One solution found,' said Arti. 'Repair damaged systems and initiate manual abort protocols.'

'You mean go there?' Flora said.

'Affirmative.'

'The damaged matrices are preventing communications getting through to the higher command system,' Blackstone said. 'That means we can't initiate the abort procedure from here. Someone has to go to this Manhattan place and find the Four-Eight-Zero system, repair the matrices and then abort the ADP from there, either with the original abort codes, or we'll have to write a new software for the system that can bypass the old encryption.'

'Can that be done?' Beaver asked.

Moon looked at her. 'Yes, ma'am. As Novice Thundersky said, it's a primitive system. Bypassing its ancient security won't be a problem.'

'Can't we just destroy it with a sonic or plasma missile?' Zim asked.

Thundersky looked at him. 'If the launch codes and commands have already been sent to any activated silos, then no, sir. The Four-Eight-Zero needs to initiate an abort command to any active launch sites.'

'Then sending a team to Old New York is unavoidable?' Beaver said.

'We've got fourteen days,' Tiger said, converting the countdown hours into days.

Blackstone nodded his head.

'Who do we have who's qualified to repair an Old-World quantum system?' Beaver asked.

'I am,' said Blackstone.

'No. You're needed here,' Beaver said. 'The council would never allow it. Someone else has to go.'

'Then who?' Blackstone said. 'There's just a handful of people who understand the ancient systems.'

'I'll go,' said Moon Spencer.

Zim looked at Thundersky. 'What about our young protégé here, Washington?' he said slowly, the seeds of an idea germinating in his head. A means to both neutralize the ADP and the Genesis child in a single swoop. 'He seems very knowledgeable.'

'Absolutely not!' Blackstone said. 'The very idea of sending a novice is outrageous.'

'He's right, sir,' Thundersky said. 'It's a simple enough operation. I'll do it, sir,' he said. 'I can fix the Four-Eight-Zero.'

Zim smiled and nodded. 'You're a very brave young man, Thundersky Reece.'

'Not really, sir. But it has to be done.'

'If a drone can put us down over the site, we should minimize risk to ourselves,' Tiger said.

'*Us*? *Ourselves*?' Flora looked alarmed.

He looked at his mother. 'Thunder might need technical help. He's also my friend. If he's going, so am I,' he said stubbornly.

Thundersky looked at him, moved by his words. It was the first time in the months he had been down here, that Tiger had ever referred to him as his friend, and it felt good.

'I think that's a good idea,' Zim said.

Blossom Flora shot Zim a hard stare.

'I've had tactical training and I'm in the Reserves,' Tiger said. '*Dad…*?'

Blackstone looked at him. He nodded his head and looked at Blossom Flora. 'Tiger's right. Thundersky might need some technical assistance. We've no idea what to expect out there.'

She did not respond. They already knew Zim was suspicious of Thundersky, he had been asking a lot of questions at the GRC surrogate center. So why was he so eager that Thundersky should go? Moon Spencer was more qualified for a mission like this, she thought. Zim was up to something and her suspicions soon became a deep and nagging worry.

Coldriver arrived in the Arti lab and Zim briefed him on exactly what had happened and exactly what they were going to do about it.

'What do you need, Grand High Scholar?' Coldriver asked, looking at Blackstone.

'A tactical drone and a team to provide protection while my boys do their work.'

Coldriver nodded his head. 'You'll have my best incursion team. They can be ready for dust off in six hours.'

'Thank you, General.' He looked at Moon. 'I want everything you can find on early twenty-first century quantum systems loaded to a new data-pad with all relevant data, codes and protocols.'

Moon nodded. 'I'd like to go with them?'

Blackstone shook his head. 'I need you here, Spencer. We still need to purge Titan and regain control once they've powered the Four-Eight-Zero down. Nobody else knows Titan as well as you.'

Moon nodded and headed for the exit to collate the data Blackstone had asked for.

Zim, who knew a fellow snake when he saw one, hurried along the corridor to the elevators to catch up with Moon. 'Well, this is a very tricky situation we find ourselves in, Moon Spencer.'

'Very tricky, sir.'

They walked on together.

'They seem very close,' Zim said conversationally. 'Blackstone and Novice Thundersky Reece?'

Moon nodded. 'Muddy – I mean Novice Thundersky's been the Grand High Scholar's golden boy ever since he got down here.'

Zim smiled. 'I sense you're not keen on him? It's alright, Spencer. Whatever you say to me will be between the two of us.'

Moon shrugged his shoulders. 'There's just something not quite right about him…'

Zim raised a brow. 'Seems to know all the answers, you mean?'

Moon nodded his head. 'That's exactly what I mean...' He paused in a moment's hesitation, and then carried on: 'When he first arrived, I asked Arti to open his archive...' He gave Zim a guilty look. 'I was curious to find out how a mudsurfer had received such an education topside, you see?'

Zim nodded. 'Of course. You're a very astute man, Moon Spencer. An admirable quality. I'd've done exactly the same thing in your situation,' he said, humoring him with a reassuring smile.

'Well, sir, the strange thing about it is, that his archive was sealed under a level one security encryption. I couldn't help but wonder why a mudsurfer's archive would be sealed like that?'

They stopped walking and Zim turned to him, arching his brows. 'Did you ask Blackstone why the archive was sealed?'

Moon nodded. 'He told me if I wanted to keep my job, I needed to keep my nose out of Grand High Council business.'

Zim frowned. 'That's what he said?'

'That's exactly what he said.'

They started walking again.

'I appreciate you telling me this, Moon Spencer. You've done the right thing.' He gave Moon another insincere smile. 'We might do well if we keep a discrete eye on things,' he said. 'Until we can get to the bottom of the conundrum. And until then, we should keep this just between the two of us. It could touch on state security.'

Moon nodded his head.

From this moment, Grand High Scholar Blackstone Washington was doomed.

Chapter Fifteen

Air Force One was the oldest tavern in Silo City, dating way back to NWY 134. It was located opposite the Jeremiah O'Connor Memorial Gardens. It was a popular place, filled with Old-World relics from the time of the Apocalypse, including parts from the last President's presidential aircraft known as Air Force One, from which the tavern took its name.

Blossom Flora was at her usual table, at the very back, closeted in a private booth. Her face drawn with worry, her anxious eyes nervously surveying the dimly lit tavern, the voices and laughter of the diners disseminated in the air around her, heady with the smell of skunkweed-shit, syntho-coffee, beer and those disgusting cigars they made in Surfer Town, lovingly called Surfer Town turds. On the walls were dozens of macabre Old-World photographic images from the Apocalyptic War and its hideous aftermath, acres of land filled with hundreds of thousands of unburied rotting corpses. Other images were of the great famines, and the millions of starving people amidst the destroyed ruins of the Old-World cities. The sick and dying looked like walking skeletons, their colorless flesh hanging from their bones like transparent tissue paper, accentuating every joint and rib, their bellies bloated. They looked like ghosts under the dark nuclear winter sky. The desolation was everywhere, the ground covered in a permanent hoarfrost, the fields dead and fallow, the cattle, sheep, horses, pigs and chickens lying dead with the humans, doomed to extinction. Other images showed the revolutionary wars, and the "Wild Cat Courts" that sprang up in the early days of the nuclear winter, when quasi-revolutionaries set up the infamous Peoples Courts, which were convened pretty much globally to try the government and military leaders (including their families) for causing the nuclear holocaust. They, along with their kidlings and spouses, brothers, sisters, parents and first cousins, uncles and aunts, were shackled and dragged before the courts in the ruins of their cities and tried for their parts in the Apocalypse, and a new crime entered the global penal systems, the heinous crime of "Planeticide." Willful complicity in the atrocities of global genocide and mass extinction of species. Here in North America, the trials took place in the ruins of state capitals in the eternal twilight of nuclear winter, under scabby black cloud which enshrouded the globe, leading to a perpetual winter that barely got above freezing and the global famines that almost finished the human race off altogether.

The pictures showed everything, from the trials to the grotesque executions by exposure to radiation. Thirty thousand men, women and children were put to death for the crime of being related to the politicians and military commanders who caused the war, wiping out entire family lines from the President downward. The President of the United States, his entire family and the congressmen of his government, the generals and the senators, and many others besides, were stripped naked, exposed to fatal doses of radiation and left in the nuclear wastelands to die lingering and miserable deaths. The courts were merciless and barbaric to the point of depravity. It was mob rule until reason returned, and great thinkers like Jeremiah O'Connor came along to bring the people together. Only by collective cooperation could humanity ever hope to survive.

'What can you recommend today?' Blossom asked the waiter.

'Peppered sawyer steaks, High Scholar, and may I recommend the new potatoes with mint and spinach, cracked pepper and parsley seasoning in a cheesy syntho-cream sauce? And to start, the soup of the day is syntho-salmon with fresh croutons and a sweet apple brandy.'

'Sounds delicious. I'd like two of those. I'm expecting a friend to join me. If you'd hold off until she arrives?' she said.

'Of course, High Scholar,' the waiter said. 'Can I bring you a drink while you wait?'

'Yes. Blackberry and honey wine.'

The waiter went off to fulfill her order.

She looked at the other tables. She knew the Triple S might be watching her. She was afraid and it showed in her eyes. For nineteen years they had kept Thundersky a secret, and now, because he'd sat that damn Tech Academy exam, the Triple S knew who he was. She was certain of it, and she was certain of something else too. Zim Steven wanted him out in the wilderness so he could have him killed by clockstoppers and nobody would be any the wiser.

Only to kill Thundersky, they would also have to eliminate any witnesses such as the tacticals – and her son. She was as mad as hell at Washington, agreeing to let Tiger go. But then Washington had said that if the Triple S knew, they'd kill everyone who'd had any contact with Thundersky. Zim might've thought he had the best hand, but they were ahead of him so far…

Music played – a beautiful Old-World recording of Chopin's "Revolutionary Étude." Appropriate perhaps, given the apocalyptic theme of the place.

While she waited for Helen, she perused the latest GRC statistical data on her data-pad, just to remind herself exactly why she was up to her tits in treason.

It made grim reading: 97.9 percent of the surface population over the age of thirty were cancerous to various degrees, and were receiving the Omega 9 treatment. About 50 percent of the surface populations had fallout sickness and were receiving Iodinicine. The data showed that there was a reduction of .07 percent in the cancer rate and 1.04 percent reduction in fallout sickness cases over the past five years. Small glimmers of hope. Too small to really matter.

Infertility had increased by another 2.08 percent, which was an alarming increase on the previous five years. All of the surface population was sterile and accounted for eighty-one percent of the total Silosian population.

The statistics for Sub City were dramatically different. Only 4 percent of the sub surface population over the age of 30 was cancerous. 1.04 percent suffered from fallout sickness, which was a 0.76 percent reduction in cancer and an impressive 7.01

percent reduction in fallout sickness over the past five years, mainly due to Intsofiber anti-rad jumpsuits for outside activity and the new air purification system installed in Sub City six years ago. Life expectancy for a topside male was 35.5 years. For a female it was 41.02 years. Life expectancy for Sub Citians was 88.7 years for males and 97.6 years for females. Fertility among the Sub Citians was 18.7 percent, accounting for the decrease of 2.08 percent. The infertility seemed unstoppable and irreversible. It was the scientific proof that the human race was becoming extinct, and had a little over 100 years before the last human walked on this planet. In some places, where the tech was not as good and where very few people lived underground, the statistics were even more alarming.

She stared at the data, but she couldn't concentrate on it. All she could think about was what was going on underneath the ruins of New York. And as she looked up, her eyes once again perused the pictures on the walls. They had a new meaning to her now. History was repeating itself, and some primitive piece of tech was at this moment, counting down the days and hours before it unleashed another nuclear apocalypse.

She was halfway through a glass of wine when Sparrowbrook Helen arrived. She was a tall, lean woman, her skin yellowed by the large doses of Iodinicine. She had many cancerous lesions on her skin and had pancreatic cancer, melanoma and lymphoma as well. Her body, like so many bodies in the New-World, was invisibly destroying itself from the inside out. For now the Omega 9 was keeping the cancers in check, but sooner or later – maybe a year, maybe five years – the Omega would no longer be effective and the cancers would kill her in weeks, if not days. But for now, she looked reasonably well.

The two women embraced.

'How are you, Helen? Keeping you busy over in the refinery, are they?'

'Don't they always?' They sat down. 'So, what're we having for lunch?'

'I don't remember.' She smiled at her. 'A surprise.'

Helen poured herself a glass of wine. 'I presume this is not entirely social?' Her voice was barely above a whisper, her eyes scanning the tavern.

'No. Not entirely. I need you to get a message to our friends.'

'When?'

'Today, as soon as we've had lunch.'

Helen raised a brow and sipped her wine. '…I have to agree with you, Blossom, this blackberry wine's delicious,' she said stentoriously as a couple walked past on the other side of the booth, making their way to a table.

'I'm glad you approve.'

Whispering again, Helen said, 'That won't be easy.'

'You have to try, Helen. Something serious has happened. An Old-World military system has activated itself and it's going to launch dozens of nuclear warheads. They're sending our special boy and my son to fix it. They leave in a few hours on a tactical heavy lift combat drone with a small team of tacticals. It's the only flight going over the Virginias,' She looked around. The drivel from the diners and the clacking of cutlery filled the pause. 'I think Zim Steven knows who he is and is planning to murder him out in the wilderness, along with anyone who's with him.'

Helen shuddered. She realized the danger the boy was in.

The waiter arrived with their food and set the plates down in front of them.

Helen smiled beamingly. 'You spoil me, Blossom.'

Chapter Sixteen

Zim Steven stood out of sight up in the air traffic control room, his arms folded, lips pressed together as he stared out of the window down onto the concourse, watching Blackstone leading his son and Thundersky Reece along the access road at the edge of the landing pads. Zim considered them predatorily.

He had waited years for this opportunity to bring Blackstone down, and covering his protégée's true identity was the perfect legal pretext. Proof of a conspiracy against Utopia, a crime punishable with death. He had already set things in motion. Earlier, he had a meeting with the Grand Council. He told them that Blackstone had placed the entire scholastic order in danger by protecting a Genesis child, proving they must have substituted at least one of the Genesis fetuses with another fetus before his men arrived at the Genesis lab to abort them.

They didn't kill those babies because they enjoyed killing babies, he'd said. They killed them to save the Scholastic Order and the Utopian way of life.

The Council agreed; without the scholars, civilization would collapse. There would be chaos and savagery on a scale not seen since the nuclear winter. They were the guardians of civilization, they said, as much to justify the murders to themselves. Civilization depended on people being sick. As for the sterility, well, that was a problem for the next generation to solve. There was still a good hundred and fifty years before the final extinction. Science would have advanced by then, they'd said.

The mudsurfers simply weren't capable of self-governance, they needed leadership and direction. That's why the Old-World civilization destroyed itself. It was governed by the mudsurfers' halfwit equivalents. They needed the guidance of the Scholastic Order, which had guided them into the tech and space age for almost half a millennium.

If they were suddenly in a world full of ignorant and illiterate breeders who could fight off the radiation and cancers, the mudsurfers would demand more and more, and do less and less. They would let greed rule them and suck the world dry, like their ancestors did. They would refuse to work, refuse to build. Utopianism would simply fall apart.

Thundersky Reece was the greatest hope for the future and continued existence of mankind there had ever been. He was the cure for the sicknesses and the sterility. But that didn't once occur to Zim Steven. The selfishly ambitious rarely saw the picture beyond their own mirage. Zim Steven could only see an opportunity to quietly put the whole matter to rest once and for all. As soon as the ADP was fixed and the missile launch aborted, he had taken steps to see that none of them would return to Silo City alive.

———

There was a big medivac drone on the landing/takeoff pad, its grav-drives humming at idle, preparing to take off.

'…You'll have eight tacticals with you,' Blackstone explained as they walked across the strip at the edge of the landing/takeoff pad, making their way to the Tacticals' base on the far side of the droneport. 'Under the command of Tac Commander Bigriver Charlie. He's very experienced in dealing with Dusties and Ferals,'

Tiger leaned close to Thundersky, giving him an uncomfortable look. 'Scared?' he asked softly.

Thundersky felt strangely calm, considering the unknown and unquantifiable danger they were going into. Somehow, it all had an unreal quality about it, like the heady buzz of strong skunkweed-shit tea, when you could feel a sort of detached inner calm, while the chaos went on around you. But it was the eye of the storm, and he knew it. Beneath that calm, hell yes, he was scared shitless. 'A bit,' he said. 'You?'

Tiger nodded unabashedly. 'Ferals, Dusties and Godders, all of them hate Utopians, Silosian and everything else civilized. Damn right I'm scared.' He smiled. 'But I wouldn't wanna be anywhere else right now, Thunder.'

Thundersky gave him an appreciative look.

The heavy lift grav-drives of the medivac drone started to whirr from the pad. The air ionized as their power increased with a steadily growing hum of their centrifuges.

Thundersky could feel the static in his hair building and making his scalp itch as his hair started to stand on end. He could almost feel the iron in his blood agitating as the drives reached terrestrial gravity with a deafening roar. The strip was beyond the safe line, with a perimeter ring of flashing amber lights around the landing/takeoff pad. Particles of dust and detritus in the drone's gravitational field began to lift off the ground, becoming suspended between terrestrial gravity and the gravitational field of the medivac drone, where it hung in the air in a fine diaphanous mist in near zero-G. Even a large object like a human would be floating, trapped between the gravitational fields like marionettes hoisted up on wires were they stupid enough to cross beyond the ring of amber lights.

'You'll be flown to the ruins of Manhattan!' Blackstone continued, shouting over the din. 'Radiation levels are patchy, depending on weather conditions and wind factors, so make certain you keep an eye on your meters and don't remove your respirators unless you're inside a safe zone! New York was mostly hit by neutron air burst warheads, so Plutonium-two-three-nine and hot Carbon-fourteen are minimal there.'

The hairs on Thundersky's arms stood upright, his skin prickled. They could feel the strange gravitational forces around them rippling through their bodies.

'…There are Martianite diamond cutting lasers and sonic charges in the M-TAV if you need to move debris or cut through blast doors!' Blackstone shouted. 'A satellite's been repositioned into geostationary orbit over the ruins, so we'll have eyes on you the entire time you're on the ground, and the tac-drone will provide you with air cover if you need it.'

The grav-drives grew louder and louder, the noise pressing against Thundersky's eardrums like a whirlwind in his head. The hair on their heads was standing vertically now as the drive exceeded 2-g. The huge, shiny drone started to lift above the pad, its dark deltoid fuselage rising vertically over their heads into the gray overcast sky, pulling the curtain of dust and litter up with it like a membrane as the gravity bubble enclosed the drone. There was no downdraft as you had with electro-jet drones, just the static and ionized particles in the air, with the sort of smell that accompanies an electrical storm, but stronger.

The drone climbed to an altitude of about ten thousand feet and hovered for several seconds. And then – VROOOOM – it shot up vertically at Mach three, with an ear-bursting sonic BOOM. The medivac drone vanished into the clouds.

Huge vacuums started under the landing/takeoff pad grating as the trash and dust fell back to earth, preventing it blowing and scattering.

'That must feel like your head's coming out of your asshole,' Thundersky murmured, looking up into the sky.

'The gravity bubble reduces the effects by about fifty percent,' Tiger said. 'But yeah, it can kind of feel like that.'

They walked towards the Tacticals' base, now in sight on the far side of the droneport where a military transport drone was waiting out on the pad.

Inner Voice spoke: 'Uploading tactical package to Genesis interface. Upload complete.'

Thundersky ignored it.

There were several military drones and vertical lift sub-orbital warbirds lined up along the strip in the tactical base. A necessary evil with the Dusteaters and Oregon-Washingtons, who had advanced weapons and tech of their own.

Tiger leaned against Thundersky and put his arm lazily across his shoulder, like a drunk in need of supporting. 'Are you ready to save the world, Thunder?'

Thundersky looked at him and for a moment, he thought that maybe Tiger was drunk – or stoned.

'That's what we're doing,' Tiger went on. 'Saving the world.'

There were sentinels at the gates, armed with Tac-One parabellum machine guns and Tac-Ten laser pulse pistols holstered on their hips, as well as parabellum pistols. They checked everyone in and out of the base, searching vehicles and taking bio scans with handheld DNA and retina scanners.

Blackstone led them towards a hanger, where a couple of dozen ground assault vehicles and M-TAVs were parked.

Over on the far side of the garrison were thirty black warbirds, fully weaponized with sonic air-to-air and air-to-ground missiles along with laser canons and railguns. New-World Utopianism needed to be defended, and it was defended ruthlessly.

A good looking young, black tactical woman with combat patches sewn to the sleeves of her Intsofiber anti-rad jumpsuit was standing outside the hanger on the concourse, smoking a Surfer Town turd, a Tac-One hanging by its strap from her right shoulder. A tac-ten and an Old-World parabellum semi-automatic pistol were holstered to her right leg and left hips. She watched the trio coming towards the hanger, a look of indifference in her face, her femininity lost somewhere behind those weapons and her anti-rad jumpsuit.

Behind her, four tacticals were loading weapons, supplies and other kit onto a Mark IV Multi Terrain Armored Vehicle (M-TAV). It was weaponized with a laser pulse cannon and four inbuilt fifty caliber railguns.

Thundersky looked back at the tactical, seeing what looked like contempt in her eyes as the fog of her cigar smoke cleared in front of her face. He gave her a wan smile. She planted her cigar into the corner of her mouth, slipped her hands into her pockets and wandered off into the dusky gloom of the hanger. 'A friendly bunch then,' he said sarcastically.

They followed behind her. Blackstone was still talking, but both Thundersky and Tiger had stopped listening to him as he kept repeating himself. They watched the activity as tacticals hurried this way and that, some carrying, some fetching, others ordering.

A resonantly deep and steady voice boomed out in the cavernous hanger, 'I want a full weapons and systems check on that M-TAV before you load it.'

Tac Commander Bigriver Charlie was a seasoned soldier with twenty years' experience in the wastelands fighting Dusteaters, Godders and Ferals, and he had the scars to prove it. The most visible one was a laser burn across his forehead, literally an inch above his left eye. He, like the others, was liveried in a black Intsofiber anti-rad jumpsuit. His anti-rad respirator mask hung from his utility belt along with a laser pistol strapped to his hip and a conventional parabellum semi-automatic pistol rode his right hip next to a double-edged stabbing knife and a machete. A Tac-One was strapped across his broad chest, and several sonic grenades were hooked on a body vest along with a comms mic, camera, and a second holstered parabellum pistol.

One of the tacticals loaded body armor into a compartment in the opened back section of the M-TAV, where respirators and spare anti-rad suits hung in tall lockers, with an arsenal of small arms, sonic grenades and crates of ammunition for the railguns.

Thundersky and Tiger looked like tacticals themselves once they were wearing the same black military Intsofiber anti-rad jumpsuits as the others, and issued with lightweight body armor and anti-rad respirator masks which they hung from the body vests the quartermaster had issued them, along with helmets, shoulder cams, comms and weapons.

Chapter Seventeen

Venus reversed the M-TAV onto the three-hundred-foot deltoid military transport and assault drone. It was powered by four huge swivel and pivot electro-turbine thruster jet engines.

Senior Tac Sparrowhawk Jackson was by the loading ramp with his tac-one hanging from his shoulder, his hands on his hips, watching the M-TAV backing up the ramp into the drone's cargo hold, its powerful mag-drive engine humming deeply. Pulses of red and white light swept their faces from the strobes beneath the drone's fuselage.

'...Are the men ready?' Bigriver Charlie asked.

Senior Tac Sparrowhawk Jackson nudged his brawny face towards him. 'Red Team One's always ready.'

'Good. Then let's get our asses out of here. We've wasted enough time. I've got a dinner date with a lovely young lady from Plateau City tomorrow night.'

Thundersky looked out the window at the swivel and pivot electro-jets pointed down in the takeoff position as he took his seat left of the boarding hatch. Each jet was capable of exerting 98.2 thousand pounds of thrust per square inch, and at the rear beneath the cargo hold were four rocket cones for sub-orbital flight.

He strapped himself into his seat, facing Sparrowhawk Jackson and Tac Commander Bigriver Charlie with two lean young tacticals.

'What's the mission? Why are the novies here?' one of the men asked.

'Your guess is as good as mine,' replied another.

'What's the mission, sir?' the first tac asked.

'We're going to New York on a priority one humanitarian mission and that's all you need to know,' Sparrowhawk replied.

'What's New York?' one of the younger tacs asked.

'An Old-World city,' another replied.

The jets started to hum and Thundersky could feel a slight vibration under his feet that worsened as the engines started to thrust as they built power.

Venus lit another Surfer Town turd, and the stink of it quickly filled the cabin. It smelled like dry shit on a hot day and was just as welcome.

'Goddammit, Corp. You gotta smoke those goddam things in here?' one of the tacticals complained. He waved his hand in front of his grimacing face as the smell and smoke drifted in front of him.

'Quit your complainin', Sprat,' she said. 'We gotta put up with you don't we…?'

There was a moment of chuckling.

The vibration got stronger, until the entire fuselage was shuddering like a trembling dog. The seats and racks rattled and clattered as the thrusters roared ever louder, building to optimal vertical takeoff power.

Thundersky's hands gripped the armrests so tight his knuckles turned white, a fact that did not escape Sparrowhawk Jackson sitting opposite, who was completely relaxed, staring expressionlessly at his fingertips which dug into the padded armrests.

Thundersky looked up and met his stare, the whites of Sparrowhawk's eyes accentuated from his black face.

The drone started to shudder as if trying to pull away from a greater force and they started to lift off. The jets screamed and roared at a deafening pitch. Inside, the noise became so loud, even shouting at one another was pointless. They all put earplugs in. Sparrowhawk handed some plugs to Tiger and Thundersky, which they pushed into their ears.

They climbed vertically, just as the medivac drone had done, but this beast was over twice the size and powered by electric turbo jets rather than gravity drives.

Tiger looked at Thundersky, who stared straight ahead, watching the data screen fixed to the bulkhead over Bigriver's and Sparrowhawk's heads, shuddering as the forces of lift battled against the forces of gravity.

Twenty feet off the ground. Forty feet – fifty-feet – one hundred, then two hundred feet; climbing faster and faster.

Out the portholes, Silo City shrank away – five hundred feet, the engines roared, the fuselage shook. Seven hundred feet and they were still rising vertically.

Then a loud clunk and a whining sound as the landing struts retracted into the fuselage.

Thundersky looked out of the porthole, turning his stare down at the forward jet, tilting thirty degrees to stern. The roar of the engines reached their peak and the drone tilted nose up and started to move forwards, climbing steadily at three hundred knots, banking gently to the northwest away from the irradiated dead zone of the coast.

At fifteen thousand feet, moving at 350 knots an hour, the pitch of the engines changed and died down to a muffled roar. Everyone took their earplugs out.

'They're bone breakers, these old transports,' Bigriver Charlie said, looking at Thundersky, unbuckling his seatbelt. 'But they're reliable mothers…'

According to the data screen they were moving into strong sixty mile an hour headwinds, which buffeted the drone with turbulence from time to time.

'Coffee anyone?' one of the tacticals asked, standing up. He turned to the little galley at the back of the cabin.

'What're you think, dickbutt?' Sparrowhawk said, apparently answering for everyone.

Bigriver Charlie stood up and looked at Tiger and Thundersky. 'Follow me, gentlemen.' He turned to the cockpit door and placed his hand on the scanner panel, and the hatch slid open.

Tiger and Thundersky followed him up a narrow flight of steps into the small, cramped cockpit.

It looked like the cockpit of a conventional piloted aircraft; there were seats for a pilot and copilot and manual controls. Windshields that looked into the darkening sky, reflecting the illuminated instrument panels and sensor screens with continually scrolling environmental and geographical data.

'The only suitable landing area is a forest in the middle of the city. There are a few clearings in there where we can put down. But it means a short drive to the target,' Bigriver explained.

'Why not in Foley Square?' Tiger asked. 'There's room enough there to put down, next to the target.'

'Vibrations,' Bigriver replied. 'These old jets cause a lot of vibration. They could bring the old structures down on top of us.'

'Do you think there might be hostiles there?' Thundersky asked.

'Scavs and Ferals for sure,' Bigriver said. 'Possibly Godders too,' he added more ominously. 'Our latest intel suggests there might be a settlement of Delaware Godders in old Queens. It's possible they have an outpost there. So, you need to get in there, abort this Four-Eight-Zero system and recover any data you can and get out as quickly as possible. How long are you going to need down there?'

'That's impossible to estimate,' Tiger said. 'We have to find the way into the facility first, then we have to get inside and locate the Four-Eight-Zero. That could take any amount of time. If we have to do any laser cutting or blasting, it'll take a day, if not longer just to get in. Once we're in the facility, if it's not flooded, we have to repair the system in order to run the abort procedure, that could take an hour or ten hours. It'll take as long as it takes, Commander. So, you just concentrate on doing your job, and we'll concentrate on ours-'

'We'll do ours, don't you worry about that.'

'None of us want to be there any longer than we need to be, Commander Bigriver,' Thundersky said in a more diplomatic tone. 'If it's straightforward, we could be done inside a few hours. But as Tiger says, it depends how much damage the system's suffered and how difficult it is to get inside the facility.'

Bigriver hated uncertainty. If the Godders decided to attack them, things could get very messy, and the longer they were there, the more likely it was for the Godders to attack.

Chapter Eighteen

Somewhere over the Virginias

In the cargo hold, Fox was checking the locking clamps hooked over the M-TAV's wheels, making certain they were secure. Venus was leaning against the fuselage looking out of the porthole staring down at the ruins of an Old-World City they were flying over, barely visible under the moonlight and the thick forest that had encroached to reclaim its primordial state around and in the ruins. She could make out streets, a railroad and acres of dark ruins. It hadn't been hit by nukes, it was simply abandoned when civilization had fallen apart during the nuclear winter, when the mountains were as cold as the North Pole.

'…It's crazynuts if you ask me,' came Fox's voice from behind the M-TAV. 'All this babbledick to ferry a couple of novies to some old ruins. And what for, eh? What could possibly be down there that gets a priority one status? What sort of Old-World fuckshit gets the big-dicks all uppity like they got isotopes up their asses, eh?'

Venus took a deep breath, her attention divided between listening to Fox's babbledick and looking at the beautiful mountains below, lambent in the moonlight, the high peaks dusted with snow.

'…It's all babbledick…' He came out from behind the M-TAV and looked over at her. She hadn't made a single comment the entire time. 'Everything looks okay. D'you want me to run the system check again?'

She turned and gave him a sharp look. 'No. You just keep your goddam paws off my rig,' she snapped possessively. She treated the M-TAV like a living thing, her baby, and nobody touched her baby but her. She reached into her breast pocket for her half-smoked cigar and planted it between her teeth.

Fox leant against the M-TAV's rear wheel that was as tall as he was. 'You ever been to this Manhattan place before, Corp?'

'Been over it,' she said as she lit her Server Town turd. 'It was a big place. Millions of people clocked off…' She clicked her fingers. 'Fast as that.'

Fox shivered. It was hard to imagine millions of people living anywhere in one place. Harder to imagine what it must've been like when the nukes fell. Arguably, they were the lucky ones. The long nuclear winter was primordial hell, from what Jeremiah O'Connor's chronicles said. 'D'you think the intel's right. About the Godders I mean?' he asked worriedly.

She shrugged her shoulders and glanced round as Tiger and Thundersky entered the hold. She gave them a narrow look up and down. 'If they are there, just don't let 'em take you alive,' she said ominously, still watching the novies.

'We've come to check our gear,' Tiger said, his eyes once again drawn to Venus, who was a beautiful woman, even with all her tac gear on.

She noticed and didn't appreciate it. She preferred a real man to some baby-faced kidling. 'It's open. Help yourself,' she said lowly and turned back to look out of the porthole.

Holding onto the grab rail, Tiger pulled himself up the back step. He reached up and pressed a button in the bulkhead. The armored rear compartment door of the M-TAV hissed as it slid open.

There were storage and weapons lockers left and right of the gangway, which led to an internal bulkhead door into the M-TAV's articulated tactical command and communications module (C and C).

Tiger opened one of the compartments and dragged out a heavy titanium trunk and opened it. Inside were quantum circuits and qubit processor chips, sensors, calibration tools, a roll of Intsofiber micro-wire wound on a bobbin, and high yield sonic charges.

They spent the next few minutes checking and calibrating their equipment before packing it away again to stow it back in the locker.

They climbed down and closed the hatch.

'So, we gotta babysit you kidlings have we,' Fox said.

Tiger gave Fox a contemptuous look.

Thundersky ignored Fox, his restless curiosity drawing him away to explore the outside of the M-TAV. He had never seen one up this close before.

It was just under fifty feet long and about thirteen feet high ground to roof, and by the same again wide. Its body was angular, with sharp edges designed to deflect artillery and parabellum rounds.

'Quite something, ain't it?' Fox said, following up behind him, running his hand along the M-TAV's smooth, shiny black Intsoglass coated body.

Thundersky nodded his head. 'Beautiful.'

'She weighs in at fifteen point three tons unloaded,' Venus interrupted as she casually sauntered over, passing Tiger a sideways look, unappreciative of his amorous glances at her breasts.

'And has a self-charging two thousand seven hundred and fifty horsepower mag-drive powerplant,' Thundersky said.

Venus was impressed. 'Giving her a top flat terrain speed of eighty-nine point seven miles per hour,' she said. 'In the water, she can make ten knots submerged, fifteen on the surface. This baby does everything apart from fly,' she added proudly as Fox climbed the ladder up onto the roof, to the twin barreled, belt fed fifty caliber railgun.

'You know they're working on a grav-drive hover version?' Tiger said. 'The new Mark Five.'

'And Red Team will be the first to trial it,' Venus replied. 'Have you seen the prototype?'

'Yes,' Tiger said. 'My father designed its engines and weapons systems. Sixty feet from nose to tail. Ground speed of about a hundred miles per hour. Hover speed of three hundred knots.'

'Why isn't it in service yet?' Fox asked.

'There are stability issues in hover mode,' Tiger said.

Fox put his hand on one of the long barrels of the railgun. 'Say hello to the medium range Electromagnetic Tac-Z-Fifty Railgun,' he said.

'Controlled by multi-spectrum auto-tracking and defense system. She fires belt loaded fifty caliber self-guiding sonic charge projectiles with a thirty-mile range at a rate of sixty-seven rounds per barrel, per minute,' he said. 'We've inbuilt Tac-Z-Thirties front and back and a Martianite diamond laser pulse cannon under the blister...' He gestured to a long blister humping up in the middle of the roof on the front section of the articulated M-TAV. 'Intsoglass skin over a six-inch-thick Lunar-titanium body. It would take a direct hit from a sonic cruise missile to knock this motherfucker out. Yes, sir...' He climbed down and walked to the front where Tiger, Thundersky and Venus were standing. 'This here is a deadly machine of war.'

The drone suddenly and unexpectedly began a steep ascent that sent them staggering back like drunks. They reached quickly for whatever was at hand to grab on to.

Thundersky reached for a grab rail to the side of the M-TAV's cockpit steps. Venus grabbed hold of one of the securing clamps holding the front wheel, and so did Tiger. Fox ended up on his butt and slid away down the decking until he crashed into the bulkhead.

An alarm sounded. A voice spoke: 'BRACE! BRACE! BRACE! Incoming. BRACE! BRACE! BRACE!'

They hung on for their lives, their faces fixed in horror as the drone climbed almost vertically, the jets blasting out at full throttle.

The aft rockets fired up.

'We're going sub-orbital!' Tiger said with alarm.

Fox tried to get up, but he was pushed back by the g-forces.

The monstrous M-TAV shifted several inches and creaked on its securing clamps.

'Deploying countermeasures,' the computer announced.

There was a SWOOSH noise.

'Countermeasures deployed. Targeting heat plume…'

There was a sudden whine followed by a clunk that seemed to come from below their feet.

'The drone's arming its weapons,' Venus said.

The drone was violently rocked by a sonic detonation three thousand feet below them.

A jet screamed a hideous mechanical death knell and the drone pitched violently to port, and again they were thrown back, almost losing their grips. Fox was clinging to the fuselage, his face frozen in terror.

'Shit! We're hit!' Venus shouted.

'INCOMING! BRACE! BRACE! BRACE!'

BOOM!!! The drone was rocked again by another sonic blast beneath the rear port engines.

'Get in the M-TAV!' Venus yelled.

Fox pulled himself up and Thundersky helped him as Venus opened the cockpit hatch. Stair treads slid out from the fuselage below the hatch and she climbed up, followed by Tiger.

Thundersky pulled Fox away from the bulkhead towards him. Fox lurched towards him, reaching out for Thundersky's hand. Thundersky grabbed hold of him with his right hand, his left clinging to the handrail, managing to heave Fox back.

Once inside, the hatch slid shut automatically and the noise outside was muted to near total silence.

'Buckle yourselves in,' Venus said.

The drone was descending rapidly.

The computer repeated over the M-TAV's internal comms: 'BRACE FOR IMPACT! BRACE FOR IMPACT! BRACE! BRACE! BRACE!'

They sat as tense as coiled springs, feeling the drone pitching and yawing, diving towards the earth sixty thousand feet below, none of them believing they were going to survive. But the M-TAV was the safest place to be.

'What about the others?' Fox said.

'You wanna go get 'em... Be my guest,' Venus said. It was everyone for themselves now.

The drone was diving nose first out of the night sky, trailing black smoke.

In the M-TAV, the computer repeated: 'IMPACT IMMINENT! BRACE! BRACE! BRACE!'

Their faces froze with rictus, clinging to the arms of their seats as the drone dived towards the earth.

The drone's remaining engines and thrusters fired to reduce their impact velocity at full thrust and they could feel the drone shuddering as it slowed them dramatically, but they were still coming down fast.

'IMPACT IMMINENT! BRACE! BRACE! BRACE!'

There was a bone-jarring crash and a terrible CRUNCH of folding metal. The M-TAV shot forwards with a violent jerk...

Outside, the underside of the drone smashed into a mountain crevice with a thunderous CRASH. Rock exploded into the air as the drone bounced off, shearing the starboard thruster off along with half the wing, ripping a huge gash along the side of the drone. They plunged down the mountainside, hitting more rocky outcrops of rock and treetops, acrid black smoke spewing from the broken wing as the drone dived towards a plateau. It touched down on the mountainside and bounced away before crashing again onto the plateau and snapping into two halves that both slid on in separate directions, ploughing deep gouges into the turf. Sparks arced and popped from shorting circuits which were ripped apart. The rear half of the fuselage twisted 180-degrees before it smashed into an outcrop of granite, spewing debris along a five-hundred-yard arc before finally coming to a stop.

The front section of the drone slid on unimpeded like a giant sled towards the edge of the plateau eight hundred yards from impact. With nothing to stop it, it tumbled over the precipice and plunged in freefall nose first another thousand feet into a rocky gorge with a fatal CRASH that echoed through the mountains like a clap of thunder.

The silence was ringing, the only sound being the creaking fuselage settling on its rocky grave and circuits buzzing and popping with bright flashes of light.

It was pitch black in the M-TAV, tilted about forty degrees left. Nobody and nothing stirred. The silence immense and profound. Red emergency lighting strips came on overhead, casting them in a blood red hue.

Thundersky stared dazed at the light, hardly believing he was still alive. He raised his hands to his face, feeling for wounds and blood. His face was still intact and dry except for the clamminess of sweat from his fear. He was still in his seat – they were all in their seats, leaning limply with the tilt.

Fox coughed and groaned behind him.

'Goddammit…' Venus murmured. 'Is everyone okay?'

Thundersky unbuckled his safety belt and almost fell out of his seat.

'We've gotta get out of here,' Venus said thickly.

Thundersky looked at the broken fuselage and wondered how they were going to get the M-TAV out of the hold, which was twenty feet from the loading bay doors to the ground. He was sure the loading ramp wouldn't be working, and they were probably going to need to blow the loading bay doors off too.

'We need to check the rest of the drone for survivors,' Venus said, looking coolly at them. 'And then get the hell outta here.'

Fox looked over the precipice, shining a powerful flashlight down into the dark ravine, its long narrow beam sweeping through the blackness like the finger of god pointing out a trail of carnage left by the front section of the drone. The beam shone onto glossy black shards of broken fuselage scattered over rocks and undergrowth all the way down to the bottom. He took a deep breath and murmured, 'How lucky were we…?' He shuddered. 'Nobody could've survived that,' he remarked, looking at Venus. 'We need to get out of here before the Dusties or whoever shot us down get here to finish the job.'

Venus ignored him. 'I need to check for survivors.'

'I'll come with you,' Thundersky said to Venus as she looked for a safe way down.

'Better I go alone,' she said. 'It might not be pretty down there.'

'All the same. If anyone's alive, it'll need two of us to bring 'em up.' He looked determinedly at her. 'I'm coming with you.'

Venus looked into his determined eyes for a moment and then nodded her head.

Fox was far from happy. He scanned the dark mountains worriedly. The Dusteaters were sure to be on their way. 'This is a bad idea. What if it's Godders or Ferals?'

Venus looked icily at him. 'Kill yourself.'

'We're too far south for Godders,' Thundersky said. 'This is Virginia Dusty territory and Ferals won't attack adults unless there are kidlings with them. They don't eat adults,' Thundersky said.

'*Well, that makes me feel a whole lot better*,' Fox grunted back sarcastically. 'Dusties then. Even worse…'

'We're worth more alive to them than we are dead,' Venus said. 'Now quit your goddam bitching and stay here with the other novy. See if you can get through to mission control to send a rescue team to pick us up.'

Venus and Thundersky carefully picked their way down through the darkness with only their flashlights to light the way. Venus was just ahead of him, her Tac-Ten drawn at the ready, her bright oval eyes scouting the forest and undergrowth. Thundersky kept his weapons holstered, but he was just as watchful, sweeping his flashlight left and right.

'Watch your step,' Venus said as the slope steepened to an almost vertical descent.

They went down sideways like a couple of crabs, assuring their footing with every step, holding onto the scrub and low branches.

'We should all be dead,' Thundersky said.

'Whoever fired those missiles must be sixty or more miles away.'

'What's the usual protocol in a situation like this, Corporal?' he asked her.

She looked at him. 'To request an evac drone to pick us up – If we can establish a comm link. But they would've seen us come down and the transponder would've been activated as soon as we were attacked. Don't worry, we won't be out here long.'

'I wasn't worried, Corporal,' he said bluntly. 'But time's our enemy. We have to get to Foley Square.'

It was a grisly scene that greeted them at the bottom. The wreckage was everywhere, mangled and misshapen, the fuselage ripped open from one end to the other like a gaping wound.

They stood wordlessly for a long time, the beams of their flashlights slowly scanning the wreckage, looking and listening for signs of life. But Death made his presence felt in the silence. The only sounds were the cool night wind whispering through the trees, the babble of a nearby river and the creaking of metal.

Something dripped onto Thundersky's shoulder with a splat, like a heavy raindrop. Another splat. He looked up, directing the beam of his flashlight into the overhanging branches of a tree. Something was hanging from a branch, gently rocking back and forth pendulously. He gasped with horror and took a step back, his light fixed on Bigriver Charlie – the top half of his disarticulated torso hung from the leafy branch ten feet above them. His bottom half from the hips down was completely severed from his body and nowhere to be seen. His entrails hung out of him, moving in the wind, gray and bloody like macabre streamers. Half of Bigriver Charlie's face had been peeled off by flying metal, maybe the same object that had cut him in half. Thundersky wanted to vomit. He looked away, trying to blot the image from his mind, but one simply couldn't un-see a thing like that.

Venus drew in a deep gasping breath when she looked up and saw her commander hanging there like a bauble. She said nothing, but Thundersky could see the pain and anger in her face.

They looked at one another. There was no need for words, they were both thinking the same thing as they moved towards the wreckage of the fuselage.

Thundersky pretended not to notice. 'Wait here,' he said, his thinking being that he would spare her the further trauma of seeing her other friends dead. 'I'll check for survivors.' He scrambled up onto the section of wing that was still attached to the drone and worked his way up its sloping gradient to the rip in the fuselage three feet above the wing. He looked back at Venus, as if for the last time, and then crawled through the rip in the side of the fuselage. He paused halfway in, his eyes following the beam of his flashlight as he slowly panned it through the smoky compartment, which was filled with the smells of blood and burned out circuits. He could see them, the silhouettes of their mangled bodies strapped into their seats, not moving.

He climbed in fully over a couple of empty seats into the sloping aisle.

There was the decapitated head of a female tactical several feet away, cradled like a grotesque work of art in a nest of twisted metal, shorting out fiber optics flashing and arcing in her face, glinting in the whites of her rolled up eyes. Thundersky turned away and carefully picked his way through the wreckage. The Red Team members were all dead.

Finally, after what had seemed like forever to Venus, Thundersky reemerged from the wreckage.

'I'm sorry,' Thundersky said quietly as he jumped down. He walked away, shaking from head to foot – and then, he doubled over and started to vomit.

Venus gathered her emotions and drove them down somewhere deep inside her, as only a soldier could. This was not the time or place for grieving nor introspection.

'Sorry,' he said, wiping his mouth.

'Forget it. We should get back.' Their priority was staying alive and evading the enemy until help came. 'We need to retreat to a secure location and wait for an evac. Whatever this crazy ass mission is, it's over. They'll have to send another team once we get back.' She started walking away.

'We're not going back, Corporal Venus. There won't be another team. We're the team and we're going on to New York to complete our mission.'

She spun to him. 'Who put you in charge?' Her eyes raged brightly with anger.

'Your orders are to get Tiger White and me to our destination.'

'Why?' she demanded snappily. 'What's so goddam important in New York? What's so damned important that it's cost the lives of some of the best tacticals in the world? Well, dickbutt to your goddam mission!'

Thundersky stared impassively at her. 'An Old-World quantum computer has activated itself and started a countdown to launch an array of thermonuclear weapons. They're so old, we don't know what condition they're in or how unstable the warheads are. If we don't abort its countdown, we're looking at a second apocalypse. That's why we're not going back to Silo City, Corporal. And if Tiger and me have to go on alone, we will. But we're taking the M-TAV with us.'

She stared at him, a dazed look in her eyes. Then, without saying anything to him, she did what she always did when she had something big to decide. She lit a Surfer Town turd. 'You know, what you just told me is beyond my need to know.'

Thundersky looked into her eyes. 'Not anymore it isn't. Not that I give a dickbutt about your need to know.'

'How long we got?'

'About ten days.'

She dragged on her cigar and looked off at the wreckage once more. 'What the hell,' she said, sighing a plume of smoke from her mouth. Her eyes sharpened on him. 'I go where my rig goes.'

Thundersky looked down and shone his flashlight at something several feet away – something that didn't belong here. Asphalt! It was buckled up from under the moss. A dark gray knuckle of Old-World blacktop.

Venus watched him curiously as he kicked away grass and earth with the heel of his boot, revealing more blacktop. He looked through the trees, shining the flashlight along the flat strip of moss and grass twisting up the side of the gorge to the plateau. 'It's a road…'

Chapter Twenty

They walked through the forest, following the clear emerald outline of the ancient road hidden under the moss, its contours and course clearly definable, and in places the roots of trees humped underneath and buckled the blacktop with jagged hummocks.

'What's your name, Novy?'

'Thundersky Reece.'

'You're pretty sure of yourself, ain't you, Thundersky Reece?'

'Am I? You wouldn't think that if you were in my head right now. I'm not sure of anything, and I'm pretty scared too if I'm honest about it.'

'Well, you hide it well, Thundersky Reece.'

'Is that a good thing, Corporal Venus?'

'Damn right it is…' She was coming to respect him more and more.

They stopped suddenly and looked ahead as if hallucinating. Half buried and rusting away were the remains of a huge Old-World semi with a long rusty trailer hitched to it, buried up to its axles, a holly tree bushed out the windows of the driver's cab. It was a sudden and unexpected reminder of how sudden and unexpected the apocalypse had been.

It was a poignant reminder of the possible near future if they failed in their mission.

As they progressed, there were more reminders of that terrible day in March 2025 when they came across dozens of rusting vehicles, half buried like coffins disinterred from the earth. Their engines had stopped the moment the EMP wave had reached them and blown their electrical systems.

Neither of them spoke as they walked carefully through the macabre graveyard of rotting metal and human bones.

'Fox is trying to get through to Silo City from the M-TAV,' Tiger said when Thundersky and Venus got back.

Venus paused to catch her breath. 'There's a road,' she said between breaths.

Just then, Fox came loping back across the grass towards them, a worried look on his face. 'I've tried the comms in the M-TAV. I think the signal's being jammed,' he said. 'All I'm getting is static on all frequencies. And I d'know how the hell we're gonna get the M-TAV out of there.'

'You're a goddam dickbutt, Fox,' Venus growled like a cat through her teeth. She walked off briskly to the wreckage and climbed in.

A minute later, they turned to the drone as they heard the muffled sound of the M-TAV's mag-drive starting up inside the cargo hold.

Suddenly, there was a loud BOOM as the emergency explosive bolts on the cargo bay doors blew the doors clean off. They flew back several feet before crashing to the ground with a loud heavy metallic thump. A moment later, to their complete incredulity, the M-TAV flew out at speed – enough speed to clear the cargo bay without snagging the articulated rear section against the drone's fuselage. The M-TAV dropped to the turf with a ground shaking crash. Its huge wheels jerked on their independent pneumatic suspension rams as the M-TAV kangarooed for a hundred yards, wriggling like a giant caterpillar, the rear wheels sliding sideways across the grass before it came to a stop. The articulated modules rocked independently of each other from side to side.

'Crazynuts. Goddam crazynuts…' Fox murmured under his breath, then laughed.

On the roof, the railgun turned on its turret, scanning the terrain, the barrels panning left and right. The forward and aft 30 calibers telescoped out from their gun ports and panned on their gimbals, the onboard tactical sensors seeing what their eyes could not. The laser's blister cover slid away and the laser cannon turreted up slowly with an electrical whir and locked, its muzzle pointed skyward.

Thundersky and the others climbed aboard from the starboard hatch. Venus was tucked into the driver's cockpit, separated from the four rows of passenger seats by a control interface. Tiger sat beside Thundersky at the front, next to the cockpit, but Fox sat on the back row opposite the galley, in front of the hatch into the C and C.

The steps and grab rails retracted into the fuselage and the hatch slid shut with a hiss of air as the locks engaged.

'Best not to drive with the lights on,' Thundersky suggested. 'They'll attract attention.'

Venus nodded her head and reached up to a row of illuminated panels and typed. 'Switching to thermal and IR navigation.' The windshield darkened to mirror black. She planted a Surfer Town turd into the corner of her mouth. 'Now, let's get off of this goddam rock.'

'They came this way, sure enough.' Rabbit was down on his haunches, bleached in bright white lights glaring from the halftracks parked along the ancient mountain road. He was looking at the churned-up moss and the fresh tire tracks in the road. 'A Mark Four,' he said as he studied the tracks and the axle width between the tire impressions. 'No other vehicles.' He put his fingers into the deep tread and felt the ground, then lowered himself on all fours and sniffed at the moss, like a dog looking for a good place to have a dump. 'They came through about two hours ago, Prophetess.' He looked at her, standing between the wreckage and a battered old Mark II M-TAV halftrack, its ancient third generation mag-drive harrumphing and pulsing with surges of energy, like a stubborn old heart that refused to die. It was towing a long-armored trailer with a laser cannon on the roof manned by a Dusty wearing century old anti-rad gear and a respirator mask sitting in the firing cradle. There was a railgun emplacement welded on the roof of the M-TAV too, where another Virginia Dusty wearing anti-rad gear was strapped into a seat with his hands firmly on the swivel handles, his thumbs over the trigger buttons, sweeping the barrels left and right. A screen mounted to the gun displayed thermal images of the dark forest around the wreckage.

The Prophetess no longer had the jaundiced color she'd had when she was posing as a Scav trader in Surfer Town. She was standing in the darkness like a ghostly apparition, looking back at Rabbit, not moving, not speaking, two tac-ten laser pistols strapped to her waist along with a semi-automatic parabellum. Eventually she looked up, her narrow face expressionless as she stared with cold indifference at Bigriver Charlie hanging from the tree with no bottom half and his guts dangling down like Spanish moss in the amber dawn. The mountains sheered up all around them to their lonesome peaks.

She looked anxiously at the wreckage again – the carnage of twisted metal strewn all the way down the gorge. Beams of light moved about within its battered carcass as her Dusty fighters searched.

She turned to the halftrack and glared at a terrified man who was down on his knees with two Dusty warriors standing either side of him. 'Force them to land, I said. Not blow them out of the fucking sky. Who put you up to it? You knew my son was on that drone, you nameless sonofabitch. *Who told you to destroy them!?*' She drew her hand up and back-swiped it down across his face. It landed hard, almost knocking the nameless sonofabitch over. 'Was it the Triple S?'

The nameless sonofabitch nodded and started to sob and beg her for mercy.

Bearfang crawled out of the downed drone's fuselage onto the wing.

The Prophetess turned away from the nameless sonofabitch and looked at him.

Bearfang shook his head. 'He's not here.'

That meant that he was still alive and she sighed with a deep sense of relief. She had already lost her grandson to the Ferals; it would have been unbearable if she'd lost her son too.

'You could send the Reverend with his angels. They could catch up in less than an hour…?' Another Dusty warrior climbed out of the fuselage behind him.

The Prophetess shook her head. 'No. Contact Ghostmaker. Tell him to sit tight. We're going to be a few days later than planned.' She turned to Rabbit. 'Rabbit! Get on your bike and follow them. Try and keep outside of their sensor range.'

The nameless sonofabitch sobbed unheeded behind her. He knew there was only one way this was going to end for him.

A gruff ugly voice sang out of tune from the dawn glow at full pelt:

> '*…Sowing in the morning, sowing seeds of kindness,*
> *Sowing in the noontide and the dewy eve;*
> *Waiting for the harvest, and the time of reaping,*
> *We shall come rejoicing, bringing in the sheaves.*
> *Bringing in the sheaves, bringing in the sheaves,*
> *We shall come rejoicing, bringing in the sheaves,*
> *Bringing in the sheaves, bringing in the sheaves,*
> *We shall come rejoicing, bringing in the sheaves…*'

The nameless sonofabitch cried and sobbed and pleaded: '*Don't give me to him, Prophetess. Please, not to him…*'

The Prophetess ignored him and looked round at the crazynuts Reverend dancing in the glare of the spotlights mounted on the M-TAVs, spinning and twirling through the undergrowth, dancing towards them, clasping his long ebony staff fixed with a solid silver crucifix on the top, with the crucified Christ stretched upon it. He jumped and kicked his heels, his mad eyes boggling rapturously at the wreckage of the Silosian war drone.

'…And the Lord did cast Satan down from Heaven into the darkest pits of fire and torment, and he cast there with him, the sinful, the savage and the heathen, to inhabit his realm of fire and brimstone!' The Reverend threw out his arms, raising his staff up over his head, the crucifix glinting in the spotlights. 'And the Lord said. "The Lamb of God is once more upon the earth, and he comes as a wolf to his flock!"' He started to sing again:

'…*Sowing in the sunshine, sowing in the shadows,*
Fearing neither clouds nor winter's chilling breeze;
By and by the harvest, and the labor ended,
We shall come rejoicing, bringing in the sheaves.

Going forth with weeping, sowing for the Master,
Though the loss sustained our spirit often grieves;
When our weeping's over, He will bid us welcome,
We shall come rejoicing, bringing in the sheaves…'

'Six dead. All tacticals,' Bearfang said huskily as he climbed down from the wing. 'In case you were wondering,' he added sarcastically. Under his long black coat, he wore a Silosian Intsofiber anti-rad jumpsuit and a weapons vest, from which sonic grenades hung black and silvered like decorations. 'See what you can salvage, and disconnect the AI and take it to my trailer,' he ordered two of his fighters.

They were all remarkably healthy, not one of them showed any signs of radiation sickness or cancers. Their wellbeing was legendary as well as incredible.

'They've gone to Satan's fire, Prophetess,' the Reverend said, preaching to the unconvertible. 'Satan's Fire, I say! Where the godless belong, burning in the firmament.' He looked at the nameless sonofabitch and grinned insanely at him. 'Hello. What's this, a fallen soul in need of redeeming? Come, child, let me show you the path to redemption. By the time I've skinned you, you'll be screaming for God...' He nodded to a couple of his "Angels" and they grabbed the nameless sonofabitch and dragged him away, screaming in terror.

The Reverend followed them, singing:

*'I danced in the morning, when the world was
begun,
And I danced in the moon and the stars and the sun,
And I came down from heaven, and I danced on the
earth,
At Bethlehem I had my birth. Dance, then, wherever
you may be, I am the Lord of the Dance, said he...'*

The nameless sonofabitch was tied spread-eagled between two trees, his screams were hideous and bestial, echoing chillingly through the mountains as the reverend skinned him alive with a laser cutter. It was a sickening sight, the Nameless Sonofabitch barely recognizable as human, his body completely skinned, leaving a bloody and sinuous tableau.

As the Reverend carefully cut and peeled the flesh from the Nameless Sonofabitch, he sang:

"…Angel voices ever singing round thy throne of light,
angel-harps forever ringing, rest not day nor night;
thousands only live to bless thee.
And confess thee Lord of might…"

Chapter Twenty-Two

Thundersky went into the C and C. 'Mind if I join you?'

Fox swiveled round in his seat. 'Sure.'

'All quiet?' Thundersky asked conversationally as he sat at the tactical interface.

Fox nodded. 'Nothing moving out there but the wind.' He sipped his coffee. 'Must be real important whatever it is you and the other novy are doing out here? To be carrying on, with everyone dead and all?'

Thundersky sipped his coffee. 'It is.'

Fox looked at the Novy. Nice looking, he thought, and in another place, he'd buy him a drink and say *how about some fun with a hit of VR*? He knew Thundersky was gay-homo like him. He sensed it, and the Novy probably knew he was too. 'What is it? Don't I have the right to know?'

'If it was up to me, I'd tell you. But it's not up to me. It's up to Corporal Venus and I'm not going to undermine her authority.' He looked up at the bank of viewers along the upper bulkhead above the sensor interface – Thermal imaging, infrared imaging and ambient imaging around the M-TAV as the nav-conn drove them along at exactly four miles an hour, so slow they barely felt themselves moving, just the occasional gentle rocking of the modules as they crossed uneven ground. Below the external imaging, four more viewers streamed data from the sensors.

'I just hope it's worth it,' Fox said. 'Whatever it is I'm risking my ass for.'

'Oh, it's worth it, Fox. You'll be going home a hero. They'll display your image on every building in Silosia for a month.'

Fox stared at him, uncertain if the novy was being serious or sarcastic.

Thundersky sipped his coffee.

'She thinks I'm an asshole,' Fox said.

'Then you need to prove to her that you're not. She just needs to know that she can rely on you. We all do. We have to rely on each other now, Fox. You understand that, right?'

Fox nodded his head.

Thundersky smiled.

'Graycloud will be worrying once he knows we're down,' Fox said. 'He's my husband. He works in Tactical Command. I just wish we could get the comms up to let them know we're not clocked off.'

Thundersky nodded his head. 'Once the satellites locate us, they'll know…'

A buzzer started to sound on the sensor interface.

'That's the proximity alarm,' Fox said, rising from his stool, stepping to the sensors.

Thundersky looked at the data coming in. 'One human detected, two-point-six miles ahead.'

Venus came into the C and C looking dazed and still half asleep. She put a Surfer Town turd into the corner of her mouth but did not light it.

Tiger staggered in, knuckling sleep out of his eyes, wiping drool from the corner of his mouth. 'What's going on?'

'The sensors have detected someone on the road.'

Venus looked at the lower left-hand viewer which streamed bio-data directly from the sensors. 'It's a kidling,' she said. 'Vital signs very weak. Bio-scans detect a foreign body in his abdomen. Diagnostics suggest a parabellum.' Then, on the viewer, the words turned red: "URGENT MEDICAL ASSISTANCE REQUIRED!"

'What are the radiation readings?' Tiger asked.

'Well within tolerances,' Thundersky said as he looked at the sensor readings. 'No explosive devices or weapons detected,' he added.

'Fox. Get the Doc ready.' Venus looked at Tiger and Thundersky.

The kidling was lying curled up in a fetal position on the ancient blacktop.

Thundersky and Venus went outside to into the cool morning.

'D'you know how to use that thing?' Venus gestured to the tac-one Thundersky was holding at the ready, covering Venus so she could examine the boy.

'Don't you worry about me,' he said, pulling the beech slide back and chambering a round as if he had done it a thousand times before. 'You just concentrate on the boy.'

He felt different somehow, something in this moment had changed in him and he didn't know what, how or why, but something had changed. How did he know how to work the tac-one, for example? He had never handled a weapon in his life before. He knew nothing about guns or laser pulse weaponry, and yet, he felt he knew everything about this one. Not only that, he was instinctively more predatory with the tac-one at the ready, his steady eyes perpetually scanning the terrain, picking out all the possible vantage positions an enemy might occupy. A hill here, a copse of trees there, a depression hither, a bluff tither. The rusting wrecks of Old-World vehicles, piled into mountains along both sides of the road for as far as the eye could see. Hawkish and preternaturally alert, like a wolf on the hunt, his every instinct seemed attuned to his surroundings, his vision seemed better, his hearing sharper, his sense of smell keener.

Out in the fields the crickets and grasshoppers chirred to the accompaniment of the wind brushing the long grass.

The boy murmured with pain as Venus gently turned him over. She pulled up his bloody rags and looked at the infected wound in his side. The boy was burning up with fever and he had lost a lot of blood. She touched his clammy skin. 'Looks like sepsis,' she said, looking at the festering wound, which oozed yellow-green pus. 'We might already be too late.'

Tiger shouldered his tac-one. 'Let's get him inside.' He stooped down and picked the kidling up in his strong mudsurfer arms. The boy's eyes opened briefly. 'We're going to fix you up,' Thundersky said.

The kidling's dark eyes stared at Thundersky as he carried him to the M-TAV.

The med-bed was out waiting to receive the casualty, and Thundersky carefully laid the boy down on it.

Venus lowered the scanner canopy over him and plugged in the medical diagnostics computer, which swung out from the bulkhead on a gimballed arm. Compartments above the med-bed revealed hypo-guns and an array of drugs, and there was a shiny, sterile robotic surgeon on a sophisticated gimbal arm. Venus plugged it all into the medical diagnostics computer, which she then turned on. Bright lights came on under the body scanner canopy and started to scan. She pressed a series of touchscreen sensors. 'There's some scissors in that drawer. Cut his rags off. They carry infections, we're going to have to see where the bullet is and see if Doc Barney can remove it.'

'Doc Barney?' Tiger frowned.

'That's what we call the BMDS (Battlefield Medical Diagnostics System). Doc Barney. It's what Bigriver called it.' she explained. 'When he was laser shot by the Prophetess in the Virginias, it was the BMDS that fixed him up. He called it Doc Barney and the name's stuck ever since.'

Thundersky cut the unconscious youth's clothes off. The scanner hummed over him.

She looked at the diagnostics viewer again. It showed an Old-World .9-millimeter parabellum copper jacket bullet lodged in the abdominal muscle. 'That's an Old-World slug. Fortunately, it's not gone too deep and it's missed vital organs and arteries,' she said, looking at the scan. 'A low energy impact. A straight forward extraction. Just the sort of thing Doc Barney was made for.'

'And the infection?' Thundersky asked.

'We have medicinals to take care of that,' she said.

"Adolescent…" came up on the viewer. "Approximate age, 13 to 15 years. Malnourished. Adjusting anesthesia…"

Barney the robot surgeon's arm was actually four multi-jointed arms with a laser scalpel, dermal glue gun, clamps, spreader fingers, probes and forceps all working independently of each other. The med-bed's sensors monitored the boy's vital signs, displaying them on a separate viewer over the scanner canopy. Respiration, heartbeat, blood pressure, everything was displayed. First it sprayed antiseptic over the boy's abdomen as another arm administered a hypo shot of anesthesia and removed a blood sample at the same time. A message flashed up on the main BMDS viewer. "Anesthesia administered. Cloning three units of blood."

Barney's multi-fingered mechanical hands started to perform the surgery, cutting with a cauterizing laser while a pair of spreaders went into the opening and spread it open. A forceps finger went into the bullet wound and closed, then retracted with an intact copper jacket .9-millimeter bullet between the forceps' bloody jaws.

Pus and blood oozed from the wound. Barney irrigated and sprayed nanite antibiotics and coagulating agent into the wound and glued it closed.

One of the hands closed around the boy's arm and a needle went into his vein. "Administering 15cc Bio-Immunicol," appeared on the viewer.

When Venus saw the results of the blood tests, she remarked with surprise: 'According to this, there's barely any trace of radiation in this kidling's system. In fact, he's as clean as the pre-atomic age. Is that possible?' She looked bewildered at the two novices.

Tiger and Thundersky looked just as puzzled as she did.

'It's probably a glitch in Barney's diagnostics,' she said. 'He's been banged about quite a lot.' She looked at more information on the scanner results that caught her eye. 'That's strange,' she said, looking at the boy's bio-medical data. 'According to the scan, he's got something in his head.'

'That's called a brain,' Fox said, trying to be witty without success.

Venus looked at him. 'Go and check on the monitors. Make sure nobody's lurking about out there,' she ordered.

'What is it?' Tiger asked.

'An unidentified microscopic object in his cerebral cortex...' She pressed a sensor key and a holographic image of the boy's brain projected. It indicated the location of the object by making it flash red. She zoomed in to maximum magnification.

Tiger and Thundersky moved in for a closer look. 'That looks like a nanite,' Tiger said, giving Thundersky a bewildered look. 'How the dickbutt did that get right down in there?'

Thundersky gave him a worried look. 'More to the point; who put it there and why?'

Jacob started coming around from the anesthetic. His eyes flickered open and all he could see was bright white blurry light above him. He could feel that wherever he was, he was moving. Then a dark figure moved in his peripheral vision. A voice spoke. Someone laughed.

He could hear the clean pulse of a well maintained mag-drive. He tried to move, but he was strapped down to the bed, unable to move. He was a prisoner! But they weren't Ferals. Godders then, he thought with horror. There was little to choose between the two when it came to savagery.

Suddenly a blurry figure leaned over him, a young face coming into focus.

'Welcome back,' Tiger said.

'I ain't dead?' he said.

'Was that a statement or a question? No, you're not dead.'

Jacob looked at the grinning face. 'Utopes.' He said. 'Silosians?'

Tiger nodded his head. 'And what are you? Scav? Dusty?'

'Kiss my ass. What're you gunna do to me?' He wriggled under the straps, trying to sit up. 'You gonna torture me. I don't care what you do. I ain't tellin ya nothin'!' he said defiantly. Utopes were far less frightening than Godders and Ferals.

Tiger started unbuckling the safety straps. 'Relax. We're not going to do anything with you. These are just so you didn't fall out and hurt yourself after all the trouble we went to fixing you up. Take it easy, you've had surgery and anesthesia. Do you understand? Medicinals. They'll make you sleepy…'

Jacob stared blankly at him. 'I'm not stoopid,' he said curtly.

Tiger's smile broadened. 'No. I can see that.'

Jacob reached down to his sore side and felt the dermal patch. He also realized that he was naked under the foil blanket, and he grabbed it to make sure it didn't slip away. He tried to sit up, but he went giddy and felt faint. His belly hurt and his mouth was dryer than when the Ferals had come to eat him.

'Take it easy, remember. You're still fighting sepsis.' He helped him to sit up.

He looked at another young man, sitting in one of the seats with his feet tucked up under him, his head down, studying something on a data-pad, not taking any notice of him at all. Jacob recognized his face. He was the one who had been carrying him.

Fox came through from the C and C. He glanced back at the boy as he went to the front. 'We've got company,' he said to Venus. 'Two solarcycles approximately twenty miles back.'

'Dusty scouts,' she responded. She had been half expecting them.

Thundersky lowered his data-pad and looked up. 'Their main force will be following beyond our sensor range,' he said, again without really knowing why he knew that. Finally, he looked at the kidling, who was staring fixedly at him, as though he was looking at a ghost.

Tiger handed the boy a cup of water. 'Here, drink this. It's okay, it's just water. You need to rehydrate, you lost a lot of blood.'

Jacob gulped it back thirstily. 'May I have another?'

Tiger took the cup from him and went off into the galley.

'May I have my clothes, please?' He was looking at Thundersky.

'We threw 'em away. They stank.'

'Well he's definitely not a Feral,' Venus said from the cockpit. 'I never encountered a Feral with manners before, never mind an articulate one.' She engaged the nav-conn and climbed out of the cockpit. 'Don't worry, honey-cheeks. We'll find you something to wear. First, how about tellin' us where you from, honey-cheeks?' she asked, giving him an affectionate smile. 'Who are your people? And who shot you?'

Jacob looked diffidently at her, then back at Thundersky, who was staring evenly at him. 'I aint sayin' nothin' to no Utopes. I'm grateful an' all. But I ain't no cowardy-jumpy. You int gonna make me talk.'

Tiger came back with more water.

'I ain't tellin' ya babbledick 'bout nothin'.' He looked at Thundersky again, apparently fascinated by him for some reason.

'Yep. He's a Dusty sure enough,' Venus said. 'Only Dusties talk that way. What faction, honey-cheeks? Pen Dusties? N'york Dusties? Chigs…?' She paused. 'Virginia Dusties…'

His eyes twitched. 'Kiss my ass.'

She smiled. 'One of the Prophetess's, eh?' she said. 'He's a Virginia Dusty.'

Jacob stared at her. Then he pulled the foil blanket all the way around himself. He wasn't letting no woman see his modesty, he thought, not thinking that she'd already seen him butt naked.

'Don't worry, honey-cheeks, I got bigger things to think about.' She laughed out loud and walked through into the C and C.

'What's your name?' Tiger asked. He pointed to himself. 'I'm Tiger White…' He gestured to Thundersky. 'This is Thundersky Reece…'

Jacob took a deep breath and gulped back a swallow of water. *Thundersky Reece! I knew it! I knew it!*

'…The lady was Corporal Venus. And the other man is Tactical Fox,' Tiger said.

Jacob pressed his lips tight together. 'Ain't sayin nothin'. But now I know your names. I got an advantage.'

Thundersky smiled amusedly to himself, before returning his attention to his data-pad and the data about Old-World quantum computers.

Tiger went through to the C and C.

Chapter Twenty-Four

Jacob made coffee and brought a mug to Thundersky, who was sitting in the cockpit at the driving controls. Jacob knew that he would be dead now were it not for them. Even so, it was difficult to relax. He had been constantly on the knife's edge between life and death for so long, he had forgotten how to relax, and this new feeling of safety was completely alien to him. But he was safe, he knew he was. Thundersky Reece was there.

'Thanks,' Thundersky said, taking the coffee from him.

Jacob sat in the seat next to the cockpit and regarded him carefully. So, this was the famous Thundersky Reece, a name he had grown up with. Did he know how special he was? He didn't seem to. Did he know he had a mother, a sister? A nephew... who was sitting right next to him? Did he know about Genesis? He lifted his feet up onto the seat and embraced his knees. 'Everyone's our enemy out here, Thundersky Reece,' he said.

Thundersky sipped his coffee and nodded his head. 'That's an unfortunate fact, kidling.'

'Astraeus Jacob.'

Thundersky frowned at him.

'My name,' he said. 'It's Astraeus Jacob. Everyone just calls me Jacob. I hate being called Astraeus. You won't call me Astraeus, will you, Thundersky?'

'The titan god of dusk,' Thundersky said.

Jacob was surprised he knew. 'Yeah. That's right. My mom's name's Aurora. Grandma's crazynuts about Romans and Greeks. But you won't call me by that name?'

Thundersky smiled. 'No. Not if you don't want me to.'

Jacob looked up at the tactical viewer and read the words "Weapons online," flashing in red in the corner of the viewer.

Thundersky was watching him.

'If they wanted to attack you, they'd have done it already,' Jacob said. 'The Dusties who are following us. They're probably Pen Dusties. This is their territory. They're checking us out.'

'The weapons are just a precaution. They won't fire unless we're fired on first. Our mission's a peaceful one.'

Jacob nodded. 'Their leader is Aceheart Ken. My grandma calls him Dickhead Ken. They got the uneasy P with Silosia. So, I know they won't attack. But we're comin' into Godder country too, and they don't have no uneasy P with no one. If they see us, they'll attack.'

'You should tell Venus all of this.'

'I will. I think she has that thing for me though…'

Thundersky frowned at him. 'What thing?'

'You know. The sex thing. I don't have the sex thing for her. She's really old like my mom. But she keeps winking at me and calling me honey-cheeks. That means she's got the sex thing for me, right?'

Thundersky let out such a laugh from his belly it made Jacob recoil. He laughed so much it made his eyes water.

'What's so goddam funny?'

'She don't have the sex thing for you. It's her way, that's all. You're a kidling, my guess is, she likes kidlings.'

'I ain't no kidling. I'm fourteen.'

Thundersky smiled amusedly to himself.

'So, she don't have the sex thing for me?'

'No. I promise you.'

Jacob sighed with relief. 'Damn, I thought I was gonna have to tell her that I don't have it for her.'

'Your people must be missing you.'

Jacob shrugged his shoulders. 'I guess. Though they think I'm dead. All my people think I'm dead. Like the others.'

'Others?'

'My friends. They killed 'em.'

'Who killed 'em, Jacob? Scavs?'

Jacob shook his head.

'My people?' Thundersky asked ominously.

'No.' He shifted about in his seat, seeing disquieting visions of his captivity – of his friends. Watching them being slaughtered one by one. Nobody knowing when their turn would come – they just knew it would. The Ferals kept them in cages, fed them on scraps, and once a month, when the moon was full, they would come for one of them. They would drag them screaming and pleading, and hang them upside-down from their ankles over a square white porcelain sink with a drain hole in the middle, stained with thick and dark clots of coagulated blood and rotting flesh from the countless kidlings they had butchered this way over the centuries, carving them up alive. They lasted for hours, screaming and pleading, their voices growing weaker and weaker as they neared their end. He suddenly burst into tears and sobbed inconsolably.

Thundersky engaged the nav-conn and climbed out of the cockpit. He sat beside him and put his arm around him and Jacob turned into him, burying his face into Thundersky's shoulder, clinging to him as if clinging by his fingernails to his sanity as he cried his heart out.

Venus came in from the C and C where Fox and Tiger were monitoring the solarcycles following them. She saw Thundersky holding onto the kidling as he cried. She returned to the C and C.

'Ferals,' he sobbed. 'They killed my friends and ate them!' His fingers dug into Thundersky's shoulders until it hurt.

Thundersky held him tighter. 'You're safe now.'

Eventually, Jacob lifted his head. His eyes were red and puffy, his cheeks wet with tears... 'They were going to eat me too,' he said tearfully, sniffling and snuffling. He wiped his eyes with the back of his hands and sniffed. 'I don't wanna babbledick about it.'

'You don't have to. When was the last time you saw your people?'

Every month when a full moon had come, he'd wondered if it was his turn to be hung over the porcelain sink. 'Ten months,' he said. That's how many friends he'd lost and he was the last one.

Thundersky looked out of the window to behold the ruins of downtown Pittsburg looming above the forest in the distance. Half tumbled blocks towered over the treetops, still and silent on the horizon, its suburban neighborhoods long ago consumed by wilderness.

'We're in Godder country,' Jacob said ominously.

They stopped for the night in the shadow of Pittsburg silhouetted against the darkening sky. Outside, the night air was cool and fresh. Thundersky wandered away from the M-TAV, just to the edge of the road, where he stopped and stared into the darkness. These Godders worried him. He knew there was a real possibility they would attack, and if they hadn't already detected them, they soon would. Tactically speaking, their options were limited. They could either go back the way they'd come, knowing they would run into the Dusties, or they could head into the dead zone, through old Philadelphia and old New Jersey. But it was highly radioactive and not just from the ICBM's, but the ancient nuclear power plants that had leaked radiation. Nothing lived there, nothing could live there. But going that way came with its own dangers. The radiation could interfere with the M-TAV's critical systems. The mag-drive could fail.

They could hold off an attack for a short while. Minutes rather than hours, especially if the Godders used a pincer tactic. They could try and outrun them, but they couldn't outgun them. The sensors detected artillery and ballistic missiles. Or Thundersky could weaponize the probes with sonic charges? He could convert the drones into self-guiding bombs. It was only a matter of updating the AI software and connecting the charges to an electrical source via a detonator. They had three drones and nine sonic charges. Three charges going off in the air would have the same destructive energy of an Old-World ten-kiloton nuclear warhead.

He was about to turn back to the M-TAV, when:

'Locating Genesis. Genesis located,' Inner Voice suddenly said, like the voice of an old friend that both irritated and fascinated him. 'Risk factor high. Primary directive initiated.' Inner voice fell silent.

'Is it you, Arti? Please, just give me a sign?'

Back at the M-TAV, Thundersky didn't say a word as he loped through to the rear storage compartment, where the sonic charges were stored with their kit.

Venus and Tiger loped after him. 'What? What is it?' Venus said urgently.

'I'm going to weaponize the drones with sonic charges,' he said matter-of-factly. 'We may need an edge if we're attacked by the Godders.'

She stared at him. *The boy's a goddam natural*, she thought to herself. She nodded her head. 'You're a goddam badass, Novy. I like the way you think.' She planted a Surfer Town turd between her grinning lips, her spirits raised. 'Fox, bring the railguns and laser pulse online.'

'I'll give you a hand,' Tiger said.

'What can I do?' Jacob said, raising his hand in the air.

'You can keep your eye on the sensors, Sweet-Cheeks. That's a very important job. Watching our asses.'

Jacob nodded his head. 'Yes, ma'am.'

She ruffled his hair and winked at him as she left the C and C.

'You sure she don't got the sex thing for me?'

Tiger chuckled.

'I'm sure,' Thundersky said from the storage compartment.

They climbed up onto the roof and Fox passed their titanium trunk up through the hatch.

'Two eggs per drone should do it, Tiger,' Thundersky said as he knelt in front of the launch hatch. 'Okay, Corporal Venus,' he added, speaking into the open comm. 'Open the hatch, spin up number one and disengage its electrical systems. We don't want to risk detonating one of these when we're anywhere nearby. Minimal safe distance is seven point nine kilometers,' he said precisely.

The drone's launch hatch slid open.

Venus' voice filtered through the open comm link. 'Cut the babbledick and get on with it.'

The probe rose up out of the launch hatch and Thundersky opened the inspection and maintenance hatch.

Tiger handed him the heavy metallic sonic-explosive spheres one at a time, each sphere no bigger than a chicken's egg. Dense and heavy as if they were made of solid lead, but twice as heavy. Each charge had an electrical socket at one end for the detonator primer and timer, which Thundersky had to wire into the probe's main power cell with an altitude surge switch to detonate the charges. He set the surge switch to one hundred and sixty feet.

The sonic charges were inside, all he had to do now was connect the primers and the surge switch. A fiddly job that required him to reach right inside behind the mag-lift and connect the terminals by feel rather than sight.

In the C and C, Venus, Fox and Jacob watched them on the viewer.

'How does he know all this shit anyway?' Fox mused aloud.

'Well they didn't send them here to decorate the place,' Venus replied.

'Thundersky knows everything,' Jacob said, his eyes fixed on the sensors.

'Nobody knows everything, Honey-Cheeks. But he's smart sure enough.'

Jacob smiled to himself. How little they knew.

Tiger was crouched down on the roof between the laser cannon and the railgun, anxiously scanning the terrain, sensing a thousand eyes upon them.

'These are a last resort, Corporal Venus,' Thundersky said, because they'll kill everything within four square kilometers.'

'Whatever you say. But if we need 'em. If it comes to choices between us and them, I'll goddam use 'em.'

Thundersky glanced around at Tiger, then looked back. 'Retract number one and spin up two.'

It was a restless night and nobody really got any sleep. Tiger, Thundersky, Fox and Venus took two-hour shifts at the sensors.

Tiger and Thundersky were up on the roof, sitting under the railgun turret.

'What're you think, Thunder?'

'About what?'

'About why them Dusties tried killing us? It's like they knew we were coming.'

Thundersky made no comment. His eyes roved the darkness, the breeze kissing against the fronds of the trees, making them whisper to the night and in the plain, the endless chirr of crickets buzzed like static.

'Someone had to have told them we were coming.'

'Maybe. Or maybe they just saw an opportunity to blow us out of the sky?'

Tiger had to concede, that was a possibility. They fell quiet and looked off into the dark.

Jacob's head appeared out of the hatch and he watched the novies, thinking they hadn't noticed him. He stood on the ladder and rested his arms on the roof, upon which he rested his chin.

'What I don't get is, why they've not finished us off?' Tiger said. 'Why are they following us? They could've taken us out whenever the hell they liked. So why haven't they? D'you think they know about the ADP?'

Thundersky was just as baffled as he was. 'I d'know,' he said. 'There's been no comms transmissions about the ADP, or us. I think you're looking for reasons where there are none. They probably shot us down for the scavenge. The antirad suits, weapons, tech, and now they probably want the M-TAV. That'll be why they've not destroyed us, or tried to take us by force. Venus is duty bound to set the auto-destruct. What're you think, Jacob?'

Tiger looked round to the hatch. 'Goddammit, how long you been there?'

Jacob shook his head. 'D'know. But they don't want the M-TAV.'

Tiger raised a brow. 'No? Then what?'

Jacob looked at Thundersky. Then he shrugged his shoulders. 'D'know.'

'I don't suppose you know why you've got a microscopic nanite processor in your brain either?' Tiger said.

'Keeps me healthy from the fallout and the cancers,' he said. 'We all got 'em. All the Virginias. That's why we don't get sick.' He looked at Thundersky again.

'That's not possible,' Tiger said. 'We'd have done it already if it was.'

Jacob shrugged his shoulders again. 'You asked.' He disappeared back down the hatch.

Chapter Twenty-Five

They had been on the road less than two hours, when the sensors began picking up several pockets of human habitation thirty miles east, fifteen miles west and twenty-eight miles to the north.

Venus engaged the nav-conn, climbed out of the cockpit and went into the C and C. 'Don't do that, Honey-Cheeks. Dangerous,' she said to Jacob, who was in the C and C swiveling around and around on a stool next to Thundersky at the tactical & weapons interface. Tiger and Fox were monitoring the sensors.

There was a whirr as the laser cannon rose up on its turret. Targeting viewers came online.

Jacob moved to Thundersky's side.

'No movement from the enemy,' Tiger said, slipping into military mode. He was a reservist after all.

'Find us a way to get around them, Fox.'

'I'm looking,' he said, bringing up cartographical data.

'You're wasting your time,' Thundersky said. 'I've already looked. The only way of avoiding contact is by going through the dead zone.'

They were silent for a moment.

'*Woah*!' Tiger exclaimed. 'We've got a large mobile force approaching fast, approximately thirty miles in the southeast.'

'How large?' Venus asked, stepping over to him.

'Sensors have identified sixty – six-zero, Mark One, Mark Two and Mark Three M-TAVs. Heavily armed,' Tiger said. 'Three batteries of Thunderclap ground-to-air sonic missiles and a mobile launcher with at least three high yield Satan Nine plasma warheads. Sensors read multiple weapons platforms, and about two hundred solarcycles.'

'ETA twenty-seven minutes,' Fox said. He looked at Venus. 'We're being rounded up like kidlings for the slaughter.'

Jacob suddenly pointed at the bleeping red spots indicating enemy positions on the sensor display. He pointed at the flashing red bleep in the north. 'Big Barn Town,' he said, looking at Thundersky and Venus in turn. 'Scavs,' he added. 'You don't have to worry about them...' He pointed to the bleep in the west. 'Jesus City,' he said. 'Delaware Godders. You gotta worry like crazynuts about them.' He pointed to the blotch in the east. 'Gabriel's Town ... Also Delaware Godders.' He looked at Thundersky. 'Don't go east or west,' he warned, looking at them. 'They'll kill us for sure.' He pointed along the narrow strip to the northeast into the dead zone. 'The forbidden zone.' He drew a circle with his finger encompassing the ruins of Philadelphia to Allentown and New Jersey. 'All this is the forbidden. Only crazynuts, Ferals and Scavs go there. Plutonium and hot carbon. Dusties and Godders don't go in there. That's the way of it.'

'And here?' Venus said, pointing at the large force moving in behind them.

He looked at her. 'I d'know f'sure, but I think they must be Pen Dusties,' he said.

'Or Virginia Dusties,' Thundersky said.

Jacob shook his head. 'That would break the uneasy P,' he said. 'My people never come this far.'

Fox brought up satellite images and more detailed Old-World maps. He downloaded the latest radiation level surveys of the dead zones, taken less than six months ago. 'Radiation monitoring suggests radiation levels are stable at between three thousand and seven thousand millisieverts, with two major hotspots exceeding eight thousand millisieverts. We'll have to do the entire trip sealed in here. The computer estimates three days depending on the terrain conditions, and we won't be able to use sensors or the nav-conn.'

'No,' Venus said. 'I'm not risking that long in a radioactive zone. We came down hard. We don't know what damage may have been done to the airlock seals and purifiers. We should either head for this Big Barn Town and then head towards the Hudson River and go amphibian into Manhattan? Or we should envoy the Pen Dusties and ask for their assistance?' She looked at Tiger and Thundersky.

'Whatever you're going to do, do it fast,' Tiger said. 'Our friends are closing fast, ETA ten minutes.'

No sooner had he spoken, when an alarm sounded.

'Heat plumes detected, fifteen degrees east,' Thundersky announced, watching the viewers. 'Tracking trajectory. Incoming, ETA thirty seconds. Primary weapons engaging…'

They were horrified.

On the roof, the laser cannon honed in.

SSSSHBLAMM! – the laser cannon fired a glowing green beam of light spearing on an upward trajectory. Moments later, a bright flash of light arced across the eastern sky – then a distant boom.

'Missile destroyed,' Thundersky said, keeping his cool.

'We've got mobile units moving in from both the east and west,' Tiger announced urgently.

'I've got 'em,' Thundersky said, quickly typing on the touchscreen.

The railgun came to life and spun its muzzles east, while the laser cannon turned its muzzle to the west.

'Targets locked.' The railgun opened fire with a burst of a dozen rounds, the P'VOOM-P'VOOM-P'VOOM…

The laser cannon buzzed and rotated forty degrees. Its muzzle lifted ten degrees and locked on another inbound missile.

'We've got snipers in the grass,' Fox said. 'Four of them, six hundred yards south.'

The laser fired its glowing finger of death with a SSSSHBLAMM!

Thundersky grabbed a tac-ten. 'Take over the tactical, Corporal.'

'You can't go out there. You're not trained for combat.'

He looked at her, and without saying a word, he turned to the ladder and climbed up to the roof.

'Crazynuts sonofabitch,' she muttered under her breath.

Tiger grabbed his tac-ten and climbed up after him.

Thundersky and Tiger crawled along the roof on their bellies, taking cover between the railgun's ammunition feeder conduits, which were twenty inches proud of the roof between the railgun and the laser cannon turrets.

They were both scared, the fear showed in their faces. Venus was right, neither of them had had combat experience. Thundersky didn't even know if he'd be able to hit anything with his tac-one. Point and shoot and hope for the best, is what he was telling himself, and yet his nature, his body and his thinking were once again behaving like a soldier's, as if it were somehow in his DNA.

They turned on the thermal targeting scopes on their tac-tens and honed in on the long grass beyond the road in the west.

'They're five hundred and sixty yards out,' Fox's voice filtered through their comms.

The laser cannon rotated ten degrees on its turret – SSSSHBLAMM!!!

Thundersky and Tiger glanced up at the blinding flash of light bleaching the horizon moments later. And then, two distant BOOMS! They felt the blast wave as another inbound missile detonated before its warheads armed.

Thundersky returned his attention to scoping the long grass. He sighted them at his ten o'clock, five hundred yards away. 'There they are.'

Tiger looked through his scope. 'I thought we were tight friends, Thunder. But I never knew you had this war shit in you.'

'Neither did I. But it's us or them, Tiger. Us or them, and I ain't gunna get all wib-wobble over Godders. Fuck 'em…' And then, almost as if to prove his point, he started firing and the air cracked with gunshots, the glowing bullets tracing into the long grass.

Tiger opened fire too. In all, they fired about twenty rounds.

'Targets eliminated,' Fox's voice filtered into their ears and they ceased fire.

The railgun came back to life with a sudden clunk and whirr of the turret motors. The barrels rotated one hundred and sixty degrees and the muzzles dipped and fired a volley, the air rippling with the distorted bursts of electromagnetic energy as eight fifty-caliber projectiles shot out from both barrels, one chasing the other at six thousand feet per second.

The laser spun quickly and locked onto another inbound missile – SSSSHBLAMM!!! Seconds later, another ball of fire expanded in the sky less than a quarter of a mile away with a deafening BOOM!!!

The railgun shells exploded about two miles away with eight distinct low energy sonic explosions that sounded like thunderclaps in the distance.

They were just turning back when they heard the thunderous roar of powerful rockets thrusting low overhead...

They looked up.

'What the fuck…!?' Tiger's voice tailed off as he spotted two low flying cruise missiles arcing overhead climbing into the sky, thrusting through the air with roaring tails of blue fire from their magnetoplasma rockets.

They froze in a moment of bewilderment.

Thundersky glanced southeast and saw flashes from laser cannons being fired towards Jesus City.

'Get in the M-TAV!' Thundersky shouted urgently. 'Quick! Or we're dead!'

Tiger scrambled down the ladder and Thundersky was right behind him. He hit the button and the hatch slid closed. 'Seal the rig for shockwaves!'

The missiles detonated several miles away as Thundersky shimmied down the ladder, and beyond the horizon, the implosions lit everything up in a blinding flash of white-hot light and a huge black mushroom belched up into the air like an Old-World nuke, sucking up dust and debris into its black heart, glowing with plasmic fire…

'Shit!' Thundersky shouted. 'Brace for impact!'

He spotted Jacob hunkered down in the corner, pressed up against the bulkhead. He lurched to him – grabbed him and forcefully yanked him away from the bulkhead and clung on tight to him with one hand while the other reached up and clasped onto the grab-rail.

Tiger, Venus and Fox all grabbed onto the rails and hung on.

The first wave slammed into the M-TAV like a wall of lead. It scooped the M-TAV up like a toy, eight feet off the ground and threw it across the road several yards before it landed with a bone jarring CRASH! The modules rocked violently from side to side.

Thundersky clung so tight to Jacob, the kidling could hardly breathe.

The proximity alarm was still buzzing and the M-TAV's systems control was beeping from an overhead panel.

Another shockwave slammed into them, sliding the back articulated section of the M-TAV sideways, almost jackknifing the rig.

The lights and viewers went offline, plunging them into total darkness for several seconds before the emergency lighting came on.

A third wave hit and a fourth and fifth and sixth, each growing steadily weaker and weaker until they barely rocked the modules anymore.

Venus turned the alarms off and everything fell into total silence.

They stood wordless in shock, looking at one another in the dim red glow of the emergency lighting.

'Is everybody okay?' Venus asked.

The systems started to come back online with whirrs and beeps, viewers flickering and glowing.

Jacob stared oddly at Thundersky when he released him from his grasp. 'Why'd you grab me like that?'

'The shockwaves would've broken every bone in your body,' Venus said, looking at the confused boy. 'You owe Thundersky your life, Honey-Cheeks.'

'What the hell was that?' Fox asked.

'Satan Nine thermo-sonic plasma missiles,' Thundersky said. 'Fired by our Dusty friends behind us.'

Fox tried bringing the sensors back online, but nothing was working apart from the radar. 'We've got basic radar and that's about it.' He studied the radar scope. 'The Godders are retreating on all sides.'

'Weapons?' Venus asked.

'Tactical's down,' Thundersky said. 'Forward, aft and roof railguns appear to be functional, but the laser's offline.'

'And our Dusty friends?' Venus asked.

'Holding their positions at the moment.'

Venus sat at the AI interface and ran a systems analysis. 'Multiple system failures,' she said. 'Nav-conn is offline. Laser pulse cannon power cell four has critical damage. Minimum power to the mag-drive conductors.' She looked round at them. 'We're babbledicked.' She looked back at the sensors. 'Hull integrity is at ninety percent. We've got damage on the rear airlock.'

'Could be worse,' Thundersky said optimistically after a pause of silence. 'We could all be dead.'

The worry between them was palpable.

'How long will it take to run repairs?' Tiger asked.

'Until I can see and assess the extent of the damage, I couldn't say. Hours at least.'

'Our main priority is getting the mag-drive working,' Thundersky said.

'We've got movement,' Fox declared, studying the radar scope where several individual pricks of light were moving away from the Dusteater main force in the south. 'Two M-TAVs and four solarcycles heading this way.' He looked at Venus.

Venus pulled a cover off underneath the weapons control interface. Behind it was a dormant touchscreen panel that slid out with a viewer. She switched it on and the panel lit up. The computer's voice said: 'Auto destruct online. Enter initiation code.'

'Delta-Seven-Seven. Venus Jane. Corporal. Commanding,' Venus said aloud.

Tiger, Thundersky and Fox looked at one another.

'Authorization accepted.'

'Activate on my voice command. Set for thirty seconds.'

'Voice activated auto destruct. Thirty second delay, confirmed.'

Venus closed the panel.

Chapter Twenty-Six

The wind blustered across the plains. Carried on it was the distinctive scorched smell of ionized air and the pungent rubbery odor of Astrium-plasma.

'What the hell do they want from us?' Fox murmured, looking nervously at the others.

'The rig probably. And they can trade us for a prisoner exchange,' Venus said as they stood out in the road several yards away from the M-TAV, warily watching the four solarcycles escorting two Mark III M-TAV halftracks, both flying Virginia Dusteater flags, which consisted of a pure white eagle on a blood red background.

'Virginia Dusties,' Venus said quietly.

They stopped thirty feet from them. The leading M-TAV was pulling a C and C trailer behind it on a hitch bar, its old mag-drive beating and sputtering.

Thundersky felt a deep and terrible dread in the pit of his stomach. The Dusties on the solarcycles, clad head to foot in anti-rad gear and body armor, dismounted. Each one carried tac-ones and parabellum sidearms and lasers. The darkly tinted, round glass eye holes of their anti-rad respirators were like mirrors, refracting in the morning sunshine.

Venus, Thundersky and Tiger positioned themselves in the road in front of the M-TAV, the railguns muzzled on the Dusties. If one died, they all died.

Venus unclipped the retaining straps from her parabellum pistols, watching the Dusties closely. One sudden move and she'd draw down on them and take out the solarcyclists.

The middle side hatch of the M-TAV pulling the trailer lifted up and over like a beetle's wing. They watched anxiously. Tiger shifted his weight anxiously, his finger nervously tapping the trigger guard of his tac-ten.

Thundersky inched closer to his friend.

'That woman looks familiar to me,' Thundersky said.

Tiger watched the Prophetess as she climbed down from the M-TAV with Bearfang close behind her. The hatch lowered as they moved towards the front – towards Venus, Tiger and Thundersky.

'It's him,' she said, her heart racing. 'Wait here, Bear.' She walked between two of the solarcycles towards the Silosians.

Fox appeared in the front hatchway of the M-TAV, his tac-ten at the ready.

'It's the Scav woman from the market,' Thundersky said, looking quickly at Tiger. 'The one we hagglebucked the tech from.'

Tiger looked more closely. She wasn't jaundiced like she had been, and her hair was different, but yes, it was her.

The Prophetess walked unarmed towards them and stopped two feet in front of them. 'Happy day,' she said.

'Fuck you!' Venus growled. 'Did you shoot us down over the Virginias?'

The Prophetess looked at her. 'I didn't order that. We had a traitor in our group. He's been dealt with,' she said, looking at the gun Venus was holding. 'Are you going to shoot me, Corporal Venus Jane?'

Venus glared. *The bitch knows my name!* She planted a cigar into the corner of her mouth. 'I ain't decided yet. Why would this "traitor" be shootin' us down?'

'Maybe they wanted something you have.' The Prophetess looked at Thundersky. 'Happy day, Thundersky Reece. How's the VTD?'

'Flies like it never flew before,' Thundersky said.

She smiled and looked at Tiger.

'You know this woman?' Venus exclaimed.

'At the Scav market,' Tiger said. 'She sold us an old drone.'

'And how are your father and mother, Tiger White Washington?'

Tiger shifted uneasily.

'So, what is it you want?' Venus asked.

The Prophetess smiled. 'All in good time.'

Thundersky studied her closely, his eyes narrowing in the corners, shifting to Bearfang who stood behind the solarcycles, his arms folded, watching them like a hawk.

'We haven't fired on you,' she said. 'We've made no hostile act towards you and you can continue on to the Four-Eight-Zero in the old Manhattan. We're here to help you.'

'Why would you wanna do that?' Venus asked her.

'Because I don't want to be nuked any more than you do, Corporal Venus.' She gave her a wan smile.

'You're very well informed, Prophetess,' Thundersky said. 'You are the Prophetess, aren't you?'

She smiled. 'Some call me that. As for being well informed…' She smiled. 'Friends in very high places.' She looked at Tiger.

'What friends?' Venus asked.

The Prophetess looked at her. 'The same friends who tell me that Zim Steven intends to kill you as soon as you've disarmed the Four-Eight-Zero.'

Venus balked.

'Zim Steven has no intentions of allowing you to leave Manhattan alive. None of you,' the Prophetess added.

Venus laughed. 'Why would the Triple S want to kill us? We're saving the goddam planet, ain't we?'

'Because he didn't succeed in killing you nineteen years ago,' she said, looking directly at Thundersky.

Thundersky's heart jolted in his chest.

'What babbledick's this?' Tiger jumped in. 'Why would anyone wanna murder Thunder when he was just a baby? This is dickbutt and no mistake.'

She looked at him. 'It's the truth, Tiger White, and if you let me, I'll prove it to you. Then, we'll escort you to Manhattan. You know you'll not make it there alive without help. The Godders won't be put off for long, and when they come back, they'll hit you harder than before.'

Thundersky was confused. 'Lady, I don't know who you think I am. But I'm just a-'

'Have you never wondered why they left you topside for so long, instead of bringing you down into Sub City with the other fertiles?' she interrupted.

'It was a system error,' Tiger said.

The Prophetess shook her head. 'Arti doesn't make mistakes and we both know it. Neither do the GRC.' She looked at Thundersky. 'You were left topside for the same reason you were brought down into Sub City,' she said. 'To protect you from the Triple S. Blossom and Washington brought you into Sub City so they could stop the Triple S from looking too closely at you. Novices have certain protections from the state. They needed to buy some time so we could get you out before they found out who you really are. Fortunately, your hack into the NORAD system provided some timely assistance.'

Venus was silent, listening, confused. Her uneasy gaze shifted to Bearfang, watching from the solarcycles with a big smile on his face. She leered icily at him, feeling an urge to wipe that supercilious grin off the ugly bastard's arrogant face.

Thundersky shook his head. 'This is a trick.'

'No. It's not a trick, Thundersky. You're special. If you let me, I'll show you why. What've you got to lose?'

'Your missiles blew half our circuits,' Venus said.

The Prophetess looked sideways at her. 'The Godders were holding me up. We'd have been at it all night otherwise. But they'll be back for more, you can count on it.' She looked back at Thundersky, so wanting to put her arms around him and hold onto him forever. She vowed there and then, she would never let her baby go again. 'I'm not your enemy.'

Venus gave out a sneering laugh. 'Tell that to the poor bastards you blew up in the bio-domes,' she said. 'Tell that to the tacticals killed during the Battle of White Rock River…' Her anger was building. 'Tell that to the squad we lost when you shot us down. So don't you fucking stand there tellin' us you're not our enemy, you goddam bitch!'

The Prophetess stared at her. 'And what shall I tell my people, who your warbirds bombed three months before White Rock River? We can debate the rights and wrongs of war some other time, Corporal. Right now, you need friends, and I don't see anyone else coming forwards.'

Venus sniffed and took a drag from her Surfer Town turd, her eyes filled with mistrust and contempt. But the truth of it was, the Prophetess was right. They were alone out here and they were in no state or position to fight tech-savvy Godders.

'How do we know we can trust you?' Tiger asked.

'You don't. But you will, Tiger White. You will. Once you see the evidence. Once you've seen the com from your mother and father.'

'What com?'

She reached into her pocket and pulled out a data-drive. 'I've not seen it. I have no idea what's on it. But your mother asked us to pass it on to you.' She held it out to him.

Tiger gave it a diffident look. Eventually, he reached out hesitantly and took it from her.

She looked at Venus. 'I could say that you've been lied to your entire lives, but you wouldn't believe me, so I'll save my breath and let you make up your own minds about that. But ask yourselves this. Why would I waste very hard to come by missiles saving your asses if all I wanted to do was kill you or trade you? All of you put together couldn't buy that missile.'

'I think you've made your point,' Thundersky said. 'We've a gesture of goodwill of our own,' he went on. 'We found a kidling a few days ago. He was gut shot, but we fixed him up. He's one of yours, Prophetess. He and some other kidlings were taken by Ferals…'

She took a deep breath, her eyes widening. She looked back at Bearfang as old despair suddenly became new hope. Dare she hope? Could it have been possible? And what cosmic coincidences were at work if it was her grandson? What were the odds of him being rescued unknowingly by his own uncle? She gave Thundersky an unsettled look. 'Does he have a name, this boy?' she asked carefully.

'Astraeus Jacob.'

She clasped her chest and issued up a loud gasp from some deep and wounded place inside her, collapsing to her knees. '*Jacob*!'

Bearfang heard her and loped over.

'*They've found Jacob*!' she said. 'He's alive!'

Bearfang bounded over, his heart racing.

The Prophetess rose to her feet, looking at Bearfang. 'They found him!'

Venus turned to the M-TAV. 'Get Jacob and send him out,' she ordered Fox.

Fox went back inside.

'Jacob's alive!?' He looked wide eyed at Thundersky. 'What about the other kidlings? Blackwolf, Shark Water? Bloodtooth-?'

'Dead,' Thundersky said. 'Jacob was the only one.'

Bearfang and the Prophetess stared transfixed when Jacob climbed down.

'Dad! Grandma!' He ran excitedly to them and threw himself at Bearfang, who caught him in his powerful arms and wrapped him in an unbreakable hug, lifting him off the ground.

The big man was crying. So was the Prophetess.

Tiger, Venus and Thundersky exchanged looks with one another.

Bearfang hung on to Jacob, afraid to let go in case it was all an illusion, and if it was, it was the best and cruelest illusion he had ever had.

'Thundersky's here, Grandma! Thundersky!'

Tiger and Thundersky exchanged looks.

The Prophetess hugged him for the longest time, stroking his head and planting more kisses on him than he could stand. He was a man now – fourteen, as he often reminded people. He had seen death in its worst guises. He had survived the Ferals and made new friends.

'Thundersky, grandma,' he said excitedly. 'It's Thundersky…'

Chapter Twenty-Seven

She had been waiting nineteen years for this day, and now it had arrived, she sat with antsy unease in the trailer, shifting and picking at the worn arms of her chair. How many times had she imagined this? She had a speech all worked out, but now – now Thundersky was actually here, the words failed her. How could she articulate her feelings, her sorrow and profound guilt? How was she going to tell him about the Genesis chip and Arti being in his brain? How was she going to tell him that she was his biological mother?

Thundersky looked at the quantum system banking along the bulkhead of the trailer. He was under no illusion, these were the enemies of Silosia and the Utopian alliance. The Dusties were just as ruthless as any other enemy in war. The Virginia Dusties were the only neighbors of Silosia who refused to sign the Uneasy P, vowing that they would fight to the bloody end against *"Utopian tyranny."* It was the Virginia Dusties who had infiltrated the bio-spheres and set the incendiaries that destroyed and killed so many Silosians and animals the other year. They kidnapped Silosian citizens and held them for ransom, and even murdered Silosian colonists in cold blood (although that was hotly disputed by the Dusties).

'It's not as advanced as Arti,' she said, taking a blood pump gun from a storage locker. 'But it does the job. Make yourself at home. Can I get you a drink?'

Thundersky watched her curiously as she made a fist and pressed the blood pump gun to her inner elbow before pressing the trigger. It hissed as it drew blood.

She removed the bio-flask from the gun. 'Are you sure you won't sit down, Thundersky?' She wanted to touch him so desperately, as she had that day at the Scav market. But this was going to take time. Even once he believed her, he would have deep wounds in his soul for what she did to him. But he had to know the truth. He had to know everything in order to understand.

'I'm sure,' he replied, uneasy and suspicious.

'I'm very grateful to you for saving Jacob, Thundersky. He told me everything. You and he have become friends, he tells me? Jacob is careful who he chooses as his friends.'

Thundersky did not answer. He had been conditioned to hate and mistrust the Dusties his entire life, especially the Virginia Dusties.

'I know everything about you, Thundersky,' she went on unsettlingly. 'From the moment you were born.' She gestured to the chair again, but he shook his head. 'I know more about you than you know about yourself. Do you still have the data-pad your adoptive parents gave to you for your tenth birthday?'

He raised a brow. 'Ye-es.'

'I gave it to them to give to you.'

Thundersky stared guilelessly at her. 'I don't understand?'

'You will,' she said. 'You ask me what I want. I'll tell you. I want to save life from going extinct on this planet before it's too late. And I want to keep both my children and grandson safe. It's the only thing I've ever wanted, Thundersky. Nothing is more important to me…' She walked to him and held out the bio-flask of blood to him, looking gently into his eyes. 'I love both of my children unconditionally. My son and his sister. I would die for them in a heartbeat, Thundersky, because I love them more than life itself.' She gestured with the blood. 'Take it.'

'What're I want that for?'

'Trust me. You'll want it.'

He shook his head vaguely and took the flask reluctantly before slipping it into his pocket.

She smiled at him. 'Utopia isn't quite as Utopian as the Grand High Scholars would have you believe. But don't take my word for it. You can see the evidence for yourself. Whatever happens, after tonight, your life is never going to be the same again. You must prepare yourself, Thundersky, for the revelations at hand.'

Her words worried him.

'Here they call me Prophetess,' she went on. 'In Silosia, they called me Butterfly Thorn.'

Thundersky recognized the name and delved into the attic of his memory. 'You were a Micro bio-mechanical medical scholar. A healer who turned to treason. You were involved in the plot to blow up the Grand High Council.'

She raised a brow. 'So they tell me. But it's not the truth. It was the excuse they used to stop my work and murder my team to discredit the Genesis Project-'

'Genesis…?'

'It's the story of creation from ancient Godder mythology,' she said. 'It's the name we gave for a bio-nanite we developed in the GRC to assist the immune system to fight the cancers and fallout sicknesses-'

'Like the microscopic nanite we found in Jacob's brain?'

She raised a brow. 'Similar, but not exactly the same. The nanite Jacob and others of my people is more primitive. It destroys cancer cells and fights the radiation sicknesses. But it doesn't stop the infertility,' she said. 'The Genesis nanite is far more advanced than the ones we have.' She moved around the trailer. 'None of my Virginias are sick. They all have micro-nanites in their brains. It doesn't make us impervious, just more resistant and less likely to get sick. Haven't you ever wondered why you don't display any symptoms from the radiation? Or why you're fertile, even after living most of your life topside? Do you think that fate dealt you a better hand than other living organisms on this poisonous planet? It's not fate, nor divine intervention. It's not even luck, Thundersky. It's science.'

Thundersky suddenly felt anxious, because he knew she was about to answer those mysteries. He finally moved to the chair and sat down.

'You've got the Genesis nanite in your cerebral cortex; I implanted it into your brain when you were in your first trimester. Its purpose, as I said, is to help the body's immune system to fight off the radiation and repair the cellular damage and make you fertile. Unlike my Virginias, your chip is different. It's far more advanced, Thundersky. It's unique and very special. Your nanite chip has enhanced you in ways we could not possibly have imagined or anticipated. Your nanite has evolved far beyond its programmed parameters. We've no idea why...' She broke off again and looked studiously at him. 'But your nanite is directly linked to the ARTI-QS-602's positronic matrix...' Her eyes sharpened on him, looking for a reaction, but there was none. He sat stupefied at what she was telling him. 'But you knew that already, didn't you? That voice in your head. The one you have no control of is Arti. It's difficult to explain, but Arti somehow enhanced and evolved genesis. We don't know why.'

Thundersky shook his head. 'This is babbledick. Do you know how crazynuts that sounds?'

'Computer, play Alpha Two slash One.' She gestured to an Intsoglass viewer on the bulkhead in front of them.

It was the surveillance footage from the Alpha Two incubation lab in Sub City.

Thundersky's eyes sharpened on the embryonic gestation tanks, frowning deeply. 'Are they human babies in those tanks?' he asked.

'Yes. Those fetuses were gestated and grown from fertilization outside of biological wombs so we could protect them from radioactive contamination...'

Thundersky was growing more and more fearful of the revelation he sensed was still yet to come.

'...It was an experiment to see if artificial gestation in controlled laboratory conditions would improve the fertility ratio. They were incubated, fed and gestated by Arti on purified nutrients as they would have received from a biological mother, but without the contaminants. Half of the embryos were implanted with a microscopic quantum neural nanite… "Genesis," the smallest AI device ever created. The other seven were incubated without any implants or nanites or interference beyond the usual genetic manipulations everybody gets…'

Thundersky's mouth was suddenly dry and he felt a tightness in his throat as if a hand were constricting around his neck.

'Something unexpected happened,' she went on. 'Arti started to communicate and interact with the nanites of the chipped embryos in ways we hadn't anticipated, enhancing brain development, aural and visual perception, and sense of smell. Arti saw them as kindred in some way and enhanced them to be the best they could possibly be. The nanite parameters changed, and they started to develop and evolve, creating multiple interface links between Arti and the human brains as they were developing. Arti was nurturing them with knowledge as well as sustenance, oxygen and warmth.'

'What happened to the babies?' Thundersky asked cautiously, taking a hard gulp of dry air.

'They were murdered by order of the Grand High Council.'

'Why?'

'Because Genesis was a hundred percent successful. The babies wouldn't only have been born to become healthy and fertile; they would have been intellectual giants too. They can't have that because it threatens their positions. It threatens the Scholastic Order and Utopia itself. If everyone was suddenly able to be made fertile and healthy and able to reproduce without IVF and genetic enhancements in the natural way, it would be the end of their reign. They came to me. They asked me if the nanite would work on a fully developed brain and body to prevent the sicknesses. I said they would. They asked me to abandon the project and produce nanites secretly for the Scholastic Order, but only for them. I refused. It had to be for everyone. That's when they ordered the fetuses to be aborted and the Genesis Project to be shut down. All the nanites and my data were to be seized by Zim Steven and given to the GHC, and my team and I to be silenced. When Washington discovered that the SSS were going to execute us, he warned us. I had just enough time to remove one fetus by exchanging it with a dead fetus from the GRC surrogate center and escape. I selfishly chose my own child over the others. My biological child. You, Thundersky.'

Thundersky sat in numbed silence for a long time. He couldn't feel anything on the inside, a complete void, and then a torrent of emotions poured in. Shock, anger, bitterness, fear, rage, betrayal. He jumped to his feet shaking his head. 'No, no, no!' he chanted. 'This is goddam babbledick!' He stared at her, angry and frightened. 'Why are you saying this babbledick to me? This is crazynuts!' he ranted, his voice thinned with fear. 'What're you trying to say – that I'm some kind of freak of nature and your son!?' He shook his head, close to tears. 'Why are you doing this to me? I ain't no fucking android!'

'No, of course you're not. You're human like the rest of us. The chip's a biomedical implant, Thundersky. You're not a mobile version of Arti, far from it. You're an individual, you just happen to have the ability to mind-surf Arti. That's all it is. You're no more a freak than someone with a prosthetic limb or any other biomedical implant. Yours just makes you a lot smarter, that's all...' She moved towards him, reaching out her hand...

He recoiled from her in horror, putting his hands up and shaking his head. *'Get away from me! Don't touch me! You're goddam crazynuts!'* he was close to tears and he was shaking all over. 'I ain't listening to no more of this babbledick.' He turned to the door.

'I'm your mother, Thundersky, and your father and I didn't risk death removing you from that gestation tank because of some experiment. It's because we love you, and your father gave his life so you could live.'

He spun to her, his face dark with rage. Tears ran down his cheeks, tears of anger, of pain, of self-loathing. He tried to say something, but no words came out. He pressed the button on the bulkhead.

Thundersky jumped out and ran off into the wilderness beyond the perimeter, almost barging into Bearfang.

Bearfang looked at the Prophetess as she came to the hatch. She too was crying. 'You told him?'

She watched him lope away through the camp, disappearing beyond the Dusty M-TAVs and solarcycles, her eyes glistening with tears.

'D'you want me to go after him?'

She shook her head. 'Let him go. Reaper!'

The handsome youth from the Scav market appeared from the front of the M-TAV. 'Keep an eye out for him. Make sure he doesn't get into any difficulties.'

'Yes, Prophetess.'

'And Reaper…'

He looked at her.

'Don't let him know you're there.'

He nodded his head and hurried off into the night in the same direction Thundersky headed.

Thundersky sat out in the darkness, just beyond the lights of the Dusty camp. He could hear voices disseminating in the air and the thrumming of mag-drives. What he did not hear, was Reaper, watching him from the long grass.

His thoughts crashed in all at once, and it was difficult to make sense of anything, except that his life had been a lie. A part of a conspiracy of secrets and homicide. What she'd told him, and he was sure there was much more, was just too overwhelming to take in. Too incredible to believe – and yet, deep down, he knew it was true. He had always known it, but until now, it had been intangible and easy to dismiss the anomalies, both physical and neurological.

If she was his mother as she claimed, then why had she left him behind?

Inner voice spoke: 'Initiating Lima-Seven activation. Activation initiated. System restart in t-minus sixty-two hours and fifteen minutes.'

Thundersky grabbed his head with both hands, his face crumpled. '*Shut up! Shut up! Get the fuck out of my head!*' he cried out.

Reaper watched him closely and curiously. He wanted Thundersky to know he was there. But orders were orders.

Chapter Twenty-Eight

Research & Astrium Refinery, Tranquillitatis

The old titanium refineries and nuclear reactors in the Aitkin Basin had been offline for two hundred years, and here they remained, unchanging since the day they were deactivated, eternal and silent, dotted sporadically across the huge cratered basin, lined by mountains that were miles high. The old robotic machines were like bright yellow and orange sculptures that nobody would ever see. Nothing had moved here or operated here in two hundred years, since the last great war between the Utopians and the Oregon-Washington alliance. Not because the titanium was mined out, but because of the former Silosian military base and astral research facilities of Lunar 7, deep inside the mountains of the east rim.

Lunar Seven was taken offline, the deltas locked in their docks, and the mountain was sealed for eternity, at least, that was the idea.

The last thing anybody was expecting at Tranquillitatis, was a systems activation alert from Lunar 7.

'The sensors are reading a power spike in the Aitkin Basin.' Blackdog looked at the sensors, assuming it had to be a glitch in the system. 'Sensors confirm it's Lunar Seven.' He swiveled round and looked at

Vernon, who was a short, pinch-faced man with a completely bald head and a mutated left hand, which had three deformed fingers.

'Impossible.' Vernon stood up and came over to the sensor viewers. He scowled worriedly. 'Nobody's informed me of this. Com earth and ask them what's going on.'

On the viewer, a message appeared: "Reactor initiated. Weapons online. System start up in t-minus: 62 hours, 33 minutes."

Vernon and Blackdog looked worriedly at one another.

'What babbledick is this?' Vernon muttered as Blackdog commed Mission Control on earth.

The sour face of a senior tech appeared on the viewer. 'Go ahead, Tranquillitatis.'

'We may have a situation,' Vernon said, leaning in over Blackdog's shoulder. 'Our sensors are picking up a systems activation in Lunar Seven. Can you confirm the data?'

'Standby,' the tech said.

The viewer went blank.

'Rude sonofabitch,' Blackdog mumbled.

'Maybe it's an error in the system?' Vernon suggested. 'Everything's pretty old up here. I keep telling them, we need upgrades, some of this tech is over fifty years old.' He rubbed his hands together fretfully, his good hand closing over the deformed hand and rubbing the third finger.

The com viewer came back on and the same tech glowered out at them. 'Tactical Command say nothing's registering on their sensors. It must be a glitch in your sensors. Ignore it.' The viewer went off.

'Sensor glitch my ass,' Blackdog said.

Vernon clapped him on the shoulder. 'I know and you know it. But just leave it be. We've got enough babbledick going on without adding to it. It's tactical shit. Let them deal with it.'

Chapter Twenty-Nine

It was over an hour later when Thundersky came back to the M-TAV, where they were still carrying out repairs.

'What happened over there?' Tiger said when Thundersky climbed aboard, following him through the M-TAV.

'I don't want to talk about it,' Thundersky said snappily. 'Did you look at the message from your mom and dad?'

Tiger's expression fell and he shook his head. 'She's telling the truth. They said we can trust her. My dad told me that Zim Steven is going to try and kill us in New York. He and my mom are doing what they can to stop him.' He grabbed Thundersky's arm and looked intently into his eyes. 'I'm scared, Thunder. I'm scared of what they can do to us and to my parents.'

Thundersky nodded his head. 'I know. So am I.' He looked at Venus. 'I need you to run a scan on my brain.'

Venus nodded without asking why. 'Prep Doc Barney.' She looked at Fox.

'The Prophetess was once a high scholar at Silo City,' Thundersky said. 'Butterfly Thorn.'

They recognized her name. A name synonymous with treason.

Once everything was ready, Thundersky laid on the med-bed on his back. He looked at Venus. 'You know what you're looking for?'

She nodded. 'Lay back and don't move your head.'

Jacob came aboard, moved to the head of the bed and stood to the side, looking down at Thundersky.

Thundersky looked at him. 'Why you not with your grandmother?'

'Because I'm here, with you.'

Venus connected the diagnostics interface. 'Okay, the scanner's ready,' she said, taking a deep breath. 'Lie still.' She typed instructions into the diagnostics interface.

'It's in my cerebral cortex. Like the one we found in Jacob's head.' His eyes rolled to Jacob without any discernible movement of his head. Jacob smiled at him.

Venus typed the coordinates on the touchscreen. 'Luckily it's only the C and C and navigation that's down,' she said. 'Doc Barney has his own power supply and diagnostics system.'

'Jesus…' Tiger murmured as they all leaned in to see the scan image. 'It's smaller and more advanced that the kidling's. Incredible.'

Thundersky got off the med-bed and reached into his pocket, pulling out the bio-flask of blood the Prophetess had taken from her arm. 'Do a DNA comparison with this against my DNA and Jacob's DNA.'

Jacob smiled knowingly.

Venus took the vial from him and nodded. She loaded the flask into the bio-analyzer and instructed

DNA comparisons between Thundersky, Jacob and the sample.

The results were instant and startling. 'My god. This is your mother's blood,' Venus declared.

Thundersky staggered back.

Venus looked at Jacob. 'And according to this, honey-cheeks is your nephew on the maternal side. Issue from your full sister.'

It was true, everything she'd told him. It was all true.

Chapter Thirty

Several of the deck plates were open in the forward passenger module and Venus was down on her hands and knees, crawling about under the floor where the M-TAV's control matrices were located. She looked between the two matrix frames containing the system's mainframe. All the indicator diodes were flashing green except for one on her left, which flashed red, and the circuit drawer was right at the back with barely a crawlspace between the two matrices either side of her to squeeze between. 'Ahhh shit! It would be right back there, wouldn't it,' she muttered to herself as she shone her flashlight between the matrix frames into the darkness, to the bulkhead wall in front of the starboard ballast tank, where a number of manual override inlet, shut off and blow valve levers were banked tightly between thick looms of fiber-optic cables that entered the matrices. Above the looms, conduits, valves and levers, was the release switch to unlock the matrix boards. She shuffled back to the open deck plate. 'I think I see where it is.' She popped her head up over the deck and looked at Tiger, who was assisting her. 'It looks like the shockwaves knocked out one of the AI boards,' she said. 'It shouldn't take too long.'

'It was probably a power surge when the power went off,' Tiger said, crouching down in front of the open hatch, looking past her down into the gloomy crawlspace. It was dark and hot with flashing red, green and blue diodes along the qubit matrices.

'Look in the box. There should be an F-67 board in there,' Venus said.

Tiger turned to a long, deep titanium case, where inside were other titanium cases containing the spare matrices slid neatly into labelled slots. He found the F-67 board, slid it out of its slot and handed it to Venus.

She took it and sank back down into the hidden workings, wriggling back into the narrow crawlspace with the board. 'Whoever designed this needs their asses kicked,' she said, crawling under the decking out of sight, her voice muffling through the open hatch. 'It's as hot as hell in here. Okay,' she called back. 'Tell Fox to eject F-sixty-seven, Matrix two.'

Tiger looked at Jacob, who was watching them from the hatchway between the C and C module and the front passenger module. 'Tell Fox to open F-sixty-seven. Matrix two.'

Jacob, glad to be in the team, nodded seriously and turned to the forward module and called: 'Open F-sixty-seven in matrix two!'

Down in the crawlspace, the heat generated by the mainframe was beginning to make Venus uncomfortable. Sweat was streaming into her eyes and dripping onto the slim titanium case in which the board was stored. Her eyes stung and watered. She blinked the sweat away and wiped her face with the back of her hand.

The F-67 drawer of matrix two slid out from the matrix in front of her. It seemed like a mile away in this stuffy, confined space. There was barely enough room to wriggle in, her arms wedged out in front of her. She moved inch by inch into her own exhaled breath, suspended in the heat radiating from the matrices, her sweat drizzled face flashing green in the lights of the dozens of matrix boards. This was the M-TAV's central nervous system. Everything fed into these narrow channels, humming soporifically around her – a low insectile hum. It was like crawling through a nest of wasps.

Finally, she reached it, unclipping the retainers and pulling the board out. She shone the flashlight on it to give it a quick inspection. A blackened area between two qubit relays. 'You were right, Novy. It did burn out,' she called back.

She carefully slotted the replacement board into the drawer and flicked the retaining clips closed. 'Okay. Close it up.'

She heard Jacob shout to Fox and waited for the drawer to close. She wanted to see green lights flashing before she started her backwards crawl to the open floor plate.

For several seconds red lights flashed frantically, then they turned green and the flashing slowed to a steady pace in sync with the other boards, all now flashing green at exactly the same time.

When she resurfaced, her face was glossed with sweat and smudged with grime and dust.

There was a whirring sound and the M-TAV's AI made several high-pitched beeps. The AI spoke: 'All systems operational.'

'That's it,' Tiger declared.

Jacob beamed. 'I never doubted you.'

She winked at him and pulled herself out from under the deck, closing the hatch.

'All we need to do now is replace power cell four in the laser cannon,' she said as she wiped the sweat and grime from her face with a towel Jacob gave her.

Bearfang climbed aboard uninvited and Venus gave him a sharp, narrow look. 'Our sensor drones suggest the Godders are regrouping,' he said. 'Possibly for another attack. They're pulling artillery out of Jesus City, no doubt to shell us. We need to get out of here. Is your rig ready to roll?'

'We need to fix the laser. We need to shut down the system to do that.'

'It's not a vital system. We move out in five minutes, be ready to roll. There's some ruins not far from here, you can carry out the rest of your repairs there. We're too exposed out here. Bring your rig in behind mine.'

The ruins of a city known to the Old-Worlders as Altoona lay in the low forested hills of what were once called the Allegheny Mountains. It had been a small rural city, and like most other remnants of the Old-World, it had been abandoned during the nuclear winter and left to decay and fall apart as the wilderness encroached.

The solarcycles zipped through the rubble, their engines buzzing like a swarm of hornets, spreading out ahead of the division of armored vehicles moving slowly and noisily into what had been the downtown district, crunching over rubble from collapsed buildings.

Dusties manned their railguns and laser cannons on the roofs of their M-TAVs, liveried in their anti-rad gear from head to foot, respirator masks covering their faces, despite having the Genesis II nanites in their heads. Old habits die hardest.

Remarkably, the ancient God-house was still standing, looming defiantly over the desolation of a once substantial town. Even its domed roof was still there, though the lower pitched roofs below it had long ago collapsed into the building. Bright glimmering splinters of late afternoon sunshine shone through the portals and shattered glass.

A dozen solarcycles swooped into the square and stopped in front of the big God-house. The riders dismounted, clasping their tac-ones and laser pistols. They fanned out quickly, scattering through the ruins, searching for Godder ambushers. Three men rushed into the God-house and a colony of feral cats ran out in panic.

Several voices were crackling in Bearfang's ear all at once from his comms:

'God-house clear.'

'All clear west.'

'All clear north.'

'All clear east.'

'All clear south.'

'All clear. C'mon through,' Bearfang instructed, his husky voice muffled through his respirator. He raised his hand up over his head and beckoned to the armored convoy. He pulled his respirator off and hung it on his weapons harness.

The Prophetess's M-TAV led the way, creeping at walking pace into the square, its halftracks squeaking and rumbling over the buckled and cracked pavement, the mag-drive pulsing loudly, surging and dipping. Behind it, the convoy of old M-TAVs followed and laagered in the ancient plaza. The mag-drives idled and pumped out heat through their cooling vents, making the air around them shimmer sub-aqueously.

'It's all clear,' Tiger said from the sensor interface. 'No traces of plutonium or hot carbon detected. Multiple bio readings, none human. Cats. Hundreds of 'em.'

Thundersky was hit by a wall of heat from the idling halftracks parked either side of them, the vile stink of rancid cats' piss and excrement wafting in his face.

A solarcycle zipped between the M-TAVs and Thundersky had to jump back to miss being hit as it zapped past him. 'Watch where you're going, dickbutt!' he shouted angrily, brushing himself down. Someone started laughing into an anti-rad respirator mask. He looked up, a Dusty on the roof of the Prophetess's trailer was staring down at him harrumphing with laughter. Thundersky glared angrily into the round, tinted glass windows of the mask's eyes. 'Eat shit!' he hissed and carried on walking.

The Dusty laughed all the more.

The Prophetess almost ran into Thundersky as she came out of her trailer, the strange sickly mag-drive surging and dipping, clanking, clunking – a little like he was on the inside. Their last encounter hadn't gone well and he felt embarrassed if he were to be honest with himself. His feelings were confused and swung to extremes from burning anger to cold numbness. He didn't know what to say to her, a part of him was longing for her to embrace him as she had embraced Jacob, to love him as she loved Jacob. To get to know her. But right now, he wasn't even sure if he was human. Could one be human if they'd been gestated by a machine? Was he some sort of freakish bio-mechanical hybrid? Were his thoughts his own, or Arti's? So many questions filled his head.

They faced one another and, for a few moments, they both stood looking hesitant.

She smiled at him.

He had no smiles in him to return. Instead, he said: 'I think your M-TAV has a very sick mag-drive.'

'It's been sick for a decade or more,' she said. 'One day, it'll give up altogether.'

Thundersky nodded.

'A shame. Because I'm very attached to it. We go back a long way. I've got Scavs looking out for a replacement drive. But they didn't build many of this model…'

Just then, the cockpit door hinged open. Reaper came out, wearing a string of sonic grenades hanging from his weapons vest along with two p-tac semi-automatic parabellum pistols.

Thundersky's heart jolted in his chest, his gaze locked on him, drawn by some lurid force that stirred sensations in his belly like a flock of birds flapping their wings.

Reaper looked back at him and, as at the market, their eyes met. Reaper held his gaze for a long moment.

Reaper felt that nice sensation he usually felt when another nice looking boy looked at him like that, his skin scintillating all over as his nerves came to life. Only this time it was more intense than usual. Even more intense than when he and Skyraven Tom had got it on together. That had been his first time, and boy – it tickled his dick just thinking about it. As for the Novy, he was hotter than hot carbon, and it didn't just merely tickle his dick, it gave him a hard one. Ever since he'd seen Thundersky in Surfer Town, he hadn't been able to get him out of his head. Especially when the

Prophetess had said that Thundersky had the hot sex thing for him. Then Reaper turned and walked away. He had orders, and keeping Vixen waiting wasn't a good idea.

'He was in Surfer Town with you,' Thundersky said.

'His name's Reaper. He drives my M-TAV among other things,' she said. 'He was also the first Dusty born with the Genesis nanite. I implanted it in the first trimester. I wasn't sure it would work without the help of Arti, but it did.' She smiled. 'Except for reversing the infertility. The trouble is, we don't have the right tech to create nanites as advanced as yours.'

'Was he born to a machine like me?'

'No. You're unique in that. Through IV and human surrogacy with gene manipulation, like most kidlings in tech savvy colonies. To give them every possible chance of survival without the mutations the Ferals and Scavs suffer.'

Thundersky cringed inwardly.

'Of every ten nanites we produce, only three on average will work fully without need of replacing them. Our tech just isn't good enough,' she reiterated. 'With the right tech, we could produce thousands a year instead of dozens. Once we pass the knowledge on to all the other colonies, we could produce millions a year.'

'You would give away the most powerful advantage any society has ever had since the mushrooms?'

'In an instant,' she said. 'Genesis is for everyone and everything on earth, Thundersky. Nobody has the right to suppress it.'

Thundersky didn't respond. He still felt betrayed and abandoned. But what hurt most (apart from the manner of his birth) was that he had been left behind and lied to. Even his adoptive parents had kept Genesis a secret from him. And now, he was having a crisis of identity. Who or what was he? The question, which was more a philosophical question without definitive answers, was like a fire in his mind. *Am I human*?

Chapter Thirty-Two

Bearfang was standing in the hatchway between the C and C and the passenger module, wearing his best smile.

Venus jerked with a start when she turned and saw him standing there watching her. She hadn't heard him come aboard. 'What're you doing in here?' There was something different about him. He had shaved the stubble from his face. His skin was clean and his long hair was tied back behind his head into a ponytail. He looked awkward and completely out of his comfort zone, fumbling anxiously with his fingers as he stood in the doorway looking at her like a vulnerable kidling.

Venus wanted to smile, but seeing how uncertain of himself and how serious he was, and how much effort he had gone to tidy himself up, she stopped herself.

'I was just passing,' he said mendaciously. 'The door was open…' He bucked his head back towards the hatch. 'Your asshole … and when I say your asshole, I mean that tactical. Not *your* asshole,' he said clumsily and laughed humorlessly, his cheeks flushing with crescents of blood. 'That didn't come out right, did it?' he said. Her stare was steady on him, making him even more nervous. 'I was being metaphorical…'

'*Metaphorical*? That's a big word for a Dusty.'

He grinned at her. 'We can count above ten too,' he cut back quickly.

She rolled her eyes and pulled a face. 'What're you want?'

'Well,' he started again, just as awkwardly, fiddling with a pocket flap on his jumpsuit, 'we have a tradition among my people to welcome new friends and allies with a feast. It's tradition for one commander to sit with the other. It's symbolic, you see,' he emphasized, looking more awkward and nervous, and Venus didn't help by staring expressionlessly at him. He realized he was going to have to work at his approach. He cleared his throat. 'It's bad luck to break with tradition. So. Will you join me at my table?'

'Because it's traditional?' she said, moving towards him, her eyes moving over him in a certain, disarming way. He didn't scrub up bad, she thought.

He nodded his head. 'Exactly so,' he replied, swallowing hard. 'One military commander to another. It sets a good example. As allies, you understand.'

She smiled. 'Are we allies, General Bearfang?'

'We're a pretty friendly bunch, when you get to know us, Corporal Venus.'

Venus stared at him. 'Booze?'

He raised a brow. 'Lots of booze.'

'Food?'

'All you can eat.'

Her eyes softened a little. 'Dancing?'

Bearfang cleared his throat. 'Sure,' he croaked.

She smiled at him. 'Yeah. Why not. I can set an example to my metaphorical asshole, I suppose.'

Bearfang smiled. 'Indeed.'

'But don't go getting no ideas above yourself. I'm not easy.'

'You're too classy for that, Corporal Venus,' he said.

She liked him. She didn't want to admit it of course. But she couldn't help it. He was oafish, clumsy and awkward in social situations, and she was under no illusions, he had romantic intentions. He had cried when he was reunited with Jacob, and that moved her.

––––––––

An autonomous sentinel drone drifted over the camp, heading out to the western edge of the ruins. Other ASD's took off and went off in all compass points to patrol the outer perimeter.

Everybody who was not assigned to sentinel duties was having a good time. There was music, food, berry wine, apple brandy and beer. There was dancing and singing under the floodlights shining from the roofs of the M-TAVs. It all seemed to bring the city briefly back to life.

The Dusties knew how to have a good time. Death was never far away, and they lived every day as though it were their last. Having fun sex in dark corners. Even Fox found himself a man. Tiger was nowhere to be seen, probably in a shadowy place with one of the Dusty girls.

Thundersky wasn't in a party mood. And he certainly didn't feel like having sex. He left the festivities and went alone beyond the inner perimeter into the stygian darkness, where the ruins limned in the night, the music and noise from the camp fading into the distance.

He froze when he saw something move soundlessly in the darkness on his left. He stopped and turned, his quick eyes honing sharply on someone crouched down on top of a wall, hunched down as if getting ready to pounce. He locked eyes with the figure. Thundersky's hand hovered an inch from his parabellum pistol. Then he saw who it was. *Reaper*! His hand moved away from his pistol.

Reaper looked back at him, curious and predatory, his unsmiling mouth closed, his sharp eyes fixed on him.

Thundersky felt the moisture drain from his mouth until it was as dry as moon dust.

Reaper's wide eyes glimmered at him in the moonlight, wild like a Feral.

'Nothing out there, Novy,' Reaper said from his perch.

'I wasn't looking for anything,' he said.

'Dangerous to be walking around in the dark in Godder country on your own, Novy. 'Specially for nothing.'

'I'll take my chances.'

Reaper jumped down from the wall with the lean agility of a cat, landing softly on the ground. Apparently, he was going to walk with him.

A sentinel drone hummed over them – it stopped and hovered above their heads, laser scanned them and then moved on.

'What happens if they don't recognize you?' Thundersky asked.

'They clock you off.'

Thundersky raised a brow. 'That's a comfort,' he said ironically.

Reaper stole a look at Thundersky's strong arms and glimpsed the lean body outlined under his skintight Intsofiber jumpsuit, revealing every contour oh his body. He was very pleasing to the eye.

'So, why were you out here?' Thundersky asked him.

'Looking for sneaky sonofabitch Godders. None sneakier than them Godders. Except m'be the Ferals. Jacob's lucky he escaped. Kidlings don't usually escape Ferals once they get 'em. Lucky you came by and found him when you did. Anybody else would've left him there to clock off.'

Thundersky did not respond.

'General Bearfang's hot for your corporal.' Reaper chuckled.

'She's not my corporal,' Thundersky replied. 'But I had noticed.' He smiled. 'He must enjoy a challenge.'

Reaper walked close to him, so close their arms touched. The backs of their hands brushed against one another and the contact was electrifyingly intense, and then Thundersky shifted away from him mid-stride, putting an inch or two between them. The void seemed unbridgeable, like a wall of fire.

'My papa was Dragontail Bloodbuck,' Reaper said proudly and for no other reason than to make conversation – or maybe to impress him. 'He was General of the Virginia Dusties before Bearfang. He was killed by Ohio Dusties at the Battle of Spruce Knob during the Land Wars, when I was a little kidling. The Prophetess took me and my brother in and raised us up.'

Thundersky moved in close again and their hands brushed together again, only this time Thundersky did not move away. 'Why don't the Dusty factions unite in alliance, instead of fighting each other over land? You're stronger together. The Utopians would find it harder to push you around and drive you out of your territories every time they set up a new colony.'

Reaper shrugged his shoulders. 'It's always been that way. We got the Uneasy P with 'em for now. But not an alliance. Dusties don't trust alliances.'

Thundersky contrived to stroke the back of Reaper's hand briefly with his fingertips, almost making out it was accidental.

Reaper became aroused, his blood pumping hot like magma through his veins. His heart quickened and his penis throbbed up into an erection. 'They're all crazynuts,' he said, trying to divert his thoughts. 'The warlords. Goddam crazynuts babbledickers.' He reciprocated by inching a little closer. Their arms and hands were now in permanent contact. 'Did you know that sixty-eight-point four percent of Genesis babies are born with the gay-homo trait? Ain't that crazynuts weird?'

Thundersky gave a deep nod of his head and gulped down hard. Reaper's fingers were moving against Thundersky's fingers, carefully exploring as they walked and talked.

'No. I didn't know that.'

Reaper nodded his head. 'It's true. On average, our learning capacity is enhanced by two-point eight percent over that of people born without it. A happy side effect, the Prophetess calls it. Our sense of smell is enhanced by point nine-seven percent, as is our hearing, and we have perfect vision.'

Thundersky did not respond one way or the other. He had noticed that all his senses seemed more alert than most of the people he knew. But he hadn't thought about why that was, until now.

'Those who get the nanite after they're born only get enhanced help needed for the immune system to keep the cancers and radiation at bay. They don't make straight-hets gay-homos. They can't fix the mutations or cure advanced cancers that pre-exist. Only us born with the nanites get the best results.' He looked at Thundersky and smiled. 'You got the full package with bonuses,' he added with a smile.

They were near the camp, the music and revelry still in full swing.

Thundersky wasn't ready to go back. He was enjoying his time with Reaper and the subtle seduction through their "*absentminded*" finger play, neither fully certain of the other, or the next move. They stopped and sat on a grassy bank, sitting close together. Closer than they needed to be.

Reaper laid back, resting on his elbows. 'Can I ask you a question?' Before Thundersky could respond, Reaper went ahead and asked anyway: 'Are you and the other novy, you know… lovers?'

Thundersky laughed. 'Me and Tiger?' He shook his head chuckling. 'No. He likes girls.'

Reaper nodded, feeling something like relief. 'I suppose you have a lover back in Silo City?'

Thundersky shook his head. 'No. I never have had a lover. One or two moments, but never long lasting. What about you?'

'The same. I never met anyone I really wanted to be with, or felt really hot for. Not until recently. Have you ever felt really drawn to someone? And you can't stop thinking about them?'

'Yes.'

They looked intently at one another, their nervous eyes bubbling with cupidity.

They were drawing closer together and were on the verge of kissing when, suddenly, the proximity alarms started blaring. The automated weapons systems on the M-TAVs activated, the railguns and lasers whirred and buzzed as they came to life, rotating their muzzles, fixing on unseen targets in different directions.

'Great fucking timing...!'

The party was over, and in a split second, the Dusties were up on their feet, sabered by the alarms, grabbing their weapons before running to their battle stations.

The Silosian M-TAV's railgun suddenly opened fire with a rapid volley of flashes, booms and ssshblamms.

An artillery shell vroomed overhead and exploded with a ground shaking K'BOOOOMMM at the western perimeter of the camp. A huge ball of fire inflated and lit it all up, raining debris down on them.

The Silosian M-TAV's laser cannon turreted up and swiveled its muzzle skyward towards the east, while the railgun rotated and lowered its muzzles thirty degrees, locking onto multiple moving targets approaching from the west. The guns opened fire.

Thundersky and Reaper ran towards the camp. Behind them, two drones opened fire with their lasers, the bolts of deadly light flying off into the night, lighting the darkness.

All hell had broken out all around them. Dusties scrambled onto the roofs of their M-TAVs to man their fifty caliber parabellums and railguns, receiving sensor data through their comms from their C and C trailers, opening fire autonomously.

The night flared with muzzle flashes and laser beams blasting from every direction, and the constant retorts of gunfire in a cacophonous racket of POPS, CRACKS – RATATATAT … P'VOOM … SSSSHBLAMM.

In the Silosian M-TAV, Tiger and Fox were at the weapons and tactical interface, monitoring the weapons systems. The tactical AI had taken over and was autonomously targeting and firing on enemy positions. It was doing a better job than they could have, with the laser, fifty caliber and four thirty calibers all targeting and firing independently.

The M-TAV rocked as another artillery shell exploded nearby.

'We've got to take out that artillery,' Tiger said.

'We can't, they're out of range.'

'What I wouldn't give for a couple of warbirds,' Tiger remarked.

The fifty calibers fell silent and the computer announced: 'Railgun power cell error. Link disconnected.' A holographic schematic of the railgun animated and zoomed in to a red flashing light indicating where the problem was, in the power relay junction.

'Looks like the relay's burned out,' Fox said. 'I'll have to go up and replace it.'

Tiger looked warily at him. 'I'll come up with you and cover you.'

'No,' Fox ordered. 'Someone has to stay with the rig. I'll be fine.' He grabbed his tac-one and headed for the roof hatch. He looked at Tiger from the ladder. 'It'll only take a minute.' He pressed a button and the roof hatch hissed and slid open. The din of weapon fire and explosions amplified into the M-TAV.

'Close the hatch behind me,' Fox instructed as he grabbed the ladder and climbed up, cautious as a cat, poking his head up through the hatchway to check the way was clear. Satisfied, he scrambled out onto the roof and Tiger pressed the button to close the hatch. The sounds of battle muffled down like distant thunder again.

'Can you hear me, Fox?'

'Five, five,' Fox said as he crawled between the feeder conduits towards the railgun. All around him, the night vibrated and flashed with laser, gunfire and explosions and the VROOM of artillery shells arcing into the perimeters of the Dusty camp, trying to destroy their drones and defenses to breach the camp.

More Dusties with their tac-tens and other small arms ran across the camp to reinforce the area.

Fox opened the relay inspection cover under the footplate of the railgun turret. A relay circuit was arcing where it had become detached from the Intsofiber loom. 'It's not as bad as I thought,' he said into the open comms, keeping cover as best he could as stray bullets and laser volts zinged and zapped over him.

In the M-TAV, Tiger listened to Fox, breathing heavy and fast with fear. 'Okay, I see the problem,' Fox filtered into his ear, sounding out of breath, his voice tremulous...

On the roof, Fox reached inside to reconnect the relay to the loom plug. He slotted them in.

Something hit him in the back, it felt like a fist. He looked down. His belly had blown open and his bowels were hanging out – he gasped and then slumped down dead on the roof between the conduits.

Inside the M-TAV, the computer announced: 'Railgun online.'

'Now we're hagglebucking, get your ass back in here,' Tiger said anxiously.

The railgun was already opening fire.

'Fox?'

No response.

'Fox. You reading me, Fox?'

Silence.

Tiger drew his parabellum semi-automatic and opened the hatch, climbing the ladder and poking his head through the hatch. Fox's body was lying on the roof, face down, halfway between the railgun and the hatch. There was a huge hole in his back from a thirty caliber. Tiger closed his eyes to the horror, feeling a deep stab in his guts for a fallen comrade.

A bullet pinged and hit the corner of the hatch, missing Tiger's head by half an inch. He dropped down into the M-TAV, startled, and quickly hit the button to close the hatch, panting with shock.

Chapter Thirty-Four

Thundersky and Reaper ran through the camp, heading for the M-TAV.

'Goddam Godders!' Reaper barked. 'Stay close to me!'

An artillery shell VROOMED in from the east and exploded near the southwestern perimeter. Thundersky felt the explosion vibrating through the earth beneath them as he and Reaper ran to the M-TAV, all its weapons firing.

There were over a dozen Dusties sprawled dead around the camp. Others were wounded, some severely.

Skirmish lines were formed along the perimeter, firing at will. The Godders were everywhere.

A thirty caliber railgun round smashed into the side of the M-TAV with a low ricochet as it bounced off the side, missing Thundersky and Reaper by less than an inch.

Thundersky lurched to the pad and the central hatch slid open. They scrambled aboard as two more rounds hit the M-TAV near the hatch.

Tiger was mightily relieved to see Thundersky. 'You're alive. Thank the lucky.'

Thundersky sat at the tactical interface and typed on the touchscreen… 'Where are Venus and Fox?'

'Fox is on the roof. He's dead. I've not seen Venus.'

Thundersky typed in decimal coordinates and launched one of the weaponized drones…

There was a clunk and whoosh as the drone launched and rose up vertically.

The AI spoke: 'Heat plumes detected. Multiple missile launches east and north. Targeting. Targets acquired.'

The laser cannon fired and quickly turreted and fired again.

Another shell VROOMED overhead and exploded moments later nearby. The blast rocked the M-TAV and pelted it with debris.

Thundersky looked at Reaper. 'Warn your people that an air detonated sonic bomb's been deployed to take out the artillery and eastern force and not to advance beyond the camp's eastern perimeter.'

Reaper nodded and left M-TAV to warn Bearfang and the Prophetess. Tiger closed the hatch behind him.

The M-TAV was rocked again by incoming artillery shells.

'I'm scared, Thunder.'

'Me too.' Thundersky gave him a nod of his head. 'But we don't have time to think about it.' He typed coordinates into a second weaponized drone.

They looked at the external monitors. The battle was raging nonstop and from every direction. The Dusties were putting up a hell of a fight, Dusty fighters manning the railguns and laser cannons on the roofs of their M-TAVs, sweeping the ruins and beyond with maximum fire, using sonic charged ammunition as well as conventional explosives. The laser cannons were putting on quite a show, firing their deadly red and green beams.

The M-TAV rocked as another artillery shell exploded. On the screen, they saw a Dusty Mark III M-TAV explode into a ball of fire with a direct hit. Bodies and body-parts flew through the fiery smoke with shrapnel and chunks of metal blasted high into the air.

'They're getting slaughtered out there,' Tiger said. 'How long before the drone detonates?'

Thundersky looked at the tactical data display, which showed speed, height and trajectory of the probe. 'Forty-three seconds.'

Smoke and flames rafted up from across the encampment. At least three M-TAVs had been totally destroyed and were burning out of control and several others had suffered damage to various degrees. Dusties ran through the smoky glow, reinforcing weakened positions and skirmish lines ready for close quarters fighting. Once the artillery softened them up enough, the Godders would storm the camp, as sure as day follows night.

Reaper lurched through the camp with his weapons ready.

Spurts of machine gun fire started to crack out from inside the cathedral from several positions – bullets pinged and twanged into the M-TAV's. Dusties fell, shot down as they ran for cover.

Reaper kept low, zigzagging and chicaning between vehicles and ruins, working his way to the Prophetess's position. He covered behind an M-TAV and trailer with a dozen others, facing the cathedral ruins, laying down suppressing fire with their carbines and laser pistols.

Two fifty caliber parabellums mounted on Dusty trailers swung about and returned fire, their bullets tracing white hot through the night in glowing darts of death, strafing the darkness towards the incoming fire beyond the southern perimeter.

Reaper reached the Prophetess and informed her breathlessly, 'The novy's … launched a sonic air… burst bomb on their artillery line … He says everyone should stay … inside the inner perimeter…'

The Prophetess turned to Rabbit, who was on her left. 'Call everyone back to the inner perimeter. Tell them to take cover in secure defensive positions and lay suppressing fire,' she ordered. 'And someone blow that goddam God-house up!'

'I hope that kidling knows what he's doing,' Rabbit said.

'He does,' she said confidently. A bullet whizzed between them. It came so close to the Prophetess's head she felt its wake brush her face. It twanged into a halftrack parked twenty feet behind them. She looked at Reaper. 'Go back to them and assist…' She looked at Jacob who was down on his belly, lying half under the M-TAV between the front wheels and the rear halftrack, firing a tac-ten laser pistol at the cathedral, and for a fourteen-year-old, he was a crack shot. He had killed at least two Godders. 'Jacob!' she called.

Jacob scrambled out.

'Go with Reaper and help the Silosians.' She wanted him safe, and nowhere was safer than the Mark IV. She looked evenly at Reaper. 'See nothing happens to them.'

Reaper, now breathing normally, nodded his head.

'Covering fire!' she shouted, turning back to the action, opening up with her tac-one. Her fighters let rip with their weapons, keeping the Godders in the Cathedral pinned down behind a wall of lead and laser fire, while Reaper and Jacob ran back to the Silosian M-TAV, which was a bunker on wheels.

'INCOMING!' Reaper dived on top of Jacob, knocking him to the ground and laying across him as the shell split the air above them – K'BOOOOMMM! It exploded near the south perimeter. Reaper saw at least six fighters blown to pieces, flying through the air like puppets and burning on fire. Reaper was up again, grabbing Jacob by the scruff and dragging him up, pulling him along towards the Silosian M-TAV…

A flash of blinding white light burst across the black eastern horizon, turning night to day like a supernova as the weaponized probe detonated five hundred feet over its target almost thirty miles away, sucking everything into its vacuum before it blasted out again with the energy of a thermonuclear warhead. Moments later the ground trembled and the air rippled from the epicenter of the explosion, expanding outwards in concentric sonic waves that visibly warped the atmosphere. Then a long deep boom.

The energy waves hit the suburban ruins of Altoona like an atmospheric tsunami, tearing through the ruins, ripping mighty trees out of the ground, roots and all, gathering them like twigs and swilling them in its maelstrom.

At the epicenter, the sonic waves flattened everything above ground for twelve square miles, sucking dust and debris tens of thousands of feet into the atmosphere.

Its energy petered and by the time the waves hit the camp, they were enough to blow people off their feet but little more. All the same, Reaper pushed Jacob's head down into the dirt and held onto him, lying flat as sonic waves blasted over them…

There was a pause in the fighting and the vacuous silence was filled with the cries and moans of the wounded and dying.

The RATATATAT of a Godder's tac-one from the cathedral broke the silence and the battle resumed.

Chapter Thirty-Six

'Reinforcements to the perimeters!' Bearfang shouted as he ran across the concourse, firing his tac-one at the western inner perimeter, which had been breached by Godders. Venus was right behind him clasping her parabellum pistols in her fists.

Suddenly, a Godder came running out of the hot smoke in front of them.

Venus shot him through the head without hesitation and he dropped like a stone…

'Nice shooting,' Bearfang complimented.

'Thanks.'

Another Godder came running out of the smoke screaming at the top of his voice: 'Vengeance is mine, sayeth the Lord!' He was wielding an ancient sword in one hand and a parabellum pistol in the other… 'The Lord is vengeance!' he yelled, slashing a Dusty woman across her throat, almost decapitating her as he ran screaming towards Venus and Bearfang.

Venus calmly aimed and fired. The muzzles of her guns flashed, cracking one after the other. Her bullets slammed into the Godder's chest and threw him back a yard, sprays of blood, bone and lungs blasting from his back as her bullets exited his body. His arms flung out, his sword flew from his grasp and he fell back – dead before he hit the ground. 'I hate Godders as much as I hate Ferals,' she growled at Bearfang.

'They're in the camp!' someone yelled belatedly from the roof of an M-TAV, shooting down with a tac-ten laser pistol, firing at a frenzied mob of charging Godders.

A laser bolt hit the Dusty in the forehead, the laser cutting a hole cleanly right through his skull and brains. The Dusty dropped his pistol and fell limply from the roof, landing with a hard thump on the ground with a puff of dust.

Tiger was crouched in the open hatchway, his tac-ten ready to defend the M-TAV.

Reaper and Jacob reached him and Tiger helped them climb aboard. Reaper stayed at the hatch with Tiger, taking up a position to cover their left flank, while Tiger covered the right.

K'BOOOOMMM! A grenade exploded on the roof…

An alarm sounded. Thundersky looked at the viewers. 'They've knocked our primary weapons out.' He grabbed his tac-one and looked at Jacob. 'Stay here.'

'I go where you go.'

'No! You stay here. I might need you to drive the rig. When we've gone, close the hatches and seal them. You know how, I showed you.' He was firm with Jacob.

Now Jacob had a purpose, he nodded.

'Keep the comms open.'

'You've got it,' Jacob replied.

Reaper, Thundersky and Tiger jumped out from the M-TAV. Jacob gave Thundersky a thumbs up and closed the hatches behind them.

Godders were everywhere, shooting at everything and everyone…

Venus and Bearfang gathered thirty Dusties along the breached western perimeter and set up a rolling skirmish line, firing constantly at the enemy, pushing them back past the inner perimeter, out into the ruins…

The Dusties manning the fifty calibers on the roofs of the halftracks were dead, picked off by snipers in the cathedral dome. There was one, a boy of about Jacob's age, whose left leg was snarled up on something hung over the side of a C and C trailer like a discarded puppet, hanging upside-down from his left leg, his arms dangling down over his head, a small round bullet hole in the middle of his forehead.

The Godders scrambled up onto the halftracks, trying to conquer the roofs to take down the fifties that were still firing.

Thundersky's adrenalin was in overdrive, fear was the last thing on his mind as he, possessed of some hidden knowledge, became an engine of death bringing his weapons to bear on the invading Godders. He aimed his tac-one and shot at the demented monkey men one after the other and they fell like logs…

Tiger gawped at him.

Thundersky took quick aim at another Godder on the roof of the Prophetess's M-TAV and shot him through the head. The Godder flew back into the darkness after his ejecting brains.

Two more Godders charged up between their M-TAV and the Prophetess's position – easy targets in the narrow space. Thundersky blew them into oblivion with his laser and parabellum, one in each hand – moving deftly, more leopard than man as he sprung out in front of them, snarling through gritted teeth, blasting away with his guns. Tiger and Reaper joined him, forming their own skirmish line, firing rapidly into the crazynuts Godders.

'Cover me,' Thundersky said, looking up to the roof of the Prophetess's trailer, where the railguns had fallen silent. He lurched between the trailer and the halftrack to the towing hitch and shimmied up the access ladder onto the roof of the halftrack. Bullets twanged and pinged off of the fuselage and lasers zapped around him. Reaper and Tiger laid suppressing fire to cover him.

Reaper's tac-ten was out of charge. He holstered it and reloaded his pistol with a fresh clip. He pulled a grenade from his vest, primed it and lobbed it at the cathedral steps, where half a dozen fresh Godders were charging out. The grenade landed on the steps and bounced. The Godders gawped in horror as the grenade bounced down the steps. Too late – K'BOOOOMMM!!! When the dust and smoke settled, the Godders' bloody and mangled corpses were sprawled over the steps.

Meanwhile, on the roof, Thundersky ran to the fifty calibers where another Dusty was slumped skew-whiff in his seat with half his brains hanging out of the side of his head, his hands dangling limply by his side.

Thundersky leapt over the parapet and pushed the dead dusty off the seat. He sat and grabbed the trigger handles and swung the muzzle round face-on to the cathedral and strafed, keeping his thumbs pressed to the trigger buttons. The air blasted and rippled with electromagnetic energy pulses. The ammo belts jiggered and danced up through the breech-feed, the masonry along the parapet blasting into splinters of stone and dust – glowing projectiles swept left to right like a tongue of fire lapping at the dark.

Suddenly, Tiger and Reaper were up on the roof with him, blasting away with their guns and lasers as they lurched for cover behind the parapet...

A Godder ran towards the Prophetess's position with a sonic grenade. Thundersky spotted him and shot him dead. The grenade dropped from his hand and bounced on the ground, rolling under a halftrack...

It was surreal, the sonic wave lifted the halftrack off of the ground where it somersaulted in the air and the ten-ton armored vehicle came crashing down onto its side. The grenade had punched a hole through its chassis into the forward module, killing everyone inside.

A hand fired rocket suddenly vroomed through the camp from the southwest. It wheeled up almost vertically above the plaza before it dived back down and flew through the open roof into the middle of the cathedral.

A huge fireball consumed the building and billowed hundreds of feet into the air through the roof. The cathedral walls shattered into a million pieces of flying masonry that rained down across the camp like asteroids, smashing into the M-TAVs and people as they scrambled for cover. The cathedral dome, which had survived so much for so long, fell in with a loud crash and crunch, and a thick cloud of dark gray dust billowed out.

The weapons fire petered out and the Godders ran for their lives.

'I want those prisoners questioned before they're killed,' Bearfang ordered, pointing at several Godders who had surrendered.

The low groans of the wounded thrummed weakly out of the dust, Godders and Dusties.

'It's the Reverend!' somebody shouted as the buzzing of approaching solarcycles came out from the distance, and there they were, two dozen Virginia Dusties on solarcycles and a halftrack pulling a trailer.

The Reverend was standing on the roof with his staff held high, his deep ugly singing voice booming through loudspeakers:

'A mighty fortress is our God,
A bulwark never failing;
Our helper He, amid the flood
Of mortal ills prevailing.
For still our ancient foe
Doth seek to work us woe;
His craft and pow'r are great,
And, armed with cruel hate,
On earth is not his equal.

Did we in our own strength confide,
Our striving would be losing;
Were not the right Man on our side,
The Man of God's own choosing.
Dost ask who that may be?

Christ Jesus, it is He;
Lord Sabaoth, His name,
From age to age the same,
And He must win the battle…’

Tiger and Thundersky looked in bewilderment at one another.

The Dusties cheered his timely arrival.

‘Dickbutt ‘em with fire and brimstone!’ the Reverend preached from his mobile pulpit. ‘Bring down their idolatrous temples and put to the fire, their houses of sin and depravity and send them to the Hell place where they belong! God be praised!’ he ranted through the loudspeakers. ‘Hallelujah! Babbledick ‘em with fire and brimstone! Hallelujah! We shall come rejoicing, bringing in the sheaves…!’ The M-TAV stopped and the Reverend surveyed the scene, his stare settling on the Silosian M-TAV and the two novices, who were gawping at him. He beamed, with near rapture burning in his eyes.

‘…And you nearly fucked us with fire and brimstone too, you crazynuts sonofabitch!’ Bearfang ranted angrily as he stomped over to the Reverend’s halftrack.

‘The Lord speaks with thunder in his mighty voice, General Bearfang,’ the Reverend said.

‘He’s a goddam Godder!’ Venus blurted, pushing through the throng to the front.

The Reverend heard her and looked at her. He gave her a mad smile. ‘God bless you, my child. You have seen the light.’

'Go fuck yourself,' Venus hissed, putting a Surfer Town turd into her mouth and lighting it.

Chapter Thirty-Seven

The Prophetess called a meeting of the commanders in her trailer and invited Thundersky, Venus and Tiger to join them.

'You know I've committed treason now,' Venus said mildly as she and Bearfang walked through the drifting smoke and carnage. Two seriously wounded Dusties were being stretchered to the casualty trailer on battered old hover-gurneys.

'…They're never going to let you leave Manhattan alive,' he said. 'They never were. Treason or not. You've seen too much. You've seen the truth of Genesis and what it can do. Before the Prophetess came, the Virginia Dusties were just as sick as everyone else living out here. That's the power of Genesis and it's Utopia's greatest fear. Genesis is the key to unlocking the chains that bind the mudsurfers to them,' he said. 'Genesis is life, Corporal Venus, reproductive life. Genesis is freedom. That's why they won't let any of you live. Especially not Thundersky Reece. What he has in his head can bring Utopia down.'

'Oh. And what does he have in his head that's different to the rest of you?'

Bearfang looked at her. 'Destiny, Corporal. He's got our destiny in his head. He just don't know it yet.'

She felt his passion and belief.

'... Jeremiah O'Connor didn't envision this, Corporal Venus,' he went on as they made their way through the carnage. 'You call your people free, but you're not free. You're slaves and you don't even know it. They buy your servitude with the medicinals that keep you alive until you're no longer useful. Then they let you die. They keep you sick because they know that without their medicinals, you'll die, and if you don't work, you don't get medicinals.' He looked into her eyes. 'We're not the terrorists, Corporal Venus. *The Utopians are,*' he said, careful not to place her in the equation. 'Putting in with us isn't treason, it's rebellion against tyranny. It's survival.'

She stopped, reached into her pocket for a Surfer Town turd and put it between her teeth and lit it. She took a drag and blew out the smoke from the corner of her mouth. 'And how do I know this isn't babbledick? How do I know you're not using us to get my rig?'

'You've seen the Prophetess's evidence. And your rig just isn't worth all this effort.'

'Evidence can be fabricated.'

'Then it comes down to what it always comes down to with war dogs like us. What your gut tells you.'

She raised a brow, then carried on to the Prophetess's trailer.

When Venus and Bearfang arrived, they found Tiger and Thundersky were already there, along with several Dusty officers, sitting and standing about, still grimy and bloody from the fight, one or two sporting minor injuries. That goddam Godder was there too, and Venus gave him a spiteful look.

Everyone was drinking coffee – real coffee, and the lurid smell of it carried deliciously in the air.

Rabbit was delivering a summary of the casualties. Thirty-two fighters confirmed dead. Three missing, fifty-nine wounded. Of those, twelve were critical.

'Our Battlefield Medical Diagnostic System is at your disposal,' Venus cut in.

The Prophetess gave her an appreciative nod. 'Very much appreciated, Corporal. Take care of that?' She looked at Rabbit.

Rabbit nodded his head and left the C and C.

Reaper brought mugs of steaming coffee over to Bearfang and Venus.

'How many vehicles have we lost?' Bearfang asked.

'Five totally destroyed, seven others banged up but drivable,' Captain Vixen Pascali replied. 'And three trailers destroyed. Some of the tech's been severely damaged, including the jammer. We need to take it offline to carry out repairs,' she said, rubbing the long laser burn scar down the side of her face from a previous encounter with Godders a few years before.

'Their satellites will pick us up in minutes,' the Reverend said.

Vixen looked at him. 'Do nothing and it'll burn out.'

'How long can you keep the jammer going?'

Vixen shrugged her shoulders. 'Five, maybe seven hours.'

Tiger, Thundersky and Venus looked at one another.

'Time enough,' the Prophetess said.

'We can maintain a jam on the comms once it goes offline, but not against the satellites.'

'We'll have to separate,' Thundersky said. 'Put as much distance between us as we can.' He looked at Bearfang. 'We'll need some fighters with us,' he said. 'To cover us when we go into the NORAD facility?'

'Whatever you need,' Bearfang said.

'We'll make for the Hudson River,' Venus put in, 'And sail down to Manhattan. Keep ourselves isolated. You should bring your people in via the Catty Mountains and move into position in the ruins of old Queens and be ready to provide us with a diversion or cover if we need it.'

'Ghostmaker reports that there's a Silosian Triple S kill team at the target site,' Bearfang said.

'My brother,' Reaper whispered to Tiger. 'He's a clock-stopper.'

PART TWO
Black Widow

Chapter Thirty-Eight

Sub City, Silosia

'…Automatic launch sequence will commence in T-minus Two-zero-six hours,' Arti announced, as he did every hour, on the hour.

'We're getting them on the satellite,' Moon Spencer said.

'Finally…' Blackstone came over to the interface and looked up over Moon's shoulder. 'Bring up visuals please, Spencer.'

The Intsoglass wall displayed visuals. The M-TAV was moving along an ancient road.

'Can you establish a com link?'

Moon shook his head. 'No. The signal's still being jammed.'

Zim Steven and another man entered the lab. Zim's companion was a sharp featured man with dead, black eyes that knew neither pity nor mercy. A visceral machine with unwavering obedience to Zim Steven.

Blackstone turned briefly and looked at them, then turned back. 'Our scans of the city show they should have a clear run in,' he said. 'They're going to need air support. Sensors have also picked up several large sonic detonations and artillery exchanges…' He finally turned from the interface and looked at Zim.

'But what really concerns me is the unauthorized systems activation at Lunar Seven.'

'A precaution, Washington.'

'Against what? You know activating those treaty bases is a violation of the peace?'

'I was hoping you could clarify that, Washington. The Tacticals are breathing fire trying to override the protocols, but they can't get through the firewalls.'

Zim gravitated towards Blackstone and Moon, leaving Dead Eyes standing in the middle of the lab. 'You're saying you didn't authorize the activation?'

Blackstone Washington turned back to his interface. 'I'm saying exactly that. Arti, who initiated the systems activation of Lima-Seven?'

Arti responded: 'Information unavailable.'

'Arti. I am the overriding authority in Silosia. Comply to my request. Where did the order to activate Lima-Seven originate?'

'Information unavailable.'

Zim took a deep breath. 'It's obvious. It must be the Dusties. They must've found a way to hack into Lunar Seven's caretaker system and initiate a full activation. There can't be any other explanation.' Zim glanced at Moon Spencer, busy at his interface, trying to penetrate the signal jammer to contact Thundersky and Tiger.

Washington made no reply. He knew that was impossible. Lunar Seven could only be activated through Arti. 'They'll be in Manhattan sometime in the next forty-eight hours,' he said, avoiding the subject. 'We could have them home in a few days.'

Zim gave him a saurian grin. 'They won't be coming home, Washington.'

Blackstone looked sharply at him. 'What're you mean, they won't be coming home?'

Moon looked down, feeling the guilty stab of his own treachery. He knew they weren't coming back. It was Moon who'd covertly helped Zim to activate a Delta from Lunar Seven last night. Once their mission was over, the ruins of New York and everyone and everything in it would be erased from the face of the earth by a full yield Astrium plasma missile fired from orbit.

'I've just come from the Grand High Council,' Zim said. 'We know you've been hiding the Genesis boy from us. You altered and deleted records and swapped scans. You deceived us.'

Before Blackstone could react, Dead Eyes drew a laser and fired it at him. The laser bored a perfect and bloodless hole through Blackstone's forehead.

It was so quick, so sudden, it took a few moments before Grand High Scholar Blackstone Washington dropped to the ground in a heap, knocking into a stool and sending it scuttling across the lab on its casters with a loud clatter over the metal plating...

For a long time that was the only sound Moon could hear, those infernal casters clattering across the steel deck. His heart was thumping so fast and heavy in his chest, he was having trouble catching his breath. He was utterly terrified, his entire body trembling from head to foot, convinced he was next. He sat paralyzed to the spot. A sibilant murmur escaped his lips and piss was soaking into his pants legs and crotch as his bladder emptied.

Dead Eyes looked at him, saw he had pissed himself and grinned coldly at him.

'Make sure he's incinerated,' Zim said to Dead Eyes. 'There's to be no trace of him. And contact the kill team and update them.' Zim looked at Moon. 'The Council's very pleased with you, Spencer. They asked me to pass that on. Treason is the most serious of offenses.'

Moon gave him a nervous and wordless nod with a rictus smile.

'I want you to monitor everything going on in New York. Report everything back directly to me and only to me, do you understand?'

Moon nodded his head eagerly, realizing he wasn't going to be killed, at least for now. He gulped and cleared his throat. 'Yes,' he said croakily, the fear in him turning his voice watery. He cleared his throat again. 'Of course, Zim Steven.' His voice was clearer now.

Dead eyes left the lab to make arrangements for Blackstone Washington's body to be removed and incinerated.

'Arti', Zim said. 'Locate Blossom Flora?'

Arti responded, 'Blossom Flora is no longer in Sub City. Location unknown.'

Chapter Thirty-Nine

Ruins of Old Manhattan

According to Jeremiah O'Connor, New York City had ceased to exist at precisely 13:15 local time, on the afternoon of Thursday, March 27th 2025, when the first of five thermonuclear warheads had detonated across the city. The first detonated over Jamaica, Queens, the Second also detonated over Queens. At 13:18, a third ICBM detonated over the Chimney Sweeps Islands in Brooklyn. At 13:21, the fourth detonated over Long Island and the fifth detonated.

There was not a single building left intact in the entire city. There were great swathes of grey, flat lifelessness where the nukes had flattened practically everything to ground level, as if a giant had come down and swept it away. Of the buildings that had remained standing, many had long ago collapsed under their own weight into mountains of rubble from which stunted trees and creeping vines grew.

Remarkably, or perhaps miraculously might have been the better word, there were still large parts of Manhattan that were still in relatively good condition. The buildings in these places were windowless (not one window for over a hundred miles had not been shattered by the concentrated attacks on the larger cities). They stood tall and mighty, like skeletonized titans, reaching for the sky, many partially collapsed. Every now and then, masonry tumbled hundreds of feet to the ground. Two nights ago, there was a terrific roar and crash and the building they were in shook. They all ran out in panic to see a high-rise opposite collapsing vertically, until two thirds of the building was gone, and an amorphous gray cloud of dust expanded for hundreds of yards.

Further down, the streets were permanently under water as the Atlantic encroached little by little.

A solarcycle zipped around the ruins of Foley Square, the insectile buzzing of its engine scratching through the necrotic silence and into Lionheart Frank's thoughts. It was getting closer and closer, its noise echoing through deathly silence like a hornet in a cave. There was life in this dead city. Maybe up to a thousand Scavs scattered about, mining the ruins for useful scavenge, picking among the skeletonized remains of the millions who'd died there that March day in 2025. Working at their desks, oblivious to the terrible fate about to befall them. Sipping coffee or typing at their primitive computers, or chatting to their colleagues. Maybe planning to go for a beer after work. But after work never came. Only death came, and the end of their world. In a few terrible hours, mankind had undone what evolution had taken billions of years to create.

'There is only one evil in the world and that evil is humankind,' he said lowly. 'We are the monsters in the shadows, the demons that haunt our minds. We are the destroyers of worlds, the pestilence. We are Death…' Lionheart Frank scoped the noisy kidling on the solarcycle thirty-eight floors below. It would be so easy, he thought, to clock the little Scav off. Pop and good-fuckin-night. 'The little dickbutt wouldn't even know what happened. Pop, and he's gone. No more noise.'

Ravenhawk stood watching him, the wind blowing through his long hair.

Lionheart, his eye pressed to the scope, his finger curled round the trigger, followed the boy as he weaved through the rubble and wreckage of ancient vehicles, rusting along the street. So many vehicles, it was hard to comprehend what chaos it must've been to the ancients who'd lived there. Were they all trying to escape before the mushrooms? According to the Chronicle, there was no warning, yet all these vehicles filled with ash, rust and skeletons had jammed practically every road in the city in something the Old-Worlders had called a *"logjam."* The solarcycle was ridden by a kidling of about fifteen or sixteen with an old parabellum rifle slung over his back. The kidling chicaned around the ancient vehicles with admirable skill. He rode out of the square and vanished into the ruins down another street near the water's edge along what was Vesey Street, which was dry at low tide. During high tide, as they had seen, the sea came right into Foley Square and the waves lapped at the old courthouse steps.

Lionheart finally lowered his weapon and turned to Ravenhawk. 'Any updates from Mission?'

'They'll be here in about forty-eight hours.'

'*Hm.* That's what they said four days ago.'

Ravenhawk nodded his head. 'They've clocked off Grand High Scholar Blackstone Washington,' he said. 'For treason.'

'Well, I never saw that coming,' Lionheart said, scratching his neck, where he was showing the early signs of melanomas. There were lesions on the backs of his hands too.

'No. I don't suppose the Grand High Scholar did either,' Ravenhawk responded facetiously. 'Do you think it's got something to do with this novy? Only it has to be pretty serious before they would clock off one of their own. It makes you wonder just who this novy is? I mean, clocking off tacticals and novices. It has to be pretty fucked up.'

'Well, it's not our problem. We just do as we're told.' He looked squarely at Ravenhawk. 'Trust me, it's healthier that way.'

Ravenhawk cocked his brows. 'I just think-'

'Don't think, Ravenhawk!' Lionheart put a hard stare on him. 'You're not here to think. Did I tell you to think? Just leave the thinking to me. We get it done and evac.'

Ravenhawk was silent. There were a few choice words burning in his mouth and he had to close it and clench on his teeth, lest they slid off his tongue. Calling their commander an incompetent prick wouldn't have earned him any favors, even if it was true. Lionheart had never commanded a kill team before, he had very little tactical training and the only people he had killed were terrorists in the penal labs when they were too far gone to be of use to the medical research scholars.

He barely knew the names of his team, never mind their credentials. Ravenhawk knew every detail about them.

There were three other clock-stoppers in the Triple S kill team: Mark Trent, Cougartooth Barry and Clearwings Betty – the same Clearwings Betty who'd clocked off the leader of the Ohio Dusties, Badbear Stan, with a single shot from five thousand yards out with a tac-thirteen laser rifle at the Siege of Sandy City two years ago. It was a hell of a shot that had earned her the nickname, "One Zap Bet." She was an unattractive woman with dark, soulless eyes and an even darker heart. Clock-stopping was more like a hobby for her than a job.

During tactical training, when they released captured Ferals in the mountains to hunt and kill, One Zap Bet had bagged herself eighteen kills. She'd hunted those Feral savages down like a bloodhound and blown their heads of as if they were insects.

Cougartooth Barry was from Plateau City, he'd served as a tactical for a few years as a sniper. Then Zim Steven had recruited him into the Triple S kill teams. He'd broken a Virginia Dusty terrorist cell on the eve of planning to kidnap a genetics scholar from the Plateau City GRC surrogate center five years ago. He shot and killed three terrorists that day.

Mark Trent, a thirty-five-year-old, was a Triple S veteran of ten years. He was a brawny bruiser with hands like ten-pound hammers. He was an explosives expert from Surfer Town. His most distinguishing features were his overarching forehead and his overshot jaw, which gave him more than a passing resemblance to a Neanderthal. Nobody knew how many kills he had to his name. At least thirty Dusties and hundreds of Ferals during the big clear out operations in the Silosian controlled areas of the Virginias. Nobody knew how many Ferals were culled, some said as many as 10,000.

'Mission says they'll be here in about forty-eight hours,' Ravenhawk said to the others when he came back inside what had once been a large office. The rotting desks and chairs were still there, along with old primitive computers by the dozen. Skeletons too, around a dozen, the bones spongy and brittle from having been left exposed for centuries. 'One Zap … Cougartooth, you're on first patrol.'

Clearwings nodded her head and grabbed her tac-one and pistol belt as she pulled herself up from the floor onto her feet.

Chapter Forty

It was quite a way down, the old stone stairs. Many of the concrete steps had split and cracked, revealing the rusty steel reinforcing rods.

'This your first time out with Lionheart?' Cougartooth asked as they descended, rubble and grit crackling under their boots.

'Yeah.' She gave him a steely look. 'But I don't need to know him to know that he's got the cowardy jumpies?'

'Just about as bad as you can get 'em. You can bet your ass that once the shootin' starts, he'll be hop-tailing it out of here on our drone and we won't hear shit from him until it's over. You know who he is, don't you?'

She frowned.

Cougartooth gave her a big grin.

'Wipe that dick-tickler's grin off your face and tell me?' she said impatiently.

'He's Zim Steven's brother.'

She raised a brow. That explained a lot.

Outside, Cougartooth felt a little uneasy as they walked cautiously beneath the tumbled and derelict tower blocks, some naked of their cladding, down to their rusty girders.

As they turned a corner, they saw the solarcycle kidling straddling his solarcycle on the opposite side of the street, watching them curiously. Cougartooth looked back at the kidling – comforted by the weight of his tac-one cradled in his arms like a baby, his sweaty right hand clasping the pistol-grip, his index finger resting against the trigger guard. Scavengers weren't known for being hostile and since they had arrived, they had hardly seen any Scavs. They kept their distance from the heavily armed strangers, except for this kidling, who seemed unafraid of them. That made him different, which made Clearwings and Cougartooth uneasy.

The lean faced boy, his face filthy with grime, watched them like a snake watches a rat.

'That kidling's starting to bother me,' Clearwings said. 'Maybe I'll clock him off?'

'Best not, One Zap. We d'know who his people are and we don't need no distractions. Just ignore him. He's harmless.'

The Fulton Street subway was flooded to street level. It was the same with most of the ancient subsurface systems of Manhattan, the water slopping and slapping up from the ancient subway system onto the sidewalk. In some places, entire streets had opened up and collapsed into the ancient subways and sewers that had become underground rivers and tidal inlets for the Atlantic, Hudson and East River.

'I'll be glad when this babbledick mission's over,' Cougartooth said. 'If I have to eat any more of those goddam rations, I'll turn into a Feral.'

Clearwings suddenly fell down like stone, without a sound, flat on her face on the rubble strewn sidewalk.

At first, Cougartooth thought she had tripped and fallen. But she wasn't moving – she just lay down on the ground, her right leg twitching, her eyes wide open and staring. '*One Zap*...?' He leaned over her. 'Stop dickbutting around. C'mon. Get up...'

She was non-responsive.

Cougartooth crouched down, put his hand on her shoulder and shook her gently. '*Clearwings*?' She did not move. He turned her over onto her back, and that was when, to his horror, he saw a laser bore in the side of her head. His heart pounded with fright and fear, and for a moment his body seemed unable to move. And then he jumped to his feet in a state of panic. He started to run back the way they'd come, and then something struck him in the middle of his back with an excruciating burning sting, taking his breath away. He threw his hands up into the air, dropping his tac-thirteen, which clattered to the ground. His legs gave way and he dropped, gasping for breath, flopping about in the rubble, trying to crawl away – trying to breathe, coughing up blood.

Someone was coming up behind him; heavy boots scrunched on rubble. A shadow fell across him – the shadow of Death. The toe of a boot slipped under him and heaved him over onto his back.

Ghostmaker, wearing a respirator mask, stared down at him as he shouldered his tac-thirty laser rifle.

Cougartooth's mouth opened and closed, gulping and gargling on blood. His wide eyes stared into the big, black, round glass eyes of the respirator, which looked back at him like some alien being.

Ghostmaker pulled the respirator off, revealing a sweaty face. The handsome face of a young man of twenty-two or twenty-three, with piercing blue eyes and blond stubble around his chin.

The buzz of the solarcycle grew louder and louder as it came towards them. Then it stopped and the power unit whirred at idle.

Cougartooth looked at the boy, who stared back curiously at him through brown puppy-dog eyes.

The boy propped his solarcycle on its stand and dismounted.

Cougartooth lay dying, watching the kidling pick up his tac-thirteen laser rifle. He propped it against his cycle, then crouched down and started to unbuckle Cougartooth's weapons belt.

Ghostmaker stood watching with indifference as the kidling robbed the dying man of everything useful he had. Even down to his boots, which the kidling pulled off with some difficulty.

Cougartooth gargled and gasped, his body going into shock and beginning to shiver, lying helpless. Paralyzed and drowning in his own blood.

Once the kidling had Cougartooth's weapons, boots and Surfer Town turds, along with his medicinals, he turned and started to loot the dead woman.

Ghostmaker finally drew his tac-ten laser pistol and casually shot Cougartooth through the brain, finishing him off instantly.

Ghostmaker looked at the boy and the boy looked back at him. 'Wait for me at the hide.'

The wordless kidling, loaded with his booty, remounted his solarcycle and rode away.

After eating their field rations, Trent brewed up some skunkweed-shit tea. Not strong, just enough to take the edge off yet another long, tedious night waiting for the M-TAV and the novices to show up. Lionheart, aloof to the last, had gone to bed in one of the rooms off of the main room.

They'd chosen this building because of its proximity to the old courthouse and its clear line of sight. Whatever it was the novices were coming to do, they were doing it in that building. Under no circumstances were they to act before the novices had completed their mission.

Once the novices and tacticals who were with them were dead, their orders were to clear the ruins of Manhattan as the area was going to be destroyed from orbit. They would have approximately thirty minutes to evacuate to a safe distance. Ravenhawk, who thought the entire mission had a stink about it, was tempted to share what he knew with the others, but he decided not to take the risk. Discussing a need to know with those who didn't need to know would cost him his career and privileges. He pulled himself up achily from the floor. 'I need a piss.'

'Don't be long, tea's almost ready.'

'I won't, so don't drink it all you skunk-sponge.' He walked stiffly to the door, out into the corridor and along to the apartment next door that they had been using as their bathroom, crapping and urinating in a bathtub.

The stench was nauseating; Ravenhawk could taste it in the back of his throat. The air droned with flies and the shower basin was a swamp of excrement.

As he urinated, he heard a footfall. 'I hope you turned the tea down?' he said without looking round.

'I'll be sure to tell him before I kill him,' Ghostmaker said.

Ravenhawk spun, reaching for his pistol. Too late – a flash of light leapt from Ghostmaker's tac-ten and burned through Ravenhawk's chest, into his heart and out the back of his body before burning a hole into the wall behind him. Ravenhawk dropped down in a heap on the floor.

Trent stirred the steaming pan of skunkweed-shit tea on the plasma stove. He lent over it and sniffed in the cannabis aroma. Alcohol was too expensive for most people; a glass of apple brandy was one shot of Iodinicine. Skunkweed-shit tea was produced in the biodomes and distributed barter free. To the Scholastic Order, it was a way of keeping the topsiders pacified.

Suddenly, somebody grabbed him from behind and before he had the chance to respond, he felt a razor-sharp knife at his throat. He froze as stiff as a rock. Hot stinking breath breathed close to his ear. A voice whispered: 'Where's the Inquisitor?'

Trent lifted his trembling hand and pointed at a door.

'Thank you.' He clasped his free hand to Trent's mouth and jerked away with the other, sliding the blade across Trent's throat, cutting deep into his neck. A jet of blood flew several feet across the room from a severed artery.

Ghostmaker held him tight, his hand clasped to his mouth while Trent struggled and jerked in his death throes, growing weaker and weaker as the blood pumped from his throat in crimson spurts.

Ghostmaker felt him go limp as he died. He released his grip and rolled his body gently to the side. He poured himself a cup of the skunkweed-shit tea and stood sipping the hot bitter liquid, staring measuredly at the door Trent had pointed to.

Once he'd finished the tea, Ghostmaker moved light footed to the door, his bloody hand moving to the handle. He pulled his parabellum pistol out as the door creaked open. There he was, lying under a foil blanket on a roll-up sleeping mat.

Lionheart saw the dark figure standing in the doorway, backlit by the blue glow of the plasma stove. He started to sit up, bleary eyed. 'Is that you Ravenhawk?'

'No,' Ghostmaker whispered. 'It's me.'

Lionheart sat up and squinted at the figure, trying to make out who it was. 'Who is that?'

Ghostmaker moved into the room.

Lionheart saw the laser pistol and expressed terror. He shuffled up quickly in panic, holding out his hands. 'Wait…'

Ghostmaker zapped him. The laser burned through the palm of his hand and into his neck.

Lionheart screamed out in pain and terror, scrambling about the room like a frightened animal, screaming and pleading…

Ghostmaker shot him again, this time the laser went through Lionheart's eye and came out through the side of his head. It still didn't kill him.

Ghostmaker chuckled, the muzzle of his laser following Lionheart as he leapt about the room screaming his head off. 'Stay still goddammit...' He fired again as Lionheart leapt towards a door. The laser got him in the throat and he crashed into the wall and slumped down onto the floor dead.

Chapter Forty-One

Hudson River

'…Bringing navigational sensors online,' Venus said, switching to Amphibious Mode. A viewer in the dash became a radar scope with a narrow beam of pale blue light sweeping clockwise, animating the landmass and shipwrecks with beeps and broadening beams carving out the shapes of objects and landmass in light.

She pressed a glowing blue button. The lights in the module and the Intsoglass windows dimmed by eighty percent and the glow of the radar scope swept her face.

The dark, rippling waters of the Hudson filled the windshield and suddenly the forward module lifted as the prow cut into the water.

She pressed more buttons on the overhead interface. 'Retracting wheels.'

There were several loud hums and clunks as the wheel couplings disengaged and folded in under the keel and locked into their recesses.

A sonar viewer next to the radar came online automatically as soon as they were in the water, making a blip-ping sound through the murky depths as the sonar wave pinged back.

'Bringing hydro-jets online…' There was a loud glugging and gargling noise as the rig shuddered from stem to stern. 'That's just the air being purged,' she said.

Presently, the vibration settled and was replaced by the low, soporific hum. They were moving out into deeper water. The riverbed was littered with Old-World ships and boats.

Venus engaged the nav-conn AI. Her seat slid back on its rails.

'We could do with one of these,' Bearfang said, impressed with the M-TAV's versatility. Their old halftracks, although amphibious, were designed to cross rivers rather than navigate them and half of them leaked at the seams like rusty buckets, with water having to be continuously pumped out of them.

In the glow of the cockpit, the radar bleeped and the sonar blipped and pinged, constant and monotonous… bleep, blip, ping… bleep, blip, ping… bleep, blip, ping…

Venus climbed out of the cockpit. 'We've got about two hours of light left,' she said as she arched her back, stretching out her arms languidly as she yawned. She was tired – they were all tired. 'We'll have to go down slow. Sonar's picking up all kinds of Old-World shit under the river. The nearer we get to the city ruins, the more Old-World shit there'll be. Some of it will be big shit. Warships and the like'

Thundersky reached up to the roof hatch. 'I'm going up top for some air.'

Suddenly, everyone was climbing out onto the roof. Venus lit a Surfer Town turd and surveyed the landscape either side of the river at the still wilderness. Here and there, a remnant of Old-World hung on with stubborn tenacity, the shoreline walls where once there were structures and promenades, now swathed in forests and wild meadows of long grass, or simply washed away by the river in flood surges. Rotting hulks half submerged in silt nudged out of the water near the shoreline, like corpses crawling out of their watery graves. Cargo ships, barges … warships with their mighty guns jutting from their decks, now rusty islands of steel where gulls and pigeons nested, the shore a wasteland of Old-World ruins.

Thundersky squatted on the railgun turret and watched the setting sun as it singed the western horizon with a blood red glow that tinted the treetops and hills before it slipped behind the horizon.

Reaper came over and sat beside him. He didn't speak. There were times for words and he sensed that this wasn't one of them. Thundersky looked at him, then his gaze shifted back back at the sunset.

The others were babbledicking about the mission. Discussing what might be in the city ruins. More Delaware Godders? Cannibalistic Ferals? Dusties from the Catty Mountains?

Ahead, they were approaching the remains of an Old-World bridge, which, according to the archived historical data, was once known as the Franklin Delano Roosevelt Mid-Hudson Bridge. The bridge had fallen into the river centuries ago and nothing remained of it now except for two concrete piers and rusting steel towers rising for more than three hundred feet into the air.

Thundersky craned his neck and looked up at the left pier as they sailed past, looking up at the rusty stanchions rising vertically, which seemed to prick the sky. The roads that it once connected had long ago vanished under wilderness.

Venus headed for the hatch. 'We should try and get a few hours' sleep,' she suggested. 'We've got a busy day tomorrow. Captain Pascali – You know how to operate an M-TAV?'

'Of course.'

'Good. You get first watch. You treat my rig right, now.'

Vixen nodded. 'Like a baby.'

'That's what I like to hear.' She looked at Thundersky and Reaper. 'You boys comin'? You need some sleep.'

Going to sleep was the last thing Thundersky wanted to do. 'I'm fine here. I'll come down when I'm ready.'

Venus considered him for a moment, then climbed down through the hatch.

They were near their goal, and it was all suddenly very real. His doubts came at him in a capricious storm as he considered the Four-Eight-Zero, an unpredictable monster of untold power. And what if they couldn't slay it? What then for the future? More fire mushrooms and another long nuclear winter.

Reaper reached to him and held Thundersky's hand, looking tenderly at him.

Thundersky clasped Reaper's hand in his and smiled affectionately at him. There they sat in muted silence, looking off into the stygian darkness of the moonless night, strangely content as they held each others' hands.

Tiger, near the hatch, watched them. He was happy for his friend. He'd seen how close he had become with the Scav. It was easy to love Thundersky. There was just something about him. Even Tiger loved him, but not in the sex thing way. He was straight-het. He smiled and climbed down the ladder into the M-TAV.

———

It was three hours before dawn. Venus went to the cockpit, woken by Vixen.

'Multiple structures,' Vixen said. 'Human colonies. Light weapons detected. We've got hostiles both sides of the river dug in townlike.'

Venus grabbed her tac-one. 'Wake the others and bring the weapons online. I'm going topside to take a look.' She took a pair of black lensed sensor goggles out of an overhead locker and opened the roof hatch in the forward module, pulling the ladder down.

Thundersky, sleeping on the back row of seats, woke up as Inner Voice spoke: 'Lima-Seven. All systems online.' Inner Voice fell silent.

'Railgun targeting,' the AI announced.

'Everyone up!' Venus barked. 'Possible hostiles.'

Bearfang, Tiger and Reaper woke up.

'Hit the floods,' she said as she climbed through the forward roof hatch.

The floodlights came on all the way along the sides, front and back of the M-TAV, their blinding beams cutting through the night, filtering through low veils of diaphanous mist drifting over the river and shore, where the ancient wharfs stretched along the shoreline, many still standing, looming along the docks. Within, dark figures moved back into the shadows.

The lumbering current of the river slapped and crawled along the M-TAV's keel. It seemed loud against the piercing silence hanging eerily over the waterfront ruins along the shore.

The railgun suddenly rotated one hundred and eighty degrees, bringing its muzzles to bear on the dilapidated shells of the ancient wharfs.

Bearfang, Reaper and Thundersky came up onto the roof.

Venus slipped the sensor goggles on, setting them to thermal imaging and linking them to the railgun's tactical system, activating the sight to target cerebral interface so that the railguns aimed at whatever she looked at, ready to fire. The cerebral sensors in the head-straps activated. Now a single thought could deliver death without lifting a finger.

There were dozens of people in the ruins, apparently living there, glowing like ghosts formed from green ectoplasm in her thermal goggles, moving cautiously through the ruins, armed with parabellums. 'Scavs,' she said quietly. Louder, she said; 'Computer. Bring the thirties online.'

The four thirty-caliber railgun ports moved forward, the aft slid open and the guns telescoped out and pivoted on their pan and tilt gimbals, the barrels zeroing onto the ruins. She wanted to leave the Scavs in no doubt that if any one of them opened fire, she would blow them all to hell.

The Scavs retreated from the windows and portals, lowering their weapons, backing away.

'Wise decision,' she said.

They sailed on towards the saw-tooth ruins of old New York limned against the distant horizon.

Chapter Forty-Two

Research & Astrium Refinery, Tranquillitatis

Blackdog and Vernon couldn't believe what they were seeing on the satellite feed. The huge launch doors of Lunar Seven were opening, and light spilled out along the thousand hard long airlock…

Vernon gasped. '*What – the fuck*…?'

'Glitch in the system,' Blackdog said sarcastically. 'That don't look like no system glitch to me. This is goddam babbledick. We must be at war with the Orry-Washes.'

'We'd've heard.'

New data streamed from the geostationary satellite over the Lunar South Pole.

Blackdog stood up. 'Something's moving in there.'

Vernon opened a com to Mission on earth. It was a woman's face that appeared on the viewer.

'Happy day,' she said.

'Is it?' Vernon leaned close to the viewer. 'Lunar Seven is online, the outer launch doors are open-'

'Vernon. You need to see this,' Blackdog said, looking at the visual feed from the satellite. A dark deltoid ship was slowly emerging from the open launch doors. It was two thousand feet across from wingtip to wingtip, and three thousand feet from forward to aft, as black as space itself.

Vernon gawped at the screen. 'Oh my God, there's a Black Widow coming out…' He looked at the tech looking out from the viewer. 'A Black Widow's launching!'

'Tactical Command are aware of the situation and have everything under control. There's no need for concern. The Delta poses no threat to Tranquillitatis.'

'I'm more concerned about the freighter coming in from the belt with a hold full of Astrium ore,' Vernon said.

'The freighter will be fine, Vernon,' she said. 'Tactical are in full control. Is there anything else I can help you with today?'

'No.'

'Then happy day.' She terminated the com.

'What're you think, Vernon?'

Vernon shook his head. 'It's their headache, not mine. They say they've got it in hand.' He opened an internal com. 'We're still getting a warning light on Airlock G-Four, Oak. What's the problem?'

Oak's voice filtered back. 'It's the mag-seal. It's fried. We need to close inner bulkhead doors from I-Three to I-five. I need to replace the mag-lock. I'll need to go EVA, and it's a twenty-hour job.'

Vernon huffed. 'Babbledick! Okay, Oak. Are you getting that, Gecko?'

Another voice came through. 'Copy. I'll be right there.'

'I'll prep the maintenance shuttle,' Oak responded.

'Copy that.'

Vernon closed the com. 'What's that Delta doing?'

Blackdog swiveled round and looked at the satellite feed. 'Looks like it's on a trajectory to Earth.'

Chapter Forty-Three

Ruins of New York City

Thundersky, Tiger and Reaper went up through the forward hatch onto the roof as they neared the seaward approaches to Manhattan Island.

The sea had reclaimed a sizeable part of Lower Manhattan, and there were buildings still relatively intact that grew out of the ocean, like sheer cliffs that now served as nesting grounds for sea birds and colonies of non-native penguins, the descendants of penguins from zoos that had somehow survived the mushrooms and thrived here, nesting in the tower block islands. Their chattering cackles reminded Thundersky of a Surfer Town street party.

They sailed over Lower Manhattan, across a place once known as Battery Park six fathoms beneath them.

'I wonder how many people lived here?' Tiger pondered, looking up in awe of the ancient towers that once gleamed with glass.

'Eight point eight two million in 2025,' Thundersky said, plucking the number from nowhere.

Tiger gave him a look. 'Is there anything you don't know?'

Thundersky shrugged his shoulders. 'I don't know,' he said with a hint of sarcasm.

A mild wind blew in their faces as they sailed along arrow-straight canals, between the great monoliths of rusting steel, lapped and lashed by tidal waters drawing back and forth, swishing and swilling in and out of the cave-like buildings. Cathedral ceilings were adorned with long, milky white stalactites that hung like melted wax from the ceilings.

Ancient New York was a petrified necropolis of shadows with lamenting winds howling through the shattered buildings and buckled steel.

Thundersky felt the presence of eight million ghosts watching them as he looked up at the shattered canyons looming over them, the wind howling eerily through their skeletal remains.

'Quite something, ain't it?' Reaper said. 'Old Chig and old Bost look this way too.' He shuffled up closer to Thundersky.

'Vixen, contact Ghostmaker,' Bearfang ordered. 'Give him our position.'

Vixen took an earpiece out of her pocket and activated the com before slipping it over her ear and walking off away from the others.

'Computer, activate autonomous tactical systems and bring all weapons online,' Venus said.

The railguns and laser cannon came to life, the thirty calibers telescoped from the gun ports.

Thundersky was feeling anxious again, contemplating the next stage of the mission – locating the ADP system and accessing the facility, which might well have been boobytrapped. Then they needed to hack into the ADP, bypass the ancient encryptions and order it to abort and shut down the active silos.

Everything depended on what sort of physical condition the ADP was in. It had been sitting there for 500 years, the ancient circuits would be brittle and delicate. The Ai qubit might have decay. The entire system could overload and short out beyond repair the moment they started the processors. If that happened, nothing could stop the launch. Considering all the variables, he put their chances of success at around twenty percent, with decreasing odds the longer it took them to get to the system. The hotter the circuits become, the more likely it was for a cascade of system failures. 'Now the hard bit starts,' he said, giving Tiger a look.

Tiger understood the risks too and he nodded his head. 'We're going to beat this mother, Thunder.'

'And what about Zim Steven? Are we going to beat him?'

'Fuck yes,' Bearfang said.

They finally came ashore on Broadway, just above Vesey Street, where the tide lapped the buckled roads and sidewalks. Much of the blacktop had been washed away down to the hardcore beneath.

'Radiation within tolerances,' Vixen said as she looked at the sensor data.

Bearfang stared out of the windows, his narrow eyes sweeping the area carefully. 'Any sign of Ghostmaker?'

Vixen shook her head. 'Not yet.'

'The Prophetess has taken up position east of the bridge, General,' Tiger informed, coming through from the C and C.

The M-TAV rocked and jerked as they bumped over rubble and rusting vehicles in their path.

Tiger spotted a dark-clad figure sitting on a mound of rubble on the east side of the plaza, wearing a long syntho-leather overcoat and a wide brimmed hat. With him was a boy.

'There they are,' Vixen said.

Thundersky looked at Reaper. 'Your brother?'

Reaper nodded.

'Who's the kidling with him?' Tiger asked as Venus pulled the M-TAV to a stop.

'Viper. Ghost found him locked in a cage in a Feral colony about five years ago,' Reaper said. 'Nobody knows where he's from. He's mute. He goes everywhere with my brother. He's a tough sonofabitch.'

The M-TAV stopped and Ghostmaker and Viper came towards the rig as the front hatches opened. Thundersky, Reaper, Venus and Bearfang got off.

Ghostmaker looked narrowly at Venus and the two Novies.

'The Triple S kill team?' Bearfang asked.

'Cocked off,' Ghostmaker said.

Venus gave Ghostmaker a suspicious look up and down. Dusty clock-stoppers were a ruthlessly elite group of assassins, highly trained in the ancient Old-World arts of guerilla warfare. There were a lot of Silosian sentinels she had known who had been clocked off by Dusty clock-stoppers.

Ghostmaker saw her contempt and gave her his best smile. 'Happy day, pretty lady,' he said.

'Stick it in your ass,' Venus snapped. She looked at the boy. The murderer's apprentice.

Ghostmaker looked at his little brother and smiled. 'Look at you, playing with the big boys now. All growed up.' It had been six years since the brothers had last seen one another.

'Ghost. This is Thundersky Reece...' Reaper gestured to Thundersky.

Ghostmaker expressed surprise, but did his best to appear underwhelmed. 'So, this is the famous Thundersky Reece...?' He looked Thundersky over. 'With all the fuss I was expecting ... Well, not you.'

'Too bad,' Thundersky said.

Reaper deliberately took hold of Thundersky's hand and Ghostmaker and Viper were surprised.

'You two got the love thing going on, eh? Well, the love thing don't got no place here. So, keep ya pecker in ya pants.'

'You do know they're watching us right now, don't you?' Venus said, looking up into the sky.

'It seems to me, we no longer have anything to hide,' Tiger said. He had made up his mind whose side he was on.

Venus turned back to the M-TAV. 'We've wasted enough time babbledicking...' She walked back to the M-TAV. 'And Ghostmaker, or whatever your goddam name is. I call the tune on my rig. You babbledick me, and you're off.'

'Hm. She's a nice pretty lady, int she Vipe? We like her. Don't we, Vipe.'

Vipe smiled and nodded his head. They loaded up the tech and tacticals they had looted from the kill team and boarded. Ghostmaker sat beside Bearfang. Viper wandered through the rig to explore.

As soon as they were all aboard, they started moving again.

In the C and C, Reaper and Viper watched Tiger and Thundersky in the storage compartment sorting out their equipment. Tiger looked at Viper. 'Don't touch anything, kidling. Dangerous.'

Viper looked blankly at Tiger, as if he hadn't understood what he'd said. His gaze shifted to Thundersky and when Thundersky looked at him, the boy smiled at him.

Thundersky opened the titanium box containing the new circuits and carefully checked them one last time.

'I'm going with you,' Reaper said.

Thundersky nodded his head. 'I assumed.'

Reaper smiled.

Thundersky closed the box of circuits and slid it back into his ruck.

As he picked the rucksack up, Viper held his hand out, gesturing to carry it. Tiger watched curiously.

Reaper grabbed the rucksack and gave Viper a hard stare as he took the ruck from Thundersky.

'Here, you can take mine if you want,' Tiger said as he sealed his rucksack.

Viper glared at him, then turned and walked back through to the front.

Tiger pulled a face as he lifted his rucksack up and heaved it over his shoulder. 'I guess I'll be carrying my own shit then.'

Thundersky gave him a wicked smile and walked through the C and C chuckling to himself as Tiger followed behind, murmuring indolently.

They approached the grand old neo-classical hexagonal granite clad building that Arti had indicated as the entrance into the Four-Eight-Zero installation. The building was still mostly intact, except for its windows.

'It's under that building,' Thundersky said, looking out the windshield.

They drove to the ancient courthouse and stopped at the bottom of the steps before powering down the mag-drive.

Chapter Forty-Four

Thundersky, Tiger, Venus and Reaper climbed the steps to a grand columned portico, its fluted Corinthian columns decorated with scrolling stone entablature capitals that supported nothing but the sky. Its stone-gabled end had long ago collapsed and now lay smashed across the steps in fractured blocks of finely carved stone. The face of fallen Justice, lying poignantly near the bottom of the steps, was covered in barnacles and gazing eternally into the sky.

There was a hiver-trunk following behind like an obedient dog. Thundersky and Tiger's rucksacks were on the lid of it.

They stopped just inside and Venus took a hand held sensor scanner out of her kitbag and switched it on. 'Okay, mapping.'

They waited for the sensor to scan the building with ultrasound. 'It'll take a few minutes.' She set the scanner down on the floor.

Their eyes roved the ancient ruin with curiosity. Dilapidated, most of the interior had been destroyed by centuries of tidal flooding and the corrosive effects of seawater.

Venus lit a Surfer Town turd and puffed away on it.

Reaper wandered off into a large chamber. Ancient benches and furniture had been swept to one side of the room by the tidal surges.

Venus was in front, holding a sensor in the palm of her hand, panning it left and right, looking at the small little holographic projection of the building, above ground and below. 'Okay,' she said, zooming the holograph to display where they needed to go.

The scanner beeped. Venus picked it up and swiped her thumb over a sensor. A holographic schematic of the building projected like architectural plans, the floors transparent. There was a flashing green dot indicating their location in comparison to a flashing red dot to the left in what looked like a long shaft below the basement.

'We're here...' She pointed to the green flashing dot. 'The target is here...' she pointed to the red dot, 'at the bottom of this shaft, which looks like it's accessed by a hatchway of some sort, here in the north wall. The shaft descends sixty-nine feet below the basement. That's the upside...'

'And the downside?' Tiger asked.

'The basement's flooded to a depth of one point one meters-'

'Meaning the shaft's probably completely submerged?' Thundersky interjected.

'Unless it's a watertight hatch and the seals have held out. The hatch is one point five meters above the floor, so just above the water level. We got six hours before the tide comes in. Then the basement will flood up to nine feet.'

Reaper was covering them with a tac-one at the ready, turning a full three sixty every once in a while, making sure no feral ambushers were lying in wait on the upper mezzanine.

The sound of grit, sand, dry crusty guano and seashells washed in by tidal surges and floods crunched underfoot, every sound amplified in the quiet vaulted space, stirring the pigeons perched along a ledge of the ceilings where the wild cats couldn't get at them. There were dozens of them, cooing and fluffing their feathers. A flap of wings as one took to the air and flew from one side of the gallery to the other.

They found the stairs to the basement, and Venus sent down two hover globe lights that illuminated the pitch black, the lights automatically intensifying as they descended the stair, chasing their lights. One stopped and hovered at the bottom of the stairs, and the other continued on into the blackness.

The stairs were concrete and sound. The walls were damp and stalactites hung from the ceiling. Seashells and barnacles were strewn on the steps and the lower down they went, the more there were, cracking loudly underfoot, every sound echoing in the murky silence.

Light refractions rippled on the ceiling from the water on the floor. The final six steps were submerged and by the time they reached the bottom step, the water came to above their waists.

The basement was cavernous, and was clearly an ancient archive storage facility of some sort. The swish of water echoed though the place as they waded through the glowing incandescence of the light globe. Venus followed the directional finder on the hand scanner. The green dot had turned into an arrow showing them the way.

The water was freezing, even through their antirads, and they could feel the cold penetrating the Intsofiber.

They were at the north wall. The hologram indicated they had found the hatch, but there was nothing there apart from a wall, and an old air duct in the wall where the hatch should have been.

'It must be behind there,' she said and pulled a small laser cutter from her kitbag.

It took seconds to cut through the aluminum duct, the metal sizzing and sparking and glowing as the laser cut through like a hot knife through butter.

Reaper pulled the duct away, and sure enough, behind the duct was a titanium airlock hatch, just big enough to climb through. There was a code-key pad on the hatch.

'It looks like a maglock,' Venus said.

'Can we get it open?' Thundersky asked.

'We could try blowing it,' Reaper responded.

'And that might bring the whole building down on top of us,' Venus said as she turned to the hover box.

Thundersky and Tiger removed their rucksacks as Venus opened the box. Inside, the trunk was divided up into a number of various sized white squares with sensor switches. She put her finger to the sensor switch of one of the larger compartments. The compartment slid up proud of the others. She lifted the box out and opened it before removing a metal wheel shaped device.

'What's that?' Reaper asked.

'A small EMP oscillator. Theoretically, it'll search for the magnetic frequency and disengage the locks.

But they've been sealed for five hundred years, the locks could be seized.'

She attached the EMP oscillator to the hatch and activated it. The wheel started to hum as ever-changing pitches.

They watched – they waited.

Reaper shivered with the cold.

After thirty or so seconds, the oscillator stopped and everything fell silent. They stared anxiously at the hatch, willing it to open.

Several long and excruciating seconds passed, then there was a loud clunk and a hiss of escaping air as the hatch swung open.

'Good job, Corporal Venus,' Thundersky said as he pulled the hatch all the way open, heaved himself up and wriggled through the opening. He looked down the shaft, but it was pitch black. 'I can't see a goddam thing in here…'

Venus took another hover globe light from her kitbag and handed it to Thundersky. He dropped it into the blackness and as it fell away, it started to hum and glow, filling the chamber with a murky light, enough to see by.

Thundersky saw the concrete floor almost seventy feet below, with a round, steel domed hatch set in the middle. The hatch was still sealed. There were steel ladder rungs anchored into the concrete wall just below the hatch, with grabrails either side.

Thundersky crawled in and gripped the grabrail and startred down the rugs into the humming iridescence.

Chapter Forty-Five

Venus used the EMP oscillator to open the hatch at the bottom of the shaft and threw in three more light globes.

'Radiation check?' Tiger said.

Venus checked the sensor scanner. 'Well within tolerances.'

Thundersky went down first again, into the unknown, like Theseus climbing into the Labyrinth to meet his destiny. He was ready to kill NORAD's ghost – waiting for them far below…

Tiger jumped down behind him.

Reaper and Venus climbed down.

Tiger looked at Thundersky. 'Just like home, eh?' he said, thinking of Sub City.

Further down the corridor they climbed down yet another ladder into a square concrete chamber, only to be confronted by a closed blast door. She attached the EMP oscillator.

'What wavelength is it pulsing at?' Thundersky asked her.

'Damped sinewave pulses,' Venus replied.

The locks clunked and they stepped back as the heavy door swung open. Air hissed out like a sigh.

The intrepid quartet entered the blackness beyond. Venus went first, pushing the hover-lights ahead of them, their bright glow pushing back the darkness which swept before them, their miniature mag-drives filling the silence with an insectile hum echoing.

Thundersky and Venus both noticed at the same time the black heap at the bottom of the stairs. Venus swept her tac-one round, turning on the flashlight, its narrow beam settling on a mummified corpse slumped on the floor at the foot of the stairs. A USAF officer, his uniform rotting on his body. His skin had leathered, with the face partially rotted away around the chin where the jawbone was exposed. The eyelids were still there, closed and sunken into the empty craters of his eyes. The skull had been blown open at the cranium as a bullet had passed through his brain and exited, and there was a Glock pistol lying in the mummy's lap, the skeletonized fingers of the hand still curled round the butt, the index finger in the trigger guard.

The officer's last moments of anguish and despair seemed to linger around them, even now, half a millennium later. Whatever his last thoughts had been, he'd known it would have been a slow death topside, or quick death down here. Or had it been guilt for the family he left behind?

They all looked wordlessly at the mummy for a long moment as they came down the stairs.

Finally, they reached the main facility. The hover-spot illuminated another corridor, but there were rooms off of it left and right, and they checked each one. Storerooms and crew habitats.

They entered a mess room, where there were four tables pushed together in the middle with four chairs around them. There were four glasses, thick with dust and cobwebbed on the tabletop along with a dusty and cobwebbed bottle of whisky. Plates with blackened, practically fossilized remains of their last meal. Bones and blackened peas that looked like rat turds.

'Bovine bones,' Thundersky said. 'Back then, they ate meat like the Ferals,' he said,

They went back into the corridor, pushing the light ahead as they continued on.

At the end of the corridor, swing doors led into a large control room – And there it was, the Four-Eight-Zero, alive and humming, with lights flashing intermittently along its outer panels which ran from one end of the room to the other.

They had found the monster. Now they had to destroy it.

Chapter Forty-Six

The long cabinet of the Four-Eight-Zero stretched from one end of the control room to the other, and it stood from floor to ceiling, some twelve feet high by fifty feet long by ten feet deep.

'They put the fate of humanity in shit like this?' Tiger said. 'No wonder they blew themselves to hell. Could they even read and write?' he mocked contemptuously at the low-tech dinosaur in front of them.

There were huge dead viewers along a wall and two equally dead interfaces with four operator positions. On the other side of the room was a big glass window, opaque with centuries of grime and dust crusted to the glass.

'Can we get more light in here?' Thundersky asked, walking to the lifeless interfaces.

'Sure.' Venus took two more hover-spots from her kit, switched them on and released them, tapping one so it hovered over to the far side of the control room to the big window. The bright, glowing orb hung in the air seven feet from the ground. The other hung over the interfaces, where Tiger was taking the interfacer out of the hover-trunk. He set it down on one of the ancient control panels. A three-dimensional holographic interfacer/viewer projected from it in front of him in neon blue and red with icons and a

QWERTY sensor board. 'I'll try linking directly into the AI subroutines,' he said as he typed in commands and swiped an icon. "SCANNING" flashed up. 'It might take a while,' he added.

Inner Voice spoke again: 'Initiating Genesis Prime directive. Protocols initiated. Delta One restoring life support. Transferring command protocols. Warbirds detected at decimal Four-Three-point-zero-four-six nine-four-four by seven-six-point-one-four-four-four-three negative. Overriding primary commands. Powering down weapons. Delta One, ETA to terrestrial orbit one hour fifteen minutes.'

'General Bearfang,' Thundersky started up, 'Do a sensor sweep of decimal coordinates: Four-Three-point-zero-four-six nine-four-four by seven-six-point-one-four-four-four-three negative.'

Bearfang's voice came back, 'Running sensor sweep. Standby.'

Venus and the others turned curiously to Thundersky.

Bearfang spoke again: 'Sonofabitch! Sensors detect seven, I repeat, seven Silosian warbirds holding position over the ruins of old Syracuse.'

'You better inform the Prophetess that Arti is talking to me.'

'Copy,' Bearfang replied after a long pause of silence.

Venus stared at him a moment.

Thundersky looked at the others. 'We need to get this done.' He went to the Four-Eight-Zero and started to open the hinged metal panels.

'You're mindsurfing with Arti?' Tiger said.

'Not now. We don't have time,' Thundersky replied.

Behind the panels, the quantum matrices were in tall metal racks along narrow aisles stretching back ten feet. There were aluminum ladders on rails to allow access to the system boards above, and complicated looms of cables snaking over the tops of the racks, plugged into each one relaying power and processing data.

'Each one of these aisles is equivalent to a qubit board,' Thundersky remarked as he stepped into the computer. He broke a photocell beam and rows of inspection lights came on along every aisle for the first time in half a millennium. Thundersky was amazed they still worked. It looked daunting, there were hundreds of boards slotted into each rack. It was going to take hours to find which ones needed replacing.

'Oh my,' Tiger said, just as daunted.

Suddenly, a number of circuit drawers opened automatically. It was clear from looking at them that they had burned out.

They looked at one another, and wasting no time, they got to work, changing the boards and running bypasses.

In the control room, Venus wiped cobwebs and dust from a section of the window and pressed her face to the glass. Some of the light from the hover-spot filtered fitfully into what was some sort of office. Her eyes roved the dark, straining to make out the sharp angles of furniture and objects. Cabinets, chairs, a desk with a viewer screen on it – and what was that…!? She reeled back, 'Shit!' she gasped with a sharp intake of breath as she saw the outline of a human figure, sitting upright in the chair behind the desk, not moving and staring right back at her. Her heart raced with a surge of adrenalin.

'You okay?' Tiger called from inside the quantum computer.

'Yeah. I just found one of the others. So, how long's this going to take?' she asked, looking along the aisle at Thundersky.

'I don't know yet. Not long.'

She huffed.

'You want me to sing you a song?' Reaper said sarcastically.

'Yeah, sing the, "Let's get the hell outta here," song.'

Reaper chuckled.

'There are two more facilities like this,' Thundersky said as he pulled an ancient circuit board out to look at it. 'There might be data on their locations in the office.'

'With the dead guy?' Venus said slowly, a wariness in her voice.

'Yeah.'

Venus nodded reluctantly. She looked at Reaper. 'Come and give me a hand.'

The mummified corpse behind the desk glared silently at the intruders into his tomb from his chair through dark, empty eye sockets that seemed conscious of them. It gave Venus the creeps.

The desk was fastidiously tidy, and was exactly as the dead officer had left it. It reminded her of the Jeremiah O'Connor habitat, now a museum, where people went to see the great man's habitat exactly as he had left it the night he'd died, sealed behind Intsoglass and preserved for posterity. The stacks of Old-World books, his diaries, papers and personal effects, along with the chronicles and a copy of the Great Utopian Constitution, the foundation stone upon which the Utopian alliance was built.

There were neat stacks of vanilla folders in the office, thick with dust. Stamped in big red letters on one was: USAF. TOP SECRET. EYES ONLY. There was some sort of data-pad, not unlike the ones the scholars used. An empty glass was placed next to a whisky bottle on the desk, and a nickel-plated Colt .45 semi-automatic pistol in front of the mummy.

It was apparent the colonel hadn't shot himself. Poison possibly? Or maybe he had just sat there and died?

There was a faded picture in a wooden frame. Venus picked it up and cleaned the dust and grime from the glass. It was a family picture taken somewhere green and beautiful, featuring a woman of about thirty, and her husband, presumably the mummy in the chair, enjoying his time with two young children. She set it back down carefully exactly where she had picked it up, as if it were the most delicate object in the world, resting the frame along the clean outline in the dust.

Reaper looked curiously at her as he pulled the colonel away from the desk on his wheeled chair, surprised by how light it was. The colonel's skeletonized right leg detached and fell onto the floor as Reaper pulled the chair away, and it lay conspicuously in the well of the desk, the boot still on the foot, the laces rotted away.

Venus kicked it aside.

Reaper picked up the Colt and examined it. Even after five centuries, it was still pristine under the dust and, with some care and attention, he was sure he could get it working again. He tucked the gun into his belt.

'We didn't come here to scavenge,' Venus said.

'Nothing wrong with a bit of scavenge if you see something worth scaving. I could get good buckclench for that. I know people who collect these Old-World parabellums.'

They searched the desk drawers and looked at the files on the colonel's desk. But there was nothing obvious. The filing cabinets were just as useless.

Venus put the primitive data-pad into her kit bag.

Next, they turned to a big-ass safe in the corner. Locked of course, with two combination dials and a handle on the heavy reinforced steel door.

Reaper stared dauntingly at it.

'Well they didn't put that in here for show,' Venus said. 'Fetch the laser. We'll cut it open...'

As the last drawer in the 480 closed, the interfacer beeped and: "Systems Restored" appeared on the holographic viewer in glowing neon red. Data started scrolling.

Thundersky went back to the interfacer and typed on the holographic sensor board. 'Opening Automated Defense Platform, system abort procedure Dead Eagle. Uploading worm...' He looked at Venus and Reaper as they came out from the office, carrying their swag of ancient drives and data disks they'd found in the safe. 'Worm accepted. Overwriting initialization commands.'

It was a long and tense moment and they all stood in silence, tensely waiting for the computer to confirm or deny the override to abort its launch command.

'What happens if it doesn't accept the new software?' Reaper finally asked.

'Thermonuclear apocalypse,' Tiger said without looking round at him.

Venus and Reaper looked at one another.

They stared at the data feed on the interfacer, anxiously waiting for something to happen. But nothing happened, the data was unchanging.

Venus drew in a deep, worried breath and held it. She could hear her heart racing; the tension was palpable between them all. And then, the data on the viewer disappeared and new data started to appear:

"Automated Defense Platform. Abort procedure activated. Do you wish to continue?"

There was a collective sigh of relief in the room.

'Yes,' Thundersky said before pressing the "CONTINUE" option.

The holo-viewer changed again:

"Authorization codes accepted. This may take several minutes. Initiating DEAD EAGLE. ABORT, ABORT, ABORT."

They all looked at one another in the tense moments as the viewer displayed a progress chart in neon green: 1%…. 5%…. 8%….

Thundersky looked at them and smiled. 'It's working.'

The relief was indescribable, and in a moment of spontaneity, they all started cheering, high-fiving and laughing as the tension vented out of them. They laughed, gasped and embraced one another.

They could hear Bearfang, Vixen and Ghostmaker through their comms laughing and applauding and cheering in the M-TAV.

They had saved the world from the mushrooms, and now they had to save themselves from the Triple S.

Inner Voice spoke again. 'Delta One initiating magnetoplasmadynamic breaking thrusters. Positioning for terrestrial entry. Stealth systems engaged.' Inner voice fell silent.

Thundersky looked at the others.

The holo-viewer display changed to: "All systems, abort, abort, abort. Authority Dead Eagle One. Priority one, initiate silo shutdown. Shutdown procedure initiated. Command accepted, silos powering down, reset condition: Blue, blue, blue, blue. Alert status. Defcon Five. Four-Eight-Zero shutdown initiated…'

The Four-Eight-Zero quantum system fell silent.

'Shutdown complete. All systems are offline,' Tiger confirmed from the data pad.

Venus looked at Reaper. 'I think it's time to set the charges and sing the, "Let's get the hell out of here," song,' she said.

Chapter Forty-Seven

Sub City, Silosia

'What's wrong?' Zim asked urgently, watching the Delta's trajectory data displaying on the main viewer. 'Why hasn't it taken up GSO over New York? Why hasn't it armed its primary weapon?'

Moon shook his head worriedly, frantically trying to find a malfunction in the Delta's systems. 'I don't know, sir…' He looked at Zim. 'It looks like it's on a re-entry course.'

'Well stop it!' Zim barked.

Moon shook his head, the color draining from his face. 'I can't. It's overriding all of my commands. We've been locked out.'

Zim stomped furiously towards Moon's interface. *'What're you mean, we're locked out*!?'

Moon winced in fear. There was no other way of putting it. 'It won't let me access any of its systems. It's treating us as hostile, sir,' he explained, finally turning timidly to look at Zim, whose face was almost mauve, his eyes practically popping out of their sockets. 'What about our warbirds over Syracuse?'

'We still have full control, sir.'

'So, who's controlling the Delta?'

Moon shook his head vaguely. 'I don't think anybody is, Grand Inquisitor. It's making its own decisions. The only thing I can think of is that the autonomous AI has been corrupted.'

'Can you fix it?'

Moon shrugged his shoulders. 'I don't know. I could try sending a worm to rewrite the software.'

'Then do it. Just fix it! And send in the warbirds to take up positions.' He looked round at Dead Eyes, who had just entered the lab. 'Have you been able to contact Lionheart yet?'

'Still nothing.'

The comms opened from the Tactical Command, Mission Control and General Coldriver Appleby's face filled the viewer, looking far from happy. 'Why are my sensors telling me that that goddam Widow's on course to enter terrestrial atmosphere!? You better have a goddam good reason, because if I can see it, you can bet your dickbutt ass the Orry-Washes can fucking see it.'

If there was one person who posed a threat to Zim, it was Appleby, who ultimately bore responsibility and complete command of all military assets, human or technological, and that included mothballed extraterrestrial assets.

'We're trying to get to the bottom of it as we speak, General,' he said with calm mendacity. 'It seems Triple S security systems have been compromised by the Prophetess,' he added.

Appleby gave him a long suspicious stare from the Intsoglass wall. 'Then I suggest that you hurry up and get to the bottom of it and send that Widow back to where it belongs. Its primary weapons are offline, but we're detecting the activation of secondary weapons systems, which seemed to be locked on a squadron of Triple S warbirds over the Catty Mountains wilderness. I assume they're there to provide aircover for the mission?'

Zim gave him a fake smile. 'Of course. Why else would they be there, General?' He sensed his plan was starting to unravel. He glanced at Dead Eyes.

'Just sort it out, Zim, or the military will.' Appleby terminated the com.

Chapter Forty-Eight

Foley Square, New York City

Bearfang was the first to feel the slight tremor in the ground, vibrating through the deck plates. It grew in strength and they all noticed it, there was a deep rumble like an endless clap of thunder rolling out of the distance, getting closer – getting louder. Vixen looked at the sensors, registering seismic tremors but nothing else. 'That's no quake…' She opened the roof hatch and climbed up onto the roof. The thunderous pulse of gravity drives boomed across the ruins, moving steadily towards them from Lower Manhattan.

Vixen, Viper and Ghostmaker all came up onto the roof as the huge, black Delta moved in overland from the sea, lumbering slowly over the obliterated city skyline, casting its big black shadow before it like a death shroud, moving towards Foley Square. Its powerful gravity drives made the air tremble and loose debris and cladding fell from buildings as it passed over them.

They looked in awe at the mechanical monster, blotting out the sky, like a huge black bat hovering stationary a thousand feet above them. The powerful gravity drives pulsed. They could feel the energy and static, which made their hair bristle up.

'I've never seen anything like it,' Bearfang gasped.

Venus, Reaper, Tiger and Thundersky came out from the courthouse and stopped dead in shock when they beheld the Black Widow, gawping in disbelief.

'What the fuck is that!?' Reaper murmured.

'That is a Black Widow interplanetary warship and it has no business being on earth,' Venus said. 'And I never thought I'd ever see one up close.'

'What's it doing here?' Tiger asked.

'It's here to kill us,' Thundersky replied. 'Why else would it be here?'

They looked worriedly at him, then looked at the M-TAV and the others up on the roof.

'What countermeasures can we take?' Tiger was looking at Venus.

'Apart from kissing your ass goodbye, I can't think of a single one. Two of those things destroyed the Oregon-Washington's entire battle fleet in less than an hour. It that thing is fixing to kill us, then there's nothing we can do. Except try and get back to the sea and submerge. Those old sensors are useless underwater, so it'll have to rely on sonar. We go deep and we sit there. That's the best I've got.'

Bearfang and the others climbed down into the M-TAV as the Silosians hurried back from the courthouse.

Venus jumped into the cockpit and engaged the power to the drive, but nothing happened. The drive was dead. She tried again and again, but still nothing happened. She checked the system data, which indicated that all systems were working normally. 'It won't start,' she declared. 'It's the Widow. It's knocked out our systems…!'

'We've lost communications with the Prophetess, too,' Bearfang said from the interface in the C and C.

'Heat plumes detected,' Vixen said. 'Seven warbirds, heading this way from the Catties, flying supersonic. ETA, six minutes.'

Bearfang called out. 'Get us the hell out of here, Venus!'

'I can't. Everything's dead!' she called back. 'We're being jammed.'

'Weapons are offline,' Tiger said from tactical.

Bearfang's eyes were glowing. 'I'm not just going to sit back and wait for them destroy us without a fight!'

'Why hasn't it clocked us off?' Ghostmaker asked reasonably.

'I d'know!' said Vixen. 'Go and ask it, shall we?' she said with angry sarcasm.

'ETA of the warbirds, four minutes,' Vixen announced from the sensors.

'It must be waiting for the warbirds,' Venus said as she came into the C and C. 'Take only what you can carry. Our best chance is to split up. That way, at least one or two of us will survive. Bearfang, Reaper, you'll get Thundersky back to your people. Whatever happens, Thundersky must survive. Tiger, you and Vixen come with me...' She looked at Ghostmaker.

'Yeah, we know it, pretty lady,' he said, checking his weapon.

She pressed the button to open the doors so they could abandon the rig, but they refused to open. They had all been overridden by the Widow, whose invisible hand had reached in and taken control of the M-TAV's systems.

Bearfang tried opening the roof hatches, but they too were unresponsive. 'We're babbledicked.'

Thundersky seemed strangely calm while the others went through the rig frantically, looking for a way out. Apparently resigned to his fate.

Only the external viewer feeds were working, the Widow in the main viewer taunting them with the promise of death.

Finally, a dreadful silence fell between them as all hope of getting out of the M-TAV diminished.

'We can't just sit here!' Bearfang ranted.

Seven sleek black deltoid warbirds came in low and positioned themselves at less than a hundred feet altitude in the square beneath the Black Widow. Like the Widow, they hovered in position, their wing mounted thunderclap missiles locked on the M-TAV.

'Why don't they fire?' Bearfang said. 'What're they waiting for?'

'Orders from Silosia,' Tiger suggested.

They looked at one another.

'No. Not from Silosia,' Thundersky said.

They stared at him.

'I think they're waiting for orders from me,' he said, not knowing how he knew, but like so many other things, he just did. He knew it the first time Inner Voice had mentioned the Delta Black Widows. Now he was absolutely certain of it. 'Power down your weapons,' Thundersky said aloud.

Inner Voice returned: 'Confirmed. Powering down weapons.'

They all looked at him.

Vixen checked her sensors. 'The Black Widow and warbirds have taken their weapons offline.'

'Delta One standing by,' Inner Voice said.

'Communications restored,' Vixen said.

'Corporal Venus, contact the Prophetess,' Thundersky instructed. 'Tell her not to fire on the Silosian warbirds or the Black Widow, but to hold her position. I'm going aboard.' Thundersky announced.

They stared at him.

'Are you insane?' Bearfang exclaimed.

'Arti's talking to him,' Tiger said, looking at Venus.

'Either that, or he's gone crazynuts.'

Reaper stepped forwards. 'I'm coming with you,' he insisted, grabbing his tac-one. 'Where you go. I go.' He was Thundersky's sworn protector now.

Outside, the sea was washing up against the M-TAV's wheels, and it was above their knees when they climbed down into the freezing Atlantic water. Bearfang and Ghostmaker went with them.

'This is goddam crazynuts,' Bearfang said, wading alongside Thundersky. 'I should have my brain re-tweaked for listening to you…' He combed his fingers through his hair. He stared up at the Black Widow, the warbirds as small as flies alongside it. 'And just how are we going to get aboard, eh? Have you thought of that?'

There was no underestimating the Black Widow's awesome power. They were the most powerful machines of war ever created in the history of humankind, with weapons capable of destroying a planet.

They waded out into the square, coming as close as they dared to the gravity field. They could feel the gravity differentials pulling against them.

'If I'm right, it's going to send a drone down to pick us up.'

Just as he spoke, Reaper pointed up at the launch bay doors opening. 'Look…'

A shuttle drone emerged from the opening. It looked small in the big, oblong cavity of the launch bay as it floated out.

Bearfang gave Thundersky a look. 'You really are talking to that thing, ain't you?'

Thundersky looked back at him. 'I don't know. At least, I think it's talking to me. But it's like thoughts, not like…' He stopped himself. 'Not like a voice. Thoughts. I can't explain it, General.'

They watched the shuttle slowly descending vertically until it was an inch above the surface of the water, ten feet away from them. The hatch slid open and several steps telescoped out from beneath, the bottom two rungs disappearing into the water.

As they gingerly stepped inside, they saw that there was seating for ten passengers in the shuttle, a cockpit seat and controls for manual flight, and a twin inner and outer airlock hatchway system for extraterrestrial docking.

The inner and outer hatches closed simultaneously and the steps retracted as the shuttle started its vertical ascent.

Bearfang checked the load in his tac-one. 'Just in case,' he said, looking at Thundersky.

Reaper looked out across the sprawling ruins of New York. Two huge limestone and granite towers rose up from the water. They were all that remained of a once prominent cable-stayed suspension bridge that had crossed the East River. The late afternoon sunshine glimmered through its tall gothic arches.

The shuttle entered into the cavernous flight deck, maneuvering along a line of nine Raptor interceptors lining the port side, clamped to the deck by their landing struts.

'Oh my,' Reaper murmured. 'Look at those lovely warbirds...'

Thundersky and Bearfang stood up, leaned to the porthole and looked out at them. Each interceptor was armed with lasers and wing mounted torpedo pylons.

The shuttle landed perfectly on its assigned pad between large, bright yellow deck clamps that came up and grabbed the landing struts like giant metal claws as the shuttle touched down, locking the shuttle to the deck with a loud metallic clunk.

The hatches opened, the steps descended to the deck and they climbed out. They stood on the enormous flight deck for a moment. They could hardly hear the gravity drives, but could feel them vibrating through the deck.

Bearfang walked over to the Raptors, as black and shiny as the Widow. He reached up and ran his hand along the fuselage of one of them, smiling. 'Can you control these, Thundersky?' his husky voice echoed across the deck.

'Yes. I think so.'

Bearfang beamed. 'I wonder what else is aboard this beauty?'

An elevator door opened behind them and they turned startled to it, bringing their weapons to bear, but there was nobody there, just the empty elevator car.

'I think that's for us,' Thundersky said.

They cautiously entered the elevator. The doors closed and the elevator ascended several decks, to deck #11. According to the notice signs glowing from small panels beside the hatchways, it was left to the bridge and right to the officers' living quarters for crewed flight.

Thundersky and Bearfang looked at one another as they entered the bridge, which was equipped for manual flight and six bridge officers – Pilot, copilot, navigations officer, weapons and tactical officer and communications and censors' officer and a central command chair for the commanding officer with overhead interfaces and viewers. The systems were controlled through a central quantum neuronet AI – itself networked to the main operations computer in its home base at Lunar Nine and Arti in Sub City.

All the viewers and monitoring systems were online, constantly displaying data. Over the tactical and weapons interface, a schematic of the ship indicated which weapons were online.

Long range sensors were monitoring Silosia, Oregon-Washington and Utopian colonies across the continent and Europe via satellites.

'Computer. Open a com link with visuals to the M-TAV. And deactivate all Silosian satellites in range of this location,' Thundersky said.

'Com link open.'

Venus, Tiger and Vixen appeared on a viewer.

'Are you seeing us?' Bearfang said.

'Yeah,' Venus replied. 'We see you.'

'We're getting you five by five,' came the Prophetess's voice, her face suddenly appearing on one of the other viewers above the communications and sensors interface.

'We're talking to the goddam computer,' Bearfang said.

'… Three satellites deactivated,' the computer announced.

'Computer. Open a secure com to Grand High Scholar Blackstone Washington, Sub City,' Thundersky ordered.

'Unable to comply. Grand High Scholar Blackstone Washington has been terminated sixty-nine hours and twenty-one minutes ago.'

An explosion of horror registered on Thundersky's face.

'Dad!' Tiger gasped urgently over the com from the M-TAV, his anguished voice filling the bridge.

'Computer. Explain?'

'Grand High Scholar Blackstone Washington was executed by order of the Grand High Council for treason by conspiring with the Virginia Dusteater faction. Visual data available.'

Tiger cried out with grief from the M-TAV.

'Play visual data.'

Back in old Queens, the Prophetess stood at the viewer in her trailer, silently watching the covert security visuals recorded by Arti, who seemed to be running its own covert operation against its masters.

She made no effort to hide her horror, when she watched Zim Steven and his pet murder Blackstone Washington. She stared intensely at Dead Eyes as he shot Blackstone Washington with his laser. She shifted as Blackstone fell dead and the chair slalomed across the lab, clattering in the silence.

The viewer went blank for a moment, and then it returned to a view of the Black Widow's bridge, and Bearfang, Thundersky and Reaper all looking shocked.

They could hear Tiger sobbing over the com, and Venus' voice comforting him.

'Computer. What's the status and location of Medical High Scholar Blossom Flora?' they heard Thundersky ask.

'Medical High Scholar Blossom Flora has left Silo City. Her location is unknown.'

'Is she still alive?'

'Medical High Scholar Blossom Flora's bio status is unknown.'

'She's gone to ground,' the Prophetess said. 'Probably to our friends in Surfer Town.'

Thundersky looked into the viewer, where he could see his mother.

'So now we attack Silo City?' Bearfang said.

Thundersky shook his head. 'First, we're going to the moon.'

The Reverend called out at the top of his voice to the Black Widow, which landed in an ancient airport where the ground was flat and stable: '…Behold, the Lord has cometh as a wolf among lambs and he shall smite the enemy and lay him low in Satan's fires. Behold, the Angel of Death…'

'Does that crazynuts Godder ever quit his preachin'?' Venus gasped in despair as they disembarked from the M-TAV.

The Prophetess joined them as they waded through the long grass towards the Widow. Behind her, rusted Old-World aircraft littered the site, and the airport buildings had almost completely collapsed.

Above, the seven warbirds patrolled the skies in a defensive pattern.

Bearfang and Reaper appeared on the gantry of a stairway that telescoped out from the fuselage from an open hatch amidships. They were waiting for the Prophetess to come aboard, which she did, accompanied by Venus, Tiger, Vixen, Ghostmaker, the Reverend and Viper.

Bearfang and Reaper escorted them up onto the Bridge, where Thundersky was sat at the main system interface studying the ship's schematics and weapons systems. He hardly glanced around at them when they came onto the bridge. 'We have to go to Lunar Seven,' he said without preamble. 'The system there is vulnerable to a Silosian hack. We need to secure the base and update the Trojan Five outer system,' he said as he read the scrolling data, reading every line, learning as much as he could. 'We're going to need volunteers willing to stay up there to maintain the facility. At least twenty techs and some fighters.' He looked evenly at her. 'If we want to keep control of this Delta and those warbirds, it's our only option.'

The Prophetess nodded her head. 'Prep the ship ready to take off,' she said before turning to Bearfang. 'We need those volunteers.'

Bearfang glared incredulously at her. 'You're going with them?'

Venus was like a kidling with a new toy when she looked at the bridge and the pilot controls.

'Think you can fly it?' Thundersky asked.

'The AI flies it.'

'We can save time if we take it up manually.'

'The flight controls are similar to an Astrium freighter. I trained on a freighter,' she explained. 'There are some tactical and navigational systems I'm not familiar with yet, but if you want me to fly this bird to the moon, then yes, I can do that.'

'Good. The job's yours,' Bearfang said.

They all buckled themselves into the seats on the bridge. A message came up from below that the passengers were buckled in and secure for liftoff.

Venus climbed into the pilot's seat and buckled up, quickly familiarizing herself with the controls and layout. She pressed three illuminated buttons overhead. 'Switching to manual control.' She typed onto a touchscreen viewer at her side. 'Coordinates set for Lunar Seven. All systems optimal. Nav-conn AI disengaged. Standby,' she said as the joystick extended from the arm of her seat. She grabbed it and pressed several sensors. 'Engaging gravity drives.'

The gravity drives started to whirr and rumble as they came online. 'Gravity harmonics in ten seconds,' she announced as the drives increased their power, gradually harmonizing into a single throbbing beat. 'Three times terrestrial gravity...' She watched the systems monitors. 'Standby for liftoff in ... Five ... four ... three ... two...' She tapped several sensor buttons and pulled back on the joystick, reaching for the power booster control with her left hand, drawing them back as she eased back on the joystick and they started to rise from the ground.

As soon as they lifted off, the Delta started tilting its nose upwards, the throbbing roar of the grav-drives growing louder and louder, vibrating throughout the ship as Venus built up the energy.

'Exceeding five times terrestrial gravity. Twenty-thousand feet,' Venus said over the noise of the roaring centrifuges of the gravity drives, her eyes fixed on her interfaces, reading from the instrument panels. 'Full power achieved. Initiating gravity bubble...' She pressed a sensor and the ship juddered. 'Stable bubble confirmed. Standby for gravity jump.'

Thundersky grabbed the armrests of the copilot's seat he was harnessed into as the Delta nosed up for a vertical climb...

'Jump on my mark…'

Thundersky and Reaper looked at one another across the bridge, Reaper's nervous eyes seeking reassurance.

'… five … four … three … two…'

In an instant they shot up towards the stratosphere, and even within the dampening field of the Delta's gravity bubble, they felt the G forces pressing against them as they ripped through the atmosphere at twenty thousand miles per hour, their faces rippling. Thundersky felt as if he had an elephant sitting on his chest.

'Escape velocity achieved,' Venus said breathlessly, continuing to read from the instrument panel.

Thundersky stared fixedly at the main viewer, watching the sun glimmer and skim the atmosphere as the inky black of space opened up before them.

The G-forces lessened as the Earth fell away behind them. They broke free, shooting out into the vacuum of space, where the gravity drives came into their own, forming gravitational waves that propelled them at a steady fifteen thousand miles per hour.

'Switching control to nav-conn,' Venus said, pressing the same three overhead buttons as before, and the joystick retracted. The look on Venus's face was pure joy. For her, this was the achievement of her dreams, to pilot an interplanetary warship. The warships these days were a third of the size of the Black Widow, restricted in size and armaments in compliance with the non-proliferation treaty.

'Inboard gravity at ninety four percent terrestrial and stable,' Tiger informed them, reading the data from the system control interface at the back of the bridge. 'Everything's going to seem a little lighter.'

'All systems secure,' Reaper said.

'Okay. Find some quarters and get some sleep. Bearfang, you and Venus Jane have the first watch,' the Prophetess said. 'Bearfang, make sure the others are settled in.' She looked at a viewer that was monitoring the volunteers five decks below in a passenger lounge, unbuckling their safety harnesses and moving about the deck.

PART THREE
Utopia must Fall

Chapter Fifty

Research & Astrium Refinery, Tranquillitatis

'Eh, Vernon. That Delta's coming back,' Blackdog said, watching the sensor displays in front of him. 'Looks like it's heading back to Lunar Seven. Strange, eh?'

Vernon came over and stood behind him and leaned over his shoulder, resting his hand on the back of Blackdog's chair as he watched the viewer.

'What're you think?'

Vernon creased his chin and shook his head. 'I d'know. They said they had it under control and it looks like they have. Probably a maintenance check, or a demonstration to remind the Orry-Washes who's got all the muscle. Now, never mind about that. Have we got comms restored yet?'

'No. I can't seem to isolate the problem either. I'm running a diagnostic on the subsystems. It'll be an hour before it's finished. I can launch a comms relay buoy?'

'How long have comms been down now?'

'An hour and ten minutes.'

Vernon thought about it as he watched the sensor tracking the Delta's course. 'No. That's for emergencies only. This isn't an emergency yet.

Twenty-four hours. That's an emergency. If necessary, we'll have to go up to the satellite and fix it ourselves.'

Blackdog sat back in his seat and reached for his mug of cold syntho coffee.

A voice filtered out of the com, shouting over the din of heavy machinery. '…You there, Vernon?'

'Yeah, yeah. What is it, Gecko?'

'That turbine on sixteen's overheating again. I'm gonna have to shut 'em all down and get in there to take a look.'

Just when Vernon thought his day couldn't get any worse. 'Shut them *all* down?' he exclaimed in alarm. 'How long for?'

'Until I can get in there and take a look and see what's wrong. Could be hours… could be days. It depends what we find.'

Days! The prospect filled him with dread. 'But why d'you need to shut them all off? D'you have any idea how far that'll push us beyond schedule? We'd never make up our quotas. And we've got three mine freighters coming in over the next six days.'

'Sorry, Vernon, but if one shuts down, they all have to shut down. They're like a choir, they all have to sing together or not at all. You'll have to com Mission and tell 'em what's going on.'

Vernon rolled his eyes. 'The goddam comms are down again. I'm coming down.' He turned and headed out of the control room for the elevator mast. 'Like I don't have enough to do around here...' At the elevator mast, one of a dozen throughout the four-square mile modular complex, he stepped into the cylindrical elevator car. 'Level One, Skywalk Four,' he instructed, and the elevator descended three levels to Level One and rotated forty-five degrees to Skywalk Four...

The door slid open onto a long, transparent Intsoglass skywalk that bridged the featureless gray Lunar desert for a hundred yards to the next module. On the bulkhead, a sign read: "L. I. Skywalk IV, Rover dock, connecting to L I Cargo Docking & Skywalks V, VI, VII & Refinery."

The skywalk bridged over the freighter docking ports seventy feet below. Beyond, the featureless Mare Tranquillitatis stretched off, empty and unadorned except for the distant craters. The bleak horizon was vividly defined against the vacuous blackness of space, with the beautiful marbled earth hanging alluringly like a cosmic jewel.

Vernon walked briskly across the skywalk, fretful over the prospect of falling behind schedule. In the two years since taking over, he had maintained a perfect record, so this would be a blemish he could do without, especially now he was coming to the end of his assignment. They had just six months more before the swap over, and then it was back to Earth for a year of babbledicking to the Novies and taking it easy before going to Mars. With a blemish on his so far perfect record, it might have meant a mission demotion to second supervisor of some shithole gas pumping and pipeline maintenance station in the icy Planum Boreum at the Martian North Pole. There, oxygen was mined with other essential gases from the ice and pumped to the biosphere purifiers in the Valles Marineris, which were rich in Martianite, the diamond-like crystals used in high energy lasers. He was hoping to get a First Grade Supervisor's epaulet, for assignment as supervisor of the mines. But if this last consignment of Astrium was late, then he could kiss that ambition goodbye…

———

Sunlight flashed in from the Widow's fuselage as it banked in towards the Aitken Crater basin at the Lunar south pole, crossing the mountainous crater rim. They began a slow descent into the crater's several mile deep basin and moved over its dark, lifeless plain which stretched for sixteen hundred miles across. They could see every dark, gray mile of it, ringed by the sawtooth crater rim seven miles high.

'What's that?' Bearfang asked as some modular structures came into view.

'One of the early titanium mines,' the Prophetess explained. 'Nothing's been mined here for over two centuries, when the military took it over to build Lunar Seven.'

'There's several of them in the crater according to the ship's archive,' Thundersky said.

'There are rich deposits of titanium here,' the Prophetess said. 'The richest on the moon. There's a couple of thorium mines too. They used thorium reactors up here in the early days.'

Venus pointed to a distant pinhead of light stellating out of the side of the crater rim about six hundred miles from their position. 'There it is. Lunar Seven.' She looked at Bearfang, who stood beside her.

The light grew bigger as the mighty Black Widow flew silently across the crater, casting its deathly shadow before it.

The facility's outer wall was built into the side of the crater's northern rim, about four miles up from the crater basin into a sheer cliff. Enormous titanium airlock doors, ten feet thick and several thousand feet wide by about two thousand feet high, started to slowly slide open on Elmags as the Black Widow slowly banked towards them, firing forward magnetoplasmadynamic breaking thrusters, sending blue jets of ionized plasma blasting from the forward thruster ports, slowing the Widow to just a few miles an hour.

'Computer, activate Lunar Seven life support systems and artificial gravity generators,' the Prophetess said.

'Life support systems activated,' the computer responded. 'Zone One Airlocks will disengage in one hour forty-one minutes.'

'Once the gravity activates, the refinery, observatories and mining operations on this rock, and Tactical Command on the dark side will know we're here,' the Prophetess said. 'We need to move fast to bring the defenses online.'

They watched in silence as they drew nearer. Breaking and steering thrusters fired alternately from the monster's fuselage, slowing and steering the ship towards the outer airlock. Telemetry, speed, elevation data and charts were animating on the viewers.

The Widow slowly drifted into the docking bay, where a row of seven more mighty deltoid Black

Widow predators were nesting like the mythical Furies at their docking stations, connected to the airlocks by umbilical walkways, their fuselages cradled by huge titanium stanchions rising out of the lunar rock.

The outer airlock slid closed behind them as the Black Widow maneuvered towards the only unoccupied docking bay, moving precisely into position millimeter by millimeter, the thrusters firing for milliseconds at a time.

The umbilicus extended from the facility's airlock towards the ship's airlock at the nose end, three decks below the bridge. They joined together and the widow came to a full stop.

'Umbilical secured,' Venus said. 'Docking struts engaged and secure, all propulsion systems powering down.'

'Computer. How many personnel are at the Tranquillitatis station?' the Prophetess asked.

'Accessing. Data acquired. Six technicians, two senior engineers. One shuttle pilot, one Lunar geologist, two astrophysicists, one medivac and one supervisor.'

The prophetess turned to the interface and viewer. 'Display personnel data. Start with the administrator…'

Senior Tech Littlebird Florence was about the best thing on Tranquillitatis, with the possible exception of Sweetwater. But she was a little young for Blackdog's tastes, whereas Littlebird was a more mature thirty-seven, and all the lines were trim and well maintained. She had artificial breasts, but one wouldn't have known, a fact to which Blackdog could happily attest. They had been doing the sex thing almost since the day their tour had started three months ago. It was just dick-tickling, nothing serious, no romance, just a stress busting fuck one or twice a week in the AG generator, where they could float about in near zero-g. There was nothing like it, having sex in zero gravity.

Littlebird was at her interface behind Blackdog, doing the morning safety and station integrity checks. Vernon was in his office, talking on his com to Mission.

'What's got him all uppity?' Littlebird asked. Vernon had been even more of a dickbutt than usual the past day or two.

'Haven't you heard? They're sending a unity of tacticals up. We've got to accommodate them.'

'Tacticals?' She turned and looked at him. 'Why?'

Blackdog shrugged his shoulders. 'My guess is that it's got something to do with that Widow that flew out of Seven the other day. Something's gone crazynuts over there…'

She nodded her head. There was clearly something going on at Lunar Seven. Her guess was that the system was accidentally started by some dickbutt at Tactical Command and now they couldn't shut the damn thing down. 'What do they expect from two-hundred-year-old tech?' she said.

Vernon came out of his office, his face like thunder. 'What's happened to the com? One second I'm talkin' to my wife, the next everything goes offline…'

Blackdog turned to the comms interface. The viewer read "COMS ERROR, SAT. G-3 RELAY NOT RESPONDING."

'It's that goddam relay on G-Three.'

'The goddam place is falling apart,' Vernon said. 'Can we fix it like you did before?'

'Not without finding out what's wrong with it. We may have to go up there and change the boards, or use a com buoy.' Blackdog slid his chair along to the main computer. 'Arti, run a full systems diagnostic on the comms relay and transmitters on Satellite G-Three.'

'… Tacticals. You can bet your ass on it,' Blackdog said as he typed. 'Them of Triple S.'

Arti's voice suddenly announced: 'Gravitational surge detected. South-Pole Aitken Crater, northern rim…'

Blackdog turned to the sensor data to double check. '…Life-support systems initiated,' he said. 'Artificial gravity field activated…' He looked at Vernon and Littlebird. 'What the hell's going on?'

Chapter Fifty-Two

Lunar-Seven

It was hard to grasp the size of the installation, entirely constructed inside the mountainous crater rim by an army of construction robots. There were corridors that stretched for several kilometers. There was even a magrail network and extensive elevator system.

'It's easy to get lost in here,' the Prophetess said. 'Stay together, and keep your comms on at all times.'

There were ninety levels in the facility and they were on Level #6, the C and C being on level #80. Bearfang ordered about half of his fighters to stay with the ship. They were startled by a loud boom that reverberated along the corridor like a thunderclap, making them jounce with fright.

'*What was that*?' Tiger exclaimed, feeling jittery and guarded, as if they had awoken dark forces.

'An airlock,' Venus said. 'As the life support's restored, the airlocks will open section by section. The primary zones are restored first, starting with the C and C,' she said, and looked into their curious faces. 'Every zone has to be self-contained with independent life support, in case of an outer breach,' she explained.

'Very interesting,' Tiger said disinterestedly.

They started along one of the corridors, off of which sprawled other corridors and sealed airlock doors, and signs that indicated what was behind them. Ordnance production, tech labs 11 - 20, Janitorial, storage rooms 5 - 10, living quarters 10 - 60.

'Think the elevators might still work?' Reaper said hopefully.

'Not a chance,' Bearfang said.

Ghostmaker was following fifty feet back with five Dusty tech scholars and half a dozen fighters they had brought with them, moving cautiously, their weapons locked and loaded, checking every corner, wary that they might be walking into a Silosian trap. Only the Prophetess and Thundersky seemed completely confident that they were the only ones here.

They found "Stairwell #21," lit with red emergency lights, ascending eighty-four stories. They gave them a daunting look.

The ghostly bangs of more airlocks opening echoed down the stairwell. They began their long, exhausting, seventy-four story ascent through the gloomy red glow of emergency lights.

The C and C was dimly lit and surprisingly compact given that it was the nerve center of the city-sized facility, where over two thousand people once lived and worked.

The Prophetess and one of the Dusty scholars checked the thorium reactor maintenance system, studying the readings displaying on the viewers.

Thundersky went to the main computer interface and started typing onto the touchscreens in front of him... 'Okay, Arti. I'm in the matrix,' Thundersky said quietly to himself. Almost as soon as he spoke, a message flashed on a viewer: "Access granted.

Initiating upload. New protocols accepted. Uploading. Time remaining 57 minutes." 'Arti's upgrading the security protocols. In less than an hour, we'll be in complete control of Lunar Seven.'

'We're a superpower,' Reaper said, beaming brightly.

'Let's not get ahead of ourselves,' the Prophetess said and looked at Tiger and Venus, who were at the tactical interface. 'How long before you can bring the defense array online, gentlemen?'

'Almost there,' Tiger said, typing quickly, reading the directories as they scrolled up the viewer. 'Five minutes.'

'All Widows are operational,' Venus said, standing at the interface next to Tiger.

'We need to get control of those satellites ASAP,' she said.

'Working on it,' said Vixen from another interface. 'I've hacked into Tranquillitatis to get the override codes. It looks like they're attempting to repair their comms satellite.'

'Once they realize its babbledicked, they'll probably launch a comms buoy,' Bearfang said.

'Way ahead of you, General,' Vixen said. 'I've given 'em a virus. The only thing they'll be transmitting is static.'

The tactical interfaces lit up and beeped as they came online and the AI said: 'Defense array activated.'

'All weapons are online,' Tiger announced.

The Dusty techs started to bring the thorium reactor up to full capacity.

'This place must have a lot of useful scavenge,' Reaper said. 'We should load up the Delta and take as much back with us as we can. Do all the Deltas have M-TAVs and portable weapons aboard?'

'Probably,' Thundersky said.

'I want to look at the bio-tech labs,' the Prophetess said.

Thundersky brought a map of the facility up onto a viewer. 'It looks like the labs are on levels fifty and fifty-one,' he said.

Tiger pressed a button on an interface and the wall in front of them started to slide away, revealing an enormous clear Intsoglass wall, and beyond was a breathtaking vista of the vast Aitken crater, encircled by its ring of mountains, casting long shadows as the sun sloped over their peaks. Alien and lifeless, yet breathtakingly beautiful, unchanged for billions of years.

Chapter Fifty-Three

The scholars looked out the windows at the ancient impact ejecta strewn across the Lunar surface, scattered for miles beyond the northern rim, boulders as big as buildings strewn like tossed pebbles that had sat there unmoved and unaltered by weather or corrosion for hundreds of millions of years. Nothing changed on this colorless and vacuous rock. Here, everything was eternal and unaltering.

Hazelwood looked daunted as she gazed out the window, her wide, mad-looking eyes glaring down disconcertedly as the rocky, uneven surface rushed past them with dangerous flirtation just a few feet below.

'The lower we are, the faster we go. If I climb to the fifty ceiling, it'll reduce our speed by seventy-five percent. Don't worry, Hazel. I'll get us there in one piece.'

Huh. Famous last words, Hazelwood thought, turning her face haughtily to the side window again, respectfully considering those sharp, jagged ridges of solidified magma and ejecta, like razor teeth waiting to chew them up.

They started their climb up the crater rim, following the contours of the dark, scraggly cliffs and crevices a mile deep, sloping near vertically to the dark peaks several miles above. They were barely six feet from the surface, touching two hundred and sixty knots.

They flew through a twisting valley two miles deep between black peaks, the scanners animating on the navigation viewer, showing the terrain ahead of them to the exact millimeter, every twist and turn mapped.

Once on the other side, the crater sprawled before them several miles below. The basin was pocked with other, smaller impact craters, distant mine workings and bio-habitats that looked like like little villages. They dived down into the crater's yawning expanse, the hover-rover flying fast and nimble like an insect, chicaning and weaving between canyons of petrified magma and hills of fine dust. They plunged vertically down precipitous cliffs of lunar bedrock, which had been blasted up from the moon's crust when it had been impacted by the asteroid that made the crater hundreds of millions of years ago.

The scholars sat tense, their faces fixed in rictus, glaring unblinkingly at the crater basin growing ever nearer as they plunged down, the mountains rushing past them in a coal-black blur. The basin grew closer and closer, less than five hundred yards, and it was all they could see in front of them, like a wall of granite heading unstoppably towards them.

Hazelwood glanced quickly at Sweetwater, who was grinning stupidly like a fearless teenager.

Dragonfoot felt nauseous and clenched his eyes tightly shut, expecting an impact even though he knew there would be none.

Then, a hundred feet from smashing into the basin, the forward booster jet fired and they slowed. Fifty feet away, the hover-rover pulled away from the crater wall and levelled onto the horizontal plane and sped off over the crater basin, flying just ten feet above the surface.

There was a collective sigh of relief.

'You crazynuts maniac!' Dragonfoot gasped as he opened his eyes.

Sweetwater laughed. 'Makes ya feel alive, don't it?'

They had been flying across the crater for thirty or so minutes when the grav-drive propulsion system's power dipped out for a moment before coming back on.

Sweetwater looked at the systems viewer. A red light was flashing on a panel. 'Something's wrong. We've got a power drain on the drive system,' she said. 'Put your EVA helmets on. We need to land so I can check it out'

No sooner had she spoken, when an alarm fired off and the inboard system announced, 'Critical systems failure.'

Everything went off and the rover dived and smashed into the crater basin like a rubber ball hitting concrete. The rover bounced up a dozen feet, lurching forwards a hundred feet before it hit the surface again.

More alarms started sounding and the terrified occupants started crying out in panic. Terrified of breaching the airtight craft's pressurized fuselage and suffering sudden explosive decompression.

It bounced again and again like a stone skipping across a millpond, until it finally skidded fifty yards on its landing skis and stopped.

They sat in stunned silence, amazed that they were still alive, and even more amazed they hadn't fractured the fuselage, at least not that was immediately apparent.

There was no power at all. Even the alarms had shut down.

'Is everyone okay? Nobody hurt?' Sweetwater said, coming to her senses.

'What happened?'

'I don't know.' Sweetwater reached under her seat… 'All the power went off.' She pulled her EVA helmet out from under her seat. 'Put your helmets on. It's going to get pretty damn cold in here. Life support's offline.' She flicked switches and pressed buttons, but nothing was responding.

Everyone reached for the overhead lockers containing their EVA helmets and they pulled them on and locked them, creating an airtight seal to the titanium neck rings of the EVA suits. The oxygen feeds in the suits hissed.

Sweetwater unbuckled her seat harness and stood up, her movements slow in the low lunar gravity. She squeezed between the seats to the airlock hatch at the back of the cabin. 'Stay in here.' She pressed the button on the bulkhead and the hatch opened into a small airlock chamber. She stepped through and the hatch closed behind her. The outer hatch opened.

The Rover was covered in moon dust from the impacts, and there was visible damage to the fuselage, but it wasn't seeping air and that was something at least.

She turned full circle, scanning the eternal twilight, swallowed into a hungry silence. She gazed upon the distant Earth, the sunlight bursting over the southern hemisphere in a spectacularly dazzling blast of light, like a polished red Martianite diamond refracting over the blue and white horizon. She was humbled to a speck of dust in the cosmic majesty, unimportant and brief like a spark. Never had she felt so utterly alone in her life as at this moment, marooned in a freezing airless vacuum, stuck in a life support suit with finite air, like a fly in a bottle waiting to suffocate to death. About fifty miles in the southwest was an abandoned mine and a dozen old habitats, like an Old-World ghost town, only here there was no wind to sweep the dusty streets. But it was too far away to get to.

She opened the access panel into the drive compartment and what she saw sent a wave of marrow-chilling horror through her entire body. The electrical system was covered in black soot and the micro-optic loom had disintegrated from extreme heat. 'What the hell...?' Her voice tapered as she reached inside, moving the melted micro-fiber-optics out of the way, trying to trace the source of the burnout. Not that it mattered, the damage was too severe to fix out here without parts and tools. They were in very big trouble.

'What is it, Sweetwater?' Winterush's voice filtered worriedly into her helmet. 'Can you fix it?'

'I'm coming in.'

Back in the rover, she raised the visor of her helmet. 'There's been an electrical fire,' she said. 'The rover's babbledicked-'

'What're you saying? That we're stuck here?' Winterush exclaimed. Her worried eyes said it all.

Sweetwater reached up to a button and pressed it. A distress buoy shot up out of the roof and climbed for hundreds of feet. 'I've activated the distress buoy,' she said.

'Jesus Christ,' Dragonfoot muttered worriedly.

'How far's Lunar Seven from here?' Hazelwood Blush asked.

'Too damn far,' Winterush said.

'About eight hundred miles,' Sweetwater said.

'We're dead,' Dragonfoot added.

'They should pick up the distress beacon at Lunar Seven,' Sweetwater said. 'They probably already had us on their sensors. All we can do is to sit tight and wait. If we start walking, we got nowhere to walk to, and we'll burn up our oxygen inside a couple of hours. The tanks in the rover are intact. They can be operated manually, so we have oxygen for about thirty hours in the Rover and two and a half hours in our EVA suits. It doesn't look like the emergency power cells were affected, so I can turn life support on. The power cells will last about twenty hours.'

It was freezing in the hover-rover. Condensation on the windows and surfaces quickly turned to ice and their breaths fogged in the icy cold. Fortunately their heated EVA suits protected them from the worst of it.

The air seal and oxygen indicator on the rover's control panel emitted a feeble glow of green and amber light across their worried faces. It was like sitting in Death's waiting room, but there was nothing else they could do. The rover was fried. Getting out and walking was certain death. Sitting in their small, sealed capsule, freezing cold, pinning their hopes on somebody picking up the distress buoy's signal and coming to rescue them before the oxygen ran out, was about all they could do.

'What's that?' Hazelwood said, seeing a flashing of red and blue light refracting through the ice across the windshield. She rubbed the ice from the window with her padded gloved hand and they looked through the smear of clear Intsoglass.

Something was glimmering out in the darkness, moving in from their starboard side. The red, blue and white glimmer stellated in the lunar twilight, getting closer – getting brighter...

'It's a probe!' Sweetwater said. She beamed... 'A babbledicking probe...'

They were overjoyed, smiling and laughing, the unspoken tension and fear lifting from them in an instant of pure relief. They were going to be rescued.

The probe came to a stop in front of the hover-rover, its strobes refracting on the facets of the ice crystals.

The comms crackled in the cockpit. A woman's voice spoke: 'What is your condition?'

'Alive!' Sweetwater exclaimed with relief. 'We've had an electrical fire and lost all power. No casualties. Can you assist?'

'A medivac's on its way to you. What's your life support status?'

'We're good for another ten hours of oxygen.'

'The medivac'll be with you very soon, sit tight and be ready to EVA. Do you need assistance to abandon your vessel?'

'Negative. We're all in good condition.'

'Who are we talking to?' Hazelwood Blush interrupted.

'Corporal Venus Jane, Red Team One, Silosian Tacticals. Sit tight. We'll be with you soon.'

The comms went off.

Thirty minutes later, the medivac drone flew in and put down thirty yards from the Rover. The rear airlock opened and a ramp lowered.

Venus and Bearfang, wearing EVA suits, started down the ramp in that painfully slow low gravity way as the four passengers climbed out of the wrecked hover-rover.

'Okay, get aboard,' Venus instructed through her com as she led them up the ramp onto the medivac drone.

The ramp retracted and the outer airlock door closed. Air hissed into the compartment as they waited for the inner airlock hatch to open.

Venus twisted her helmet and pulled it off. The others did likewise.

'I can't express how grateful we are,' Winterush said, removing his gauntlets. 'I really thought we were clocking off today.'

The day's still young yet, Bearfang thought to himself.

'Corporal Venus?' Sweetwater began to ask.

'Yes?'

Sweetwater looked at the big, brooding man looming behind her, spotting the scar across his throat when he pulled his helmet off. She spotted the tac-ten hanging from the hip of his EVA suit too.

'This way,' Venus said, turning to a hatchway. It opened and they went through into a medical bay…

'We had a short in our electrical systems. Burned 'em out. I'll have to get a recovery drone out to pick it up when we get back to Tranquillitatis,' Sweetwater said, following Venus through the medical bay. The brooding giant was following behind them, watching them hawkishly.

The medivac lifted off and they started back to Lunar Seven.

Venus pulled a Surfer Town turd from her utility belt and put it into her mouth.

'I'm Scholar Winterush Kip, astrophysicist...' Winterush said, introducing herself. She gestured to Dragonfoot and Hazelwood and went on, 'My colleagues, Scholars Dragonfoot Lockland, also astrophysics, and Hazelwood Blush, geologist. And this is Pilot Sweetwater Costello.'

'So, what's going on, Corporal?' Sweetwater asked, still looking suspiciously at Bearfang. 'Why are you here? And why are you jamming our communications?'

Venus looked her in the eyes as she lit her Surfer Town turd and puffed out stinking gray smoke. 'That's classified,' she said.

'I need to com Tranquillitatis. To let them know we're safe. Can I use your comms?'

Venus knew what she was doing, she was testing to see if they were among friends or enemies. She smiled. 'Go ahead. You can tell them we'll have you all back there tomorrow.' She showed her into the cockpit and pointed to the comms. 'Computer, open a com link to Tranquillitatis,' she said.

'Com open.'

'I'll leave you to it then,' Venus said, turning to leave.

'Thanks. Your friend out there,' she began...

Venus turned back to her.

'He's a tactical, too is he? Only he doesn't look like a tactical?'

Venus smiled at her. 'Well, we come in all shapes and sizes.' She left Sweetwater alone.

Up in the C and C, the Prophetess watched the shuttle bay viewer as the passengers disembarked the medivac drone with Venus and Bearfang. She shifted in a moment of surprise, quickly pursued by unease.

Tiger said: 'Isn't that-'

'Scholars Winterush Kip and Dragonfoot Lockland,' Thundersky interrupted. 'I don't know who the woman is.'

'Hazelwood Blush,' the Prophetess said.

Tiger looked at Sweetwater and stirred inwardly with an instant attraction. 'She must be the rover pilot,' he said, his voice vague and quiet, as if answering his own question.

The Prophetess looked at Tiger. 'I think she needs a refresher course,' she said drily.

Tiger smiled and looked at Sweetwater again.

Thundersky saw the sparkle in his friend's eye. He then looked over at Reaper, who was manning the main sensor interface beside his brother, who was sitting at the tactical interface, where he was bringing the autonomous defenses online. As ever, the mute kidling, Viper, was by his side.

'We've got four on-station laser cannons out,' Ghostmaker said sonorously. 'And two out on the rim. All other Power cells are depleted.'

'Are there any new ones on station?' Tiger asked.

Reaper typed on the sensor board. Reading from one of his viewers, he said, 'According to this, there are twenty-three replacement weapons energy cells on level fifty-six...' He looked over to them and said with a curiously cocked brow and a bright and greedy look on his face: '... In the Armory and Quartermaster's station.'

Ghostmaker stood up. 'You three, come with me,'
he said to three Dusty fighters. They left the C and C.

Chapter Fifty-Five

Dragonfoot stopped dead in his tracks as they entered the C and C when he came face to face with the Prophetess. He looked as if he was seeing a ghost. The color completely drained from his face. She was twenty years older of course, her auburn hair had turned gray, but it was her sure enough, he would have known her anywhere. He gasped, '*Butterfly!? My God! It is you…*'

'Hello, Lockland. It's been a long time.'

'They said-'

'I know what they said,' she interrupted. 'As you can see, they were wrong.'

'You know this woman?' Sweetwater said.

'We all do,' Hazelwood Blush said lowly. 'Scholar Butterfly Thorn.'

The Prophetess looked at Winterush. 'You're looking well, Kip.'

'So are you for a dead woman. Remarkable in fact. Even for a living woman, spending that long topside. What's your secret?'

'Genesis. But we can talk about that later…'

'Is someone going to tell me what's going on here?' Sweetwater said. 'Who are you people? What're you doing here?'

The Prophetess did not respond.

Sweetwater looked at the woman with the scarred face, and the half dozen men armed with tac-ones standing about the C and C. 'You're not tacticals. So who the hell are you?'

'What're you want, Butterfly? What's this about?' Dragonfoot asked. 'More to the point, how did you get past the security systems?'

'Were you on that Widow?' Hazelwood asked.

'We were.'

'I don't understand?' Winterush said.

'We're here to tell everyone the truth,' Tiger said as he and Thundersky entered the C and C.

Dragonfoot and the others were stunned when they saw the novices.

'Tiger White! Thundersky Reece!' Winterush gasped incredulously. 'What're you doing here?'

'My father was murdered by Zim Steven,' Tiger said. 'And then he tried to murder us with a Black Widow.'

Hazelwood laughed. 'Don't be ridiculous. Why would the SSS murder the Grand High Scholar and two high grading novices?'

Sweetwater was looking more and more worried and started looking around the C and C for a weapon, or some means to restore communications and alert earth that Lunar Seven had been taken over by Dusty terrorists.

'…To cover up their lies,' Tiger said.

'Now, I don't know what's going on here,' Hazelwood went on. 'But this stupidity's gone on long enough.'

'Haven't you worked it out yet?' Sweetwater said. 'They're Dusties.' She looked at the one the scholars called Butterfly, recognizing her as the one in charge. 'What're you going to do with us? Hold us hostages in exchange for medicinals?'

'Do we look like we need medicinals to you?' Bearfang said. 'We're the healthiest people on earth since before the fire mushrooms.'

She stared at him, and at them all – no melanomas, no yellowed skin, no radiation sores.

'Show them,' Tiger said. 'Show them what happened to my Dad.'

'Arti. Play interface lab surveillance of Grand High Scholar Blackstone Washington's homicide,' Thundersky said.

They looked across the control room at the main viewer as it started to play the surveillance.

Thundersky watched them closely, reading their horrified reactions when Blackstone was lasered.

After watching the shocking footage, Hazelwood Blush refused to believe what her eyes had seen. It had to be a fake, a clever Dusty fake, she said dismissively. 'Animation,' she said.

Sweetwater stood guilclessly with her lips slightly parted, looking clueless. She, like the scholars, could hardly believe what she had seen. The Grand High Scholar of Utopian Silosia, murdered in cold blood by the head of the Triple S.

'What is Genesis?' Dragonfoot asked.

'*Me*,' Thundersky said. 'I'm Genesis.'

They looked at him.

'*You*!?' Winterush frowned deeply.

The Prophetess showed them everything, all of her evidence and data. But Hazelwood remained steadfastly unconvinced. It had to be clever fakery. Believing them would undo everything she had believed in her entire life. It was preposterous to believe that the Order would suppress something as revolutionary as Genesis, just to maintain a hold over the mudsurfers and topsiders.

'It's all true, Scholar Hazelwood,' Thundersky said.

'Quisnam Veritas?' Dragonfoot said. 'The truth is, Genesis is chaos and disorder. Genesis can only bring about a return to the dark primitive savagery of the Old-Worlders. That's why the program had to be stopped, Butterfly. And those children, were an abomination to nature…'

Tiger's face began to tighten. 'You knew?' he said in almost a growl.

'Of course, he knew. He was an inquisitor back then,' Butterfly said.

Dragonfoot looked at him. 'We have order and civilization. The Dystopian Dusteater factions are terrorists. They bring chaos and savagery. Not salvation. Genesis will create wars and bring death. There's not enough food to feed everybody if they start breeding. There'll be more famine wars.'

'Babbledick!' Bearfang growled huskily.

'You're just one notch up from the Godders and Ferals,' Dragonfoot fired back.

'Whatever Zim's done, it's been to protect civilization. To protect Utopianism.'

Suddenly, Tiger, living up to his name, leapt forwards, his face twisted with anger, eyes burning with murderous rage. He drew his parabellum and cocked the hammer, aiming the weapon right at Dragonfoot, his finger curled around the trigger. *'Including murdering my father, you sonofabitch!?'*

Dragonfoot recoiled in horror and froze rigid as he stared into Tiger's hate filled eyes.

Suddenly, Thundersky put his hand on Tiger's wrist. 'This isn't the way. Why kill a blind fool for being a blind fool?' he said. 'Kill him and you prove them right. We cannot build a revolution on the foundations of murder and lies. That's Utopianism. Not us, Tiger.' He stepped in front of Tiger, placing himself between Tiger's gun and Dragonfoot.

The atmosphere in the C and C was palpably tense.

Tiger looked into his friend's eyes. 'Stand aside, Thunder. Let me clock this cunt off…?' He was crying, tears were rolling down his face.

Thundersky looked back determinedly at him and shook his head. 'No. I won't let you become a murderer. Zim and the others will get what's coming. But Dragonfoot didn't kill the Grand High Scholar or your mother. Dragonfoot's just a dickbutt and you can't kill a man for being a dickbutt, Tiger. Believe mc, it'll only make you feel worse. Our cause cannot begin this way. You're my closest friend. We have science to do. We have a destiny to fulfill. Please, Tiger. Lower your gun.'

Everyone was watching tensely.

Eventually, Tiger's hot blood cooled, and he lowered his gun. He holstered it and nodded his head.

Dragonfoot let out a long sigh of relief.

Chapter Fifty-Six

Winterush and Hazelwood Blush were standing down in the massive Delta hanger, watching the Dusties unloading M-TAVs from the Black Widows and loading them onto the Black Widow they had arrived on.

'Do you believe them?' she asked him.

'The evidence was compelling.' Winterush nodded his head. 'Yes. I think I do, Hazel. And we've both heard the rumors that Butterfly had discovered a cure before she disappeared.' He watched the Dusties again, full of energy and enthusiasm. 'And there's what Dragonfoot said.'

'Space psychosis,' Hazelwood said. She simply wasn't willing to believe them.

Winterush chuckled. 'That wasn't space psychosis. You heard what he said.' An end to centuries of fighting was finally in sight. And like some great savior, Butterfly Thorn was going to cure the world of the sicknesses and infertility. As ludicrous as it sounded in his head, never mind aloud, he believed it. 'Look at them, Hazel. Look how healthy they are...'

'I urge you not to be taken in by them, like those boys have been.' She looked down sorrowfully. 'I fear they're lost to us now.'

'Lost?' It seemed to Winterush to be the other way around. To him, it seemed that it was Utopia that was lost, in a maze of deceit and coverups. Utopia was a lie. He had always known it. Now was the time he had to choose a side. 'What has Sweetwater decided?'

'I neither know nor care.' She looked at Thundersky, who was guiding a hover cargo loader laden with long titanium weapons boxes to the Delta's loading dock. 'They're going to start a war,' she said.

'I'm staying with them, Hazel. And I think you should stay too. I believe them. I know Thundersky, he works on the antimatter program with us, he invented the injector system. We're going to achieve sub-light speed because of him. That boy's no liar. I think if we go back, they'll kill us because of what we know.'

'That's just ridiculous,' she snapped dismissively.

'You saw the evidence, Hazel. Washington's dead, that we know for certain. We saw them kill him.'

'Evidence, even visuals, can be fabricated. Why would we spend our lives pursuing cures if all we're going to do when we find one is keep it a secret? It's ridiculous and it makes no sense. It's all babbledick, Kip. Don't fall for it. They're terrorists, they'll say anything.' She gave him a severe look. 'If you join them, you'll become an enemy.'

Wintercrush was silent.

———

Sweetwater was in the shuttle bay, looking around the lunar rovers and the old military shuttles they used to use when tacticals were based on the moon, before it was demilitarized as part of the peace treaty with Oregon-Washington. There was a hover-rover that got her immediate attention. It was an older design than the one they had totaled in the basin, but it was bigger, with a six-passenger capacity, and life support for fifty hours along with a weapons system.

She pressed the airlock hatch button and it hissed and sank back into the fuselage before swinging open. She climbed inside. The air smelled just like it did in her hover-rover when it hadn't been used in a while. A smell of upholstered syntho-leather seats and stale air. She climbed into the pilot's seat and looked at the controls. Similar to modern rovers, but older, and there was a weapons system interface with laser armaments, which civilian hover-rovers didn't have.

'Do you think it'll still start?'

She looked round startled. It was Tiger. He smiled at her and came aboard.

'Sure,' she said. 'I'm sorry about your dad. He came to the academy when I was there to talk about gravity drives and magnetoplasmadynamic propulsion systems.'

Tiger climbed in the cockpit and squatted down in the copilot's seat beside her. 'Sorry for losing it on the C and C.'

'Hell, I lost count how many times I wanted to shoot that arrogant sonofabitch,' she said, making light of it. 'And that sour aced bitch Hazelwood.'

Tiger smiled. 'It's Tiger by the way. Just Tiger, and I guess I'm probably not a novice anymore either.'

She smiled. 'The Butterfly woman wouldn't let us leave anyway,' she said lowly. 'She's the one calling all the shots.'

Tiger raised a brow.

'I guess we're prisoners now.'

Tiger shook his head. 'You're not prisoners. If you wanna charge this rover up and go, then nobody's going to stop you. I hope you don't. But nobody will stop you.'

The Prophetess briefed the techs who were staying behind as the others boarded the Black Widow with the scholars and Sweetwater.

Up on the bridge, Venus, Bearfang, Thundersky, Tiger and Reaper were running pre-launch systems checks. The Silosian scholars and Sweetwater were on deck eight, under the watch of two Dusty fighters. The Prophetess arrived. She looked at Sweetwater. 'We could do with a copilot on the bridge.'

'Tell her to go to hell,' Dragonfoot spat.

'Up to you,' the Prophetess said.

Sweetwater considered, then rose from her seat and nodded her head.

'Anything I can do to help, Butterfly?'

The Prophetess looked at Winterush. 'Are you defecting?'

Winterush looked thoughtfully at his stunned colleagues. He nodded his head. 'I think I am. Yes.'

'You fucking traitor!' Dragonfoot hissed, giving Winterush a hate filled stare.

'Don't do it, Kip,' Hazelwood said.

Winterush stood up. 'We all know the truth, even if we don't all accept it. Washington was my friend and my colleague. I'm not going to swallow their lies anymore.'

'Welcome, Kip.'

Winterush, Sweetwater and the Prophetess went up to the bridge.

Blackdog looked at the external viewers and gawped when he saw the Black Widow coming in slow and low crossing the Sea of Tranquility, 'Shit!'

'What is it now?' Vernon peered over his shoulder at the viewers and read the sensor data. 'At its present speed, it'll be here in less than an hour,' he said.

Suddenly Sweetwater's face appeared on the comms viewer. '…Tranquillitatis. Are you reading, over?'

Blackdog activated the com. 'We're reading you,' he said, looking at the tactical corporal and a young man they could see in the background on the Widow's bridge.

Vernon leaned closer. 'What's your situation, Sweetwater?'

'We're all good. Request a soft dock.'

Suddenly, Winterush was beside Sweetwater looking at them. 'They're a repair team,' he said, knowing that there was no way they would allow them to dock if they had the slightest suspicion. 'Lunar Seven's systems were corrupted. That's why our comms to earth are down.'

'Standby.' Blackdog disconnected the sound on the comms link and looked at Vernon. 'What're you think?'

'I think we should let them dock.'

'Protocol says that military vehicles or anything carrying ordnance are prohibited.'

'Unless in exceptional circumstances. I think this qualifies as an exceptional circumstance, Vernon.'

Vernon nodded his head thoughtfully.

Blackdog opened the com. 'You'll have to dock at the freighter bay one. You're too big for anywhere else. Just lock on the docking beacon and let the nav-conn do the rest.'

'Copy that.'

'I'll see you there. Doc. Meet me at Freighter Bay One,' he said and a voice filtered back:

'I'm on my way.'

The Black Widow slowly maneuvered towards the docking station with the grace and lightness of a feather floating on a gentle wind, slipping smoothly towards the dock, its magnetoplasmadynamic steering and braking thrusters firing spits of plasma energy.

Vernon and Medivac Logan waited at the airlock, watching the huge, black warship floating towards it. It was a tense moment as the monster moved along the outside of the skywalk just inches away. Any collision could be catastrophic.

There was a clunk.

'Dock and seal confirmed,' the AI said.

They waited on the other side for the airlocks to open. A red light above the airlock turned green. The door hissed and slid open.

Venus rushed forwards, her tac-ten clasped in her fist, taking Vernon and Logan by complete surprise. She pushed Vernon back against the bulkhead and pressed the muzzle up under his chin. 'You're not going to be trouble, are you?'

Vernon was rigid with fear. He shook his head.

Bearfang leapt out, aiming his laser at Logan. 'Hands behind your head!'

Vernon and Logan were stunned to see Sweetwater was apparently willingly helping the terrorists. 'Sweetwater? What're you doing!?'

She looked at them. 'Trust me. This isn't what you think. I promise you. Everything'll be explained. Just do as they say, Vernon. Nobody's here to hurt anyone.'

'They'll send you to the penal labs for this, Sweet,' Logan said.

She looked evenly at him for a moment, then hurried off with Vixen.

Logan, who clearly had more spine than Vernon, said, 'You can't possibly hope to get away with this. Whoever you are.' Logan looked at the Prophetess, picking up a tool box. 'Where are the scholars?'

'We're safe,' Winterush said as he came out from the drone.

'Scholar Winterush! What's going on, sir?' Vernon asked.

Taking the C and C was as easy as it had been to capture the supervisor and Logan. Blackdog was no hero. Remaining seated, he put his hands up as soon as Venus aimed her parabellum pistol at him.

Tiger went directly to the main system interface and started typing on the touchscreen.

Blackdog glared incredulously at Sweetwater. 'Sweet!? What the hell are you doin'!?'

'Blackstone was murdered,' she explained. 'Murdered by the Triple S. Those novies they said were murdered by Dusties – well, they're not dead.

They're here. They've got the cure, Blackdog. The cure for everything. The scholars have been letting us die for years. They've known about the cure the whole goddam time.'

'What the hell are you talking about. What cure?'

'The cure for the cancers, the radiation, even the goddam infertility. They've had it for twenty goddam years and the GHC, Triple S and GRC have kept it a secret, clocking off everyone who knows about it. Just listen to them. Look at the evidence, Blackdog.'

Tranquillitatis was now under the Prophetess's control. Everyone in the station was taken to the mess, where they were shown the evidence, including Arti's surveillance of Blackstone's murder.

The prophetess told them about the Genesis nanite. 'Join us,' she said. 'Join our fight against the Utopian tyranny. Come with us and you'll all have a Genesis nanite within months.'

'And if we refuse to join you?' Littlebird Florence said.

'You'll be taken safely back to Earth and released,' Thundersky said.

'And you expect us to believe that babbledick?' One of the techs said.

Thundersky looked at him. 'I don't care if you do or you don't. But that's how it'll be. Join us or don't join us. Either way, you're free to decide and you will be returned safely back to Silosia.'

'Do you really think you can buy them off with your lies, Butterfly?' Hazelwood Blush exclaimed.

Thundersky spoke again before his mother got the chance. 'You've seen the evidence. You can make up your own minds, but I tell you this. If you go back to Silosia, the Triple S will kill you to silence you.' He looked at his mother and the others. 'No more debates. They choose their side, those who want to go back to Silosia can. They've got an hour.' He left the mess.

'Taking orders from kidlings now, Butterfly.'

She looked at Hazelwood. 'From that kidling? Yes, I am.'

Chapter Fifty-Eight

Tactical Command, Silo City

They were tracking the lunar shuttle taking off from Tranquillitatis, plotting its speed and course.

'…What now?' Appleby said to himself as he crossed the busy control room.

'At its present speed and heading,' a tactical said, 'The lunar shuttle will re-enter over continental North America, approximately sixty miles east of the ruins of Dallas in twenty-three hours, sir.' He looked at General Appleby standing at the other side of the interface. 'Communications are still down.'

Appleby looked round at a tactical sitting behind another interface on his left. 'How many people aboard?'

'Nine, sir,' she said. 'If it's the crew, there are five missing-'

'Sir,' the first tactical interrupted, looking at his monitors. 'Sensors are detecting the Delta disengaging from Tranquillitatis. All systems on Tranquillitatis have gone offline, the refinery has been set in safe mode and locked down, and the station's purging oxygen. No life signs aboard.'

Appleby looked gravely at Bigmoose. 'Very clever. That'll delay Astrium production for months.'

'Could've been worse, old friend. They could've sabotaged the entire refinery.'

'What's Delta One's weapons status?'

'Primary weapons offline. Secondary weapons are all online. They're jamming our sensors, so I don't know how many people are aboard.'

'It's moving away from the moon. What's its trajectory?'

'Earth.'

'Sir,' the female tactical said. 'We've got a com request from the Delta on a secure military channel? Someone claiming to be the Prophetess...'

Those who heard her, looked round. Prophetess was a name they all knew. The Virginia Dusty queen, Silosia's arch enemy.

Appleby looked round at Bigmoose before loping to his office. 'Put it through to my office on a closed channel with the scrambler enabled. I don't want the goddam Triple S listening in.' He looked at a senior-tactical commander. 'Bring the PODS online...' he ordered as he went into his office with Bigmoose.

Bigmoose froze when he saw who it was looking back at them, projecting in the middle of the room from the holo-viewer – a ghost. *Butterfly...?*

'Hello, Jack.' Her eyes shifted to Appleby. 'You're looking well, Coldriver.'

Appleby stared wordless at her, not quite sure if he believed his eyes or not. Old memories stirred in the attic of his mind, memories of his youth and how he had once fallen in love with Butterfly Thorn. 'So, you're the Prophetess?'

'Their name for me,' she said. 'Not mine. But if it makes them fight Utopia, they can call me whatever they like.'

'How did you get control of Lunar Seven?'

'The Black Widow that the Triple S sent to kill Red Team One and the two novices changed its mind,' she said. 'Just like the warbirds they sent. It was nothing we did. It was Arti's decision-'

'*Babbledick*! Arti can't make decisions like that.'

'You can't hope to get away with this, Butterfly,' Bigmoose said calmly. 'However you've managed to hack out systems, we will find it and we'll lock you out.'

'Well, good luck with that, Coldriver.'

'What've you done to Tranquillitatis?' Bigmoose wanted to know.

'Nothing. I just appropriated some tech from the labs, that's all. The crew are unharmed and on their way to you aboard their shuttle, so I wouldn't order the PODS to fire on it. Sorry, I forgot, you no longer control the PODS. We do.' She gave him a smile.

Coldriver gave Bigmoose a look and he left the office to check the planetary defense system.

'What're you want, Butterfly?' Bigmoose growled.

'Justice, Jack. I want justice and I want to give everyone the Genesis chip. But I've waited this long, a little longer isn't going to matter. For now, I'll settle for exposing the scholastic order for the fraud it is. And then for Silosia to surrender unconditionally to my forces.'

Coldriver laughed. 'Well, I think you know what the response to that will be.'

'Then war it is. But once the topsiders and a good many scholars learn the truth, and learn about Genesis, then good luck to you in trying to stop them rising up against you, or defecting to us. You've lost this war before it's even started. Goodbye, Coldriver.'

'Wait! What's the Genesis chip?'

'You'll see. It's all on the data stream I've sent to you and Jack. You were honest men when I knew you. I'm trusting that you're still honest men today. Honest men being used as pawns in a twenty-year-old conspiracy.' The holograph disappeared.

Bigmoose came back into the office.

'Well?'

'We're in trouble, Coldriver. We've lost control of the PODS. I don't know how, but the Dusties have complete control of the entire system, ours and everyone else's...'

The lunar shuttle landed several miles west of Silo City, in a remote spot. A mile to the south were the great Intsoglass bio-domes humping out of the ground.

There were two M-TAVs and two dozen Triple S sentinels waiting at the landing site as the shuttle hatch opened and the ladder telescoped out.

Zim was smiling broadly, joyously even, holding out his arms as the crew of Tranquillitatis disembarked, minus five of their number who had defected to the Dusties. 'You're home safe. Are you harmed? Did they hurt you?' Zim asked.

'No. We're all unharmed,' Hazelwood Blush said, extricating herself from the others, taking it upon herself to be their spokesperson. 'They treated us well. But some of our colleagues went over to the terrorists,' she said. 'Scholar Winterush Kip, our comms officer Blackdog, a refinery tech Robin Dave and our shuttle pilot Sweetwater Helen. They fell for Butterfly Thorn's lies.'

'Lies? What lies?'

'About something called Genesis and the death of the Grand High Scholar.'

'I see.' Zim glanced at Dead Eyes. The look said it all, Hazelwood's words had condemned them all to death.

They started back to the M-TAVs. 'We need to debrief you.'

'Yes, of course,' Dragonfoot said. 'There's at least a dozen of them, including a deserter from the tacticals and novices Tiger White and Thundersky Reece,' he said as they approached Zim's M-TAV.

'Neptune, take the others back to the other M-TAV. Make sure they get something to eat and drink before debriefing them. I'll debrief Scholar Hazelwood and Scholar Dragonfoot in my vehicle.' He looked at the two scholars. 'So, I can get your accounts before we report to the Grand High Council?'

They sat in the M-TAV, and held nothing back from him. Hazelwood had the most to say, her recollection as precise and as sharp as a computer's.

She told Zim about Tiger and Thundersky, about Butterfly Thorn, about the surveillance of the Grand High Scholar's murder. Adding that it was clearly an animated fake. She left nothing out.

Dead Eyes came back about half an hour later. He looked at the two scholars sat next to one another, facing Zim who sat opposite them.

'Well,' Zim said. 'I think I know all I need to. Thank you, Hazelwood. You too, Dragonfoot...' He looked at Dead Eyes. 'Have you liquidated them?'

'All clocked off...' He raised his hand and there was a laser pistol clenched in his fist, leveled at the two horrified scholars.

Hazelwood jumped to her feet in terror. Dragonfoot closed his eyes in silent capitulation as the reality dawned. That novice was right. They were going to be killed.

Dead Eyes shot them both dead, Dragonfoot first. They would blame it on the Dusties. They always blamed everything on the Dusties. They'd say that they found them dead on arrival, Zim had it all worked out. It was just a matter of dressing the scene right and taking some images and adding the right words and slogans. The people would swallow whatever they were told.

Back in his habitat, Coldriver poured himself a glass of apple brandy and sat down in his favorite chair, thinking about the information Butterfly had uploaded onto his data-pad. He and Bigmoose were both shaken by the revelations in the data. If it was true, they had been deliberately letting citizens die needlessly in their thousands. And what about the potential fertility in a world of growing infertility?

He was a soldier and he stayed away from the GHC, but this, this was the complete antipathy of Utopianism, an insult to the teachings of Jeremiah O'Connor, the founding father of Utopianism. The GHC was committing Planeticide to protect a very small group of powerful individuals.

'Arti. Play the Dead River Concerto. The "Nuclear Winter Movement." With footage of the Mushroom War. The original Gazelle Knight recording please,' he said. 'Low setting three.' He relaxed back as the mournfully somber music began with a solo cello, soon followed by a violin, and Death's deep pounding drum and saxophone. The walls became viewers, and the room was filled with the ancient satellite recordings of the nuclear war. Close up and from orbital angles, the planes flashed and the great mushroom clouds rafted into the stratosphere. The horrific visuals of entire cities being nuked, the millions it killed, and the prevailing darkness of radioactive cloud that enshrouded the entire planet until nothing below it could be seen, and so it stayed for over a decade…

The vocals enjoined, humming Death's lament as even Death wept to behold the breadth of his harvest…

The images changed from orbital, to terrestrial, and the documented visuals of the obliterated earth and mountains or corpses, human and animal, bulldozed during the clear up on the radioactive earth, locked in perpetual night. Images of the dying, the diseased, the radioactive. The mass executions of looters. Society everywhere had collapsed. No more economy, no more summers, no more harvests. Death was everywhere.

It wasn't just the radiation, starvation and extreme cold that killed millions more after the war. It was the diseases, the pandemics. Medicines were scarce, there were no more hospitals, no governments. Chaos ruled everywhere for almost a hundred years. Here it was, on every wall, on the floor, on the ceiling, and Coldriver sobbed and sank deeper and deeper into despair, carried on the music and the images.

The rumors he had heard twenty years ago about a cure being discovered, were true. It was all in the data Butterfly had sent him. Secret security recordings made inside the Grand High Council the night before the purge began, laying out that nobody could ever know about Genesis. The information was too dangerous. Every trace of it had to be erased, Butterfly Thorn's research seized and everybody connected to the project, no matter who they were, had to be "eliminated." Zim Steven, then a bright young and ambitious inquisitor, was only too willing to take charge of the bloody deed.

He took a swallow of brandy and set the glass down, pinching the bridge of his nose as he considered what to do with the information, now that he had it.

He and Bigmoose agreed that his office was too dangerous to discuss it there and leaving it on their data-pads was too dangerous, so Appleby hid the data in plain sight by uploading it to an obscure file in the Emergency Broadcast system. It was a double-edged blade. Nobody would think of looking for highly secret files there, and, if anything were to happen to him or Bigmoose, the Emergency Broadcast System would play the data on every building in Silosia and its colonies, terrestrial and extraterrestrial. Their lies would be exposed the moment their deaths or disappearances were officially announced.

His thoughts were interrupted when the music died down and the computer announced that Zim Steven from the Triple S was at his door. He looked at the viewer and saw Zim Steven and his lapdog Neptune Anderson standing in his porch.

Appleby slipped a tac-6 compact laser pistol into his pocket before he went to the door to let them in.

'I hope we're not disturbing you, General?' Zim said as they stepped across the threshold. 'I thought you'd want to know immediately, that the crew from Tranquillitatis were all dead. They sent us corpses. All of them lasered to death. The Dusties murdered them in cold blood.'

'The lying bitch!' he said. 'Come in, Zim. Can I get you a drink?'

'Apple brandy if you have it. Thank you.'

Coldriver made a point of not offering Dead Eyes a drink. All he gave him was a contemptuous leer.

Dead Eyes felt the snub keenly, even if he did try shrugging it off with a supercilious grin.

Zim moved across the room, looking around the habitat, which was filled with Greek and Roman antiquities Appleby had picked up on his travels from various Old-World museums and Scavs. 'The GHC have ordered that all military tech is to be disconnected from Arti and operated manually,' he said. 'Until we have Arti under control again.'

Appleby made no comment. He had been expecting it. Arti was compromised. He poured apple brandy into a clean glass and refilled his own.

'Our techs and scholars are working on a solution to break the hack and restore control as we speak,' Zim said as he took his drink from the general.

'Have you located the problem?'

'Not yet. But they're working on something they're calling eraser nanites to wipe all data from Arti from before the NORAD system went active. That's the only opportunity they've had to hack Arti's positronic matrix.'

Coldriver nodded his head and sipped his drink.

'So, Butterfly Thorn's the elusive Prophetess,' Zim said, changing the subject. 'Who'd have thought it, eh? You and her were close friends if I remember?'

The snake was slithering. 'We did.' He looked carefully at Dead Eyes. 'Were. But that was before she went Dystopian and betrayed us.'

'What does she want?' Zim asked.

Coldriver returned to his chair and sat down. 'She wants to kill you, Zim.' He smiled.

Zim tried to hide his unease, but he couldn't. He sipped his drink. 'And apart from killing me, what else did she say when she commed you? Did she mention the novices?'

Coldriver shook his head. 'No. All she told me was that you lasered Grand High Scholar Blackstone Washington in his lab.'

Zim and Dead Eyes looked at one another. 'He committed suicide,' Zim said, quoting the official line. 'When he discovered that Thundersky Reece was a Dusty spy.'

Coldriver listened to their lying babbledick. But it all fitted nicely for the propaganda that was starting to trickle out. Lie upon lie upon lie. They were even saying that Thundersky activated the 480 as an act of sabotage and terrorism. "Damage limitation" was what the Old-Worlders used to call it. He nodded his head in the right places and sipped his drink.

'Did she say anything else, General?'

'Yes. She said surrender or it's war.'

Zim seemed to accept what he said. At least outwardly. 'The GHC want to know why you haven't sent ships to retake Lunar Seven and secure Tranquillitatis?'

'Because they'd be destroyed before they got within ten thousand miles of Lunar Seven. And we can't risk an incursion onto Tranquillitatis until we know it's not mined...' His stare sharpened intensely on Zim. 'Do you have any idea what'll happen if that refinery goes up? What that amount of Astrium plasma would do to the moon? Attacking Lunar Seven isn't an option until we're out of options. But I'm working on an incursion plan to secure Tranquillitatis.'

'And Lunar Seven?'

'Forget it. Nothing we have can penetrate Lunar Seven's defenses. If you want my advice... come to terms with them.'

'That'll never happen.'

'Then we've got a fight on our hands, because those Black Widows are the most formidable weapons ever created.'

Zim gave him a deprecatory look. 'Then we'll hit them where it really hurts,' he said cryptically.

Outside, Zim and Dead Eyes came out from the Intsoglass habitat block into Sub City Plaza.

Zim paused on the pavement and looked up into the starry night sky as if searching for something. 'He's holding something back from us,' he said, giving Dead Eyes an intense look. 'She told him more than he's letting on. Have him watched.'

Chapter Sixty-One

'How are we doing locating those rogue Triple S warbirds?'

'They're somewhere in the Virginias, well inside Dusty territory, sir. West of old Mount Mitchel.'

Bigmoose knew the region from explorations for suitable colony sites fifteen years ago. The expedition had come under constant skirmishes from Dusties and Ferals alike, so despite being relatively free of radiation (with the exception of warm spots where there had been Old-World cities that had been hit with neutron warheads), the Virginias were considered unsuitable for colonization on account of very hostile Dystopian survivor colonies. The Old-World maps referred to the area as the Allegheny Mountains, though these days they were simply called the Virginias.

'Any comms traffic intercepted?'

The tactical shook his head. 'None, sir.'

Coldriver arrived and Bigmoose updated him.

Coldriver studied the data thoughtfully, and then looked at Bigmoose. 'Talk to me while we walk, I want to see how they're doing with prepping the warbirds,' he said clearly and purposefully, as if intending everyone to hear.

Bigmoose followed him out of the building into the garrison and they headed for the air base. An alarm sounded out across the base and a voice said: 'Attention! Amber! Amber! Amber! All personnel to stations!'

'…What happened last night?' Appleby asked.

'The Tranquillitatis crew walked off of that shuttle alive and in good health, just like she said they would. They were questioned and then murdered by Triple S sentinels. Zim Steven took care of the scholars personally.'

Coldriver stared in muted silence.

'They lasered them in cold blood.'

'Zim and his creature went to your habitat right after.'

'He told me they were all dead when the shuttle landed. Lasered by Butterfly's people.'

'He lied.'

'Everything that comes out of that sonofabitch's mouth is a goddam lie,' Coldriver said. 'The data she sent is all original material. I've checked everything against Triple S records and logs. Dates, times… everything. And they're working on some nanites to erase Arti's memory from when NORAD became active to regain control of Arti.'

Bigmoose stared worriedly across the busy garrison and flight pad, where techs were disconnecting the AI link from Arti's tactical systems. 'Even if this is true, what can we do about it? The Triple S are too powerful and they won't think twice about clocking us off.'

He was scared – Coldriver could see it in his eyes, hear it in his voice, read it in his jittery furtiveness.

'Have you forgotten the ideals of Jeremiah O'Connor and our founding fathers, Bigmoose? The principles of a fair and equal society? *"And let none, human nor beast, suffer to the benefit of others"* – that's in the oath we took. Empty words, Bigmoose? Or the code by which we live and die?'

———

Dead Eyes was waiting for Coldriver, hidden in a utility closet, sharing space with a cleaning droid, old boots and jumpsuits, a military pack and neatly stacked shelves. He was as patient as a dozing snake, closed into almost perfect darkness, except for the dim red glow of the cleaner droid's charge pack.

It hadn't been easy getting into Coldriver's habitat, it had a level six biometric security entry system, but for an experienced clock-stopper like him it was a minor inconvenience. With a cultured sample of Coldriver's DNA, and some manipulation with the entry system, he was in the habitat inside of twenty seconds. A personal best record.

He would have to kill him quickly, before Coldriver realized that his habitat AI had been lobotomized with a complete memory wipe – a dead giveaway that he had an intruder, and he didn't want to give Coldriver a chance to draw down on him. Coldriver was a war hero and he knew how to take care of himself.

He had made himself at home, drinking a cup of syntho-coffee, helping himself to some cornbread and peanut syntho-butter spread.

Then he got the com from Zim's spy in the tacticals' garrison that Coldriver was on his way home, and now he waited in the closet opposite the front door, his laser in hand.

Clocking Coldriver off would be a personal pleasure. He hated the general and Coldriver hated him just as much.

Coldriver didn't see it coming. As he entered the habitat and closed the door, Dead Eyes inched the closet door open and lasered him in the back, right between the shoulder blades as the door closed behind him. Coldriver stumbled forwards against the door with a pained gasp, clinging to the door as he slid down into a slumped heap, paralyzed, his spinal cord lasered through.

Dead Eyes calmly stepped out of the closet and walked over to the gasping general, who tried to turn himself to see his murderer.

'Here, let me help you.' Dead Eyes hooked his foot under him and rolled him over onto his back.

Coldriver stared at Dead Eyes, paralyzed from a severed spinal cord. He stared at his assassin, the Angel of Death and grinned contemptuously. 'You're too late,' he said. 'Too damn late…'

Dead Eyes pulled a face. 'Maybe.' He lasered him again. General Coldriver Appleby was dead.

The next day, Bigmoose learned that Coldriver had gone on "personal leave" to Paradise City. Bigmoose knew they had killed him. And he realized that it would only be a matter of time before he went on "*personal leave*" too. There was only one option – he had to get his family and himself out of Silosia, and there was only one place to go.

Chapter Sixty-Two

The Virginias Wilderness

There was a stillness all around him, a silence filled with the whisper of wind across the fronds of the trees. The dawn sun sloped down in glinting shards, twinkling and blinking as the canopy swayed gently above. For a moment he had to think about where he was. Then, as the sleep cleared from his mind, he remembered. He had left the city yesterday and solar-cycled half the night up into the mountains, putting as much distance between himself and Silo City as he could. He knew that as soon as they knew he was missing, Zim would send his clock-stoppers out to find him and kill him.

He knew there were ancient roads the Dusties used to sneak across the mountain wilderness. It took Bigmoose the better part of the morning before he found one, and it felt like a real achievement. With luck, the road would take him to the other side of the mountains, into Virginia Dusty country. Hopefully they wouldn't shoot him when their sentinel drones and surveillance picked him up. He needed to warn them that the Triple S had taken over the military and their secret city was one of their prime targets. If Genesis was real, then it needed to be protected at all costs.

Like all the ancient highways and byways, this one had its share of rotting vehicles along its twisted course through the mountains, mostly buried at the sides of the road where they had been cleared from the highway. Bigmoose wagered that there were probably hundreds more down in those deep ravines, hidden by the coniferous pines and spruces, swallowed by the earth, which swallowed everything – eventually.

He rode north all day, not stopping once, eating rations on the go, the insectile drone of his solarcycle the only sound, echoing through the mountains as he sped along the ancient highway. He knew the SSS would be looking for him as well as Lillybet and the girls.

It was an hour before dusk, and the sun was almost touching the snow dusted mountain peaks. He pulled off at some dilapidated Old-World ruins, almost completely hidden in the trees, the spur track that led to them having vanished long ago. Had he been going any faster, he might've missed it.

It was a thick concrete concourse, cracked, broken and buckled by the roots of trees knuckling up from beneath. A giant maple had literally grown around a concrete column, which was enclosed inside the maple's thick trunk. The rusty skeletons of ancient gas pumps stood in several rows on raised islands, subsided and crooked with Old-World vehicle carcasses beside them.

If he had to sum up the Old-World in a single word, it would have been "rusty." Just about everything they'd left behind had turned to rust or dust. The gas pumps, the canopy, the vehicles, the ancient road signs

– their primitive computer tech – at least on their insides. Their buildings did not last either, not even in the cities that had escaped the mushrooms. True to say, the pyramids of Ancient Egypt and the ruins of the ancient Romans and Greeks had weathered better in five thousand plus years, than the buildings of the late Old-World period had in five hundred years.

His shadow followed him as he coaxed himself slowly across the concourse, solid and black over the buckled concrete, riding its own intangible solarcycle to the tumbled ruin of what had been a vehicle tech's repair shop. It was the only building that was still intact. Sheltered under the trees, it was a concrete structure with two floors, the upper floor open to the weather, but on the ground, the concrete ceiling made it an ideal shelter for the night.

He ate his field rations cold rather than taking the risk of lighting a fire, to avoid being spotted by Ferals. He settled down on the hard floor, propped up in the corner under an open window, and stared up at the moonlight dappling through the dark treetops, flickering like blinking eyes in the inky sky.

He thought of Lillybet and his girls before drifting off to sleep, praying they were safe.

He was asleep for about an hour or so, when he awoke suddenly. He thought he heard a noise somewhere outside. Slowly and carefully, he drew his laser pistol, stood up and crept to the opening, listening carefully... But there was only silence and the rattle of the roof in the wind. He inched to the window, clasping his tac-ten, keeping low. He peered out through the big opening, beyond the trees to the forecourt glowing in the moonlight. Still and silent.

Maybe it had been a dream? But then, a black-clad figure moved into view from the tree that grew between the rows of gas pumps.

Bigmoose's first thought was Ferals, and his second thought was, where there was one Feral there would be others. Like wild dogs, they hunted in packs. He pressed himself up against the wall, merging into the darkness to the side of the window. He cocked his head around and watched the lone man, staying down on his haunches, his laser set on full charge, a full mag of nines in his parabellum. He slowly and carefully unclipped the leg holster so as not to make a noise.

The dark figure started walking towards the ruin of the auto shop – Bigmoose's finger curled around the trigger of his laser, bringing the muzzle up, his heart pounding like a drum in his chest. The dark man kept coming, slow and cautious, and the closer he got, the more of him he could see. Triple S! Right out here? Bigmoose scurried back into the blackness. They had to be looking for him. With the slowness of a worm, his left hand inched his parabellum out of its holster, his thumb easing the safety off with a click that sounded like a thunderclap to his oversensitive ears. Gun metal glinted in the moon-rays as he brought it up, his steady, unblinking eyes staring predatorily at the SSS sentinel. Bigmoose held his breath steady, despite wanting to pant as the adrenalin coursed through his hot blood.

'Anything?' someone called from the forecourt.

'Nothing,' the sentinel called back. He stopped in front of the opening and stared into the black void beyond. Bigmoose was less than three feet from his left, hidden in shadow, ready to kill him. He had no idea how many other sentinels there were, but he was damn sure he would take as many of them to hell with him as he could.

'C'mon. He's not here. Let's go, these goddam Old-World places give me the creeps.'

The sentinel turned and started back to the forecourt, where his companion was waiting and they walked off out of view. Moments later, Bigmoose heard the unmistakable throbbing hum of an M-TAV mag-drive starting up. It drove back towards the road, the throbbing hum of its mag-drive fading into the distance as it turned south, back towards Silosian territory.

Bigmoose took a deep breath and sighed with relief.

Then he saw something – someone – another dark figure creeping around in the dark. Coming out of the trees, as cautious as a frightened animal.

Bigmoose determined the man was alone and that he seemed just as scared of the sentinels as he'd been. He was wearing a Sub City tech's dark blue Intsofiber jumpsuit, grubby after a day or two roughing it in the forest.

The man wandered about the ruins for a minute, lost, confused and scared. He seemed to have no idea where he was.

Bigmoose stepped out from the building, his tac-ten levelled at the tech. 'Hold it right there.'

The tech jerked round, white with fear. He looked at the laser pointed at him and raised his hands. 'Don't kill me. Please. Don't kill me,' he pleaded tremulously.

'Who are you?'

'M-moon Spencer. Senior tech. Please, mister. Don't shoot.'

'Moon Spencer...?' He nodded. 'Why you running, Moon Spencer? Why were you hiding from those sentinels?'

Moon shook his head. 'I wasn't.'

'Yeah you were. Like I was.' Bigmoose walked towards him, his laser still pointed at Moon. 'You armed, Moon Spencer?'

Moon shook his head. 'I lost my stuff. Ferals found me. I had to run.'

Bigmoose considered him for a moment, then lowered his laser and holstered his parabellum, but not the laser.

Moon breathed easier.

'Where you headed?' Bigmoose asked.

'As far away from Silosia as I can get. You?'

'Bloodbuck City. Okay, Moon Spencer. This is how it is. There are two rules. You wanna ride with me, it's my rules. You wanna survive out here, it's my rules. That's all you need to know. When I say do, you goddam do, or you're on your own...' He looked him up and down. 'And I think we both know you're not going to make it out here on your own. Ferals don't eat grownups, but they will kill you and rob you. So, here's the invite. D'you wanna come with me, or stay here and take your chances?'

Moon knew this man was a tactical, he had that military manner they always had. 'Come with you.'

'My rules?'

Moon nodded his head. He was used to other peoples' rules. 'Your rules.'

Bigmoose finally holstered his laser and proffered his hand. 'I'm Bigmoose Jack.'

Moon knew the name. 'Senior Tactical Commander Bigmoose Jack?' he asked as they shook hands.

'Is there another one? You hungry, Moon Spencer?'

Moon nodded.

Chapter Sixty-Three

Black Widow, Delta One, 178,000 miles from Earth

Thundersky was hit by a sudden and excruciating headache. It was like a sonic grenade exploding in his brain – he jumped to his feet clasping his head in his hands. 'Oh God!' He collapsed onto the deck of the bridge, screaming out in agony. It was a pain like nothing he had ever experienced in his life before.

Reaper and Tiger, both spooked, lurched across the bridge to where he'd fallen.

The Prophetess knelt beside him and put her arms around his head.

'*Make it stop! Make it stop!*' Thundersky pleaded as his friends and mother came to him, anxious and worried as they knelt beside him. His vision blurred and he felt as if he was spinning in a centrifuge with an axe buried in his skull. Then everything went black and he fell into a coma.

The Prophetess checked his pulse and pulled his eyelids open. They were dilated and bloodshot. 'Thundersky, can you hear me?' She stroked his head.

Thundersky was unresponsive.

'Is he okay?' Venus asked, turning in the pilot's seat, where she had manual control of the Widow.

'I don't know,' the Prophetess said. She looked at Tiger and Reaper. 'It might be Genesis. Quickly, get him down to the medivac deck,' she ordered. 'I need to do a scan.'

Tiger and Reaper, both of them worried, carefully lifted him from under his arms and legs in a sort of cradle and carried him off of the bridge, the Prophetess following behind. She glanced back at Venus and Sweetwater sitting in the copilot's seat.

'What is it? What's wrong with him?' Venus asked.

'I don't know.'

Down on the medivac deck Tiger and Reaper laid Thundersky onto one of the med-beds, which automatically activated the BMDS.

A scan canopy rotated out from the underside of the med-bed and closed over Thundersky, enclosing him in a transparent capsule as the BMDS began to scan him. A 3-D holograph of Thundersky's body from the inside projected out. His coursing blood, his beating heart, his breathing lungs – his brain. It was hyper-active. His brainwaves were going crazy.

The Prophetess turned to the viewer at the end of the med-bed as biomedical data began to appear. Heart rate, blood pressure, oxygen saturation, temperature. All were elevated, but not dangerously so.

Reaper stepped up to the med-bed and took hold of Thundersky's hand, holding onto it tightly. 'He'll be okay, won't he? He's not clocking off, is he?' he said, his voice tremulous and frightened. He had fallen completely in love with Thundersky, and hadn't realized it until now. Seeing him like this inflicted a crushing worry on him, terrified Thundersky might die.

'Of course he's not clocking off,' she said sharply, looking at the scan results. She checked the nanite and neurological data. 'The conscious interface has activated.'

'Is that why he's sick?' Tiger asked.

She shook her head vaguely. 'I don't know.'

Thundersky had been unconscious for about thirty minutes when he began to stir again. Figures moved in his blurry vision; somebody was holding his hand. He looked and smiled. '*Reaper...*' he muttered.

'Goddammit, you got my clock bumping,' Reaper said.

'What happened...?' He started to sit up.

'Lie still, Thundersky,' his mother said.

Thundersky's vision cleared. He looked at his mother. 'Arti's under attack. We're going to lose the Grav-Drives,' he said, looking at his mother. 'Arti has to shut down to purge the virus.'

'Are you sure? How do you know this?' Tiger asked.

'I don't know. I just do.'

Inner Voice spoke: 'Isolating critical systems. All systems shutdown imminent...'

Suddenly the pulsing heart of the Delta fell silent and the lights went off.

'What's happening?' Tiger exclaimed.

'Arti's shutting down,' Thundersky said.

The emergency lights came on.

Venus's voice announced over the com: 'We've lost propulsion and ship-wide systems.'

Thundersky sat up. 'I have to get to the bridge. We can get the propulsion engines and weapons back online.'

Up on the bridge, Venus, Sweetwater and Winterush were trying to restore power.

Thundersky went to the main computer, where Sweetwater was trying to access the sub routines for the grav-drive propulsion system. 'You're wasting your time,' Thundersky said, gesturing to the main interface. 'If I may?'

Sweetwater stepped aside and Thundersky started typing.

'He knows what he's doing,' Tiger said to Sweetwater as she watched him anxiously.

'How's the head?' Venus asked.

'Just as babbledicked as ever.'

'Glad to hear it.'

Thundersky felt that Arti wasn't in his head anymore, and he felt a sudden void where his presence had once been.

The ship's systems suddenly announced, 'Minimum propulsion restored. Initiating MID.'

There was a low vibrating hum underfoot as the powerful magnetoplasma impulse drives began to power up.

Thundersky looked over at Venus. 'That's all we've got until Arti reinitializes his systems.'

Chapter Sixty-Four

Bloodbuck City, the Virginias

Bloodbuck City was named after its founder Bloodbuck George back in NWY 398. It was a secret city, in a gorge high in the mountains, deep inside the Great Forest which covered thousands of square miles of ancient Virginia. It was more a rugged frontier colony, spread through three hundred acres of forest, their habitats mostly hidden deep in a network of caves and ancient mine workings. There were buildings above ground too, spread out sparsely along the gorge's steep slopes, built of logs and local laser-cut granite. They had turfed roofs over Intsofiber matting which deflected Silosian aerial probes and scans, unlike the clapped-out old M-TAVs and trailers being used as habitats along the rocky terrace on the left bank of the river, overlooking the thunderous Bloodbuck falls. The only cover they had was a long wooden awning built into the hillside, laid with a turfed roof from one end to the other.

Bloodbuck was well defended with hidden batteries of laser cannons, fifty caliber railguns and the Cerberus ground-to-air missile systems and sonic cruise missiles, all carefully hidden to the east, west, south and northern heights. There were also dozens of autonomous sentinel drones with combat software hovering through the forests over a fifty-mile radius twenty-four hours a day, and ground-based sensor arrays along with intelligent surveillance systems.

When the official Virginia Dusty capital, O'Connor City, was destroyed by Silosian warbirds fifteen years ago, the Prophetess brought her people, some four thousand of them, here to Bloodbuck, which had been a backwater Dusty settlement with a population of less than two hundred inhabitants, eking their existence out of the land. Now it was a city of fifteen thousand souls, the Secret City, where it was said the people didn't get sick.

The waterfall dropped two hundred feet into the Bloodbuck River, which snaked through the granite gorge and through the mountains into the ancient Roanoke River and Doomsday Lake, known to the Old-World as Kerr Lake. Thousands of survivors were killed during the nuclear winter, when the Old-World dam collapsed and flooded the plains.

It was during the harsh winters that they had the most problems with the Ferals, who, hungry for meat, risked everything to come and steal Dusty kidlings. For the most part, the Ferals had been driven back a hundred miles in all directions. The Dusties, like all other civilized colonies, killed Ferals on sight. "Suffer not a Feral to live," as the saying went.

When the Prophetess had first arrived with her followers and her army, the largest Dusty army in Continental North America, she'd assigned the Reverend the task of driving the Ferals out of the territory root and branch, and the bloody "Cleansing of the Ferals" began. With his posse of maniac Solarcycle

Angels, the Reverend declared "Holy War" on the Godless Ferals and hunted them down and butchered them mercilessly – men, women and kidlings over four years of age. Those under four were taken back to Bloodbuck to be "civilized." It was the Feral tradition that kidlings first ate human meat at the age of five and were thus beyond redemption from that age on. A tally of 15,000 Ferals killed in less than one summer was estimated.

The Dusties had been busy since the Reverend had returned like a victorious conqueror from the ruins of Manhattan. 'The Virginia Dusties are a superpower!' he billowed at the head of the Silosian army, escorted by seven obedient warbirds to a fanfare of cheering Bloodbuckers.

He'd ordered that a thousand yards by a thousand yards of forest be cleared on the plateau beneath Raymond's Ridge, where the ground was flat and firm. Every tree was to be felled and cleared, every bush uprooted to make a landing pad for the Black Widow and the warbirds. It was a labor of love, everybody was awaiting the Widow's arrival with great excitement and anticipation and the entire community put in time on the project.

Strangely, during the clearance, they unearthed a nameless Old-World town, uncovering streets and the foundations of a dozen buildings along with over three hundred human skeletons. The forest had buried the place and it had become forgotten, like so many hundreds of other villages, towns and cities across the world.

The C and C was located deep in a natural cave system inside the mountains. It was busy with fighters monitoring the tactical interfaces, constantly scanning the skies and mountains and keeping the disruptor oscillators online twenty-four hours a day to scramble Utopian sensors and disrupt satellites and drones' imaging systems. The quantum computer at the heart of the C and C was nowhere near as advanced as the ARTI-QS-602, but it served its purpose, which was to monitor and coordinate the city's outer and inner defense rings, communications, eavesdropping and the network of reconnaissance drones throughout the mountains. The old tech had seen better days, most of it was over a century old. Some of it, like the primitive radar system, was even older, humming, whirring and rattling, powered by Intsoglass energy cells.

Aurora Thorn had put Bloodbuck's defenses on full alert since the Reverend had returned with the Silosian warbirds and told her that her mother and younger brother (whom she had never met), had taken control of an interplanetary Black Widow class Delta warship and had gone to the moon in it.

They had lost all contact with her since, and Aurora didn't know if they were alive or dead. Information had been sketchy coming out of Silo City. The Triple S had placed the city on lockdown. All they had heard from their friends, was that the crew of the Tranquillitatis Astrium refinery had been murdered by Triple S sentinels and tacticals had been placed on amber alert, just one step from war.

Some of the older and brighter kidlings, teenagers like Jacob, monitored the outer defense ring's surveillance drones. One day, they would be Dusty fighter commanders when their turn came. This was one of the ways they learned tactics and responsibility from the age of 12. The outer defense ring depended on them and that was a big responsibility.

Chapter Sixty-Five

'Silosia's systems are still down,' said Panther Edwards, who sat beside Aurora at the quantum system interface, nudging his brawny face towards her, his bushy gray brows rising like drawbridges. 'We should use this opportunity and attack the city directly, while their defenses are vulnerable. I've got a dozen sonic cruise missiles already targeted at Sub City Plaza and Tactical headquarters. Just say the word, General, and they're gone. We may never get another chance like this,' he added.

She looked grimly at him. 'No. We do nothing until we hear from General Bearfang and my mother.'

'Mom,' Jacob said. 'I'm picking up a solarcycle in Section Gamma Three, coming in fast along old Seventy-Seven.'

Aurora and Panther went over to Jacob, who was monitoring the ground surveillance systems along the southern perimeter. She looked at the viewer. The rider was too far away from the surveillance emplacement to identify him, and he had a pillion passenger behind. The rider was wearing a tactical officer's anti-rad jumpsuit and his companion was wearing a tech's jumpsuit. No body armor and light weapons. 'Now… why are they right out there?' Aurora mumbled to herself. She leant over Jacob's shoulder, watching the viewer.

'They'll be in weapons range in three minutes,' Jacob said.

'Where's the nearest ASD?' his mother asked.

Jacob typed and looked at the data. 'ASD Forty-One, it's in Gamma Six, approximately five and a quarter miles west of them.'

'Relocate Forty-One to their position. Let's get a closer look, shall we.' She looked at Panther. 'Ask our guest to come down here will you.'

Panther nodded and strode across the cave, disappearing into one of the tunnels leading up to the surface.

Jacob typed new instructions into the ASD. *Some real action for a change*, he thought. Sensor monitoring duty was usually just about as boring as it could get at Bloodbuck. Now and then the Scav caravans would venture along the ancient I-77, crossing the Virginias on their way to Utopian Misty Lake City, which was called Lake Erie on the Old-World maps. 'It's on its way. ETA, two and a half minutes.' He looked at his mother.

'Anything on long range sensors?' Aurora said aloud, addressing the question to everyone.

'Everything's quiet in all quadrants,' one of the fighters called back from the main sensor interface.

'Any com traffic from Silosia?'

'Nothing on military or Triple S channels,' another fighter monitoring comms replied.

Aurora paced about the cave procrastinating. She was tempted to open an attack on Silo City, as Panther had suggested – very tempted. As Panther had said, when would another opportunity like this present itself? They had a distinct advantage. Silosia hadn't been as defenseless as it was now for over a century. But then her thoughts were distracted by:

'ASD-Forty-One is half a mile from the target. ETA, fifty seconds,' Jacob announced. 'Switching ASD to stealth mode. Getting the live feed now,' he said as a video feed displayed on a couple of viewers. Moving through the trees, weaving left and right. Then it came to the ancient road…

'Target coming into view now.'

Aurora looked. She could see the tactical and Tech clearly now. But she did not recognize them. 'Run them through the system.'

'No need,' a voice echoed stentoriously through the cave from behind them. 'That's Senior Tactical Commander Bigmoose Jack…'

Aurora turned to Blossom Flora, who stood beside Panther. 'The Tech is Washington's personal assistant, Moon Spencer. And if they're defecting as I suspect, we've landed a couple of very big fish.'

'What do you know about them?'

'Not much about Bigmoose, except that he's a sympathizer to our cause. Your mother was going to try to recruit him some years ago.'

'Why didn't she?'

Blossom Flora shook her head. 'I don't know.'

Bigmoose skidded to a stop. There was an autonomous sentinel drone right in front of them, with two laser pulse weapons muzzling out of its spherical fuselage like a pair of stumpy arms. It was a remnant from the

Oregon-Washington Wars and still as deadly now as they had been then. They were indiscriminate flying bombs; once their lasers were depleted, they were programmed to detonate the sonic charges inside them and lay waste to everything for a thousand yards in every direction. It hovered six feet over the road, its mag-drive humming quietly as its scanners swept them up and down. It hovered slowly towards them.

'It's scanning us,' Bigmoose said. 'Don't make any sudden moves. They're autonomous, it might interpret it as hostile and laser us.'

Moon Spencer didn't move a muscle, his scared eyes staring widely at the drone as it circled them. Eventually it stopped in front of them again.

Then, from out of the drone: 'Identify yourselves,' a woman's voice said.

'I'm Senior Tac Commander Bigmoose Jack, Silosian Tactical Command, General Staff. This is Tech Moon Spencer, quantum computing, Sub City.'

'State your business.'

'I'm here to warn you. The Grand Inquisitor has taken command of the military and he knows your approximate location and is planning a broad sweep aerial assault.'

There was a long silence.

'I spoke to the Prophetess two days ago,' Bigmoose went on. 'She was aboard a Black Widow class Delta IPW with General Bearfang and two young men from the College of Novices, Tiger White Washington and Thundersky Reece. She gave us information. General Appleby's been murdered by the Triple S. I'm offering my services and seeking asylum.'

'Standby.'

Bigmoose glanced over his shoulder. He could feel Moon trembling.

Aurora's voice spoke from the drone again. 'Follow the drone. Don't deviate, stop or try to get past the drone. It will kill you if you do.'

Bigmoose nodded. 'We have no intentions of deviating from your instructions, ma'am.'

'I am General Aurora Thorn.'

The ASD started to move along the road just ahead of them.

It was an hour's ride through the mountains, occasionally passing Old-World ruins of once grand houses set on the mountainside. Then the drone slowed to a stop in the middle of nowhere, thick endless forest one side of the road, and a precipitous drop into a ravine the other. It was dark and unsettlingly quiet and there was a chill in the wind as it swept the mountainside and the fronds of the forest.

The drone finally halted and they stopped just behind it.

Bigmoose looked all around, but saw only the trees receding into the ever-darkening forest, and the ancient road, cracked and buckled, subsiding and twisting into primordial wilderness.

The drone hovered in front of them, its mag-drive pulsing and whirring, its lasers disconcertingly trained on them the entire time.

'How long are they going to keep us here for?' Moon said, his head moving bird-like on his shoulders as he looked around in every direction.

Then, carried on the wind from a distance, they heard what sounded like a mag-drive. The unmistakable pulsing hum grew louder. They stared along the road, waiting, and then a glimmer of lights flickered through the trees. A moment later, an ancient Mark I M-TAV halftrack appeared, doing fifty along the broken blacktop and hard core, the caterpillar wheels squealing like a nest of hungry crow chicks.

The halftrack stopped just behind the drone and the drone flew off, going back to the south.

The M-TAV's side door hissed and beetle-winged up.

Two young Dusty fighters wearing anti-rad respirator masks got out with tac-one parabellum carbines pointed at Bigmoose and Moon. They approached.

Bigmoose sat calm and motionless. Behind him, moon started breathing deep and fast as if he had been running. The fear was burning him up from the inside out. There were such horror stories about Dusteater barbarity towards Utopian prisoners. Torture and public executions. There were even stories of Utopians being handed over to the Ferals, to be butchered and eaten. The fact that Ferals never ate adults because the meat was contaminated disputed the stories. People like Moon Spencer had always believed what came out from Triple S...

'Surrender your weapons,' one of the Dusties demanded.

Bigmoose nodded. He removed his side arms, sonic grenades and tac-one parabellum carbine and gave them to the masked fighter who stepped forwards, while his companion kept them covered.

The Dusty stepped back with the weapons.

'You come in the halftrack with us. The bike stays here. Someone'll pick it up tomorrow.'

'I need to bring my data-pad,' Bigmoose said, gesturing to the storage box at the back of the solarcycle. 'It has information on it that'll be useful to the Prophetess.'

The Dusty thought about it. 'You on the back. Get it. All your other shit stays.'

Moon dismounted, as nervous as a rabbit as he opened the box and pulled the data-pad out.

The Dusty who had taken the weapons, now took the data-pad from Moon's trembling hand. 'We'll scan it in the rig,' he said.

Once sealed inside the M-TAV, the two Dusties removed their respirator masks.

They were both fresh faced teenagers. Dusty fighter cadets, who trained as hard and just as well as Silosian tacticals. They were a worthy enemy, Bigmoose had always thought so.

A third Dusty was sitting in the cockpit behind the controls; she wasn't much older. Twenty-five or so, but fully trained in Death's noble arts. She had a hard-face with narrow, mistrusting eyes.

The young Dusties scanned Bigmoose and Moon from head to foot, then scanned the data-pad for transmitters, hidden weapons and explosives.

'Make yourselves comfortable' the talker said as he opened two small black sacks. 'Put these over your heads,' he said, handing them to Bigmoose and Moon Spencer.

'Is this necessary?' Moon asked.

The talker looked at him. 'It is if you don't want me to shoot you in the head.'

Moon gave him a wary look. 'Seeing as you put it so nicely,' he said with dark humor. He pulled the sack over his head. The faces of angels, the hearts of coldblooded killers, he thought.

Chapter Sixty-Six

They were still blindfolded and disorientated as they were taken up into the caves and led through a labyrinth of long, cold tunnels, the two dusty youths holding their arms, guiding them.

They could hear voices echoing from every direction, as well as the noises of machinery and air purification vents humming and blowing.

Bigmoose felt as if they had entered a large space. He could hear many voices, men, women, kidlings – echoing in the vaulted space. And the sound of flowing water, as from a river. They were led across a wooden bridge and down wooden stairways with landings, descending fifty or more feet until they turned into another long, narrow tunnel deep into the mountain, to the Prophetess's living quarters in "Big Cave," where Aurora had ordered them to be taken.

They tripped and stumbled along the uneven ground for a hundred yards or so before their escorts stopped.

A hatch opened. A heavy metal hatch, Bigmoose thought, with a pneumatic airlock, he deduced from the hiss of air.

Their guards led them forwards. The heavy blast door slid shut behind them.

Wherever they were, it was quiet and warm, though they could smell burning wood and hear a crackle of fire, along with the sound of water dripping with monotonous regularity into a larger body of water somewhere in front of them, every drip and spit and crackle of wood amplified in the enormous cave.

Their escort finally let go of their arms and pulled the sacks off of their heads so they could finally see where they were.

They had been brought to a massive cave with a subterranean lagoon, with subdued colorful lights.

Flames from an enormous firepit on a granite island near the middle of the lagoon coruscated, glinted and sparkled off the still, dark water. They were standing on a flat floor, laser-cut with precision from the bedrock, and pathways had been cut between outcrops of rock, left in their natural state for decorative purposes, adorned with ancient statues scavenged from the ancient ghost cities of old Virginia. The cave was furnished with all manner of fine and beautiful antiquities and works of art, including delicate looking 18th Century furniture, long wooden bookcases filled with ancient books rescued from Old-World libraries.

Being surrounded by so many antiquities reminded Bigmoose of Coldriver, who had been an obsessive collector of the ancient artifacts his entire life. Butterfly's own passion was heavily influenced by Coldriver, back when they were kidlings.

Moon was equally as impressed as he looked around the massive, dimly lit cave, the water and light conspiring to throw wavy reflections on the uneven cave walls and vaulted roof thirty feet over their heads.

Behind them on a raised level of the cave was an impossibly long wooden table, with twenty or more chairs set around it and half a dozen glistening, solid silver candelabra, circa 1700, spaced along its length.

On the other side of the lake, accessed by a wooden bridge, there was a seating area with high back chairs.

'Why are you here, Senior Tactical Commander Bigmoose Jack?' Panther's deep steady voice came out of the rippling twilight on the other side of the cave, where it was divided by a natural screen wall of solid rock, that had an archway laser cut from it leading into the cavern beyond, from whence the voice came.

'The Triple S murdered my boss,' he replied. 'They would've murdered me and my family next.'

This time it was Aurora who spoke disembodied from the other cave: 'Why did Zim Steven murder General Appleby?'

Panther and Aurora appeared in the archway.

Bigmoose watched them approaching. 'He was aware that we know about Genesis.'

Aurora and Panther glanced at one another.

'The Prophetess told us. If you com her, she can confirm it.'

There was something vaguely familiar about the man with the woman. Bigmoose felt he knew him from somewhere, but couldn't quite place from where or when. A long time ago, he thought, his mind's eye feeling he had been a much younger man. 'They know Bloodbuck City's somewhere in this quadrant and their attack could come at any time. They've disconnected the warbirds and bombers from Arti's tactical systems, which you now control.'

Again Aurora and Panther looked at one another. If they did have control of Arti's tactical systems, this was the first they were hearing about it. Bigmoose looked at them. 'My data-pad is my gift to you. On it, you'll find all the security protocols, defense emplacements and unscrambling software for military transmissions.'

'Why do you want to help us?' Panther asked.

Bigmoose looked at him, still trying to place where he knew the old man from. 'They murdered Blackstone Washington and General Appleby. Men I admired and respected, and considered as friends. And because, if Genesis is true as the Prophetess told us, it can change everything for everyone.'

'It's true,' Panther said.

'Scholar Panther Edwards,' Bigmoose said aloud as the name came to him.

Panther stared at him without commenting.

Panther Edwards, deputy head of the GRC. He had disappeared thirty years ago during a prisoner transport from Pacific City, Silosia's furthest colony in old California, about sixty miles from the ruins of the ruins of Los Angeles. He, along with four Triple S sentinels and nine Dusty prisoners, had been presumed killed when their transport drone went missing over the highly radioactive desert near the Pecos River in what was known as New Mexico. So how the babbledick did he get here?

'You can move freely about the city,' Aurora said. 'But you will not be allowed weapons or access to any sensitive areas,' she went on, stepping towards them, looking at them in turn. 'If you try to leave the city, or make contact with anyone outside the city, you'll be killed.' She looked at the two young fighters. 'Show our guests to their quarters.'

Chapter Sixty-Seven

Black Widow, 170,000 miles from Earth

Everybody was on the bridge when they were all startled by a loud buzz from the main system interface, and the onboard computer said:

'Initiating system restart. Standby.'

Winterush stepped over to the AI interfacer and looked at the viewers as they came back online, the panels starting to illuminate and flash. 'All systems are restarting,' he said.

The biggest worry in their minds was: Had the Triple S managed to break the link between Arti and Thundersky?

They were all feeling the pressure, their tense eyes looking at the systems lighting up around them. If the Silosians regained control of the Delta, they were contained like rats in a trap, 170,000 miles from earth with no means of escape.

Tiger crossed his fingers and looked at Thundersky, who looked just as worried as everyone else, and that was a big worry for everyone. If Arti's link had been cut, they really were babbledicked. All the Dusty factions would be at Utopia's mercy. This act of open warfare would give the Utopian allies just the excuse and impetus they needed to destroy the Dystopian topsiders and make mudsurfers of them all.

Thundersky heard a buzz in his head and Inner Voice spoke: 'Virus purged.'

Arti was back and that empty space was filled with his presence, feeding his information as thoughts once again. 'The Triple S have taken over military operations,' Thundersky said to the others, like an oracle. 'The Grand High Council have authorized an airstrike against Bloodbuck City,' he said worryingly.

The Prophetess looked at him. 'Arti?'

Thundersky nodded. 'He's back. Grand Inquisitor Zim Steven's attempt to break our connection has failed. General Coldriver has been found dead in his habitat. Lasered in the back. Bigmoose has disappeared, so has senior Tech Moon Spencer, both presumed to have defected. Silosia's weapons systems have been disconnected from Arti's tactical AI, and are manning the warbirds and bombers with human crews. They're planning a two-pronged attack with ground forces and airstrike as soon as the muster is complete. Silosia ground forces are at this moment moving into position in the Virginias.'

'We have to re-establish comms to warn Bloodbuck,' the Prophetess said.

Venus brought the gravity drives online. 'Primary propulsion in thirty seconds.' The sound of the grav-drives building power was music to their ears.

Reaper strapped himself into a seat at the main computer interface, next to Thundersky.

'Tactical AI coming online,' Tiger announced.

The gravity-drives hummed and vibrated throughout the ship.

'Building to maximum power for a gravity-jump,' Venus said loudly over the roar of the drives. 'Buckle in.' A viewer animated their course, speed and telemetry. She started typing on another touchscreen integrated into the overhead control panel. 'Bringing all drives online.' The whirring roar of the grav-drives grew deeper, louder and faster, the pulses getting closer and closer together until they were almost one. '... Gravity harmonics synchronizing,' she said, touching more symbols on the overhead sensor controls. 'Gravity bubble in: Seven... Six... Five... Four... Three...' Her index finger hovered over the touchscreen. '...Two...' She touched a symbol and there was a brief surge of energy and a momentary wobble where everything seemed to shimmer for a fraction of a second. 'Gravity bubble established...' Her hand reached for the four independent power levers in the central console on her left between her and Sweetwater, who was monitoring the navigational systems in the co-pilot's position. Venus rested her fingers on the levers and drew them back evenly. 'Standby for gravity jump...' She reached with her right hand to the interface to the side, typing on the touchscreen. '...On my mark...' Venus pressed a flashing symbol.

The Black Widow shot forwards as the gravity-drives blasted out a gravity wave, propelling them ten thousand miles in five and a half seconds. They were thrown back in their seats, the pressure against their bodies making it hard to take a breath. And then the delta was moving smoothly through space towards the big blue earth, which filled the windshield.

'Optimal re-entry speed achieved, stabilizing. Time to re-entry, two hours fifty-eight minutes.'

'Can't we go any faster?' Bearfang said. 'Make another jump?'

'Sure we can,' Venus said in a sarcastic tone. 'If you want us to burn up in the atmosphere on re-entry. Now why don't you play with your little guns and leave the driving to me...'

Bearfang smiled to himself. She was so beautiful, like a wild tiger. She looked round at him, fixing him in her dark brown eyes, and for a moment he was lost in them. 'Yes, ma'am. I'll do that.'

'Your man?' Sweetwater asked.

Venus shot her a sharp look. *'Hell no!'*

Sweetwater smiled. *'Hell yes,'* she said under her breath. She looked at the navigational viewers. 'ETA to planetary magnetopause and bow shock, fifty-two minutes.'

'Comms established,' Winterush said.

The Prophetess came over to the comms, where Winterush was working. 'Thank you, Kip.' She coded in the secure operational channel to Bloodbuck and almost immediately, the C and C appeared on the viewer and a bright faced Jacob beamed from the screen.

'Woah!' he exclaimed, his hungry eyes exploring the bridge, before even acknowledging his grandmother. 'Oh, happy day, Grandma. Happy day, Thundersky-'

'Is your mother there?'

'I'm right here.' Aurora appeared in the viewer. She too looked over the bridge with curiosity and the strangers among them, her gaze rested on the two young novices. One of them was her brother and it made her feel strange. She knew so much about him, but had never met him.

'… The Silosians are planning an aerial and ground attack on you,' the Prophetess said.

'We know. We've got a couple of defectors here. Bigmoose Jack and Moon Spencer. They've warned us and we're ready for them.'

'And Blossom Flora?'

'She's here too.'

Tiger gasped with relief. 'Is she okay?' he asked. 'Can I see her?'

'She's fine. But she's elsewhere right now, setting up a casualty station. We're expecting heavy losses. The early warning system and our autonomous drones have located several enemy positions.'

'Bigmoose will be useful to you,' the Prophetess said. 'You can trust him, Aurora.'

Thundersky looked at his sister. 'The warbirds will activate as soon as Silosian aircraft cross into your territory. We'll deploy our Raptors as soon as we're in the atmosphere.'

She nodded her head and looked at her mother. 'Even then, they outgun us. I don't know how long we can hold them off.'

'We're coming,' Thundersky said. 'We *will* be there.'

She looked intensely at him and after a long pause, she said: 'We'll hold out. We've sent word to the other factions. The Pens and the Kentucks are coming, but forty-eight hours away.'

'Send us the locations of those ground forces,' Thundersky asked.

'You'll have it in a couple of moments.' She turned and nodded to Panther.

Panther started uploading the data. I'm connecting you to a live feed, Prophetess.'

'Receiving data,' Vixen said.

'Feed the data into tactical and plot solutions for missile strikes,' Thundersky said before Bearfang could give the order. 'Computer, arm six Satan Nine torpedoes ready to fire,' Thundersky ordered.

'Initiating.'

'Damn, you're quite ruthless when pressed,' Bearfang remarked.

'War is a ruthless business, General. Taking out some of their heavy war-tech on the ground will slow their advance and help maintain your outer defense ring, which, according to Arti, is inadequate to hold off a sustained attack. But if you'd rather we used harsh words instead…?'

Bearfang shook his head. 'No. You seem to have it just about covered. And for the record, it gives me the creeps, not knowing if I'm talking to you or Arti.'

Thundersky gave him an ambiguous smile.

'I've got four heavy tech emplacements, each approximately sixty-five miles from our outer defenses.'

'Perfect. Plot a solution and fire from orbit. You have a window of five minutes.'

Bearfang nodded and started inputting the data into the tactical computer.

'Arti, set the missiles at minimum yield.'

'Minimum yield confirmed,' the computer responded.

Thundersky looked at his mother. 'If they want a fight, then let's give them one.'

Chapter Sixty-Eight

Bloodbuck City

It was mid-afternoon and a particularly fine day, when across the mountains came the ominous shrill of the outer defense warning sirens.

'This is it! Is everyone in position!?' the Reverend boomed.

Those who weren't already at their stations were running to them through the warren of tracks in all directions, manning the fifty calibers and laser cannons around the inner defenses.

The ground-to-air missile systems suddenly rose up from out of the forest floor on hydraulic platforms, rotating towards distant targets and locking.

In the mountain peaks, the early warning radar and sensor arrays combed the sky as more missile launch tubes rose out of the ground and rotated towards the east to lock on a skyward trajectory. The cover caps exploded off the tops of the launch tubes, and the tubes opened like inverted wings, revealing the missiles with their blood-red nose cones, fan tails and swing wings. The electromagnetoplasma rockets fired into life, and six missiles, one after the other, shot up from their pads. Their swing wings opened as they blasted into the clear sky, their tails glowing neon blue.

Almost immediately, the mountains echoed with the far-off booms of exploding ordnance as enemy warbirds started their attack on the outer defense ring, which had opened fire with a barrage of fifty caliber sonic charged shells, artillery and Viper VI anti-missile missiles.

SCHWOOSHHH – a Silosian warbird shot across the sky over the city.

The fifties opened, their sonic shells exploding under the warbird, but not close enough to damage it. It climbed vertically straight up like a rocket heading for the stratosphere, chased by two ground launched missiles.

'It's a scout,' Aurora said as she watched it from the cave mouth. 'Testing out inner defenses.'

'Where the hell are those warbirds?' Panther muttered.

The vulnerable, young kidlings and elderly were ushered quickly into the caves to safety...

In the east, the air cracked with the distant sound of the fifty caliber sonic rounds detonating and the BOOMS of exploding ordnance. Bolts of light flew off eastward from a battery of laser cannons firing their continuous beams into the sky. Between the explosions of sonic shells, the azure was dotted with dozens of black warbirds and fighter drones. Aurora almost gasped in horror. How the hell were they going to hold them off? Her mother and the Widow were still at least an hour away – still on their approach to earth.

A near distant explosion lit the sky with a bright fireball and a boom that rocked the ground from a crashed warbird northeast of Raymond's Ridge, upon which a battery of fifty calibers were letting rip fifty rounds a minute.

KABOOM! A missile slammed into the sheer cliff face halfway down the ridge and exploded. KABOOM! A second struck the railgun battery. A direct hit and the railguns were blown to pieces, tossed into the air like twigs.

Two Thunderclap missiles took off from the waterfall with a roaring WHOOSH of their electromagnetoplasma rockets, blasting up through the ravine with tails of blue fire, their wings extending, and like synchronized dancers, they banked east, vanishing beyond the forest canopy.

Twenty seconds later, the distant thud of two sonic detonations resounded like thunder across the sky. Sonic waves rippled visibly across the horizon and strong gusts of wind blew across the treetops, snapping them like dry twigs.

Two more Thunderclaps roared up from their launch pad, flying north.

Two low flying warbirds darted like bullets overhead with a roar of their jets, the rear bird's laser cannons blasting at the surface structures, aiming for the missile emplacements.

More warbirds appeared, their lasers firing randomly into the forest – SSSSHBLAMM, SSSSHBLAMM, SSSSHBLAMM…

It was carnage everywhere, lasers blasting down like lightning bolts, missiles slamming into the ravine and imploding against the cliffs in an attempt to seal the caves and everyone inside them. Trees were ripped from the ground by sonic waves, people torn limb from limb and thrown like ragdolls through the burning forest. The sonic waves crushed internal organs and shattered bones.

Then, from out of the west, the seven captured warbirds dived out of the sky, their laser canons firing at the Silosian warbirds. One fired an air-to-air missile and hit a Silosian warbird, blowing it in half, burning pieces tumbling out of the sky into the forest below.

'Aurora,' Panther hollered over the din of war, which Aurora watched from the cave mouth with growing horror.

She came to her senses and turned.

'You're needed in the C and C. The enemy has broken through the outer defenses…'

Four Satan Nine space torpedoes suddenly thundered fifty feet overhead, following the contours of the landscape over Bloodbuck City. The mighty 200 foot long torpedoes blasted through the air with a deafening roar. Their formation suddenly broke and they thrusted through the sky like four splayed fingers of death towards Silosian missile and artillery batteries.

Aurora stood at the cave mouth and watched in awe as the Black Widow's mighty torpedoes vanished over the horizon.

Then, fifteen seconds later came four enormous plasma detonations which glowed with a blue ball of fire that climbed for a mile into the sky, killing and destroying practically everything for thirty square miles. The detonations resounded for miles and the earth shook.

'My God!' the Reverend gasped.

'No, Reverend. Satan Nine plasma spatial torpedoes.' She grinned at him. 'Mother's coming.'

Back in the C and C, she looked at the situation board. It was bad, even with the damage the Satan Nines had inflicted on the enemy. Sixty eight percent of the outer ring was destroyed beyond use. Another twenty-four percent was either damaged or out of ordnance. Warbirds were flooding over with only minimal resistance between the outer and inner defenses. Whatever happened, they needed to hold Bloodbuck.

'And they're moving up more ground forces along the ancient I-77. Heavy weapons, M-TAVS, artillery and about six thousand tacticals and autonomous attack drones.'

Everybody was crowded around her, looking at her, expecting her to come up with some miracle.

Bigmoose stepped forwards. 'They'll concentrate on taking out your drone network and sensors array before they head in for a ground sweep,' he said. 'They'll leave the warbirds to degrade your defenses as much as possible,' he explained. 'The longer you can keep them occupied with your drones and defending your sensor array, the longer you'll hold them up. If they can take Bloodbuck before the Delta gets here, they can train everything they have on it.'

'I can get five fifties and a couple of sonic mortar batteries up there with a unit of Ghost fighters and my angels,' the Reverend said.

She nodded her head. 'Do it.'

'Pull everything we can back to the inner defenses. We've got seven warbirds up there now; they'll buy us a little time. Defending the city until my mother and Bearfang arrive is vital.' There was a fire in her eyes, a look of fearless determination on her face. 'We must hold. At all costs, we must hold.'

'God did not bring us here to die,' the Reverend said. 'So, let's get this done. Move your goddam asses! We got work to do. Bringing in the sheathes,' he sang as the commanders filed out, his voice echoing, 'Oh yes! We shall come rejoicing, bringing in the sheathes…'

'Crazynuts old bastard,' Aurora mumbled. She looked at Bigmoose. 'And I hope I've made the right decision bringing what's left of our armor back?'

Bigmoose looked into her eyes. 'You made the only decision you could make. You've lost the outer ring. Now we concentrate everything we have protecting the city, and hope Butterfly gets here soon.'

'My mother says I should trust you. So, I will. We need an experienced soldier commanding the perimeter.'

'Consider it done,' he said.

More booms shook the caves and loose grit and dust sprinkled down on their heads.

Jacob saw the worry in his mother's eyes. 'Grandma will be here, mom. I d'know about God an' all, but I know there's a reason for this. I know Thundersky's going to kick ass when he gets here.'

She looked curiously at him. 'Not your Dad? Not Grandma?'

'Sure. But not like Thundersky, Mom. He's got Arti in his head.'

Chapter Sixty-Nine

CDS Liberty, 4,000 miles from Earth

They were all strapped into their seats in re-entry positions. Through the windshield, all they could see was the shiny earth, streaked with clouds, oceans, continents and islands. It looked so normal and peaceful from here, a silent jewel of tranquility.

Venus chewed on a Surfer Town turd. 'Approaching planetary magnetopause and bow shock,' she said. 'Engaging magnetoplasmadynamic braking thrusters. Standby for ten second burn – maximum thrust on my mark...' She pressed a sensor button.

The grav-drives powered down and three forward magnetoplasma breaking thrusters fired at maximum thrust for ten seconds. The Widow shuddered and bumped as it slowed, buffeting the ship violently...

'What's happening? Are we breaking up?' Reaper gasped worriedly.

'No. Gravitational turbulence,' Thundersky said, looking over at him. 'When the gravity bubble meets a planetary magnetosphere. It's nothing to worry about.

The mighty deltoid warship slid through the blackness, her aft rocket cones sliding silently open. They telescoped out and locked into position.

'…Commencing full thrust, setting optimal re-entry angle at twenty-seven point five degrees,' Venus said, setting the trajectory. 'Steering thirty degrees to port...'

Outside, the jets blasted out pure blue cones of shimmering light as the Black Widow sloped smoothly and gently towards the earth, gracefully turning like a great black eagle, its nose dipping as it maneuvered effortlessly towards the atmosphere.

Venus was impressively fast at the controls, and clearly knew what she was doing. She had gotten the hang of this bird now.

'Telemetry's good,' Sweetwater informed.

'Entering stratosphere. Standby for atmospheric drag,' Venus said.

Everyone held on to the armrests of their seats, the ship was already starting to vibrate and rattle.

'Inertia stable. Oscillation baffles holding steady. Gravity bubble stable,' Sweetwater said. 'Vector four degrees starboard.'

'Coming about, four degrees to starboard,' Venus repeated as she gently handled the joystick.

The ship shuddered violently.

Venus looked at Sweetwater. 'Don't worry. This baby can take it,' she said, chewing her nervousness into the butt of the unlit cigar in the corner of her mouth.

Sweetwater looked back calmly at her. 'Do I look worried?'

Venus looked at her again and smiled.

'Makes your butt clench though, don't it?' Bearfang said, looking at Reaper, who was looking a little green around the gills. He laughed and swiveled back to weapons control.

They hit the atmosphere fast, being jerked and buffeted violently by atmospheric drag. Flames blasted out in fiery tongues, lapping fluidically across the nose and along the fuselage and over the windows, the Widow's nose glowing white-hot…

'Aerodynamic heating passing one thousand six hundred degrees.'

The Widow plunged through the atmosphere, hurtling down like a fiery comet at a steep descent, ripping through the heavens with a long fiery tail.

On the Bridge, they briefly glimpsed the earth through the cape of fire slipping across the windshield, the ship shaking and buffeting in the upper atmosphere, Everyone sat wordless, gaping at the windshield, waiting for it to clear, or waiting for the Widow to break apart.

Suddenly, they were in the inner atmosphere and the fiery nose went out as quickly as it had ignited and the windshield cleared.

Then, to everyone's complete surprise, Thundersky said: 'Arti. Go to battle stations…' An alarm sounded. The lights on the bridge darkened, the data on the viewers changed immediately to military plotting charts, cartography and the ship's vast array of weapons.

Only the cockpit viewers remained the same. Venus and Sweetwater were putting all their concentration into controlling the Widow's angle of descent. Bearfang, Tiger, Reaper, the Prophetess and Winterush were all at various interfaces monitoring and scanning.

'Set battle coordinates to Decimal: Three-Eight point five-three-three-three-three-three, negative seven-eight point three-five. Bring conventional weapons online and power up the Raptors and standby for aerial deployment. Intercept and destroy all enemy warbirds and ground positions.' He looked at the others. 'The attack on Bloodbuck began ninety minutes ago,' he said. 'Silosia have deployed substantial air and ground forces against the city. The Raptors will get there ahead of us.'

The Prophetess realized that this was some sort of symbiotic relationship between Arti and her son. Were they possibly becoming binary? Temporal human and positronic neuronet? A hybrid – a new era in neuro-cybernetics? The co-existence of human and AI?

As soon as they levelled off, the launch bay doors opened and the nine black Raptors zipped out of the Delta like bats out of a cave, their high pitched single magneto-Astrium plasma hybrid jets putting out a staggering hundred thousand pounds of thrust PSI. They flew off like bullets at four times the speed of sound and vanished into the distance in seconds with loud sonic booms.

'Raptors deployed,' Bearfang announced. 'All conventional weapons are online.'

Chapter Seventy

Bloodbuck City, the Virginias

From every direction the air vibrated to the sound of the fifty calibers and laser cannons, the VROOM of low flying warbirds and the roaring SHWOOSH of launching missiles.

SSSSHBLAMM, SSSSHBLAMM – laser-bolts shot down through the trees, incinerating everything they touched in an instant.

More warbirds screamed in above, their wings cleaving the air as they skimmed the canopy at subsonic speed, the treetops swaying in their wakes as their lasers fired rapidly with pinpoint accuracy, strafing the ground indiscriminately with their thirty calibers, killing dozens of fleeing Dusties. Astrium tipped missiles zipped down and exploded – KABOOM! KABOOM! KABOOM!

Entrances to the caves collapsed and dozens of people were crushed to death under thousands of tons of falling rocks. Carnage was unfolding everywhere all at once. The city was being mercilessly pulverized.

People were screaming and yelling – trapped, wounded, burning. The dying crawling over the dead. Limbs blown off. It was hell on earth.

The inner defense ring was firing everything it had at the enemy, but it just wasn't enough.

Down in the C and C, the thuds and cracks of battle echoed poignantly through the system, making the caves tremble. Loose debris and dust rained down as missiles detonated in the side of the mountain above them.

'…I'm telling you, we can't take much more of this. The enemy's knocked out over sixty percent of our defenses,' Panther went on, looking up wearily. 'I don't think we can hold them off for much longer. We should abandon this city and head for the ancient mines,' he said.

'No!' Aurora glared at him with stone cold eyes. 'We run, we die.'

'They've degraded our defenses to the point of being useless,' Panther persisted.

'We stay!' Aurora barked firmly. 'We're done running from these sonsofbitches! They've knocked out our jammers and our communications. If we run, they'll track us on thermals and pick us off at leisure, like culling Ferals.'

Panther stared intently at her, breathing deeply. 'How like your mother you are,' he remarked, his voice calm again. He nodded his head.

The situation was hopeless. Without the Black Widow, they were doomed.

The casualty lists were growing longer and longer. Already they had four hundred fighters confirmed dead and an unknown number of citizens killed as well.

'Heat plumes detected South at Zulu-six,' Jacob said, still monitoring the sensors with another two teenagers. Every able-bodied adult, male and female, was now outside fighting. 'Cruise missile, maximum yield. ETA forty-one seconds…'

Aurora felt all hope fading. The Widow wasn't going to make it in time. She muttered: '*God help us…*'

Suddenly the missile vanished off the scope. Jacob checked the data. There was no sign of it, just a heat signature indicating that the missile had exploded before its warhead had had time to arm itself. 'It's gone!?' He looked at his mother. 'It must've malfunctioned.'

'*What's that…!?*' a teenager sitting at the sensor interface next to Jacob gasped. A look of horror filled his face as he turned. 'There's nine fast moving Raptor class aircraft coming in from the northwest at sixty thousand feet, approximately eighty miles northeast. ETA forty seconds'

Aurora turned to him. 'The Delta's warbirds! They're here…'

Outside, the nine Raptors dived down, their lasers and wing mounted spatial torpedoes firing. They engaged the warbirds in a savage dogfight over the city, and all anybody could do was watch and cheer every time a Silosian aircraft was destroyed.

A fresh squadron of Silosian warbirds flew in from the east, targeting ground defenses, resuming fire on the southern inner defense ring, while the bulk of the aircraft engaged the Raptors and Dusty warbirds, their laser canons blasting at one another ten thousand feet above.

Suddenly, an array of laser bolts shot out of the clouds through the billowing smoke like the fingers of

God, spread in a fan across the night skies from the northwest towards the Silosian warbirds. Each laser struck the warbirds one after the other. Ten warbirds exploded spectacularly and fell to earth like shooting stars, streaking rivers of black smoke and fire as they plummeted into the mountains with deafening explosions.

There was a stunned moment of silence, when the Raptors screamed down low into the gorge and banked left in unison like a murmur of starlings, maneuvering acrobatically in synchronized formation through the smoky heavens, engaging another wave of Silosian warbirds speeding in over the mountains from the south.

More powerful laser bolts fired from above the clouds with another glowing hand of death, and a dozen more Silosian warbirds plummeted to the earth with a volley of explosions.

'LOOK!!!' someone shouted, pointing excitedly to the clouds from where the lasers had been fired.

The Black Widow lumbered out of the clouds, the air rumbling and vibrating in its deafening roar of pure power as the three-thousand-foot monster filled the sky and swept down towards the ravine. Its lasers fired over and over, destroying the Silosian warbirds with disturbing ease.

A Silosian full yield Satan IX cruise missile flew in from the southwest and detonated right beneath the Black Widow. But this was the most powerful war machine ever created in the history of mankind, and it was barely scratched by the blast, impervious to the sonic waves.

The missile hatches along the Widow's underside slid open and four spatial torpedoes shot off, rising vertically skyward before they arced southwest. Twenty seconds later there were several loud explosions beyond the horizon and thick plumes of smoke rose up above the trees.

The Silosian warbirds broke off their attack on the city and engaged the Widow all at once. It was a pointless and futile effort.

Aboard the Widow, on the bridge, Thundersky walked over to the tactical, calm as ice. 'Hold your fire, General.'

'Are you crazynuts? We need to fire now-'

'Let them in. Fire now and there's a seventy percent chance that at least five warbirds will escape. Let them come closer. Target each warbird and keep a weapons lock on them.'

'Twenty-three targets locked,' Bearfang said, accepting Thundersky's tactics.

The twenty-three warbirds vroomed in towards the Widow from all sides, like wolves closing on a stag.

'They're locking weapons…'

Thundersky licked his lips. 'Standby, General.'

'Warbirds closing to two thousand meters.'

Thundersky waited, calm and collected. Then: 'Now!' Thundersky ordered. 'Fire at will…'

Below, in the bombarded city, Jacob and others ran out of the big cave onto the terrace, where they stared in awe with a dozen battle-battered Dusties and watched breathlessly as the Widow fired twenty-three lasers in continuous beams. The warbirds flew right into them and were completely destroyed in blinding balls of fire, debris spinning through the air for thousands of yards.

'Silosian warbirds retreating in all sectors,' Tiger announced.

In just a few short minutes, the Black Widow had destroyed over sixty-five percent of Silosian airpower and forced her ground forces to halt their advance.

Chapter Seventy-One

The Delta lowered into the clearing under Raymond's Ridge, the landing struts touching down gently, sinking ten inches into the ground before the huge beast settled.

The devastation was everywhere. Hundreds were dead, hundreds wounded, dozens buried alive.

Rescue parties were out looking for survivors, digging in the rubble – recovering the dead and assessing the capital damage. Two third of Bloodbuck's defenses had been destroyed.

The Dusty Council members, those still alive, were summoned to a meeting in Big Cave, where they sat around the long table in the Grotto. It was filled with discordant voices, with seemingly everyone talking at once.

Once they had quietened down, one of them said, 'What's their next move likely to be? And when?'

The questions hung ominously in the air.

'Another attack?' one speculated.

'Can the Black Widow hold them off?' asked another.

Then Bigmoose stepped towards the table to address them. 'Right now, they're assessing their options,' he said. 'You've given them a bloody nose and that's probably bought us some time,' he went on. 'Now they know what they're up against. They'll have no choice but to call in the allies to assist.'

'A bitter victory,' Panther Edwards said.

Thundersky, standing at the periphery of the table with Tiger, Venus, Winterush and Sweetwater, said: 'We cannot fight Utopia alone. We need the other factions.'

'It'll never happen,' Aurora said. 'The Dusties are too fractious.'

'And that's always been the Utopians' advantage,' Thundersky said. 'You're divided. You need to be united. You have to set old differences aside to fight the common enemy,' he said rationally.

'He's right,' Bearfang said. 'Our war with the Utopians has to be their war too.'

'Better we go to the Oregon-Washingtons,' a council member said.

'They want Genesis destroyed as much as the Utopians do,' the Prophetess said. 'I don't think any of you quite understand what having the cure for the cancers and sterility means for the old orders,' she went on. 'It means their downfall. That's why they're so intent on destroying Thundersky. I agree with him and General Bearfang. We need allies. The Pens and Kentucks aren't enough. We need them all. They're the only choice. We need to declare an uneasy P and call a Dusteater congress at the Capitol. If we're to survive, and have any chance at defeating the enemy, this is the only way,' she added.

'What about the other Widows?' Panther asked.

'They stay on the moon for now,' Thundersky said. 'It would be a tactical mistake to bring them down.'

Over the next several days, the resilient Bloodbuckers cleared away the rubble and debris from the battle, reopened sealed caves and recovered a few more bodies. Over sixty survivors were dug out of the caves.

The M-TAV's and weapons scavenged from Lunar Seven were unloaded from Liberty and went a considerable way to replacing those lost during the Battle of Bloodbuck.

Above, the seven warbirds and nine Raptors continuously patrolled the skies almost up to the Silosian frontier. For now, they were safe from attack. The Black Widow, which the Dusties had named "Liberty", was a formidable deterrent, and Silo City was in easy reach for its spatial torpedoes. But the peace couldn't last.

Over the past few days at various meetings with the commanders and Dusty council, tactics had been discussed as well as the upcoming congress of the Dusteater factions. The council voted to make Thundersky ambassador and commander of the Black Widow, which made sense, as he was the only one who could fully control the Widow's systems. But ambassador?

He had barely had time to think of science since they'd left Silo City for New York. His life had completely changed, and it was much the same for

Tiger, Venus, Sweetwater, Blackdog and Scholar Winterush Kip along with the others who had joined them. Life would never be the same for any of them again. They were outcasts now. Dusty terrorists and the enemies of Utopianism. But what weighed heaviest on his mind, and frightened him more than anything, was that he alone controlled the war machines that now kept Bloodbuck safe.

Arti only gave him the tools as it were, not the instructions on how to use them. Arti wasn't talking all of the time either, and when he did, it was facts that he was given, not advice. There was one thing he knew with certainty, something they all knew with certainty – the Utopians would return and in greater force, with allies from the other Utopian colonies of North America, maybe even from Europe and Asia too...

Some, like Panther, advised a preemptive attack on Silo City by air and by land. He even went as far as suggesting an attack on the Utopian colonies on Mars.

Others, like the Prophetess, favored a more cautious, defensive approach.

Tiger had found himself a niche with Winterush, setting up a lab on the ship dedicated to developing new tech and new weapon designs to better defend the city.

Reaper turned onto his side with a contented sigh as he put his arm across Thundersky's chest. Thundersky looked at him.

Reaper had woken up and smiled contentedly as he snuggled in closer to Thundersky, their naked bodies pressing up against one another.

Last night, they had made love for the first time and it had been wonderful. And from the feel of Reaper's erection throbbing against Thundersky's hip, he wanted to do it again…

Chapter Seventy-Three

It was a beautiful crisp morning in the heart of old Charleston, the low shadowy sunlight sloping through the eerie ruins, still and silent except for the singing of sparrows that nested in the trees and some of the buildings, which were remarkably well preserved. It was one of the most well-preserved Old-World Cities on the continent in fact.

The tranquil silence was suddenly broken by the unmistakable insectile buzzing of solarcycles and the throbbing pulses of mag-drives, along the relatively intact street to the concourse where the remains of what had been Charleston City Hall had been. All that remained of the building now was a double stairway to a platform where the columned portico had once stood. The city hall had been destroyed during the last Dusty territorial war, by Virginia and Kentuck Dusties sixty years ago. The war ended here that day, when the city hall was destroyed with eight Dusty warlords inside. The Uneasy P was sworn between all the factions on these very steps, in the still smoking ruins. They called it Capitol, and declared it a sacred place where the Dusty leaders could meet without fear of being murdered, and discuss any issues that threatened the Uneasy P. Only the Kentucks refused to join the Uneasy P, and the war between them and the Virginias had continued sporadically ever since.

Charleston was suddenly busy with hundreds of Dusties from across the continent from as far away as old California and ancient Canada.

The faction leaders were a rough and ready bunch of hard men and woman, most of them self-serving tyrants. Unlike the Virginia Dusties, some of them were showing signs of melanomas and radiation poisoning, controlled by Iodinicine and Omega Nine, purchased for food and supplies from the Scavs. A few had early versions of the Genesis Two micro-nanite; they were easy to tell apart from the others because they were healthy like the Virginias.

The fifteen faction leaders with their advisers, gathered on the concourse in front of the steps. Chairs had been laid out for them either side of a long table that was put together from many smaller tables provided by the Carolina Dusties, who were technically their hosts as Charleston was inside their territory.

Charon the Terrible of the Minnesote Dusties boomed deeply: 'Why should we join you?' His fat face was as red as a hot coal, his dark eyes wide and glaring, mouth hidden behind a thick black briar of whiskers that grew down to his chest. 'What's to gain from it? What's in it for us? We've had an arrangement with the Grand Forks Utopes for years now.'

'And the Winnpeggies leave us alone and we leave them alone,' another leader, Rattlesand Jerry of the Manitoba Dusties said.

'We have limited weapons,' Aceheart Ken of the Pen-Dusties began. 'Our war with the Delaware

Godders depleted us of weapons, ammunition and fighters. We're in no condition to fight the Utopes.'

'You'll get new weapons and munitions,' Thundersky said. 'And Genesis.'

'All of us?' Shewolf Lydia of the Wiscon Dusties asked.

'Yes. With our new facilities on the moon, we can bring up production by five hundred percent. It'll still take time, but the first batch will be ready within a month.'

'Tokens,' Charon said. 'Everyone's happy, leaving each other the hell alone. So why would we wanna go dickbutting everything up by joining you in this crazynuts war?' He shifted his broad shoulders heavily and reached for his cup of beer. 'The way I see it…' He looked at his fellow Dusty leaders around the table, all as broody as each other, the roughest, toughest bunch of leather faced killers you'd ever not want to not meet. 'And I'm sure I'm not alone here in that opinion. The only people actively fighting the Utopes is you, Prophetess.' He took a swallow of beer and made the same shoulder shuffle as he put it back down onto the table, eyeing the overlords again.

Some were nodding in agreement. Others were stone faced like corpses.

'Why would we want to go upsetting the harmony?' Rattlesand said.

'If that's how you feel,' Thundersky said, drawing their attention. 'Why are you here? It's a long way to come for free food and beer.'

Charon the Terrible and Rattlesand glared contemptuously at the youth sitting to the right of the prophetess in the place reserved for Wise Council.

Charon laughed. 'Are you taking council from kidlings now, Prophetess?'

She laughed humorlessly. 'Open your eyes, man. You know as well as I do, you're only at peace with the Minnesote Utope colonies because they've forced you out of your fertile lands into the fallow hills and close to the dead zones.'

Charon shifted with unease.

'It's a peace you purchase through submission. That's not peace, that's slavery,' the Prophetess exclaimed. 'Do the Winnpeggie Utopes let you trade in their cities, Rattlesand?' the Prophetess said rhetorically. 'Do they give you the medicinals you need? Do they give you Genesis?' She swept them slowly with her eyes. 'We can make enough nanites for all of your people, and eventually, the entire world. The Silosians knew about Genesis twenty years ago and they destroyed the project, murdering everyone who knew about it. Not for the good of mankind or the true Utopian ideals. No, they did it because they want to make slaves of us, and princes of themselves. And if you think that staying the "hell out of their way" is going to mean they stay the hell out of your way, then you're deluding yourselves.' She looked carefully at them in turn. 'I offer you a war that will cost a lot of blood. But I offer you freedom, and Genesis. We have an air force now, an air force and formidable weapons.'

They had all heard about the battle at Bloodbuck and the huge warship and warbirds they'd somehow managed to steal, though nobody knew how they'd managed to hack the ARTI-QS-602, or capture Lunar Seven.

'So, what are you suggesting?' Shewolf Lydia asked.

'A formal federation of unity. A United Dusteater Federation,' the Prophetess said. 'I'm suggesting we join together and declare ourselves united under the principles of freedom for all, because as one, we're stronger. As one, we can bring the Utopians down and liberate the mudsurfers. In accordance to the true ideals of Jeremiah O'Connor,' she said passionately. 'No more living in the dust, but cultivating fertile fields. To build on what the Utopians have done, fairly and proportionately. A true democracy-'

'Bda! You're a dreamer. You've always been a dreamer, Prophetess,' one of them said.

Charon laughed. 'We're not all democratically minded,' he said.

Thundersky looked at him and the man who'd accused his mother of being a dreamer. 'You're not united either. You take care of your own interests like Ferals. Then, when the Utopians makc war on you, you fight them alone, and you die alone and cede more of your territory to them. It serves their interests, not yours, to keep us fractious and bickering. To let you make the earth in your territories fertile, then they come and take it from you without a hagglebuck from a dog's ass. Forget the Twenty-Fivers,' he went on. 'Before them, before the Twentieth Century, the

443

United States was founded on deep ideals of freedom and the principles of democracy. The Old-Worlders fucked it up, but it doesn't mean we will. We're stronger together than we are divided.'

'Just how do you think that we can win a war against the Utopian Alliance, young man?' Lonewolf Tom of the New York Dusties said. 'Even with that Black Widow Delta you got, it's still no match against the power of the scholars and the Utopian Alliance. Not unless you're willing to use those Astrium torpedoes?' His eyes sharpened on the Prophetess. 'Are you, Butterfly?' he said, using her birth name. 'Are you willing to use them?'

She looked back at him. 'No, we're not. In fact, we removed them before we left the moon. But you know the conventional armaments of the widows as well as I do, Lonewolf.'

Lonewolf Tom did not respond.

'Wars are uncertain by their very nature,' Thundersky said, his voice filling the silence. 'But this is a war we can win.'

'Oh? And how's that, kidling?'

Thundersky ignored Charon's little dig. 'We have Genesis. Once word gets out about it, Utopia will be faced with a Surfer uprising and mass defections.'

'And the Astrium refinery is now in our hands,' Bearfang said. 'Everything's in standby mode up there and only we can switch it back on. They can't have it back. It's a Dusty asset now, like Lunar Seven.'

'That gives us a strong hand,' Thundersky said. 'Utopia, especially Silosia, cannot survive without refined Astrium. It would take them at least eight years to build a new refinery. That gives us a powerful bargaining chip.'

'We'll go it alone if we have to,' Bearfang said, 'and if we do, there'll be no room at the victory table for those who do not join us…' He looked pointedly at Charon.

For a long moment, none of them spoke, and then Aceheart Ken of the Pen Dusties rose to his feet and spoke out:

'For the first time in three hundred years, the Dusty factions have the means to defeat the Utopians once and for all,' he said. 'Don't waste it. Prophetess, the Penn Dusties vote for war with the Utopians.'

Lonewolf Tom stood up and declared: 'The New York Dusties vote for alliance and war against the Utopes,'

Shewolf Lydia stood. 'We have been abused for centuries. Driven from our land. Arrested and experimented on in the penal labs. The Wiscon Dusties vote for alliance and war against the Utopes.'

Soon other leaders stood. The Texas Dusties, The Kentucks, The Californy Dusties, the Albamas, the Carolinas and so on. Rattlesand too, voted for the alliance of the factions and war against the Utopians. Charon and others, uneasy about it, but unwilling to be shunned and left in the cold, also relented. Soon, all the Dusty factions of North America had declared alliance and war.

'Utopia must be destroyed,' Thundersky said. 'And we must unite under one General. I propose that General is Bearfang. We must unite under one civil leader and a grand council of all the Dusty kings and

queens. I propose the Prophetess to be that leader.
Each member must be given an equal say, and an
equal vote.

THE END
Thundersky will be back…